Praise for the works of Laina Villeneuve

Birds of a Feather

This book was everything. It was cute, it was funny, and it made you want to cry, in all the best ways. I loved the relationship between Adrienne and Casey. I loved the relationship between Adrienne and her pops. The relationship between Casey and Adrienne's pops. I loved the found family, the supportive friends, and the dogs. I loved everything.

–Jessica R., *NetGalley*

I could not put this book down!

-Natalie A., *NetGalley*

This was a really cute and quirky low angst romance that kept me highly entertained.

–D. Booker, *NetGalley*

Cowgirl 101

I really enjoyed *Cowgirl 101* by Laina Villeneuve. This book has all the elements of an exceptional modern Western romance with two unique and individual main characters. The setting, of course, is gorgeous. The romance is kind of an enemies-to-lovers tale and definitely a slow-burn romance, but sweet and satisfying.

-Betty H., *NetGalley*

This is a gorgeous book. Everything about it is gorgeous, from the setting to the writing style. Her writing is so readable, so beautiful and lyrical, that it makes the story flow even better.

-Karen R., *NetGalley*

The Right Thing Easy

The Right Thing Easy is a well written romance. The writing is clean, the characters are charming, and the story keeps you entertained. Laina Villeneuve wrote the characters with a finesse and grace that I enjoyed, especially when they were struggling with tough choices.

-*The Lesbian Review*

Such Happiness as This

The novel describes Robyn's journey from grief and disappointment, through the joy of new friendships and the uncertainty of potential love. Characters are skillfully drawn, and interweave in a plot with enough realistic problems, local references, and surprising twists to satisfy.

-*The L-Word*

Laina Villeneuve

Other Bella Books by Laina Villeneuve

About the Author

Laina Villeneuve learned how to care for her pool during Covid and hopes to never hire a tech again. She is in the process of training each of her three children in the hopes that one will take over someday. Her wife has no use for the pool.

Falling All In

Laina Villeneuve

BELLA BOOKS

2024

Bella Books, Inc.
P.O. Box 10543
Tallahassee, FL 32302

Printed in the United States of America on acid-free paper.

First Edition - 2024

Editor: Cath Walker
Cover Designer: Heather Honeywell

ISBN: 978-1-64247-521-0

Acknowledgments

Thank you, Bella Books, for all you do to help a book come to life. From pep talks at GCLS to the finishing touches of a fabulous cover, you are all a dream to work with! Huge shout out to everyone at the Sapphic Story Hour. I brought such a small seedling of an idea to the group and they pitched just the right "what if" to launch the writing, and I'm ever so grateful for the magic question from Gaile that gave the story liftoff. Kay has built such a wonderful space for writers, and Cheri was a fabulous cheerleader throughout the writing process.

Valerie, thank you for helping me lean into and explore what this book had to teach me.

Thank you to my cousins for rescuing my writing crisis by stepping in to give chapter-by-chapter feedback. I had such a good time fine tuning the podcast ideas and inner dialogue of Sarah's character with my cousin. She earned the label of Sarapist by helping me keep my sanity. For her to then contribute to a main character in a lesbian love story who was going to share her name earns her even more of my immeasurable respect. Rachael's superfast turnaround for each and every chapter helped to feed the confidence required to keep slogging through even when insecurities get hungry and come looking for me. Her texts and chats and especially her larger-than-life laugh helped me keep my momentum.

Kim and Kelly, thanks for insights on blended families and suggestions on the first draft. Jaime, thanks for your awesome feedback. Hearing that the story works from a trusted writing colleague gives me confidence that the story is ready for Cath to scrutinize. As always, this is a better story for her suggestions. So grateful for the ways she strengthened the story, especially the last chapters.

I wasn't sure I had another book in me after *Birds of a Feather*. Tucking in my daughter one night, she asked what I was working on. I told her I had a vague story idea, but I wasn't sure I could tackle it. She asked what the premise was and what was holding me back. I gave the lame excuse of hating description and how I only saw one of the characters clearly. For the other, all I knew that she was the pool technician. My daughter promptly sketched out the character and named her. I asked if she always went by Jasmine. She said no and said to call her Jass. When I asked how to spell it, she said, "Like ass with a J on it." Any time I felt like I was losing momentum, I would remember that, laugh and then push on. I am forever grateful for the way she got me started and checked on my progress.

Louisa, there is no romance without you. Thank you for having the courage to tell me that we needed to reshape this hobby of mine. Thank you for our brainstorming dates and for reading the whole thing when I had a draft and for saying it's my strongest story yet. You help me grow in so many ways.

Dedication

For my own Sarah
Who has been there for me for as long as I can remember.

And

For Madeleine
Who reminded me a book only happens if you sit in the chair
and put words on the page.

CHAPTER ONE

"It's too hot," Chloe whined.

Suck it up. Sarah cringed at her crabby reaction. She'd had an entire day to herself. It wasn't her daughter's fault that she had not met the work quota she had set for herself. She should have more patience and understanding. But it was hot as hell, and in the time she'd waited for Chloe outside her kindergarten classroom, the temperature inside her Subaru had spiked even hotter. She didn't remember California hitting the nineties in September when she'd been a kid, but she did remember how awful it felt waiting for the air-conditioning to reach the back seat. She hurried her child into the car seat, careful to keep the hot metal from touching her skin.

"Can we get ice cream? Mama says when it's this hot, that's the only thing that helps."

Absofuckinglutely not. Sarah clenched her teeth, wishing it wasn't so easy for her child to light the fuse of her ever-present anger with Chloe's other mother. "I disagree. When it got this hot when I was little, my mommy always took me to the library. What do you say we go find some new books?" She combed the girl's light curls with her fingers, coaxing ringlets away from her daughter's sweaty face.

"I don't want to read." Chloe batted her mother's hand away. "I want to go swimming."

With Chloe watching her every move from the back seat, Sarah cranked the engine, rolling down the windows to let the blast of hot air from the air-conditioning out. She fought the urge to tip her head to crack the tension from her neck. "I wish you could go swimming, too, but the pool hasn't been fixed yet," she said. That was the honest truth, not an accusation. Nothing beat being able to throw Chloe in the water after school. But she wasn't about to toss her child into a green pool.

"Mama didn't fix it?"

"Not yet." She kept her voice neutral. Even with this new disappointment, she was careful to swallow any criticism, to avoid contaminating Chloe's relationship with Tricia. She recalled the words she had recorded in a podcast shortly after the divorce. "The grown-up hurt is real, but it belongs to the grown-ups, not the children. It's so important to treat and talk about your ex with respect both in their presence and when you are alone with your child. Your child deserves to have an unpolluted relationship with their other parent. Try to recall what it was about that person that once called to your heart and save the disappointments for your journal or a lunch out with your friends where you know you will not be overheard. Your children are counting on you to be the grown-up, so be the grown-up, even when you want to throw a childish temper tantrum."

Be the grown-up.

She took a deep breath and peeked in the rearview mirror. Chloe was staring out the window, her posture deflated. Sarah scrambled to find something that would reinflate her child without spoiling dinner. "We could feed the peacocks! How does that sound?"

"Hot."

"How about this. You can get your swimsuit on and run through the sprinkler until it cools down."

Sarah wished that it was as easy to improve her own afternoon as it was to fix Chloe's. She sagged into a lawn chair, spent from lathering sunscreen onto her sweaty, wiggly child. She took a long sip of her lemonade, longing to splash in some gin to smooth the edges of her frayed nerves.

"Mommy, watch this! I can do a cartwheel!"

"Mmm hmm." Sarah couldn't open her eyes. Thankful for her dark sunglasses, she said, "Marvelous, honey."

"You're watching?" Chloe asked.

"I'm watching!" Sarah aimed for more enthusiasm this time and managed to push open one lid to see Chloe's hands hit the grass and her feet swing around to the side. She'd never learned to cartwheel, herself, so she could offer no advice. Tricia should have been there to hold her hips or something to help her get her legs up above her head. She was the athletic one.

She finished her drink and sank down in the chair, half an ear tuned to Chloe's chattering. She must have dozed off because the cold hand on her shoulder startled her all the way to her feet.

"Sorry!" Chloe said.

"You're fine," Sarah said, her hand over her rapidly beating heart. "Ready to find some peacocks? Let's get your shoes and peanuts."

They held hands as they walked several blocks up and then to the left to the street where all the peacocks congregated.

"Will we see babies? I miss the babies."

"Probably not until next year, sweetie. They have to grow all summer, so when the days get shorter, they are strong enough to fly up into the trees for the night." She didn't actually know if that was true, but it sounded good, and she hoped it would settle the matter. Luckily, they found a cluster of birds who strutted over to take the peanuts Chloe tossed to them.

Sarah jumped at the slam of a door nearby. Why was she so jumpy? She shielded her eyes from the still-blazing sun. Up the block, a pool guy was leaning deep into the cab of his cherry-red truck. Not a guy, she corrected herself, noticing the bright orange shorts and the long, lean legs they housed. The figure emerged fully. So not a guy. While her orange shorts were loose, the pink tank molded to her trim figure.

She'd barely glanced in the pair's direction before unloading her cart and striding toward the driveway.

"Excuse me!"

Chloe's head snapped up at the sound of her mother's voice.

Sarah was just as startled that the words had left her mouth. But they had had their effect. The woman paused on the sidewalk.

"Stay here on the corner," she ordered her child before walking briskly toward the pool…girl? "Hi!" she said, wishing she looked less disheveled. When was the last time she'd washed her hair? She quickly scooped it up and twisted it into a knot. She scolded herself for feeling self-conscious of her faded tee, self-made jeans shorts and dirty Keds in front of this stranger. It shouldn't matter, but the closer she got to the woman glowing in front of her, the dowdier she felt.

"I'm so sorry to bother you," Sarah said, a touch out of breath. "It's just that I have a pool…" She gestured toward Chloe. "We live a few blocks from here, and our pool is green. My ex was supposed to keep up with the maintenance, but…" She puffed air through pursed lips. This woman did not need her spilling her whole sad story. She tilted her head. In recognition? God, she hoped not. What were the chances that this woman listened to her show? Not likely, she hoped.

"You want me to take a look at it?"

"How much does a pool service run?" Tricia had always said it was a waste of money to hire someone, but if she couldn't manage to keep it swimmable, Sarah would have to hire someone.

The woman pushed her wide-brimmed straw hat from her head with the back of her wrist, letting it hang behind her on a cord. She ran her fingers through sweat-soaked bangs and looked at her with the brightest brown eyes Sarah had ever seen. There was something radiant about her. In the months since Tricia had left, Sarah had shrunk back into the darkest corner of herself, building a cocoon. Even through all those thick layers, her body was reacting to this woman. "Ninety," she said. "I'd be happy to take a look when I'm finished up here." She returned to the cab and ducked inside again.

Sarah did her best to keep her eyes from lingering on the woman's smooth legs but was utterly unsuccessful.

"Mommy! I'm out of peanuts."

Sarah jumped again, her daughter startling her from behind. "We're going home now, anyway. I've asked…" She couldn't supply the woman's name.

"Jasmine Dìaz," she said, her voice full of humor. "Jass."

Was she amused by how Sarah had jumped, or had she felt Sarah ogling her backside? Or worse, had she recognized her and was inwardly laughing at how scruffy she looked? Sarah tried to shake off her insecurities. "I've asked Jass if she can fix our pool."

"Hooray!" Chloe bounced like she had springs in her shoes. "I get to go swimming!"

"Probably not today, honey," Sarah said. She lifted apologetic eyes to Jass and experienced the same intense pull.

Jass extended paper and pen to Sarah. "Jot down your address for me. I'll be there in about a half hour."

Sarah took the items from Jass, careful not to touch her. "Thank you. We really appreciate it."

"No problem!" She tucked the paper and pen into her pocket and waved as she strode up the sidewalk.

Sarah turned her attention to Chloe, so she would not get caught staring at Jass a third time. "Did you have a good time feeding the birds?"

"Do you think Jass has a magic backpack?"

"Why would Jass have a magic backpack?"

"Because she's dressed like Dora. If she had a magic backpack, maybe she could fix our pool today."

Sarah took her hand and walked home, listening to Chloe talk about all the things she could do if she had a magic backpack. Chloe. She was Sarah's whole world. She had no right to be thinking about Jass's smooth legs, no right to think about how the back of her shirt had been damp with sweat. A longing to taste Jass's salty skin cracked her cocoon. She had to patch these cracks, and quickly, before Jass came to look at the pool. She needed to pull more protective layers around her and keep her focus on raising Chloe. They were the Two Musketeers, taking on the world together.

CHAPTER TWO

"Sarah Cooper is a hot mess," Jass said. She'd called her bestie the moment she parked her cart by the pool.

Amara immediately jumped into the conversation. "What did you see? Where did you see it? And more importantly why haven't *I* seen it?"

"I just met her." With her wireless headphones, Jass had her hands free to feed the cleaning hose through the skimmer and begin vacuuming the pool that stood between her and her appointment with The Sarapist. She tapped her pocket to make sure the piece of paper was still there.

"Shut up! Where are you?"

"I was about to start on the peacock pool when she walked up the street. Hot mess."

"But hot, right?"

"So hot, of course, but also, wow, so not what I expected."

"Spill! Every detail."

Jass was thankful for the slow, methodic rhythm vacuuming required to catch the sediment at the bottom of the pool. It helped her arrange her thoughts that had scattered the second she'd recognized the podcaster. "I don't know. At first, I didn't think it could be her. She's so much taller than I expected."

"She's tall?"

"Yes! I always pictured her being my height, but she's got a good four inches on me. And she looked so normal in ripped jeans shorts and a ratty old T-shirt, not at all like someone famous."

"What else?" Amara demanded.

"She's distracted," she said, remembering how jumpy Ms. Cooper had been. Was she supposed to call her Ms. Cooper when she went down to take a look at the pool? Sarah? She wasn't even supposed to know her name. Did she assume that people would recognize her on the street, or was not offering her name when Jass had introduced herself another indicator of how frazzled she was?

"You're distracted! Why are you not telling me the whole story?"

"She was with her daughter, feeding the neighborhood peacocks."

"Feeding peacocks is not something I would condone," Amara said, "but that doesn't shout 'my life is a complete mess' to me."

"You didn't see her standing there, her face blank and her arms wrapped around herself like she's about to fall apart. Something's up with Tricia, and it's throwing Sarah off her game."

"Oooooh. She told you about the ex?"

"Almost. I get the impression that Tricia took care of the pool and it's gone to hell. I'm guessing she's got someone new."

"That's a pretty big leap you're taking there."

"Trust me. It adds up. New love is distracting. It'll easily push something like pool care off the radar. I'm headed over to her house once I finish the peacock pool."

"I had no idea she lived in the neighborhood! Ack! This is so exciting! I've never seen her in the village. Have you?"

"How are you asking me that when I called you literally minutes after I talked to her?"

"Good point. So exit Tricia and enter Jass to take care of the pool and maybe its owner."

"Don't you even!"

"What? It's exactly why you called me! This is not a difficult fantasy to spin. You get the pool back to a crystal blue, she starts taking a dip in her bikini on the day you're due to service the pool, and the rest…"

Jass rolled her eyes despite the fact that her friend could not see her. "The rest is a fantasy, just like you called it. She doesn't date. You listen to her podcast. You've heard her scathing review of selfish parents who divorce and then start dating. She is a hundred percent dedicated to her daughter. I saw it myself. She's walking all over her neighborhood on a ninety-degree day to let her kid throw peanuts to the peacocks. That kid is her world."

"That's what you say now. I expect an update after you leave. And pictures!"

"I am not taking secret photos of Sarah Cooper, and even if I did, I would never share them with a postaholic like you!"

"I deserve that. I still demand an update later."

"Of course. And we'll talk about your thing, too."

"My thing." Amara laughed. "Ask Sarah what she thinks."

"You and I both know what she'd say."

Jass heard the deep breath Amara took and felt her stomach knot. She wasn't surprised when Amara returned with her voice cheerful as ever. "Maybe she'd surprise you." She delivered the three kisses that were meant for Jass's cheeks and signed off with a "Love you!"

"Love you back," Jass said.

Finished with the vacuuming, Jass coiled the hose on her cart. She dried her hands and plucked her phone from its pocket on her cart to see if Sarah had uploaded a new *The Sarapist is In*. She was not surprised to see that the newest one remained the one she had dropped weeks ago. She thumbed through the episodes. She didn't usually listen to them a second time, but it seemed fortuitous that she'd met the marriage and family therapist when she had her own difficult decision to make.

She scrolled until she found "Biological Clock" and tapped on the family tree logo to begin play. "Welcome back, folks," Sarah began as she always did, and Jass continued her pool chores as she listened to her favorite voice. While there were base notes that confidently grounded everything there was also an uptick that conveyed how deeply Sarah Cooper listened and questioned. In this episode, Sarah was talking with a reproductive expert about the deadline a woman's body puts on childbirth.

"The fact of the matter is that we live in a toxic environment, and the longer we are exposed to these toxins, the bigger toll it takes on a woman's fertility," the guest said.

"What about women who harvest eggs when they are young?"

"There is much to think about here. Are you talking embryos? Or are you talking eggs that a woman is hoping to fertilize with her spouse's sperm? Because science is telling us that time and environment impact a man's fertility as well."

"We haven't talked about the toll time takes on the body beyond whether a baby can be made. The older we get, the harder it is to get off the floor."

The women laughed together, and Jass now imagined hearing that laugh in response to something she said. A thrill ran through her. When she had first shared the podcast with Amara, it had given them something to talk about. Though Amara found it ridiculous for a professional to use her platform to argue that a woman should have her children before thirty, she heartily used the content to engage with Jass about biology and clocks.

That had been two years ago, yet those two years had changed so much for Jass. At the time, thirty was four years away. It seemed like an eternity. Focused on the math of good childbearing years, Amara also hoped she would find someone before thirty and start a family. Jass met plenty of women but always hit a wall trying to convince them that Amara was her family and not their competition. With thirty closing in on them, Amara had begun to talk about having a baby without waiting for a partner. Jass was sure that Sarah Cooper would never endorse that decision.

The podcast carried her through the daily tasks of pool maintenance. It was time to drive down to Sarah Cooper's to see whether she could fix her pool. She felt like she was going to throw up. *Get a hold of yourself!* she chided, loading her cart onto her truck. *It's not like Amara asked you to talk to Sarah Cooper about babies!* Before she went to meet her in person, Jass took a minute to watch the peacocks strut down the street, soaking up the voice that plucked something deep within her.

Within minutes, she pulled up at Sarah's address. The house was forest-green stucco with deep maroon shutters. The yard was well kept with a knee-high hedge edging the path to the front door. She was relieved when Sarah opened the door without her having to knock.

"Do you mind walking through the side yard?"

"Not at all." Jass stepped back to allow Sarah space to descend the porch steps and cut through the grass to a white gate. She pulled a cord and swung the gate open to allow Jass to step through. "Thank you so much for coming right down. I'm sure it throws a wrench in your afternoon."

"I've only got two pools left today. This won't throw me off by much."

As she walked past Sarah, she placed her palm on Jass's shoulder. "I don't think I even introduced myself before. I'm Sarah."

The touch, though brief and chaste, sent an electrical current straight through Jass. She could not form words. She nodded lamely and let her feet carry her back toward the pool.

She followed a path of hexagonal pavers along the side of the house to the backyard. The fence was covered with climbing roses, and there were pots of all shapes and sizes filled with plants drooping in the late afternoon sun. Most of them were already cooked past the point of revival. In the backyard, Jass was happy to see that a security gate surrounded the pool.

Jass envied the outdoor living space. She was willing to bet that there was a fridge next to the built-in grille. Under a pergola with a ceiling fan, deep couches pointed toward the pool. If she had a setup like this, she'd have little reason to ever go inside.

Then she saw the pool. "Wow," she couldn't help saying.

"That bad?"

"Sorry. It's been a while since I've seen that shade of green." Honestly, she was surprised that Sarah had not yet been fined by the city whose drones made sure pools did not become breeding grounds for mosquitos. She let herself in through the gate and inspected the pump area. The equipment appeared to be new and in good condition. "Do you know when the filter was cleaned last?"

"I don't. I haven't kept track of any of it. The last few weeks, my ex said to put in a gallon of chlorine. That took care of it for a while, but..." She shrugged.

"Yeah, with such hot days, chlorine isn't going to keep algae under control if the filter's dirty."

"Can you clean it?"

"Absolutely. But it'll take me at least an hour." She glanced at her watch. By the time she was finished with her two scheduled pools, it would be too dark to start the project, and her Saturday was booked solid. Sarah tried to mask her disappointment, but Jass could easily guess that another weekend without a pool was going to be a hardship for her.

"Mommy! Can I watch another episode of..." Sarah's daughter stopped midsentence when she saw Jass. "Did you fix the pool?" she asked hopefully.

"I can fix it, but it's going to take time I don't have today. And it's not a fast fix. You're going to have to be patient after I clean the filter. It will take a few days for the green to get stuck in there."

"My mommy's out of patience," the girl said.

"Chloe!"

"You said so on the phone. I heard you."

"Go ahead and watch another episode."

Chloe looked at Jass and covered her smile with her hand before she took off running.

Jass felt fully scrutinized by the youngster and wished the kid came with a thought bubble above her head. "I feel judged by your child."

Sarah wore the same expression as Chloe and stared at Jass as intently as her daughter had. "Not judged..."

The way she said it, Jass was positive they had been talking about her without saying a word. "Out with it," she prompted as if she and Sarah were old friends.

"Surely you realize that dressed like that..." She lifted her eyebrows as if she expected Jass to follow.

Jass examined her outfit. Her shirt did not have buttons to mismatch and her fly wasn't open. She shook her head and shrugged. "How am I dressed?"

Sarah looked embarrassed. "Add a backpack and a magic map, and you could be..."

"Dora? Your kid thinks I'm Dora the Explorer?"

"She was hoping you'd bring a magic backpack to fix the pool."

Jass slapped her forehead. "I wonder how many of my clients think I'm obsessed with Dora. It didn't even occur to me. How embarrassing."

"Or charming," Sarah offered.

Flirtatiously? Jass's stomach fluttered. Sarah Cooper could not be flirting with her.

"If your other clients have young children is what I meant. I'm sure they're equally charmed."

Ah. The children. Jass smiled weakly. Sarah Cooper had a child, and that child wanted to swim. It was silly to let Amara's fantasy take root. Sarah was out of patience, not in the dating market. "My schedule is crazy busy tomorrow, but I could get the filter taken care of first thing if you don't mind me starting early."

"What is your definition of early?" Sarah asked.

"Seven, seven-thirty."

"Chloe lets me sleep until six on a good day. We'll be up, but it's really not necessary for you to add this to your already busy schedule."

Jass studied Sarah. She didn't owe her anything, and yet, she wanted to help the clearly stressed-out woman. She'd gotten so much from her podcast over the years that it seemed right to give something back. "It's no bother, and it's the best route for someone whose patience is blown. The sooner it's done, the sooner you can throw your kid in the pool."

Sarah chuckled, but without humor, and Jass had a strong temptation to hug her. She shoved her hands deep into her pockets. "Sorry. That wasn't nice."

"But it's true—my patience *is* blown. It's something I'm working on."

"Speaking of, I should get to my next pool. I'll be back tomorrow."

Sarah thanked her and escorted her to the front gate. Jass tried to switch the gears in her mind to the next pool, but she couldn't, not when she felt Sarah's gaze, most probably on her Dora the Explorer ensemble, follow her to her truck. Was she supposed to wave? She climbed into the cab and quickly threw the truck into gear, raising her hand as she pulled away. She told herself not to look in the rearview, but when she gave in, she saw that Sarah had walked to the curb and was still watching the truck, a detail Amara would never get out of her.

CHAPTER THREE

"Absolutely not," Sarah said. "You know what I think about you dating again, but to suggest that you introduce her to our child? I don't know what you smoked this morning that made you believe you would hear anything but 'No' from me."

"Mama!" Chloe ran down the hall and leapt into Tricia's arms.

Sarah rubbed her solar plexus, trying to ease the pain she experienced when the three of them stood in the kitchen together. This was how it was supposed to be, but with all of them still in their jammies. Being dressed for the day made handing off Chloe for the weekend that much worse.

"You didn't tell me you were here." Chloe rested her head against Tricia's shoulder.

"I needed to talk to your mommy about our plans for the weekend. We're not quite finished yet. Why don't you watch some cartoons while we talk a little bit longer?"

"She's had her screen time this morning. You can read one of the new library books. Make sure you packed books for the weekend, too, okay?"

Shoulders slumped, Chloe headed down the hallway.

Tricia ran her fingers through her mane of black hair. "More screen time isn't going to melt her brain, Sarah."

"I don't want to fight about it, okay? I don't ride your ass about how much screen time you let her have when she's with you, but when she *is* with you, it should be only the two of you. You get her every other weekend. Surely you can make it through two days without seeing your girlfriend."

"I don't need your permission, Sarah. I was giving you a heads-up because I don't want Chloe to come home and tell you about her weekend and have you flip out if she mentions doing something with Lydia."

"There's another way to keep our child from lying about spending time with her. Do your dating when you are not raising your child."

"This isn't healthy, Sarah. Your hostility isn't good for you, and it's not good for Chloe."

"I am not hostile! You're trying to make me feel bad for holding to my values. You knew how I felt about this when you decided to leave."

Tricia glanced at her watch and then at Sarah. The blue of her eyes had been home for so many years, but now they were like the arctic when she hollered for Chloe. "Okay, Kiddo! Let's roll!"

The two stood awkwardly, the island they had chosen together when they remodeled the kitchen now solidly between them. "Chloe?" Sarah added. When the second call still failed to produce the sound of feet, she walked down the hall. Chloe wasn't in her room. Or the bathroom. "Chloe!"

At the sound of alarm in Sarah's voice, Tricia rolled her eyes. "She's probably in the bathroom."

Sarah made a beeline up the hall. "Not here!" Her anxiety spiked. Parenting on her own was turning her into a paranoid mess. She took a deep breath. "You check the office. I'll check our room."

They went opposite directions at the end of the hall, Sarah telling herself she was sure to find her daughter in bed watching the TV in the bedroom she'd once shared with Tricia. Not so. It was empty. Untouched. Her stomach lurched.

"Not in the office," Tricia said behind her. "Did she go out back?" She strode through the room and opened the patio door.

Sarah followed, immediately relieved to hear voices. In the pool yard, they found Chloe perched on the wall that surrounded the pool pump. "Chloe!" Sarah said, her hand over her heart. "You didn't tell us you were going outside."

"But I wanted to see Dora!"

"I'm sorry." Jass straightened and looked from Sarah to Tricia and then to Chloe. "I thought she was allowed to watch. I should have checked with you."

"No, please don't..." Sarah shot a dagger-filled glare at her ex. She did not want to be seen like this—in her pajamas, fighting with her ex, losing track of her child, clearly not coping very well. She wanted to crawl into a black hole and disappear. Once she got through the next five minutes, she could do just that. "It's fine now. Mama's ready to go, so let's get your stuff, okay?"

"But Dora said I could help."

Jass had busied herself with the innards of the filter again and looked as if she was about to say something. Sarah cut her off. "This is her job, sweetie. I'm sure she can manage, okay?"

"Okay," Chloe said quietly. "Bye."

"Your pool will be super spiffy in a few days. I'm sure you can go swimming this week."

Sarah carried Chloe inside, holding her close, trying to absorb two days' worth of snuggle before she said goodbye for the weekend. She drank in the smell of Chloe's strawberry shampoo. When she set Chloe down to fetch her backpack, she could feel Tricia vibrating with anger.

"You weren't here," Sarah said.

"I said I would take care of it," Tricia said through clenched teeth.

"And I heard you. I heard those exact words come out of your mouth a month ago, but you didn't take care of it. Since you didn't do what you said what you would do, I took care of it."

Chloe returned from her room, frowning when she looked from one parent to the other.

Sarah reached for her hand to walk her out. "You have a great time with Mama, okay? Make sure she's eating enough green things at dinnertime."

"We don't like green things," Chloe said.

"We like mint-chip ice cream," Tricia said.

"And cookie-dough ice cream!" Chloe skipped to the car.

Once Tricia had her buckled in and the door shut, she faced Sarah once more. "You should have at least talked to me about the pool."

"I've tried. You're preoccupied. I thought you would appreciate not having it on your to-do list anymore."

"What, so you've hired her permanently?"

"I have." So much for crawling back into bed. She was going to have to talk to Jass about taking over the pool care.

"Have a good weekend, Sarah."

"Bye-bye, sweetheart!" Sarah waved to Chloe as Tricia swung around the horseshoe driveway out of sight.

Emptiness slammed into Sarah, and she quickly turned on her heel, heading straight to the refrigerator. She pulled out orange juice and glanced from the liquor cabinet to the clock. She closed her eyes and took a deep breath to rein in the impulse. A screwdriver was not going to resolve her conflict with Tricia. "Screw you, Tricia," she whispered, frustrated that she had to deal with the mess of the pool and worried that Tricia was off to make an even bigger mess of their child.

Steeling herself, she headed back to the pool yard. It looked like Jass was finishing up. The lid was back on the tank, anyway. "I'm sorry Chloe distracted you."

Jass looked up from her task, flushed and sweaty. Her simple gaze blasted through Sarah's protective barriers, transporting her to the early days of sweaty lovemaking with Tricia. She ached for those days, ached to lay herself bare to someone. She had to look away. It was too early for her to be bombarded with so many emotions. Why did she have to be the grown-up maintaining her resolve when Tricia was gallivanting with a new girlfriend?

"She was no bother," Jass said. "This tank, on the other hand…I wish I had a new O-ring in the truck. This one is shot. I barely got the lid back on."

"I'm sorry. I didn't know. I don't do anything at all with the pool. I'm hoping you can add us to your schedule, so I don't have to give it another thought." Jass didn't respond immediately, making Sarah feel self-conscious. She suddenly realized she was still in her cotton pajamas and felt exposed.

"I can add you to the Thursday schedule," Jass said as she moved from one side of the pump to tighten something on the opposite side of the lid. "I'll draw up a bill for this and maintenance for the rest of the month. Unfortunately, a bunch of your screens need to be replaced as well. I'll make a note of it and replace them next time I clean the filter."

"Tricia...my ex kept chlorine in the garage. Should I keep it on hand or get you to take it?"

"Depends. If you're comfortable adding chemicals, it could be good to have here if your chlorine drops in between my weekly visit."

That she'd see Jass each week should not have registered for Sarah as it did. Tricia was obviously enjoying the dating scene. What was wrong about admiring a beautiful woman? Desire. She did not need to add that to the other emotions she could barely contain. Distraction. Although with Chloe gone for the weekend... No she would not let herself be tempted. Destruction. That's what she would be doing to her career if she allowed herself personal feelings. She squished the thrill like a bug. "Thank you for coming to our aid and for agreeing to take care of the pool. Now that I have that squared away, I guess I can kick back and enjoy my freedom!"

She'd meant for that to sound lighthearted, but even she could hear the bitterness in her voice. Jass barely acknowledged her, for which she was grateful. She didn't need to have this stranger pity her. "Not that I don't have work to do. Which I'm sure you do as well." Ugh. Could she be any more awkward? With a wave, she disappeared into the house to spare Jass having to respond.

CHAPTER FOUR

Jass scanned the street but didn't see Amara's Audi coupe. Amara refused to park it in the lot, convinced that a careless hiker would ding the paint, and Jass was happy to avoid the lot fee. Despite the fact that *The Sarapist* never had new episodes drop on a Sunday morning, Jass pulled out her phone to check the website. As predicted, there was no new content, so she entertained herself by scrolling through photos she had viewed hundreds of times.

The site still had pictures of Sarah with Chloe and Tricia. Was that meant to keep Tricia anchored in her life for Chloe's sake or did it mean Sarah was swimming in the deep end of denial? "Ain't just a river in Egypt," she mumbled under her breath.

She stopped on one of her favorites of Sarah, barefoot with her feet tucked up on a couch, her soft curls styled to fall around her shoulders and brown eyes that simultaneously offered comfort and challenge. Jass now recognized that the photo had been taken on her backyard patio. Next to the couch, lush plants made it look more tropical than the desert that was Southern California.

A car horn pulled her attention away from her phone, and she recognized Amara parking several cars down. She grabbed her backpack from her car, locked it and met Amara at her car, already unzipping her pack to allow Amara to tuck her wallet, keys and water inside.

Amara pressed light kisses to each of Jass's cheeks. "Been here long?"

"I barely got here."

"Don't lie to me."

"I would never lie to you." Jass and Amara had known each other since grade school and had always trusted the other with the hard stuff. When they were young and scared, they kept secrets from each other, but the secrets were burdensome. When one had slipped from Jass's grasp, she had expected to lose Amara. Who would want to be friends with the kid whose mom sometimes bailed on her for days on end, leaving Jass to fend for herself? Instead of judging, Amara had surprised her by saying she wished her parents would leave, so she could be herself. Every minute she was at home with them, she had to perform the role they expected from her. Since then, they had confided in each other without shame. They were each other's family now. She gave Amara a quick hug and whispered, "You look like a lesbian."

"Stop it!" She punched Jass lightly and started their walk through the neighborhood of fairytale homes surrounded by oaks and masonry.

"I don't mind. But you know everyone's going to presume we're a couple."

Amara was typically dressed to the nines in clothes that required dry-cleaning and shoes that required balance. Her highlighted hair fell past her shoulders when she wore it down. Today she had it pulled through a ballcap. She wore almost no makeup. "They do even when I'm not wearing cargo shorts," Amara laughed. "At least you're not dressed like Dora today." She happily began to sing the theme song.

Jass accepted the topic change easily since she had new information about Sarah and Chloe to share. "I didn't wear a drop of pink yesterday when I went to clean the pool filter."

"You still kinda look like her, though. Dark hair, dark eyes."

"Ambiguously Latine," Jass added. "She at least didn't sing the theme song, unlike some people."

"The Sarapist?"

"No. Her daughter, Chloe. The kid kinda broke my heart." She felt guilty, now, for so glibly describing Sarah as a hot mess because of the clear impact the mother's wired state had on her child. "I didn't know her other mom was coming to pick her up for the weekend. The kid came out to the pool to hang with me while her moms fought."

"She told you they were fighting or you heard them?" Amara asked, wide-eyed.

"She told me they were having a grown-up conversation. Her body posture said it was more than hammering out logistics. There's a whole lot of tension there, and I feel for the kid. Sarah had that whole podcast about being grown-ups, so children are not pulled in a bunch of directions by divorced parents, but Chloe's still being pulled in a bunch of directions."

"Sarah?" Amara bumped her hip against Jass.

"She introduced herself," Jass explained with a shrug.

"Does it make you feel differently about…"

Jass had intended to change the topic but could see how she'd done the exact opposite. "Not at all! Chloe's moms went into parenting as a couple, and now they've split, and they have to renegotiate everything. She has two homes after having one all her life. What we're talking about is the complete opposite. We're not a couple. We already have homes and lives separate from each other, so that's going to be our baby's normal."

"Just the same, I worry about you. How do you know we won't be exactly like Chloe's moms, you wanting to date and things getting all tense like they always do when your girlfriends think we're secretly in love with each other?"

"I see it being easier the next time I date. I'll be able to explain our relationship. We wanted to have a baby, but we've never wanted to be a couple. We don't feel that way about each other."

"And yet we're raising a kid together? That's threatening. You said yourself that we look like a lesbian couple. Put yourself in someone else's shoes. I know that a single mom with an infant does not scream *ready for a relationship!* I know that I'm all in for this baby. I get what The Sarapist says when I imagine having an infant. I don't see how I'd be able to be a mom and date at the same time. But you…I don't want you to blow your chance to find someone."

"Even if I didn't carry your baby for you, I would still have to find someone who understands how important you are to me.

I can't be with someone who puts conditions on my relationship with you. I wouldn't have made it this far without you."

Amara took her hand. "I wouldn't be here without you, either."

They had reached the end of the block and turned left on the access road up to the trailhead. The steep road stole Jass's breath, giving her time to consider Amara's words and all the backstory someone would need to understand the kind of family they were making together. Her truth was that she did not ache to be a mother as Amara did. She wanted to be a fun aunt. Amara had always dreamed about being a mother, but no surgery was going to give her a womb. She pictured explaining her choice to someone new. *We grew up as close as sisters. If I had a sister who couldn't have a baby, I would carry one for her in a heartbeat.*

But Amara wasn't her sister. And they weren't just talking about using Jass's womb. They were talking about using Amara's sperm which involved a deeper level of connection. Jass understood this but nonetheless believed that she could have a meaningful relationship with a woman and be part of Amara's family as well. She tried some of her arguments in her head. *Aunts are often close to their siblings' children, and they date at the same time.* But they don't often carry the baby. What about nursing? Was she going to nurse? There were so many details that she and Amara had not discussed.

Jass was closer to Amara than anyone in her biological family and anyone she'd ever dated. Making a baby seemed natural given how much they had been through. Amara had included Jass in every joy that brought her closer to herself. Her personal identity had been so much the focus of her life that she had thrown Jass for a loop when she broached the topic of parenthood, sharing that she had banked sperm before she began her gender-affirming hormone therapy.

They finally reached the trailhead that took them out of the blazing sun. Already at ten o'clock, they welcomed the shade provided by the great oaks. The trail offered a more gradual climb, allowing both women to catch their breath.

"Did you get to see Sarah at all?"

"Yeah. Both moms came out looking for Chloe. Are you sure you want to have a baby with someone who didn't even think about whether it's okay for a kid to be outside talking to the pool tech without a parent present? How do people learn all this shit?"

"One day at a time, I guess. You clearly had your eye on the kid, so you knew she was okay. And you said she was upset. How was Sarah? What's she like on Saturday morning? Cutely rumpled?"

"She's too tightly wound to be rumpled. If she wasn't a therapist, I'd suggest she find one."

"But she sounds so together on her podcast when she talks about renegotiating parenting on her own."

"Come on. Can you imagine her suddenly starting to date again after years of telling people that they can't? How many times have you heard her tell people they have to prioritize their kids if they split up? What would she say to them?"

"Oops?"

Jass gave her friend a withering stare. "She hasn't been ambiguous about dating after divorce. Remember the slew of memes that followed her saying how children need stability, not to be strapped to the emotional roller coaster of dating."

"I've never agreed with her there. That kind of rigid thinking tells me she's put blinders on, so she can see what she wants to see instead of the complexity of real life."

"Now who's the therapist?" Jass asked.

"Definitely not me! But you said yourself that she needs one. When it comes to self-care, she has a lot to offer. That one about ditching the mean inner voice is terrific, but I hardly ever connect when she talks about parenting. Any time I've tried, all I hear is someone who hasn't healed from what she experienced with her own parents. That one about whether we keep or ditch traditions? It made me feel sad for her."

"Me, too. It's got to be hard for her to be in the spotlight, everyone waiting to see if she's going to follow her own rules."

"You can help her, Jass."

"I'll tell her about my awesome stepdad who gave my life so much more stability, and she'll retract everything she's said about sparing kids the drama of their parents dating?"

"Yes! And then she'll see how stable you are and…"

"Enough. She needs help with her pool, that's all. And I'm not even sure that's going to be easy."

"I thought you said it was an easy filter thing."

"Let's hope. Because I would hate to be the one to tell her that she's got a bigger problem on her hands."

CHAPTER FIVE

Sarah had every intention of being the best version of herself on Thursday. She had promised Joshua, the executive producer of her podcast, that she was researching an idea for the next episode and would get back to him when she had content to record.

The problem was that she didn't have an idea. How serious Tricia and the new girlfriend must be if she was wanting to introduce her to Chloe polluted her every thought. After she dropped Chloe off at school each morning, she brewed her morning tea, but instead of heading to the office, she kept ending up in the bedroom she and Tricia had shared. She hadn't been able to sleep there since Tricia left.

Maybe if she gave the room a makeover, it wouldn't feel so wrong to be the sole occupant. Maybe she and Chloe should move. She could do her job anywhere. Why not live closer to the beach? *On your income?* Her inner voice laughed off this new plan. She should really move. She couldn't afford so much house on her own, even with Tricia's child support. *You're terrible with moves, remember?* She was. The packing daunted her, especially factoring in Chloe's room. No. This was her forever home. She and Tricia had done most of the renovations before she left. She could make things work.

Another day passed with eating lunch and cleaning the kitchen her sole accomplishments. At least the pool was looking better, and she could throw Chloe in after school. That would make the afternoon easier, especially if it meant that she would run into Jass. Crossing her fingers that Jass would not come to do the pool maintenance while she ran to pick up Chloe, Sarah dashed out the door.

Her daughter slunk out of the classroom, limp as a cooked noodle. Sarah lifted her sweaty bangs from Chloe's forehead. "You look hot. Let's get you in the pool when we get home."

"I don't feel like swimming."

"What? Last week you were begging to go in the pool."

"It's itchy."

"That's because of the chlorine. A shower should help."

"It didn't yesterday."

"How about we ask Jass?"

Her daughter brightened. "Is Jass coming today? She said she would teach me how to test the water."

"We'll need to stay out of her way. I'm sure she'll be busy," Sarah said, though she, too, was looking forward to talking to Jass about the pool.

When she turned onto their street, Sarah spotted Jass's red truck parked at the curb and Jass at the back by the cart attached to the tailgate.

"Is she done?" Chloe asked, trying to unbuckle the straps on her car seat. "What if she's done!"

"Stay calm," Sarah said, though she felt as anxious as her child. She told herself that she merely wanted to express her gratitude for the work Jass had done, but she could feel her inner self rolling her eyes. *Don't kid yourself. How you feel has nothing to do with the pool and everything to do with how good-looking she is.* It doesn't hurt to admire, she told herself, following her daughter across the lawn.

She heard Tricia's defense when she had first told Sarah she was dating Lydia: *I'm divorced, not dead.* At the time, she had argued how divorce brought with it even more responsibility, not permission to cut loose. Now, though she would never admit it to Tricia, she saw some truth in the sentiment, that life continued after divorce.

"Good timing!" Jass said. "I was about to leave you a note about needing a key to the pool gate."

"Oh, stupid me! We swam yesterday, and I must have carried the key in with me afterward. Let me grab it."

"Great," Jass said, though her voice didn't match her statement.

"Can I wheel the cart?" Chloe asked, not following after Sarah.

"Come through the house with me, so you can change."

"I don't want my swimsuit. I want to help with the pool!" Chloe demanded.

"Weren't you the one itching to get in a few weeks ago?" Jass asked.

"Our pool is itchy."

Jass glanced to Sarah who shrugged. "She said the water was bothering her yesterday. I wondered if you put in a bunch of chlorine to get rid of the green."

"The chlorine shouldn't be high. Let's check and see," she said to Chloe.

"Idiot, idiot, idiot," Sarah mumbled to herself as she raced through the house, locating the key on the kitchen counter before joining Jass and Chloe at the pool.

Chloe followed Jass like a duckling and watched with great attention as Jass dipped a test strip in the water. "Hold it flat," she instructed, handing it to Chloe. "The third square should turn a shade of purple between these two arrows." She held the strip next to a bottle. "If there's too much chlorine, it's going to be bright purple like this last square."

"I don't see purple."

"Nope. That means the pool needs chlorine, not that it's too high. Tell me about your itchies." Jass removed the blue hose and attached it to a brush she clicked onto a long pole. Though her hands were busy, her attention stayed focused on Chloe.

Sarah envied how relaxed Chloe was talking to Jass. Every minute they spent together felt charged. She thought the hours that Chloe spent at school would make the hours they spent together more pleasant, but within minutes of being in the same room, she was snapping at her child and scolding herself for letting Chloe push her buttons. These days it felt like everyone was better with her child than she was.

While Jass set up her equipment, Chloe described the way her skin felt. She kept listening as she maneuvered about the pool in a mesmerizing dance of balance and agility. Sarah watched with admiration she would give anyone who clearly knew her craft. But she watched more intently than that, feeling again like she was emerging from darkness into light. As much as she was enjoying herself, she needed to detach her attention from wanting to run her hand down Jass's long smooth leg or bury it in her thick, black hair. She had to keep her focus on her child.

"Maybe your pool is getting colder," Jass offered. "The temperature is starting to drop at night, and that will suck the heat right out of the water. Could the itchies be goose pimples?" So kind to entertain Chloe as she danced around miming what it felt like after she swam. Sarah had to motivate, to buck up and be the parent.

"Chloe, let's let Jass finish up her work. We need to get a snack. How about some watermelon?"

As it usually did, the word watermelon threw a switch in her child's brain, and Chloe ran toward the house. "Works every time." She waved to Jass who would surely appreciate being able to work without distraction and followed after Chloe. She was assessing the dinner problem, mainly that she once again had to produce a healthy meal from the contents of her refrigerator, when Jass knocked on the back door.

"Everything okay?" Sarah asked.

"There's good news and bad news." Jass removed her sunglasses, parking them on top of her head revealing her warm brown eyes. Sarah would like nothing better than to drown in them.

"Good news first," Sarah said.

"I've figured out what's causing the itchies."

Sarah stepped out onto the patio and closed the door behind her. "What is it?"

"Someone resurfaced your pool at some point with fiberglass. It's breaking down and releasing shards into the water."

"My ex said that there were chunks chipping off the bottom, but since it's still holding water, she didn't think it was a problem."

"I'm surprised you don't have to add water every day," Jass responded. "And holding water or not, the fiberglass is absolutely a problem."

"I take it the bad news is that it needs to be redone?"

"Yes. I'm not sure why it's been surfaced at all. Come take a look with me."

Sarah followed her to the pool yard and crouched down next to her. Sarah should have been feeling overwhelmed by the news that she was facing a huge expense. Instead, she felt acutely aware of how close she was to Jass.

"See this white track running all along the outer rim of the pool? It's for a vinyl liner."

"I'm sorry. I don't understand." It was difficult for Sarah to concentrate on what Jass was saying when the words drew Sarah's attention to Jass's mouth. She'd read about impossibly full lips before, but she had never fixated on a pair as perfect as Jass's.

"It's a big bag that lines the pool to hold the water. They come in really pretty patterns. Once you replace it, you won't have any problems at all with Chloe feeling itchy."

"I'm sorry," Sarah said. "I got lost there. How does a liner tie to itchies?"

"Whatever someone coated the pool with to avoid replacing the liner is sloughing off in the water," Jass explained again.

These words slammed Sarah firmly back into her mothering responsibilities. "I can't believe I've been telling her it's the chemicals! I'm a terrible mother! She's complained about it before, but I've always told her a shower would fix it."

Jass looked uncomfortable, and Sarah couldn't understand why. Any parent would be upset about subjecting their child to shards of fiberglass in the water, wouldn't they? Jass chewed on her bottom lip before responding. "It never bothered you?"

"Oh, I don't swim! I don't enjoy being wet." She heard what the words sounded like too late to retract them and shook her head to recenter herself. "I get too cold. Chloe has always been more tolerant of the water temperature, and honestly, I need the break."

Jass nodded but did not respond. "I have a card for a guy who does vinyl. I could grab it from my truck."

"Okay. That would be wonderful."

They walked in awkward silence. "I'm sorry for the comment about needing a break and for taking advantage of your time earlier. I'm recently divorced, and it's such a different dynamic doing all of this on my own. I'm a little lost at the moment, and it's difficult to ask for help."

"I understand that, and it's fair to say what you said. It's not…" Jass's gaze flitted away again, clearly withholding her thoughts.

"It's not what?" Sarah prodded.

"Nothing."

Sarah crossed her arms. "It's not nothing. Have I made you uncomfortable?" For an instant, Sarah worried that Jass was trying to find a way to tell her to stop staring at her.

"I think you're being awfully hard on yourself is all. You didn't know about the fiberglass, and that doesn't make you a bad mom. Don't beat yourself up about it."

"Oh." Sarah was taken aback. That was the last thing she expected Jass to say.

Jass handed her the vinyl installer's card. "Give him a call soon. He'll have to drain the pool, and you don't want a bunch of chemicals going into your yard."

"How long is it going to take to put in a liner?"

"A month? Six weeks? It's too bad you lose the end of the swim season, but really, with night temps dropping so low, the water won't be comfortable for long. Unless you have a polar bear."

"A month!" Sarah gasped. She hadn't expected the news would be that bad.

Jass raised her hands as if to defend herself. "It's only a guess. I don't know how long it takes this guy to get the liner made. I'm sorry I didn't have better news. I didn't put chemicals in today. Give him a call. If I'm wrong about when he wants to drain it, call me, and I can swing by this weekend again. I don't live too far from here. My number's on the back of the card."

Sarah nodded, trying to process everything that Jass had said. She had hoped that Jass was going to be a weekly dose of sunshine. Now she saw nothing but clouds.

CHAPTER SIX

Jass's face burned, and it was not from the amount of sun she was exposed to servicing pools. She'd been about to school Sarah Cooper on the concept of positive self-talk which she had learned about from *The Sarapist is In* podcast. What had she been thinking? At her next house, she scrolled through the past episodes of the podcast on her phone, easily finding one that she'd played many times before. She hit play and felt her body relax to the theme music. The simple melody of an acoustic guitar never failed to soothe Jass. She had known from the first time she heard the music and Sarah's rich voice that she had found a key to helping her find inner calm.

"In this episode, I'll be exploring the way we talk to ourselves and whether that voice we hear is helping us be our best selves."

It was difficult for Jass to recall the person she imagined Sarah to be based on the podcast. Until now, she had only had the promotional photos to go by, so she had an image of Sarah being utterly put together. Her voice and ideas never failed to bring light to Jass's life, no matter how stressed she felt, so she had always pictured Sarah as being breezy, wearing pastel flowing linens. She listened now with the revised perception of Sarah, who seemed as frayed as the edges of her ripped jeans shorts.

"You look terrible in that outfit. You're an idiot. You'll never be able to…Fill in the blank. Get that job. Publish a book. Impress your parents. You can't do anything right.

"Can you imagine saying any of those things to your best friend? Or even an acquaintance? No! We know better than to say such harsh and unhelpful things to each other.

"But to ourselves? We say those kinds of things and much worse. It's no wonder that we struggle to feel good about ourselves when our self-talk is so negative and destructive."

This was one of Jass's favorite episodes. Everything Sarah said resonated with her. She had worked hard to revise the way she talked to herself. As Sarah instructed at the end of the episode, she had taken the time to fold a piece of paper in half, writing on one side the most common things she told herself.

Anyone could do the job I do.

I'll never find anyone who can accept my closeness with Amara.

I suck at relationships.

There's nothing exciting about me.

She had then challenged herself to replace those ideas with more positive self-talk.

I take really good care of every pool on my route.

My relationship with Amara is special, and there is someone out there who will understand that and not be threatened. I just have to be patient.

Relationships take a lot of work for everyone.

I am the only me there is.

For months, Jass had kept the list in her pocket to remind her that what she said to herself affected her mood and self-esteem. She shared with Amara that she wanted to be kinder to herself and was so grateful for her support and the way she would say things like, "I hope you told yourself how great you look in those jeans!" or "You told yourself you did a good job today, right?" She had an uncanny ability to offer encouragement the moment Jass's confidence was slipping.

She had gotten so much out of the idea of managing self-talk that what Sarah had said about herself really shocked Jass. Calling herself stupid, and in front of Chloe, had surprised Jass enough. But to call herself a terrible mother? If Sarah was saying things like that out loud, her inner dialogue had to be worse! It made no sense to Jass that someone who did such a good job at encouraging others to be their best selves could be so hard on herself.

It had taken great restraint for Jass not to comment. How could she when she barely knew the woman?

And she had to wonder now if she'd get the chance to know Sarah any better. She wasn't facing a minor pool repair. If she decided to put in a liner, her pool might be back up and running in a month or so, but if she decided on a cement pool? That would be a much longer project with a backhoe and rebar and time for the cement to cure. It could be months before she had the pool ready. And what if she decided to fill it in now that her ex wasn't there to do the maintenance?

The realization that her interaction with Sarah Cooper may have come to an end brought Jass an unexpected kaleidoscope of feelings. She paused the podcast. Had she been hoping to raise her own self-esteem through an association with the podcaster? She did not want to be so shallow, but she had to acknowledge how excited she had been to tell Amara about it all. Amara would be disappointed if Jass's access to Sarah disappeared. But even if she'd never told Amara, she would feel sad if it turned out that she wouldn't see Sarah for months.

She had to remind herself that she didn't actually know most of her clients well, even those she had had for years. She told herself to let it go. There was no use fretting about something beyond her control.

Two poodles, a big tan one and a small white one, shot across the yard, startling two peacocks that Jass had not noticed. Jass was always alarmed by the noise the smaller dog made.

"I hope they didn't scare you," Casey said, strolling across the patio.

"I'm not listening to anything, so I heard them coming this time," Jass said. The first few times they had raced by her without warning, Jass had almost peed her pants. Now she anticipated their unleashing. "How are things? How's Marv doing?"

Casey had moved in with Marv after he'd suffered a ministroke. When it became clear that Marv was going to need help with the pool, Casey's girlfriend, Adrienne, used her librarian research skills to find a pool tech who was a member of the queer community.

Though she'd set up the consultation with Adrienne, it was Casey Jass met at the house and Casey who had hired her on the spot. Jass enjoyed the days their schedules overlapped and was sorry that she so rarely saw Adrienne who mostly visited her grandfather on the weekends.

"He's good. He saw you come in and told me to get off my ass and offer you a glass of lemonade."

Jass laughed. What she found intimidating about the old man obviously didn't rile Casey in the least. "I'd love some."

The dogs bounded after Casey into the house. Jass had finished adding chemicals and packed up her cart when Casey returned holding a glass of homemade lemonade. "Hot enough for ya?" she asked with her Mississippi drawl.

"Getting there," Jass said.

"I don't know how you do it working outside all day long, making everyone's pool look gorgeous and not being able to jump in."

"I can't exactly get my job done if I'm *in* the pool."

Casey looked doubtful. "Seriously? A hot client hasn't ever come out to sunbathe in a bikini and distracted you?"

Jass choked on her lemonade and started coughing. Her face burned red at the image of Sarah poolside in a bikini. "Ah, nope!" Jass said trying to clear the lemonade from her throat.

"Sorry to catch you off guard."

"Not your fault. I'm distracted today. Saw a pool in the neighborhood that has a problem bigger than I can solve. I'd gotten my hopes up about picking up another client, but I'm not sure it'll happen now."

"Ah. That's a bummer. I'm sorry. I can set you up with a dog or a cat." A dog groomer by trade, Casey also volunteered at a shelter and usually had a story about a great dog or cat up for adoption.

"A pet would drain income, not add."

"Fair enough. If you want to put together a flyer, I'd be happy to hang it up at work. The pet store gets a good amount of traffic."

"I'll do that. Thanks, Casey. And thank Marv for the lemonade, will you?"

She headed off to her last pool of the day, envious of Casey and the home she had found with Marv. It confused her that Marv lived with Casey and not his granddaughter. Did Casey start dating

Adrienne before or after she'd moved in? Their arrangement didn't fit the expected, yet it worked. They had clearly figured out something special which helped Jass keep the positive self-talk that there was someone out there who would understand how Amara fit into her life.

CHAPTER SEVEN

"It's good to see you back in the saddle, Boss," Joshua said, stuffing his water bottle into his messenger bag.

"Joshua." Sarah used her best mom voice to remind her executive producer to consider his words before he spoke.

"But you are the boss. Without you, we have no content."

"I disagree. I had nothing until you sent me that article on happiness habits. I'd be spinning if it weren't for you."

Joshua perched on the edge of the small couch in the recording studio. "I'm glad that it gave you material, but I was also thinking it might help you, you know…"

"Get my shit together?" Sarah couldn't hold her friend's gaze when she said these words. She did not want to see the pity in his dark eyes.

"Yeah, something like that. I'm concerned about you in this backward town. It's a recording paradise, but is there anything out here to support you? I don't see you striking up a conversation with any of your neighbors with the lawn signs supporting the recall. Could you have a conversation with someone in favor of ousting the one board member who wants the schools to adopt anti-racist policy?"

"Such a waste of money."

"Not a topic that's going to get you invited into the moms' club, then."

"You know their opinion about moms who work." Two years ago, Tricia had convinced Sarah to leave the practice she worked for in Pasadena to devote all her time to the podcast. They moved to Revelia since it was closer to Tricia's work at a landscaping supply yard and an in-home recording studio meant no commute for Sarah. At the time, moving twenty minutes east didn't feel substantial, but it had turned out to be very isolating. Sarah tried to believe that not having much in common with the moms waiting to pick up their children didn't matter. She focused on what they did share—stable homes and loving families. That was where she lived her values, illustrating through her presence that Chloe's family was no different than theirs.

But it was different. She'd felt it when people smiled tightly at her and Tricia when they held hands on a stroll with Chloe. And now she was divorced which pretty much guaranteed that Chloe would never get any invitations for playdates or birthday parties from her classmates.

Sarah had been telling herself that it didn't matter. She had her happiness routine, her meditation and gratitude journal. She had described their importance on her podcast and believed in them wholeheartedly. She'd been surprised, then, when Joshua found an article highlighting research that happiness relied on the support of a community. As she'd shared on the podcast she'd just recorded, studies suggested that a community, like belonging to a church or a yoga group, helps maintain the positive practice.

When was the last time she'd written in her gratitude journal? Would belonging to a book club with the elementary school moms really keep her more on task? She shook herself out of her rumination. "I don't see the moms around here inviting me to a meditation circle."

"Exactly what I'm saying. How often do you see your colleagues from the Pasadena office?"

When traffic was light, she could get to Pasadena in a half hour. She and her colleagues had told each other they would meet up, have lunch halfway. They could take the metro and meet at Vroman's or see an independent film at the Laemmle theater. Sarah was certain they all continued to meet weekly, but even before Tricia left, she had never made the time to join them. "It's been months since I've even talked to anyone. I'm kind of buried here, trying to figure out how to be a single mom, manage the effing house, keep the podcast going."

"What we recorded today is going to make a killer episode. I'm glad you read the article. I hope it inspires you to start reaching out. Get a sitter for Chloe and reconnect with your friends. You don't have to do everything alone."

Sarah appreciated the sentiment, but in truth, she had to do most everything on her own. Nobody else was there to brush Chloe's teeth, make her meals, make sure her homework was done or fix the damn pool. The pool. Now that she had the recording out of the way, she had to figure out how to handle that nightmare. "Thank you, Joshua. You're kind to say that." She gave him a hug and walked with him to the front door.

Sarah headed out to the backyard to stare at the white crater of her drained pool. Two weeks had passed since Jass had delivered the bad news that had just gotten worse. She pulled out her phone and scrolled to Tricia's number. She did not need to hit dial to hear her ex's voice. *It's not rocket science, Sarah. Call someone to take care of it.*

But who? Troy, Jass's contact who installed vinyl pools, agreed that the pool was designed to be vinyl. Easy, right? Drain the water, put in the vinyl cover, and refill the pool. Easy peasy. Except that the former owners had covered the pool with fiberglass. Once Troy, who had to be in his fifties but still looked like young surfer dude, had drained the pool, he pointed out the patches on the bottom that had been chipping off, releasing the fine glass-like particles into the water. Now dry, more patches had sloughed off, creating an uneven surface inhospitable to the vinyl liner.

Sarah didn't understand why they needed the vinyl liner at all. Every other pool she'd seen in her life had been cement. Why did this one need a bag?

Troy's answer had bottomed out her stomach. Cement pools, he said, have a different structure to withstand the weight of the concrete. Since her pool had no rebar in place, it would either need to be redug and outfitted for cement or repaired for the vinyl liner. Troy didn't work in cement pools but estimated that the job would be comparable to installing a brand new pool to the tune of fifty thousand dollars. He could do a liner for less than ten thousand.

Once she fixed the surface.

She did not know where to begin. Google did not yield any results for fiberglass removal. This was her own unique problem, it seemed. She imagined an alternate world where she and Tricia had not moved away from Pasadena. One where she told her colleagues about the mess of her pool, and they rallied around her, suggesting…She laughed out loud. Her colleagues would never have suggested a work party at her house, but could someone have a suggestion for her about how to remove a layer of fiberglass? She couldn't imagine calling any of them now after such a long time. She would first have to give a full update on how things were going on her own in order to pose her question. She did not have that kind of time or patience.

If she'd joined the yoga-in-the-park crowd years ago when she'd heard the moms talking about it at the school pickup, would they have had ideas? Or would they have been willing to send their husbands to look at it? Ugh. She slammed the door on that unproductive thought. How they would love to use this as an example of how she had made her life more difficult by marrying a woman.

Tricia was handier than most of her male colleagues. Sarah pursed her lips. Would she have had tools to tackle this project? Was it something a person could do on her own, or did she need to hire it out? *You overthink everything.* Tricia's frequent complaint inserted itself, causing Sarah to grit her teeth. She engaged in the imagined taunt. *And you don't think anything through! You were the one who said that pools and kids go hand in hand. I never wanted a stupid pool! It was your idea to move to Revelia! Your idea to get a place big enough to let our family grow. Look where your impulsiveness has left me! Once again, I have to be the grown-up!*

Hands balled into fists, heart pounding, Sarah was ready for a fight, but it was time to pick up Chloe from school. Chloe who would want to hear that the pool was magically fixed. Who would ask if Jass was ever coming back.

Jass.

Would she help?

Jass had said she could call if she'd been wrong about the liner and needed the pool serviced. Could she call to tell Jass that she had been right and ask for advice? If advice was what she wanted, yes, she could call Jass. It was easy to imagine her engaged with a supportive community. The problem was that asking for help with the pool wasn't the only reason she wanted to see Jass again, and that gave her pause. Her stomach fluttered which she tried to quiet with a hand pressed to her belly. What was she doing letting her mind wander like that?

Joshua had said she didn't need to do everything on her own, and the pool was absolutely something she could not even begin to handle.

Sarah returned to the house and pulled Jass's card off the refrigerator. Text or call? There was so much information to convey, and Sarah did have to pick up Chloe. She punched in the numbers, her stomach tightening in anticipation.

"Jass here!"

Her voice was warm as sunshine, and Sarah smiled as she returned the greeting. "Jass, it's Sarah. I wondered if you might be able to help me."

CHAPTER EIGHT

Though her feet remained firmly on the pool deck, Jass felt as if she'd been thrown into the water. She had hoped Sarah would call. Dozens of times a day, she replayed the day she had given Sarah the bad news and handed her Troy's card. With her name and number on the back, right?

For days, she had waited for Sarah to call. Which was stupid. They didn't know each other. Sarah didn't owe her an update on what Troy said. Yet she had hoped and spent much more time than she wanted to admit mentally preparing for the next time she talked to Sarah.

When a week passed without a call, Jass assumed that Troy had seen the pool and drained it. How long it would take to get the liner ordered and installed? Could she text him? No. She had no business asking if he'd done the consult or calculating when the pool would be up and running again. Except for the fact that she wanted the excuse to see Sarah again.

And now she was on the other end of the phone asking for help. She flailed to right herself mentally and get back to the surface where she could respond. "What's up? Did you have Troy out to look at the pool?"

"I did. And that's why I'm calling. He can't move to the next stage until the fiberglass is out."

Jass stood with her skimmer net poised above the pool, trying to process how that could be achieved. "Did he give you any ideas for removing it?"

"No. He said he wouldn't touch the stuff. I'm worried about it, and I honestly want to run the other direction, but it's clearly not going to fix itself. I have to do something, but I have no idea where to even start."

The rush of Sarah's words made Jass smile. Her favorite episodes of Sarah's podcasts were when she got so caught up in her topic that she literally had to stop and catch her breath. This happened on her podcast when Sarah was passionate about a topic, and it touched Jass that Sarah Cooper would share her fear with her. "I've never heard of removing fiberglass, but I guess it makes sense. Would you like me to take a look at it?"

"I would be so grateful! I know it is a big ask. I…"

Jass wondered if her connection had gone out. "Sarah? Did I lose you?"

"No. I'm here. I feel bad for asking you, but I don't have anyone else to ask."

"I'm glad you called," Jass said. "And I hope I can help. What kind of tools do you have?"

"Tools?" Sarah said.

Jass understood immediately from Sarah's tone that she did not do tools.

"I'll bring some stuff. A client of mine was a contractor back in the day. I'll ask if he has any ideas."

"I appreciate it so much. You don't know…" Again there was a long silence.

Jass waited for her to finish her sentence. Sensing how overwhelmed Sarah must be, Jass said, "Is it okay if I swing by after my last pool today to get eyes on the project? I won't take up your time. I promise."

"Don't be ridiculous. You're the one doing me a favor. Come by anytime. We'll be here, and Chloe will be so happy to see you."

Jass ended the call and threw herself back into her work enthusiastically, pushing to get through her weekly checklist.

Sarah Cooper had called her!

To ask about removing an entire layer of fiberglass which sounded like a hell of a miserable job.

Nevertheless. Even though a pool without water was clearly out of Jass's wheelhouse, Sarah had reached out to her for help problem solving. Would her ex have been the one to deal with such a problem when they'd been together? Clearly, she wasn't calling her for help. And, as Jass knew from the podcast, Sarah hadn't grown up with parents who managed life's chaos. Some episodes had explored learning what not to do from her parents' example.

Who would Jass call if she had to remove fiberglass from a pool? Not her stepdad. He'd say that kind of hard labor was bound to break your back without padding your bank account. She'd learned basic pool care from Dave, but he'd always had his eye on corporate accounts with hotels and resorts. He had been disappointed in Jass for choosing residential pools, saying she'd forever be servicing the pool instead of lounging by it unless she kept her business tethered to his. She was much happier scraping by than what she considered an unhealthy outlook on business. He had swept in and rescued her mother, bringing stability to her teenage years. He had gifted her with the tools she needed to be independent.

Thank goodness she did not have to measure herself by Dave's definition of success. She smiled, remembering an episode of *The Sarapist is In* where she had described thought patterns like grooves worn by a wheelbarrow. It's easy to get stuck in the trench but not impossible to push out to create new, more positive, pathways. Jass had worked hard to reroute her thoughts to how much she enjoyed the pace of her residential route. It felt important to establish a relationship with people she saw regularly, even if some of her chatty clients threw her off schedule. If she mentioned this to Dave, his instinct was to swoop in and fix what he considered a problem. *Set a timer when you get there, kiddo. The only way to make money at this game is to be heading to the next pool in a half hour.*

Luck was on her side. She didn't need a timer to be in and out without a holdup. If she saw her clients at all, they merely waved from the comfort of their air-conditioned homes as she walked through their yards to the pool. The city streets were kind to her as she headed north from West Covina, the sun already casting long evening shadows on the panorama of the San Gabriel mountains. She drove with her windows down, despite the hot October day.

The wind whipped at her ponytail and dried her sweat again. After hitting ten pools, she was a grimy mess, but there was no time to fuss with appearance, especially since she was chasing sunlight.

Up the street from Sarah's she stopped in at Marv's house. He'd been a contractor, so she crossed her fingers that he would have an array of tools. She'd guessed correctly. He had been happy to lend her chisels and a mallet and what he called his "lady's" jackhammer, a hand-held version with several chisel heads. He also insisted that she take the safety goggles, earmuffs and an N95 mask. It was difficult for her to convince him she could handle it without his help. He had to accept her argument that Casey would be furious if she heard he was crawling around in an empty pool and her promise to be careful herself and honest about whether she was up for the task.

Her stomach growled as she pulled up in front of Sarah's. She gulped water to quell the rumbling, slipped into coveralls, and grabbed the hand tools. Sarah must've seen her slip through the gate because she and Chloe both met her by the pool. Chloe looked as cute as always, her almost-blond hair up in high pigtails. That it was paired with a blue shirt imprinted with a row of different dump trucks suggested that Sarah had Chloe's hair up to stay out of her face, not because she wanted to present her daughter as the perfect girl. Sarah was also clearly dressed for comfort in cargo shorts and roomy red top that brought out the highlights in her hair. She smiled and thanked Jass again.

"Too bad it's covered in fiberglass," Jass said, keeping her admiration aimed at the steeply curved sides of the pool instead of on the curves of its owner.

"Otherwise, we'd be up and running in about fourteen days," Sarah agreed. "Troy said that's how long the liner will take to get here *if* I can get rid of the fiberglass."

"If this was cement, it'd be a skater's dream," Jass said.

"Skaters?" Chloe asked.

"Back in the seventies, lots of homeowners drained their pools during the winter. Bored kids with skateboards put them to a different use."

Chloe's eyes went wide. "That sounds dangerous."

"It was. Sorry. That probably wasn't the smartest thing to say to a...How old are you?"

"Five."

"Well, obviously you're way smarter than a teenager."

"It's probably hormones," Chloe said, straight-faced.

Trying not to laugh, Jass caught Sarah's eye. Sarah shrugged as if she didn't know where Chloe came up with the idea, but it was clear to Jass that Chloe was growing up with adults who were honest and open with her. She filed the story away for Amara. She'd love it, especially since Jass recognized her need to plan out what she was going to say with little people around.

"Let's take a look at how hard it will be to get this stuff off, so you can swim without itchies next season."

Jass slipped on the protective goggles and N95 mask and stepped carefully down into the pool. She wedged the chisel under the edge of fiberglass and whacked the end with the mallet. A square inch chipped away. She reinserted it and got it under a bigger part, lifting up a section four inches by six inches.

"Look at that!" Sarah cried. "You're amazing!"

Jass puffed with pride despite the fact that the section was relatively tiny. Her stomach growled in protest as if worried that Jass would be distracted by the project and forget to feed it.

"Was that your tummy?" Chloe asked. "Do you have a monster in there?"

Jass put her hand over her stomach. "No monster. Lunch was a lot of pools ago," she admitted.

"My mom's making bunnies and dinosaurs. Want some?"

Sarah looked embarrassed. "Chloe's favorite mac 'n' cheese is shaped like bunnies, and the chicken nuggets are dinosaurs."

"The T-rex are the best!" Chloe said. "I bet Jass could eat twenty all by herself!"

"I don't want to keep you from dinner. You two go ahead. While the light holds, do you mind if I try another tool I borrowed? It's going to be loud."

"Are you kidding? Please try whatever you want. I will happily cook up an extra box of bunnies if you'll let us feed you."

"And twenty T-rexes!" Chloe said, bouncing up and down.

"How many do you eat?"

Chloe held up two fingers.

"Hmmm. Maybe I could eat six."

"Deal," Sarah said. "It'll be about a half hour."

"Perfect. I have just enough light if you show me where to plug in the extension cord."

"What did you borrow?"

"A jackhammer," Jass said.

Sarah opened her mouth but said nothing.

"What's that?" Chloe asked.

"A big tool," Sarah said. "Are you sure it's safe?"

"It's a baby one, not like the big ones you see with street construction. And I already got a safety lesson. I promise if it's more than I can handle, I'll stick to the chisel and mallet."

"You look like the kind of person who could handle a lot," Sarah said before ushering Chloe to the house. Jass paused before continuing around to the front of her truck. Was it her imagination, or did that sound flirtatious? Jass laughed at herself. This was Sarah Cooper she was talking about. There was no way Sarah Cooper would date Jass or anyone else, not when she had her five-year-old to raise. Nobody making mac 'n' cheese and dino nuggets was shopping for a girlfriend.

CHAPTER NINE

Sarah stepped outside to call Jass to dinner and forgot how to breathe. Her feet carried her to the pool deck where she stood, struck dumb, unable to interrupt Jass from her work.

Jass stood on the pool steps, one leg hiked up and stabilizing her arm. Sarah could too easily picture every muscle beneath Jass's coveralls. With how hard Jass was working to control the jackhammer, they would be glistening with sweat. Her whole body vibrated as she leaned into the mechanical monster. Sarah's heart hammered as loudly as the machine and sent blood thrumming through her veins, pounding where it had no right to pound.

She longed to feel this woman's strong arms around her. She wanted this woman between her legs.

Jass glanced up and the noise ceased. She pushed the safety goggles to rest on top of her head and wiped at the sweat at her temples with her wrist. Sarah wet her lips. She could not think of anything beyond how much her body wanted to be pressed close to this woman she barely knew. She did not operate this way. She was not driven by hormones or lust. She was drawn to intellect, stimulated by intense dialogue, never physical desire alone. But there was no denying the way she lost herself in Jass's brown eyes. This woman seemed to see her in a way that she had never been seen before.

Jass did not meet Sarah's eyes. "You ate all the T-rexes, didn't you?"

Sarah cocked her head, confused. What did she mean, T-rexes?

"I didn't eat any yet!" Chloe answered from behind her.

She spun on her heel. "Where'd you come from!" she said, her hand to her heart.

Chloe frowned. "The house. You didn't come back."

"I'm sorry." She pulled Chloe to her side. "I got distracted." She could not risk looking at Jass again. She'd climbed out of the pool and stood achingly close to her. *Not for touching*, Sarah's mom brain said firmly. Then she realized Jass was stepping out of the coveralls, making it all too easy to visualize her stripping down to nothing.

"Sorry I got carried away out here and didn't come in sooner," Jass said. "The jackhammer turned my arms to jelly, but it's working great!"

"Why are your arms jelly now?" Chloe asked.

"Not like peanut butter and jelly," Jass clarified. "They're tired. You might have to lift my spoon for me."

Chloe giggled and skipped inside, leaving the two adults. Sarah did not want to adult at that moment. She wanted to satisfy a very different hunger. She couldn't keep herself from admiring Jass's toned body again.

"Do you mind if I leave my coveralls out here and wash up a bit?"

Sarah snapped out of her reverie. "Not at all." She showed Jass to the closest bathroom and returned to the kitchen to plate their dinner. At least she had green beans to go along with the mac 'n' cheese and nuggets. Nonetheless, it was embarrassing to have someone witness this dinner low. Thank goodness Jass didn't appear to listen to *The Sarapist is In*.

Jass returned as Sarah had all the plates and bowls on the table. "Wine? Or Water?" she asked.

"I'm having water," Chloe offered.

"I'll go with what she's having," Jass said, sitting down.

Sarah returned with a glass of water and praise for how much Jass had done in the short time that she had worked on dinner.

"Yeah, the jackhammer will be a game changer. But it's still going to take a heck of a long time to clear all that out. It would go faster with more help. Do you have friends who owe you? If you had a bunch of folks with hammers and chisels, I bet you could get it cleared out in a weekend." She shoveled a huge spoonful of mac 'n' cheese into her mouth and moaned in appreciation. "This is so good!"

"I'm embarrassed to serve you this after you've done so much."

Jass waved her off and dipped one of her dino nuggets into a yellow sauce in the middle of the table. She moaned again.

How could she not hear how suggestive she sounded?

"Did you make this sauce?" she asked.

Sarah nodded, not trusting herself to keep the thoughts in her head safely locked inside. "It's just a simple honey-mustard sauce."

"Oh, it's delicious." She turned then and said toward the empty kitchen, "Can you say delicioso?"

Sarah flushed hot with embarrassment, but Chloe giggled and answered, "Say delicioso!"

Jass smiled, relieving some of Sarah's tension. She leaned toward Chloe and said, "She'll grow out of it."

Chloe clapped her hands. "I love that movie!"

"I've only ever seen the commercial," Jass said. "But I love this dinner. I could eat it every night."

"Me, too!" Chloe cheered. "I want bunnies and dinos every night!"

"Why not!" Jass agreed.

Sarah regarded Jass, trying to guess how many years she had on her. Not as many as she'd thought when talking to her in the glare of the sun. Across the table, she appeared carefree and vibrant, the wisps of dark hair around her face wet from the quick scrub she'd given her face, but she had the settled air of someone closer to thirty. She didn't wear a ring…Was she starting to worry about hitting milestones like being partnered or married, or was she happily making the most of her twenties, untethered and interested in keeping things casual?

"What would you eat every night?" Jass asked Sarah.

An image of bare skin and desperate kisses flashed in Sarah's mind. It took her a moment to redirect her thoughts to the topic at hand. Jass was talking about dinners. "When I'm not in survival mode?" She took a long sip of her wine, trying to recall the dinners she used to love before she had to factor in whether it would go over well with Chloe. "A spinach omelet smothered in mushrooms."

"Do you eat mushrooms?" Jass asked Chloe.

The girl shook her head somberly.

"Me neither," Jass said.

This returned a huge smile to Chloe's face. It did not take long to finish the simple meal, especially with Jass engaging in what seemed like easy conversation with Chloe. Too soon Sarah had to start Chloe's bedtime routine. She declined Jass's offer to help with the dinner dishes, given how hard she had worked on the pool.

Sarah sent Chloe to pick out clean pajamas before her bath, allowing a few moments alone with Jass.

"Never a dull moment with that one, huh?" Jass chuckled as Chloe skipped down the hall.

"Never." She thought about how different her life had been before Chloe. She wouldn't trade it for anything, but tonight she ached for the time in her life where her desires were her priority, a time when she could have taken the hand of the beautiful woman in front of her and led her to her bedroom doorway instead of the front door. "Do you think you'll have kids?"

"That's tough to say," Jass said. She combed her hair back, feathering her bangs to the side.

Sarah wanted to find out if Jass's hair was as soft and thick as it looked. *Not for touching*, she reminded herself, but oh how she wanted to. "I'm sorry to pry."

"Don't apologize. It's…Well it takes a while to explain is all."

"Maybe you'll tell me when you're on breaks?" She could tell from the pause that followed that she'd confused Jass. "It sounded like you had a plan for the pool?"

Then Jass's expression cleared. "Right! Did you remember any favors you could call in?"

"Even if I did have favors to call in, I cannot see anyone I know being of any help with this job, but I'm certainly willing to work."

Jass's eyes widened in surprise she quickly masked by looking toward the front door. "Okay. Hmm. Two people against the pool isn't the best odds…I might be able to convince someone to help out. Would that be okay? I'd be ditching the two of you for a few hours to get my Saturday pools in, but the rest of the day I could put in here."

"I would be so grateful!" Sarah couldn't help herself. She was so overcome with relief that she drew Jass into a hug. An electric current zipped through her. Every place her body touched Jass's came alive. She forced herself to step away when all she wanted to do was fall deeper into those strong arms. Jass looked startled by the gesture. Sarah rested her hand on her shoulder. "Sorry. That was…I'm sorry if that made you uncomfortable."

Jass tried to speak and had to clear her throat. "No. Not at all. That was…" She took in all of Sarah. Her gaze touched every place Sarah's body felt electric. "I'm good."

"Mommy! Ready!" Chloe sang from the back of the house.

"Duty calls." Sarah could not keep the disappointment from her voice. She opened the front door. "See you tomorrow? Tell your friend I'm very willing to pay."

"Great. If it's okay, I'll come first thing to get my friend Amara going before I need to do my route."

"That sounds good," Sarah said. She yearned to put her arms around Jass again and show her how much she appreciated Jass taking on the job. *Not appropriate!* So often she talked to her clients about how much effort it took to control their desires. It had been a long time since she had been in a situation that tested her resolve. Some viewed that inner voice as the devil on their shoulder, encouraging them to give in to the temptation. They came to therapy to amplify the voice of the angel on their other shoulder.

The trouble with that image was the binary of good and bad. Temptation and desire were not bad but did need control. The image of a spirited horse in need of control had always worked better for Sarah. No one should be forced to feel like they should get rid of their desires. She encouraged people to keep that inner spirited horse along with the reins to control it.

Sarah had never had trouble controlling her desires. She had always had a firm grasp on the reins. Tonight, though, watching Jass walk to her truck, she wanted to strip the whole bridle from the spirited horse inside her that was pawing to get free.

CHAPTER TEN

Jass's entire body vibrated with an emotion she did not want to name. She turned and looked back at the house, almost expecting to see Sarah there beckoning her back inside.

Stop with the fantasy! she scolded herself. Obviously she had been listening to Amara too much. She punched dial and waited to hear her bestie's voice through the truck's speakers.

"You must have heard me thinking about you," Amara said without preamble. "I have to call an emergency meeting."

"Tacos?"

"I'm already here."

Jass had been about to pull away from the curb but put the truck back in park to check her phone. No missed calls or texts. Yet Amara was already at Rico's? That didn't make sense at all. "Is everything okay? What's going on?" Amara was silent for so long, Jass thought she'd lost the connection.

But then Amara said softly, "I bought something at the store today that I want to give you. I've been sitting here too scared to call you."

"Okay." Amara's words calmed Jass. This had to be about the baby. Conscious that Sarah might be wondering why Jass continued to sit parked outside her house, she threw her truck into gear. "I'm on my way. Order me the fish tacos, just a side though. This is a second supper."

Jass drove on autopilot to their favorite taco place on Route 66. She spotted Amara at an outside table, stabbing her straw into her drink. They always sat outside for the amazing view of the San Gabriel mountains in the distance. They usually brought a feeling of transcendence to Jass, but today they mirrored the enormity of what she and Amara were about to discuss.

Amara didn't stand as she usually did, so Jass sat down facing outward on the bench, her hips pressed to Amara's, so she could pull her friend into a hug. It was the right thing to do. Amara clung to her and shook in her arms. "What's this about?" Jass asked, stroking Amara's soft hair.

"What if it doesn't work? Or what if it does work? Then what?"

"Then you give your life over to a new little life, the one you've been dreaming about for ages," Jass said. She moved to the other side of the table and stretched her arms across to take hold of Amara's hands. "You've wanted to be a mom so badly. We can do this. What happened today?"

Amara told Jass about the encounter at the pharmacy that had prompted the emergency meeting. She'd been standing in line waiting for a prescription when a woman with a toddler struck up a conversation with her. Amara had been obscuring the anti-inflammatory creams. Amara paused when their tacos were delivered, fish for Jass and carne asada for Amara. After a few bites, Amara continued, "When the woman found what she wanted, she looked at me and said 'Don't wait too long. The older you get, the harder it is to get off the floor!'"

"Ha!" Jass exclaimed. "That's from Sarah's podcast."

"I thought I'd heard it before," Amara said, but the quaver in her voice remained.

Jass squeezed Amara's hand. "That must have felt amazing to be seen as someone who is going to be a mom."

Amara nodded. They ate in silence for several minutes. Amara closed her eyes and took a huge breath before she spoke again. "She made me see how much I want this. I want achy bones from being on the floor too long with my kid. So I got some stuff."

"Show me," Jass said gently.

Amara pushed a bag across the table. Jass pulled out the box and found herself holding an ovulation test kit. "Shit's getting real," she whispered.

"We've been kicking it around, and I was trying to give you plenty of time to weigh whether it felt right to you. If it doesn't…"

"Stop trying to give me an out, Amara. I'm in. I've been in, and that's not changing. Got it?"

"Got it."

"Okay. Good. Don't forget."

Amara finally relaxed across from Jass. "What were you calling for?"

"What?"

"You called me. I was sitting here trying to work up the courage to call you, and you called me."

"Oh, it was nothing."

"Don't even try that with me. You think I'm going to let someone who lies cook my baby?"

Jass laughed and shook her head. She could not fit both what she had felt when Sarah hugged her and Amara's baby timeline in her head at the same time. Sarah was a fantasy. That was all. A lovely thing to imagine, but an impossibility.

"You are so stripping Sarah Cooper naked in your mind."

Jass almost spat out her soda. "What!"

"I know that look. That's your *I'm about to get laid* look. What happened?" she sang, clearly happy to move the topic of conversation away from herself.

"Nothing happened. She hugged me. That's all. I'm helping her with her pool, and she was grateful…" Jass paused, remembering how Sarah was looking at her when she'd come to say dinner was ready. Her body began to tighten again in places that ached to be touched. Sarah's words flashed through her mind: *You look like the kind of person who could handle a lot.* She would very much enjoy finding out what kinds of things Sarah would want to try together.

"Something happened. Wherever you are in your head, you're not here. And wherever you are looks fun." Amara stretched the word to four syllables.

"Nothing happened," Jass said.

"But you'd like it to. Would she?"

"I don't know. Maybe? She might have been flirting with me, but this is Sarah Cooper we're talking about. You remember, the one who says that single parents with children have one obligation in life."

"To raise their children. Yeah, yeah. Go back to the flirting part."

"I'm sure it's my imagination..."

Amara waved off her words. "Stop being evasive. Tell me what happened."

"I borrowed this jackhammer from a client, and I was chipping off fiberglass in the pool. I paused for a minute and realized she was standing at the edge of the pool. I don't know how long she'd been there, but..."

"But," Amara pushed.

"I felt like she'd undressed me, you know, in her mind. And then her kid came up and startled her."

"Because she'd been dreaming about getting her hands on your hot body. Not gonna lie. What you described sounds hot."

"I was wearing my jumpsuit. How is that hot?"

"It's so not hard to imagine what's underneath. Sometimes what's hidden is even more tempting. Had you thought of that?" Jass licked her lips.

"Yes, you have. But for you it's not what's underneath the clothes, it's what's beyond reach because of her morals. I'm going on the record now. Morals are no match for hormones, and I bet you a hundred dollars Sarah Cooper's got raging hormones for you right now." She pulled out her phone and within seconds was scrolling through Sarah Cooper's website. She enlarged one of Jass's favorite pictures, Sarah leaning against a garden trellis in dark-blue jeans jacket, faded jeans, and dusty boots.

Jass couldn't help sighing.

"I'm not even into women, and I think she's hot. Got that whole professional distance vibe going that gets you fantasizing what she's like in bed. But I bet she doesn't want to be in control. I bet this is a carefully created façade for someone who is waiting to be put in her place by the buff jackhammer-wielding pool boi."

"I'm a technician."

"Not in this fantasy, you're not."

Amara's words added fuel to the fire already burning inside Jass. What if it was true? What if Sarah Cooper had the hots for her?

Her hands itched to touch the woman in the photograph, but in real life? Could she allow herself to act on how she felt? "I don't know if I could. I mean, she's Sarah Cooper. That's some pretty major punching up there."

"Do not sell yourself short, Jass. You are one helluva woman yourself. I wouldn't ask just anyone to be my baby's mama, you know. Maybe she doesn't deserve you. Is that what you're worried about?"

"No, it's not that." Jass couldn't look at the picture anymore. She turned off Amara's phone and pushed it back toward her friend.

"What is it, then?"

"She's taught me so much about emotion. She doesn't even know how her podcasts have seriously helped me process the shit in my life. To have that focused on me?" Jass blew out a long breath. "What if she could see all of that? I'm afraid she'd touch me, and I'd come undone."

Amara turned her phone back on and continued to study the picture in a way that made Jass want to take the phone back. "She's intense. That's for sure. You might come apart, but she's smart. She'd put you back together, too."

Jass picked up the bag with the ovulation kit. She was about to start something huge with Amara. Now was not the time to even imagine what it would be like to kiss Sarah Cooper.

CHAPTER ELEVEN

Chloe danced around the living room, peeking through the curtains every thirty seconds and shouting that she didn't see her mama yet. Sarah was doing her best to keep her patience and enjoy the energy bubbling from her five-year-old. She understood from years of listening to parents struggle with their teens that this vivacious child would disappear into a sullen teenager who slept hours past sunrise. She acknowledged their frustration with a mantra she repeated to herself now. *The days are long but the seasons are short.*

Would her days feel as long if she and Tricia were still raising Chloe together? Would her days feel so long if she was present for her daughter instead of lost in a lust dream? She had been spending far too many hours thinking about how she could get Jass alone.

The racket of the jackhammer started up again, pulling Chloe from the front window to the back patio door. "I want to go watch!" Chloe grumped for the hundredth time.

"All that dust is bad for your lungs," Sarah explained. "That's why we have to get rid of it, but removing it is dangerous."

"Not for Jass."

"She has a mask to keep her safe."

"I can wear a mask. I want to help."

Sarah sat down at the kitchen table and pulled Chloe into her lap. "I know, sweet girl. But this is a grown-up project. You and Mama get to go do something fun!" Her guilt and anticipation tripped over each other. Tricia had not been happy about rearranging her plans, this not being a weekend she'd been scheduled to have Chloe. Sarah had no doubt that she was right about Chloe needing to be away from the pool project, and Tricia's argument that she should hire a babysitter if she couldn't give her full attention to their child for the day rankled her to her core. Tricia didn't plan every single day around Chloe's schedule, figuring out how to squeeze things she needed to do for herself into the limited hours Chloe was at school. She was angry that Tricia fought her so much when Tricia had so much more freedom.

But she embraced the anger because it made her feel like she was in control, which felt a lot better than feeling vulnerable asking Tricia for help. Anger felt better than guilt about wanting Chloe to be away for the day. And the night because she wanted…No this wasn't all about what she wanted. She had to be available for Jass and her friend while they worked on the pool, and she couldn't do that and focus on Chloe. It was absolutely fair to ask Tricia to have Chloe for the weekend.

And she felt guilty for wanting Jass. She held a strong grip on both emotions and looked at her hands as if imagining reins, reins for the desire she usually kept so easily under control. She could no longer ignore how desire was demanding to be set free. Since the first time she'd set eyes on Jass, she had been drawn to her vibrance. It had been the pool that had compelled her to walk up the street, but Jass's repeated kindness made Sarah certain that their paths had crossed for far more than pool repair.

"Mama!" Chloe called, breaking Sarah free from her spinning thoughts.

"Grab your backpack!" Sarah called. "Race you to the car!"

Chloe was already in motion, tearing out the front door. Sarah took a deep breath and steeled herself before going out for the handoff. She shouldn't have paused because when she stepped out of the house, she saw Tricia and Jass shaking hands.

Not right! Not right at all! her brain screamed. Sarah hustled over to the small group, weighing out who she was supposed to greet first. She couldn't even look at Jass for fear that Tricia would read something into it. God, Jass looked amazing in her form-fitting shorts and tank, orange and pink, Sarah noted. Had she dressed like Dora on purpose for Chloe? Sarah tore her gaze away and regarded Tricia who stood there like she was auditioning for the part of Elsa the ice queen in *Frozen*. "Thank you for coming to get her. There's so much going on here."

"About that," Jass interrupted. "I'm headed out to do my Saturday pools, but Amara's making great progress in there with the jackhammer. We could use some heavy-duty trash bags if you've got them."

A cold front drifted off Tricia. Sarah knew that hiring someone to clean the filter had rankled Tricia, but for her to have taken Jass's advice about the pool repair without consulting her…She was frustrated, and if she'd had superpowers, she would surely put the entire neighborhood into a deep freeze.

"If I have anything, I would have gotten it for leaves. Would that work?"

"Probably not," Jass said. "I'll stop on my way back and pick up a box."

Did she accept or insist that she would go buy the bags herself? Would Tricia read something into Jass's offer? At the same time, could she leave Jass's friend unattended with a jackhammer in her pool? What if she had an accident? That sounded like a liability.

Jass interrupted her spinning. "Let me help."

She was talking about garbage bags. Logically, Sarah knew this, but her words did not register with her body that way. Jass's words felt like a calm, steadying hand on the quivering desire Sarah was barely keeping contained. "Thank you."

"You bet. See you in a few hours," Jass said.

"Let me help?" Tricia said after she'd made sure Chloe was secure in her car seat.

"I told her that I'm juggling a lot these days and it's hard for me to ask for help." Sarah hoped it sounded breezy and not suggestive.

"With more than the pool?" Tricia asked, her eyes too focused on Sarah's. Sarah flushed hot. Could Tricia really read her? Then Tricia snickered and with a dismissive wave said, "Never mind. Forgot who I was talking to for a second."

Relieved, Sarah put on her happy face and waved to her daughter. When they were out of sight, she closed her eyes and took a deep breath, trying to regain her equilibrium. She waited for Tricia's words to extinguish the spark of desire Sarah had been nursing, but it remained, pinpricks of anticipation in parts of her body that Sarah had muted the past year. Luckily, there was a job to be done, and soon enough Sarah stood at the bottom of her empty pool, protective eyewear and mask in place, wedging a putty knife under the thin layer of fiberglass and chipping it free with whacks from the hammer.

She got the distinct feeling that she was slowing Amara down. When she stepped out on the deck, Amara had paused with the jackhammer to show her what to do. After ten minutes, she'd stopped Amara again to ask what she was doing wrong. She didn't expect to break free sizeable chunks like Amara with the power tool, but she also knew Amara had gotten more than dust when she whacked the tool with her hammer.

Amara kindly stopped again and moved her to a spot where the fiberglass didn't seem superglued on. The task took her complete attention. She learned the hard way that if her mind wandered, she smacked her knuckles with the hammer instead of the putty knife. She concentrated, all her attention directed to the satisfaction of contributing to the transformation of her pool.

She fell into a rhythm of hammering until her arms felt like putty, sweeping the mess into a pile and grabbing a drink of water. She was about to take a break when she sensed Jass's return. Sarah turned and found Jass standing at the side of the pool holding several bags. For an instant, she had considered pushing on to impress Jass, but she knew she'd likely pay with another smack to the knuckles.

Amara stopped, too, and removed her earmuffs, goggles and mask. "Hey, Boss!"

"Looks great! You two have done an amazing job while I've been loafing."

"You've never loafed a day in your life!" Amara laughed.

Jass's friend was gorgeous, tall and fit and completely at home in her body. Even in work clothes and covered in dust, she was refined in a way that made Sarah stand a little straighter. Jass, though... Sarah's eyes lingered on her strong thighs. Jass made her want to let go.

"Oh, I can loaf with the best of them when the work is done," Jass was saying.

"It feels never-ending," Sarah said, pulled from her reverie. She hoped she didn't sound like she was complaining.

"My arms are jelly, so I'm glad you're back," Amara said. "I need a break."

"Good. I brought lunch." Jass raised the bags.

Sarah felt both relieved and embarrassed. "You shouldn't have had to buy lunch when I've hijacked your day."

"There's an amazing sandwich place in Sierra Madre that I treat myself to on Saturdays. I got a bunch of different kinds. I'll set us up here on the patio?"

"Perfect," Sarah said.

"Mind if I wash up?" Amara asked.

Sarah showed her to the bathroom, quickly scrubbed her own hands and arms in the kitchen sink and returned to the back patio to an impressive selection of sandwiches and small containers of salads.

"I love the broccoli and raisin, but Amara's favorite is the three-bean. The potato salad looked good, so I got some of that, too. Hope there's something you like."

"Please add the cost of lunch when you bill this. It doesn't feel right that you bought it." Sarah's stomach growled loudly, and they both laughed. "But it does look delicious. You have to let me get dinner."

"Done." Jass handed her a paper plate and extended another to Amara.

"Count me out," Amara said, quickly filling her plate before easing herself onto a patio chair. "I'll help with cleanup after lunch, but I have that thing later, so I've got another hour in me, max."

It was obvious to Sarah that they were talking in friend code. *Please don't decline because your friend won't be sticking around. Please want to stay because she's not staying.* Sarah felt like she was in high school again when everything hinged on the person she liked saying yes to a date. And this wasn't even a date.

But Jass was blushing.

And Amara was hiding a huge smile.

It was obvious to Sarah that Jass and Amara had talked about what it would mean for Jass to stay after the work was done for the evening. Was it ludicrous to think that they had arranged for only Jass to stay in the event that there was a dinner invitation? When Jass turned her gaze back to Sarah, she knew she was right and that dinner meant exactly what she wanted it to mean. Nervous now, she served herself a light plate. Jass and Amara moved the conversation to projecting how long it would take to finish the pool. Sarah didn't care anymore. All she wanted was the workday to be over and to be alone with Jass at last.

CHAPTER TWELVE

"What do you feel like?" Sarah asked when they finally agreed to stop for the day.

"Like I am always a sweaty, stinky mess when I am here. You might regret offering to feed me." Standing on the patio, she eyed the sliding door to the kitchen. She could not possibly share a meal with Sarah without first getting cleaned up. But dinner was not what Jass wanted to share with Sarah. She had spent the last five hours running hundreds of scenarios of what would happen once Sarah called it quits in the pool. In some scenarios, they didn't even have to speak. They instinctively fell into each other's arms and knew exactly what the other needed.

More often she imagined an awkward dinner psyching herself out about misread cues and texting Amara to chew her out for encouraging her to make a fool out of herself. That scenario had presented itself so often that she thought it best to give Sarah an out, just in case.

"The only thing I regret..." Sarah's soft brown eyes held Jass's. She seemed to be running her own scenarios about what happened next. The anticipation of what she would say was agonizing. "...is how much my body hurts. I'm afraid that if I sit, I won't be able to move again!"

"A hot shower works wonders on sore muscles and joints," Jass said. She knew her face was flushing at the idea of joining Sarah Cooper in a hot shower, but if she was staying, she had to know that they were on the same page.

A smile seemed to try to take flight on Sarah's face. Jass couldn't tell if it was exhaustion or fear that pulled at the edges.

She took a shaky breath and reached for Jass's hand.

Despite having worked past the point of exhaustion, the simple gesture bottomed out Jass's stomach. She stared at their linked hands, trying to wrap her brain around how what was happening could be happening to her.

"I've never done this before. Even before I was married, I never…" She, too, had her eyes fixed on their linked hands. "I barely know you, and yet…"

Jass took a step forward and pulled gently on Sarah's hand. Sarah took the step that brought her close enough to kiss. All Jass had to do was lean forward. Her lips met Sarah's, and her exhaustion left her in a whoosh. Kissing Sarah felt like jumping into the perfect pool. Every cell of her experienced relief at the same time. She leapt from a place of doubt about Sarah's intentions and just as her body did once submerged, she came alive. Arms wrapped around Sarah and snaked up her back, pulling her closer, so she could plunge her tongue deeper into the kiss.

Sarah met her everywhere, finding Jass's tongue with her own, pressing her hips and thighs against Jass, undulating, caught in the current of mutual desire. Jass wanted to stay suspended there forever and memorize every sensation, but her body screamed for air. Reluctantly, she pulled away, chest heaving. She was afraid to open her eyes, but she was not in this alone. She raised her eyes and found a new light in Sarah's radiating "Again!"

They jumped again with the sweet knowledge that the water was not cold, that it was perfect, waiting to welcome them back. With her tongue, she explored Sarah's mouth, with her hands, Sarah's curves. She wanted more freedom. She wanted more skin.

Sarah's hands agreed, slipping under her tank to stroke Jass's belly and hips before gripping her ass tight. She did not hesitate with her body as she had with her words, and the sureness of her touch sent shockwaves through Jass. "So yes to a shower?"

"Very yes," Sarah said, her voice cracking a bit.

"Very yes?" Jass teased.

Sarah took her hand. "I can't think when I am around you. I don't want to think. I only want to touch."

Touching Jass could do, as she demonstrated when Sarah led them to the bathroom. Sarah leaned into the shower to crank on the water. Jass ran her hands from Sarah's breasts to hips. "No falling," she said, holding Sarah from behind.

Sarah turned her head, chin touching her shoulder, eyes shut. "No falling," she whispered, and Jass understood. This was about chemistry and need, nothing more. Jass pulled Sarah's shirt over her head and shuddered when Sarah reached around to unclasp her bra and strip out of her pants and underwear. She disappeared into the shower. When the water hit her skin, she groaned. Jass envied the water for having elicited the sound and stripped quickly to join Sarah. She needed to hear that sound again.

Sarah had already rinsed and turned in the shower's spray, so she was facing Jass when she stepped in, the water between them. She was proud of her body. She ate healthily and kept her muscles toned, yet she braced herself for Sarah's assessment. She stepped into the water, and it felt so good, she groaned, too. She wanted to lose herself for a moment and shut her eyes, but she kept them open, watching Sarah watching her.

Sarah's smile told her everything she needed to know. She held up a bar of soap, and Jass turned around, letting Sarah soap her shoulders and arms. Oh, her arms were tired! Her muscles reminded her of the long day of work. "You are so beautiful," Sarah said. Warm water massaged Jass's shoulders as Sarah carefully lathered her breasts. Jass's nipples, already peaked from the water, pulled tighter under Sarah's touch and made her clit pulse. As if she knew, Sarah turned Jass's front toward the spray, letting the water rinse her while Sarah's hands followed the flow of water to the apex of Jass's legs.

Instead of finding her center, Sarah stepped back and slowly dragged her hands down past Jass's hips to her buttocks and through her thighs. Jass trembled as Sarah's hands again came close to her center before retreating. Jass reached behind her and caught Sarah's hand, taking the soap. Turning to face Sarah, Jass guided her under the water, savoring the vulnerability of the moment. Sarah watched her as first her eyes and then her soapy hands glided over every surface of her body. "You are so sexy," Jass said, pressing her nakedness fully against Sarah's. "So hot. So gorgeous."

Sarah met Jass's mouth eagerly and pressed a thigh between Jass's, holding her, grinding against her enough to start gathering the wave within Jass that would build to the crash of orgasm. Jass wasn't ready. She pivoted them around in the hot water, pulling apart enough to tease Sarah's nipples, first between finger and thumb. Then with her tongue. She was rewarded with a low, appreciative groan.

"You like?"

Sarah answered by pulling at the back of Jass's head, inviting her to take more, press harder. She arched, pushing her pelvis forward in search of Jass as Jass devoted herself first to one and then the other of Sarah's breasts. "Please. I need you to touch me."

Her words, the timbre born of need, was almost enough to undo Jass. How long had it been since Sarah had been loved? She slid her hand between Sarah's legs and slipped through her hot folds. She was so open, so ready for Jass. Jass wanted to take her time. "You feel so amazing," she whispered.

"More." Sarah said, her arms tight around Jass. "Please."

Jass added another finger, and Sarah pushed against her greedily, punctuating her thrusts with unrestrained sounds of her pleasure, ahs and ohs that encouraged Jass to move faster and deeper until Sarah was shuddering in her arms.

"Yes!" she cried out when her inner walls pulsed against Jass's fingers. "Oh, fuck yes!" She pressed her head against Jass's shoulder and stilled her movement by wrapping her hands around Jass's butt. Her insides continued to flutter against Jass's fingers. She teased. She could barely move with how tightly Sarah grasped at her, but she could move in slow circles. She could feel Sarah tightening around her fingers again. Jass caught her breath and found Sarah's mouth again, kissing her languidly, now stroking her tongue against Sarah's in time with her fingers that were still buried inside.

"Let go," Jass whispered. "I've got you."

Sarah loosened her hold on Jass and ground her hips again.

"Yes, like that. Let go."

"What are you doing?" Sarah gasped.

"Listening," Jass said, pressing where Sarah's body said it wanted to be pressed, coaxing her slowly until she the magical fluttering came once again.

"God, you're good at that," Sarah said, melting against her. Breathing hard, she kissed Jass, alternating between kisses and breaths. Jass could have stayed there forever, but the hot water began to slip away.

Sarah must have noticed, too. She cranked it off and the two of them stood in silence. Water droplets tickled down Jass's body. *What happened next?* Sarah pulled her bottom lip between her teeth. She looked uncertain.

"What do you want, Sarah?" Jass asked. "Tell me."

Sarah took a deep breath and held it. She stepped out of the shower and wrapped herself in a towel. She pulled another from a cabinet and handed it to Jass. Worried that Sarah was regretting what she'd done, Jass wrapped the towel around her middle. Unhurried, Sarah dried herself, but when she was finished, she did not wrap herself away again. Without meeting Jass's eyes, she said, "I want to taste you."

Jass stepped out of the shower and placed her hand in Sarah's. She dropped the towel on the floor. She was usually fastidious about stretching a towel out to dry, but she could not take the time at the moment. "A bed might make that easier," she suggested.

Sarah threaded their fingers together. "Are you sure?" she asked, chuckling nervously. "Not about the bed," she added. "About that being okay?"

"Very, very sure," Jass said.

CHAPTER THIRTEEN

Sarah had never seen anything sexier than Jass dropping her towel and following her across the hall, completely naked.

The bed in the office had served as a futon couch for years. Pulled out into a bed, one side pushed up against the wall under a window. This room faced the street but had blinds Sarah kept shut. Sarah pulled back the covers. Wordlessly and without breaking eye contact, Jass lowered herself onto the bed. There was not an ounce of uncertainty in the way she looked at Sarah, which intensified Sarah's already burning desire. Jass grinned broadly. "Do you like what you see?"

"You know I do," Sarah said, sliding into bed and straddling her. "I have since the minute I saw you by your truck."

"I thought you might have been checking me out."

"Oh, I was. And there are so many things I have wanted to do, so many places I have wanted to touch you. But I'm so..."

"Gorgeous," Jass supplied.

A startled laugh escaped Sarah's throat. "Old. And nowhere near as toned as you are." She self-consciously ran her hand over the pooch of her tummy that had never gone back to what it had been before Chloe. Chloe. A moment of doubt crept into her mind. Succumbing to her desire made her a hypocrite. What would Tricia say? What would her listeners say?

"You are in no way old. You're, what? Five years older than I am?"

"But those have been parenting years..."

"Nope..." Jass tried to interrupt.

"And parenting takes a toll. For every regular year, a parent ages three times as much."

"Stop! You are gorgeous. And incredibly sexy."

Jass's words drowned out the fires Sarah's hypercritical brain was igniting. She traced Jass's beautiful, strong shoulders and trailed her finger between her breasts. The sight of this naked woman in her bed almost brought tears to her eyes. How long had it been? To stop to compute would require sad math, and this was certainly not the time for sad math. Jass made her days so much brighter. She hovered above Jass wanting to touch her and kiss her everywhere at once. She admonished herself. They had all night.

She lowered herself to capture Jass's mouth with her own, her breath catching when her breasts brushed against Jass. Jass arched her back, pressing herself to Sarah, begging for her attention. The cup of her breast, the warmth of her nipple against Sarah's mouth, so many sensations she had missed. She was hungry, and she could not stop herself. Once she tasted Jass's skin, sweet from the shower, she had to have more. She scooched down between Jass's legs, dragging her belly across Jass's sex, kissing and kneading her way lower. She sucked hard at the soft divot below each hipbone, relishing how Jass lifted herself in offering. Sarah paused for a moment, her chin tickling the neatly trimmed hair between Jass's legs.

All Sarah wanted in that moment was to lose herself in Jass. She ran her thumb through the warm, wet folds before following the same path with her tongue. One taste of Jass, and she was done. She could restrain herself no more. She had spent too long worrying about her responsibilities. Every day was full of must-dos, never-ending lists, and putting herself last. When she took hold of Jass's hips, she let go of it all.

She fell into Jass's silkiness and thought about nothing more than the way Jass rocked her hips and encouraged her with a whispered yes and more. Sarah had not forgotten how much she loved to pleasure a woman. She had locked it deep inside. Every stroke of her tongue brought her closer to herself. She had to feel all of Jass. She was tentative for a moment, at this first invitation into Jass's most intimate of places, but Jass met her with a thrust of her hips and pulled her in completely, slamming open the door behind which she had locked her desire. With the vision of escaped horses, their hooves pounding their way to freedom, she filled Jass. She thrust faster and faster, met each time with the sounds of pleasure she had missed so much.

Jass cried out, "Sarah. Oh! Sarah, Sarah, Sarah…" as she climaxed.

Sarah rested her head on the flat plane of Jass's stomach in dizzied triumph, gently stroking Jass's soaked folds. She could not get enough.

Jass's stomach growled loudly in her ear.

Jass pressed her hand on her tummy next to Sarah's head. "Sorry! That is not a review of any of what just happened."

Sarah forced herself away from Jass. "I'm starving, too." Perched on her knees at the side of her bed, she reached for Jass again and then nipped at her sensuous skin. "For more of this, but also for food. Let me throw a pizza in the oven. I'll only be a second."

Heart pounding, she grabbed her robe from the door on her way to the kitchen. Thankful for the stock of easy dinners she kept on hand, she chose a barbeque chicken pizza and slid it into the oven without bothering to preheat it. She filled a glass of water and drank half of it on the way back to the office. The other half she offered to Jass, who had pulled the covers up to her waist.

Jass drank thirstily and handed the glass back. When Sarah leaned to place the glass on the side table, Jass reached through the gap in the robe to trace Sarah's breast, bringing a smile to her face. She leaned into Jass's touch and pressed her lips to Jass's. Unlike the pace of their shower kisses, these were languid and gave Sarah's imagination room to explore all they could do. But then there was the timer… "How far do you think we can get in seventeen to twenty-two minutes?" she asked.

Jass sat up, pushing the robe from Sarah's shoulders. She bent to take Sarah's nipple between her lips. She swirled her tongue around the peak. Sarah grabbed the back of her head and pulled her closer. "Pretty far," Jass said huskily as she moved from one breast to the other.

As Jass suckled her breasts, Sarah shucked off the robe and moved between Jass's legs. "Are you still wet? I didn't get to feel you like I wanted before your stomach demanded food."

Jass reached between her legs as she spread herself wide. "So wet. But what about you?"

Eyes locked on Jass's, Sarah touched herself, mirroring Jass's movements. Her clit pounded underneath her fingertips. Balanced on one hand, she lowered herself to kiss Jass. Their tongues swirled in time to her fingers until she couldn't hold herself off any longer. She had to break the kiss to catch her breath. She took Jass's hand with her own, bringing both to her mouth. "We taste good together," she said. "I want to feel you now."

Jass tilted her hips and wrapped her legs around Sarah, gasping as their centers met.

"You feel..." Sarah bit her lip. "So." She closed her eyes and ground against Jass. "Good."

Jass grabbed her from behind and pulled Sarah against her again, faster this time. As much as Sarah wanted to savor the moment, she followed Jass's rhythm. Every thrust brought such an erotic grunt from Jass that Sarah quickly tipped to climax. Lost in her own inner quake, she was aware of Jass's hands clasping more tightly until she, too, shuddered underneath Sarah.

Slowly, Jass lowered her legs, and Sarah fell to the bed beside her, flopping her arms behind her. "I can't move."

"Someone needs to. The timer is going off."

Sarah lifted her head. "How long?"

"Don't know. I was a little distracted," Jass said. "Want me to go?"

Sarah pressed her forehead to Jass's and willed herself to move. "No. I know where everything is. Stay put. I'm not done with you yet."

On weak knees, Sarah slipped back into her robe and hurried as best she could to save the crisp pizza from being burnt. She scooted it onto a chopping board and grabbed wine and glasses from the cupboard. She rolled the pizza cutter to make six pieces. She'd loaded everything into her arms when she remembered napkins.

Jass laughed when Sarah returned juggling all her wares.

"Don't judge me for the box wine," Sarah said as Jass helped unload her arms.

"Never."

"Do you want a shirt?"

"If this is too distracting." Jass scanned her body before looking back to Sarah.

Sarah poured them both a glass of wine and handed one to Jass. "No. I'd rather you stay just like that. But I don't want you getting the impression that I'm a bad host."

"I'd never say that." Jass grabbed a piece of pizza and inhaled it in three bites, puffing around the hot melted cheese. Sarah knew she should be hungry and was forcing herself to take bites. Now that she had unleashed her desire, she wanted nothing but Jass.

Almost to the crust of her second slice, Jass took a deep, satisfied breath. Sarah sipped her wine and noted how relaxed Jass was.

"You skinny-dip, don't you?"

"How can you tell?"

"You're so comfortable in your body. It's inspiring." Sarah lowered her eyes and had a flash of self-consciousness. She felt awkward in the robe, but it also felt weird to remove it. She drank more of her wine.

Jass smiled unabashedly. "There is nothing better than swimming naked. You don't, do you?"

Sarah shrugged. "I told you before. I don't swim."

"Yet you live in Southern California with a pool in your backyard. That might be illegal. Tell me you eat at least three avocados a week."

"I put avocado on everything."

"Whew! We were about to be in trouble here." Jass popped the last of the crust in her mouth. "This is the best pizza I've ever had in my whole mouth."

"It's my favorite, too. Chloe says it's too spicy…"

Something shifted in the air. Jass didn't move, but Sarah could tell that every muscle tensed when she said Chloe's name. "What time does she come home?"

Sarah swirled the wine in her glass. "I hope this doesn't come off as irresponsible. Or presumptuous. Or desperate." She drank again and then ran her thumb along the rim of the glass where a bead of red had been poised to drip. She met Jass's eyes again and smiled faintly. "I asked Trish to keep her for the night."

Jass took a small sip of wine and lifted her eyebrows. "That doesn't sound like any of the things you listed. It sounds like you knew what you wanted. I'm glad it was me."

Sarah let out the breath she'd been holding. "Oh, good."

"I'm glad you're finally doing something for yourself and not stressing about what people will think."

Sarah tilted her head. "What do you mean?"

Jass didn't reply immediately, turning Sarah's spine cold. They'd known each other for weeks now. Surely, Jass would have mentioned the podcast by now if she listened.

"You know." Jass set down the piece of pizza she'd picked up. "How you say single parents shouldn't date. That always sounded really lonely to me."

Sarah backed out of the bed as if she'd been stung. "You don't."

"Think it's lonely?" Jass looked confused.

"You don't listen," Sarah said, pulling her robe tighter around her. "To my show. Tell me you don't listen to my show."

"Does that matter?" Jass asked. She started to move toward Sarah, but Sarah stayed her with an outstretched hand.

"Of course it matters! How could you not tell me that? All the things you know about me…About my life…About my breakup? How could you? Did you do this on purpose? To test my resolve?"

"No, Sarah! How can you think that?"

Sarah crossed the hall and gathered Jass's clothes. *What were you thinking?* she snapped at herself. *You weren't thinking! Clearly! What if she goes public with this? It will destroy your image. Should she call Joshua? Would he know what to do? Who could she call to fix this?* She returned to the room and held them out to Jass who was perched on the side of the bed. "You have to go."

"Please…" Jass pulled her shirt over her head. "Can't we…"

"There is no 'we' here. This happened. It was…" What could she say? Two minutes ago, she was ready to hit repeat on their night, and now she wished she could hit delete. That wasn't fair. To either of them. But there was no denying that no more could happen. She walked as she tried to process it all, her feet trying their best to carry her away from the awful feeling of reality crashing down on her. She shook her head. "…But now you have to go." She left the room, taking the wine with her. In the kitchen, she filled the glass again and drained it. She sensed Jass hovering in the doorway when she twisted the cap on the box of wine to fill the glass again.

She was halfway through the third glass when the front door clicked shut. Finished when she heard the truck's engine turn over. *What did she do now?* She'd barely eaten any pizza, and she certainly couldn't eat any now. She padded back to the office with her box of wine and her glass. Her eyes slammed shut when the smell of sex hit her. Longing neighed to its friends that had long since left the barn.

Sarah picked up her phone. She couldn't call Joshua. She didn't talk about her sex life with Joshua. She had nobody to talk to about her sex life. The only person in the world she could call was Tricia. She could not call Tricia. A tear slipped down her cheek. Angrily, she swept it away and refilled her glass.

CHAPTER FOURTEEN

Jass drove. She had no destination. She had to get far, far away from how she felt. If only she could hit rewind and say something different. Why couldn't she have left it at being glad that Sarah Cooper had picked her?

When Sarah said, "Oh good," Jass could have replied, "Yes, you are very, very…" An endless stream of "veries" stretched in her mind like the freeway in front of her. "Yes." In this imagined version, she said, "You are very, very good."

And then they would have kissed again and shoved the pizza away, and she would have tasted the wine on Sarah's tongue and would have been naked in Sarah Cooper's arms right now instead of driving to who-knew-the-fuck where in her truck. Alone.

Her insides pulled with the memory of her release. And of Sarah's. She switched the memory track away from their conversation and over to the sequence of touching Sarah. Her breath caught. How had she known to stay inside? It was like she'd touched Sarah thousands of times before. She knew there was a second orgasm ripe for the picking if she stayed. Sarah had wanted her, and Jass wanted so much more.

Numbly, she exited the 405 and headed west on the 133 to Laguna Beach. She parked at the shore. It was too dark to walk on the beach, so she grabbed the pool chair she kept behind the seat and set it up in front of her truck, settling in the warmth emitting from the engine.

She lost track of how long she'd been sitting there until the bob of a flashlight caught her attention. She watched a couple pass in front of her, hands linked. If only she'd kept her big mouth shut or used it for something better, that could have been her and Sarah.

What was she supposed to do now? With the pool halfway finished, she would have to go back, but how could she face Sarah again after what had happened? Her heart had never been lifted and smashed in such quick succession. She would have to tell Amara. Always one to rip off the bandage quickly, she pulled out her phone and dialed her.

"Tell me everything that happened after I left," Amara said gleefully.

"I am fucked."

"Yes! I knew it! She is so into you. I told you! Did I bet you? I think I bet you a million dollars. You so owe me!"

"I don't mean that kind of fucked. I mean…we did…but now I'm fucked. I can't go back there. But I have to go back to finish the pool, but I don't ever want to see Sarah Cooper again. Can't you go back tomorrow and finish the pool?"

"Slow down! Slow down and back up. What the freak happened? Start at the beginning. And where are you? Is that the ocean I hear?"

"I drove for a while. I'm in Laguna Beach."

"Honey! Why didn't you come here?"

"I'm embarrassed. I ruined everything." She outlined the time from when she and Sarah stopped work to when Sarah had told her to leave.

"It's for the best. All that sounds awful, but eventually, she had to find out you're a fan. This was the best-case scenario."

"Me sitting in the dark by myself is the best-case scenario? How's that work?"

"She was always going to find out, and if she'd found out before you had sex, you never would have had sex at all. This is the scenario where you got laid. Isn't that a win?"

"Not when I have to face her tomorrow. I can't go back there. You can't make me."

"You're absolutely going back there, and it has nothing to do with me. There's no way in hell that you could leave her high and dry to figure out how to finish that pool."

"You're coming with me, right?" Jass pleaded.

"Won't that be awkward?"

"Everything about it will be awkward. If you're with me, you can at least distribute the weight of awkward."

"I'll be there for the show."

"No. I'm picking you up, so there's no chance of you leaving me there on my own thinking that you're being helpful."

"You're no fun." Amara was smiling. Jass could hear it in her voice.

"I need you to not enjoy this. And I need you to hate Sarah Cooper. I told you she would make me come undone, and you promised she'd put me back together."

"You're not undone, honey. Sarah Cooper came undone, and she's not one to let anyone help her put herself back together. She has this vision that she has to do that shit on her own. From what you described, the two of you had a really good time. And greedy bitch that you are, you want more. Can't blame you, but c'mon. People like us have hookups with people like Sarah Cooper, but that's it. Trust me. Things could not have played out better than this. You hold your head up high tomorrow and finish the job. Do not be ashamed, and do not be angry. You can feel sad for Sarah Cooper that she is not allowing herself to have more fun with your hot self, but that's it."

"I'll try to remember that."

"You and me against the world, Jasmine Dìaz. Remember that."

"You and me against the world," Jass repeated.

"Will you be okay getting home?"

"I'll be fine. I'll pick you up tomorrow at eight. You have to do all the talking."

"You're such a grown-up." Amara signed off after making Jass promise to take care of herself.

She was right. Jass was such a grown-up. She'd been more grown up than her parents before she even hit middle school. She was used to taking care of herself, but tonight she was exhausted.

She leaned her head back and stared at the stars, wishing their light could chase away the shadows that had so darkened her evening.

The next morning, Jass and Amara rode in silence to Sarah's house. They let themselves in through the side gate that passed all the sunbaked potted plants. Amara didn't say a word when, without even knocking on Sarah's door, Jass plugged in the power cord and got to work.

When Jass engaged the jackhammer, she imagined how the rest of Sarah's night had gone. On her way to the front door, she'd seen Sarah refilling her glass. Had that helped? How much wine did Sarah have to consume to dampen whatever she'd been feeling when she asked Jass to leave?

Though Jass's arms tired quickly because of the previous day's work, she pushed on, sure the noise would draw a hungover Sarah to the pool. It took longer than she'd anticipated for Sarah to emerge, one hand to her temple, and a tall glass of orange juice, no doubt spiked to take the edge off her hangover, in the other.

Amara shot Jass a look, but Jass blinked away and kept at her work. The more she applied herself, the more likely they would finish the job in two days and be able to walk away. That had to be what Sarah wanted. She worked steadily, acutely aware of how long Amara talked to Sarah before she returned to her work with hammer and chisel.

Finally, when Jass's arms could take no more, she set down the jackhammer. After a long drink from her water bottle, she grabbed the broom and dustpan. "What'd she say?" she asked Amara.

"She said that you two hadn't had a chance to talk about whether you'd be here today. She's pretty surprised you came back."

"What'd you tell her?"

"That she obviously didn't know you. I told her that once you say you'll do something, you do it till it's done, no matter what."

"I don't know her, either. She thinks I know her from her podcast, but I don't know her at all."

"She has to pick up her daughter. She asked if she should get a sitter, so she could help with this. Hope you don't mind that I said we'd do fine without her."

Jass swept and filled a bag with debris, Amara's words tumbling in her thoughts. Amara took over with the jackhammer to give

Jass's arms a break. The noise offered relief of its own. Without it, Jass would have been tempted to ask Amara how Sarah looked. Did she look as gutted as Jass felt?

If she closed her eyes, Jass could call up the Sarah who knew what she wanted and who wanted her. She could remember Sarah's eyes hungrily roaming her body, trying to decide where to touch down first. Sarah's hands making contact and touching her exactly where and how she wanted to be touched. Sarah's mouth on her.

She took a shaky breath and shelved the memories. Amara caught her eye and mouthed *You okay?*

Jass nodded. Amara had said they would be fine without Sarah, and that was true for more than just the pool work. Amara was her lifeline and her anchor. She was so lucky. As long as she had Amara, she would be fine.

CHAPTER FIFTEEN

"I'm going to go swimming! I'm going to go swimming!" Chloe sang as she ran in circles on the pool deck.

"No running by the pool," Sarah warned.

"It's gonna be really cold." Troy ran his hand through his bleach-blond hair.

"But not itchy, right?"

"Nope! No more itchies for you. I still can't believe Jass was able to clear out all the fiberglass. Has she seen the finished product yet?"

"Not yet. It does look amazing!" Sarah had chosen a deep blue liner that made her pool look like something out of a magazine. She hadn't even texted Jass to let her know that Troy had been impressed by the job she'd done let alone that he had finished. Jass had not talked to her since the Sunday after they had…What did she call it? Hooked up? Was that all it had been? If it was just a hookup, then shouldn't she be able to appreciate it for what it was and move on?

"Let her know ASAP that it's ready for chemicals."

Sarah said she would and thanked him for getting her pool back in working order. Once she had written the final check and he was gone, she finally gave Chloe the go-ahead to jump in. She took picture after picture of Chloe playing on the step, shivering but elated.

"Watch me!" Chloe said, jumping from the top step to the next.

"I see you!"

"Feel the bottom! It's soft! And slippery!"

Sarah kicked off her shoes and sat on the edge to put her feet in the numbingly cold water. "Oh, that does feel nice!"

Jass had said nothing felt better than swimming naked.

Sarah gently chased the thought away and shut the gate. She did not need to be fantasizing about Jass naked. Troy had said to call her, but the pool needing chemicals didn't mean that it needed Jass. It needed someone who knew about pools, and Sarah would feel more comfortable if that person didn't know all about her and had not seen her naked.

But boy, did Sarah miss sex. Since Tricia left, Sarah had become pretty good at not thinking about sex constantly. Once she had come out and accepted her attraction to women, once she had given herself permission to love and be loved by women, she could not stop thinking about sex. She daydreamed about how she wanted to touch someone and how she wanted to be touched. Once she'd had sex, she would replay the encounter to savor the best parts.

In between sexual encounters, she calculated the probability of having sex like it was a weather forecast. When she'd been single, sex was difficult to predict. Would attending an Indigo Girls concert increase the chances? What about wearing Doc Martins to a poetry reading? Would her chances decrease if she picked the beef burger at the Pride-sponsored picnic in college? There was no telling.

When she began dating, though, she got quite good at predicting whether she'd have sex. Friday night brought a ninety-five percent forecast. Tuesday? Fifteen percent at best. First day of her period? Zero percent. On things like that, she and Tricia had agreed. A few days into her own cycle, Sarah's chance for sex popped back up into the forties, higher if it were a weekend.

Because the forecast was always available to Sarah, she liked to check in with Tricia. If there is an eighty-percent chance of rain, doesn't one grab an umbrella on their way out the door? It followed to Sarah that if she was eighty percent in the mood to have sex, it would be helpful to tell Tricia. Unfortunately, her weather forecasts were not well received by Tricia who said that it killed the mood for her when Sarah would ask about having sex later. Sarah tried to adapt by expressing the forecast in kisses or touches, but this did not yield anywhere near the amount of sex Sarah desired. She got frustrated. She stopped communicating in any way, and the relationship tanked, leaving her in a desert with zero chance for sex.

She thought she'd been coping with masturbation, but Jass shattered that idea. Before she'd slept with Jass, she would have said she was doing fine. She wasn't doing fine. She was staying alive, but like the plum tree that she had had to have removed after it lost all its leaves, she was not well. The trimmer she hired to remove the tree had blamed the drought. *But I water every week*, she'd argued. He had shaken his head sadly and said that watering by hose does not nourish the trees the way rainwater does. Trees need rainwater to thrive. Did she need sex to thrive?

Sarah knew she was getting by at best. Jass had said that her position on parents not dating sounded lonely, and it was. Jass was right, but that didn't mean that Sarah could call her and have her take care of the pool again. How would she be able to resist the temptation of what she had had and so very much enjoyed?

"Mommy! Will you swim in the new pool?"

Sarah smiled at her daughter, thankful for her ability to always draw her back to the present. "Maybe when it's warmer. Let's get you out. Your teeth are chattering!" Sarah stood and let her toes enjoy the warmth of the pool deck.

Chloe scampered out of the pool and into the sun-warmed towel Sarah held out for her. Parenting duties pushed all of Sarah's personal musings aside. When she had Chloe, there was a one-hundred-percent commitment to parent, and she accepted this. She wrapped Chloe in the pool towel and helped her rub dry, so they could go inside and start the bath, dinner, and bedtime routine.

Hours later, after reading *Ada Twist, Scientist* a third time, she pronounced it time for bed. When Chloe went pee one more time, Sarah pulled out her phone, scrolling through messages.

"I want to see." Chloe ran back to her bed and reached for Sarah's phone as she snuggled under her covers.

"There's nothing to see." Sarah tried to stow her phone in her pocket, disappointed in herself that she had taken it out in front of Chloe during her bedtime.

"I want to see the pictures!"

Sarah sighed and opened her camera app to show Chloe the photos she had taken by the pool. Chloe swiftly swiped through the images. She stopped on one of their feet side by side on the stairs.

"Send this one!"

"To Mama?"

"No, to Jass! She has to come see the pretty pool!"

"You think so?"

"Tell her I went swimming and I'm not itchy."

"Okay. I'll tell her."

"Send it now!" Chloe demanded.

"After I tuck you in. No phones at tuck-in, remember? I'm sorry I broke the rule."

"It's okay."

Sarah pushed Chloe's hair back from her sweet face. "No, it's not okay. I want to be here for your bedtime, not distracted by my work messages."

Chloe yawned and shut her eyes. Even though she had not been in the pool long, she was exhausted from the anticipation.

"I love you, sweet pea."

"I love you, too, Mommy."

Sarah was about to get up when Chloe added, sleepily, "I like Jass, too. Is that okay?"

This brought a smile tinged with sadness to Sarah's face. "Of course it's okay." She liked Jass too, and wished that it were as uncomplicated for her to express that. As her daughter drifted to sleep, she selected the picture Chloe had said to send to Jass. *Chloe swam today! It's cold but no more itchies! Thank you!*

She had had no contact with Jass since she'd finished up the pool weeks ago, and even that day, she'd only seen Jass working in the pool. It had stung that Jass had not acknowledged her, sending Amara to talk to her instead. Sarah had understood, though. Would Jass even be willing to take on her pool care now that Troy was finished with the repair? There was only one way to find out.

She hit send.

CHAPTER SIXTEEN

Jass studied the picture Sarah had sent. Twenty little piggies resting on a pool step. She would have liked an image of the whole pool. From what she could see in the picture of Sarah and Chloe's feet, it looked like she'd picked a nice dark liner that would pull in heat.

She read the message.

So it was finished.

Thank you was what someone said at the end, wasn't it? *Thank you* ended a transaction.

Sarah had said nothing about getting the system up and running again. Did that mean they were finished as well?

While she'd invested a lot of sweat into the pool, Jass had not thought she would hear from Sarah again. She had plenty of hours to consider whether she would feel comfortable performing the weekly maintenance on the pool after what had happened.

Most often, she thought not and resigned herself to the probability that someone else would pick up the job. Financially, another pool on her roster would be a help, but her sadness extended far beyond the lost revenue. Sarah's dating life was not her responsibility, yet Jass did not want to give up and allow her to exile herself just because she was raising Chloe.

In the ensuing weeks, Jass had listened to The Sarapist's new podcasts, hoping for a hint that Sarah was reexamining her position on dating. For as long as she'd listened to Sarah Cooper, she had felt like they were friends. So many episodes felt like Sarah was talking directly to Jass. There were times that the connection nearly brought her to tears.

Now that they had slept together, Jass anticipated feeling that connection more deeply, but the opposite happened. The content was fine, all good reminders about living an authentic life, not one influenced by expectations. Sarah's rich voice felt good in Jass's ears, but something was off. When the episodes ended, she did not feel invigorated or inspired like she usually did. She felt distanced, as if she did not know Sarah Cooper at all.

Her phone buzzed again, but not with another message from Sarah as Jass had hoped. This one was from Amara. *How are you feeling?*

Hot. That's how Jass was feeling. She lived in a small upstairs apartment with a weak air-conditioning unit. Evenings were the worst after soaking up the heat of the sun all day. At least on a fall day like today, she could open her windows and pull in the cool desert air. But that's not what Amara was asking.

Tired, she typed, propping her feet on her coffee table and pressing a glass of ice water to her cheek.

Pregnancy exhausted?

They had inseminated merely days ago. It was too early to pee on another stick though Amara had already purchased a bunch of home pregnancy tests. *Haven't even missed my period. Too early to guess.* Jass drank the full glass of water. Did she have to make dinner, or could she drink a smoothie instead? Did she have to make the smoothie, or could she justify driving to her favorite juice place? Pregnant ladies got to give into all sorts of cravings and self-care. She could be pregnant. If she was pregnant, she had to eat a better dinner, though, didn't she? She called Amara.

"What's wrong?" Amara asked.

"What if I'm pregnant?" Jass squeaked. "I'm too tired to eat, but what if I'm pregnant? Then I have to eat, don't I?"

"You have to eat," Amara agreed.

"Does a bowl of cereal count? I don't know if I have the energy for anything but a bowl of cereal."

"Depends. Are we talking whole-grain granola or Fruit Loops?"

Jass didn't want to say.

"Fruit Loops? Are you kidding me? You are not growing me a baby on Fruit Loops."

"It's too hot to think about food," Jass complained.

"Are you okay? You don't sound like you," Amara said.

"I'm good. Just tired. I'm going to rest my eyes for a minute, and then I'll figure out what to eat."

"Promise?"

"Promise. I won't be a bad baby-cooker."

"You know I love you for more than baby-cooking. Are you holding up okay after...you know. Sarah Cooper."

"Yeah. The pool's done. It looks great."

"Wait, you saw the pool?"

"No. She sent me a picture and said thank you."

"That's it? What about the setup?"

"She didn't ask me about that. I don't even know if I want to. It might be too weird. There are plenty of other pool techs out there."

"I call sour grapes on that."

"You're probably right."

"I usually am. Are you sure she didn't ask when you're available to take a look at it?"

Jass put Amara to speakerphone and returned to the text to read it verbatim. She blinked. There was another text. When had that come in? "Can you get us up and running again?" Jass read the message aloud.

"Wait, what?" Amara said.

"There was another text after the picture. She does want me to get the pool back up and running again."

"That's not what I heard. I heard she wants to get you and her up and running again. That sounds like she's regretting how she ran you off."

"She means the pool."

"Maybe you should tell her to find someone else."

"Two seconds ago, you said I should go do the setup."

"No. Two seconds ago, I was surprised she hadn't asked you to come work on the pool. There's a difference. I don't think it's a good idea for you to go back. Sarah Cooper is a big, tangled mess inside, and I'd hate for you to get caught up in it."

"What if I tell you that I was only attracted to her when she was who we thought she was from the podcasts."

"I'd call bullshit. The first thing you said to me after you met her was that she's a hot mess. You're attracted to the hot mess because you think you can fix it, but you can't fix it. You can't fix her or her effed-up life or bizzarro values. You think you can fix the wreck at the side of the road, but you've got to stay in your lane."

"You got that from Sarah."

"Sometimes she's spot-on, and right now, you can't let yourself get pulled into her mess. If you do, you'll get hurt. I don't want you to get hurt."

"You want me to push a baby out of my body for you! I'm pretty sure that's going to hurt!"

"One, that's a different kind of hurt. It's physical. Once you have the baby and heal, you're A-okay again. Plus, we already mapped out every detail to manage the emotional part. That's the part that worries me about Sarah Cooper. She may not realize that she said, 'Can you get us back up and running,' but she said us. She doesn't have a handle on her emotions."

"I know."

"What are you going to say?"

"That I'll stop by when I can bring you with me to be my representative?"

"Now that sounds like an idea. The woman does pay well. That pool job alone will cover another insemination if this one doesn't take. How are you feeling now?"

"We've been on the phone for twenty minutes. I don't feel any different."

"Call me if that changes."

Jass promised she would. She returned to Sarah's text. As hard as it would be to see Sarah with the line that she had clearly drawn between them, Jass could not say no. *It looks great!*

She hit send and chewed on her thumbnail as she weighed how to accept the job Sarah had offered. *Will swing by tomorrow to get the pump back up and running. Okay to purchase new screens for you?* She proofread the message and then deleted "you," replacing it with *the filter.* Keep the lines clear.

Whatever you need came Sarah's immediate response.

She doesn't mean me, Jass reminded herself. This is just about the pool.

CHAPTER SEVENTEEN

Sarah's heart pounded like it was her prom date that had pulled up to the curb, not Jass's pool truck. She took long, even breaths, telling herself once again that what had happened between her and Jass, while amazing, could not happen again. What she'd told herself had apparently stayed in her head but failed to deliver the message to the rest of her body. Despite her deliberate breathing, her body tingled where she longed for Jass to touch her again.

"Zero percent chance," she whispered under her breath. She tucked a bookmark in the book she'd been pretending to read all afternoon. She hoped that once Jass had come and gone, she would be able to get the focus she needed to prepare for her next podcast.

Jass had unloaded the cart from the back of her truck and was wheeling it behind her, the long, muscled legs that had first grabbed her attention quickening Sarah's pulse. Jass did not glance at the house. Would she be just as happy working on the pool without seeing her? Sarah chided herself for being childish. She had to talk to Jass. She was a grown-up. She had to acknowledge that she had come back to help her even if she said nothing about how Jass might be feeling.

"Chloe! Jass is here to work on the pool. I'll be outside for a few minutes."

Chloe tore down the hall, her red satin cape with a large embroidered "C" flapping behind her. "I want to see Jass!"

Sarah shook her head, laughing. Sometimes having a gregarious child made social situations easier.

"Jass!" Chloe yelled after throwing the door open. She ran to the pool gate and hop, hop, hopped outside.

Jass smiled at Chloe but before moving to open the gate, looked up to Sarah. Their eyes met and held. Jass's expression was filled with care, not the challenge Sarah had anticipated. It would have been easier to interact with a hurt Jass or even an angry Jass. If Jass was concerned about her, if she was thinking at all about Sarah's emotions, she was too close to Sarah's personal boundary. Sarah would have to work hard to push her back over the line of professional distance.

"Good morning, Jass," she said levelly.

"Morning." Jass opened the gate for Chloe and held it until Sarah was also in the pool yard.

The day was already warm. Sarah had to be reacting to that. She could not possibly be feeling heat from Jass standing a foot away.

As if reading her thoughts, Jass stepped toward the pool. "Gorgeous."

Jass met Sarah's eyes. Sarah's stomach bottomed out as she slammed back into the memory of Jass's hands on her naked body in the shower. Again, her body pulsed with need. She cleared her throat and dragged herself back to the present. "Troy did such an amazing job. Thank you for recommending him. I would never have known about the vinyl liner if it wasn't for you."

"It's slippery on my feet!" Chloe inserted, hopping with excitement.

The spell between the adults broke, and Sarah immediately felt the absence of Jass's attention. She curbed her desire to win it back.

"I love that about a vinyl pool," Jass agreed. "Did you get your mom in?"

"She only put her feet in," Chloe said.

"It's got to be a lot warmer to coax me in," Sarah said.

"I don't know. These hot days, a cold pool is sure inviting."

"Can you swim? Do you have your bathing suit?" Chloe asked.

Jass laughed. "No swimming for me on the job."

"Even if you're really hot?"

"Even if I'm about to melt. People pay me to keep their pools clean, not to swim in them."

"That's not fair. You can swim in our pool, right, Mommy?"

"You heard Jass, sweetheart. When she is working, she has to behave professionally. That means no swimming, as much fun as it might be." She was talking about more than swimming, and Jass's rueful smile told her she understood. Good. They were on the same page.

"What if you fell in by accident?" Chloe mused.

"Knock on wood..." Jass paused, looking around. When she found no wood, she knocked on her head. "In the fifteen years I've been doing pools, I've never fallen in."

"Fifteen years!" Sarah said in surprise. Jass did not look old enough to have fifteen years of experience.

"I tagged along with my dad when I was a kid. At twelve, I got to start sweeping the pool to earn spending money."

"Can I sweep?" Chloe asked.

Jass flexed her biceps and said, "Show me your muscles."

It wasn't meant to be sexy, but the pose reminded Sarah of how it felt to have Jass's arms wrapped around her, nonetheless. Chloe mirrored Jass's pose.

"You've got a few more years to go, kiddo. You could help me check the chemicals today, though." She took a bottle off her cart and extracted a test strip. "Do you remember what I did with this last time?"

"You dipped it in the water!"

"Yup! Can you handle that? Always check the water before you add any chemicals."

She knelt to match the test strip Chloe held against the control on the bottle. "It's not purple," Chloe said.

"Good memory! That means we'll be adding chlorine once I get the pump going."

"Okay, Chloe. Let's let Jass do her work."

"But I'm helping!" Chloe said.

"She's fine," Jass said. "The pump setup shouldn't be tricky. If you've got stuff to do..." She gestured toward Sarah.

Sarah looked at her hands and realized she was still holding the book she would be discussing in her next podcast. "I'm so far behind on my work. It's not easy to concentrate..." She looked at her daughter even though it was the way her thoughts wandered back to Jass that was the real problem.

"She's not in my way at all."

Did not having her own kids make her more patient? Chloe had always been curious when Tricia worked on the pool, yet Tricia pausing to explain anything made her crabby. She'd always asked Sarah to keep Chloe out of her hair when she was working. Could Sarah accept Jass's kindness? Would that blur the line that they were newly establishing? It would be such a relief to get some uninterrupted reading done. "Are you sure?"

"Sure, I'm sure. I've got a few new screens to bring in. You look strong enough to help with that. What do you say?" she asked Chloe.

Chloe ran to the gate.

"No running by the pool," Sarah and Jass said at the same time. They caught each other's gaze again, and Sarah felt the pull. She really shouldn't let things get too familiar with Jass.

"You must follow the pool rules if you're staying out here with Jass," she said to her daughter. Equally important was Sarah resolving to follow her own rules. "I'll be right inside. Give a holler if..." She was about to say *if she gets in the way* when Jass interrupted.

"If you get bored or too hot out here, you can always run inside."

She opened the gate, and Chloe zipped out, making a beeline for Jass's truck.

"It's kind of you to let her help, especially after..." She couldn't finish the sentence. "Thank you. You didn't have to come back to help with the pool."

"I like to see things through," Jass said.

Sarah studied Jass. She got the sense that she had faced major obstacles in the past without letting them defeat her. Jass's statement produced a list of questions Sarah wished she could ask. She wanted to know more about her seeing things through. Now, though, such an inquiry felt out of bounds.

"Jass!" Chloe called from the edge of the yard.

"Coming!" Jass's animated voice did not match her apologetic smile. She turned to follow Chloe out to her truck.

Sarah told herself to keep her eyes to herself, but they did not obey, locking directly to Jass's backside. Zero percent chance of touching that again. She would keep reminding herself until the temptation passed.

CHAPTER EIGHTEEN

Jass could feel Sarah's eyes on her as she walked away, but she did not look behind her. Sarah had made it clear that Jass was there to take care of the pool and only the pool. There was an undeniable pull between the two of them, but if Sarah said no more "swimming in the pool," then she would keep her hands to herself despite how hard Sarah was making that, wearing a loose tee that hung low on one shoulder. How was Jass supposed to ignore how much she wanted to kiss the exposed skin?

"What do you have in your truck?" Chloe asked, snapping Jass's attention back to professional. She jumped at the curb, trying to get a look at the gear in the truck bed.

"Brushes, nets, diatomaceous earth. The crates have chlorine and acid."

"Is that dangerous?"

"Not if you're careful and wear a mask and goggles. Here are the screens for your pool. You carry this one. Be careful with it. We don't want anything to poke a hole in the mesh, okay?" She handed it to Chloe and was glad to see her handle it carefully.

Chloe nodded and directed all her energy to carrying the screen protectively. She looked like a mini-Sarah which stopped

Jass short, a strange whoosh of anticipation tipping the world off balance. In five years, would the child she conceived with Amara wear an expression that mirrored her own? What was it like to see yourself in another? She had only thought of her commitment to Amara in terms of Amara's baby. In the abstract, she had not absorbed how her own genetics would be involved.

How had Sarah and Tricia decided who would carry the baby? When they split, did they decide Chloe would spend most of her time with Sarah because she had done so? Was it hard for Tricia to spend so much time away from Chloe? Amara worried about the possibility that Jass would change her mind and find it impossible to give Amara full parental rights when the baby was born. Jass had sworn that would never happen. She wasn't ready for a child yet. Maybe one day when she had met her person. Amara and Jass both knew with great certainty that they were family, not each other's person. Amara had of course dreamed about getting married and having a child with a partner, but she had not found anyone who shared her dream. She was tired of waiting, and she wanted a baby, even if it meant having one on her own. She was right when she argued that they weren't getting any younger.

Jass didn't yearn for children like Amara did. She wanted a partner, and if she was too old to have children by the time she found her, she would still be content. One thing was for certain, having seen her mother struggle as a single parent, she knew she didn't want that. She saw her mother's exhaustion etched in Sarah's face. She had looked so relieved when Jass had given her the opportunity to get some work done.

Back in the pool yard, Chloe handed the screen to Jass. "Where does it go?"

"It goes inside the tank. We need tools to loosen the lid. Check out this ratchet wrench. It's my favorite part." She got the bolt loosened to the point where Chloe could take over, and as she expected, the girl delighted in the noise the tool made as she swung the handle back after cranking the nut counterclockwise. "Righty tighty, lefty loosy is the way to remember."

She sat back, her heart pinching at the memory of Dave teaching her these basics. She was lucky to have bonded with her stepfather and could see the sweetness of passing knowledge from one generation to the next. Amara didn't have that kind of relationship with either of her parents, vowing she would do everything she could to avoid passing down the scars inherited from her parents' fighting. Her father's machismo dictated the household dynamic. He expected his only son to model his authority and administered discipline he deemed necessary to keep his kid from being a *maricón*. He refused to raise a sissy and accused his wife and Amara's two older sisters of babying him and turning him soft. Amara had always said that she wished her parents had divorced like Jass's. Their staying together meant she spent her childhood stuck in her parents' toxic relationship.

"Okay, kiddo. Let's sort the screens." If only the past was as easily tidied up as the pool screens. It was a simple thing to identify the broken pieces and replace them to get the system functioning properly. She saw how Amara's parents refusing to acknowledge the problem meant that their whole household suffered, like a broken screen allows all the debris to sweep right back into the pool. Jass's mother had identified the broken part of their family, her father, and removed it. After the divorce, her mother had found Dave, and he restored balance to their family.

Maybe that was why it made Jass sad that Sarah so firmly believed she should not date. Her train of thought gave her pause. Could she be for Sarah and Chloe who Dave had been for her family? Jass and Chloe had discarded the broken screens and taken the usable ones over to the lawn to spray clean with the hose. Jass was so lost in her thoughts that it did not occur to her that her helper might not have the most accurate aim in spraying the dirty screens. She shrieked when the cold water hit her instead of the screen she was holding steady.

She and Chloe were both laughing when Sarah opened the patio door. "Is it time to come in?" she asked.

Chloe's smile vanished.

"We're figuring it out!" Jass called back. She turned to Chloe. "Unless you're tired."

"I'm not tired," she answered.

"Good. We're almost ready for the puzzle part where we put the filter back together. It can be tricky."

She instructed Chloe to stay on the grass and ran to turn off the hose. Sarah stepped out onto the patio. "Are you sure she's not in your hair?"

Jass looked up. Sarah had removed her hair tie and her shoes. Jass often saw her customers in a more casual state. Until Sarah, seeing someone barefoot had never made her question the professional boundary. Sarah's bare feet didn't seem casual. They made her look vulnerable, Jass realized, which felt more intimate. Inwardly, she rolled her eyes. She had to get a grip. Since when did she swoon at the sight of a woman's feet? Amara was going to have a field day with that tidbit. "She's having a good time," Jass deflected.

"You're so good with her."

Jass couldn't help the flush of heat that ran through her. "Have you been spying on us?"

"No! I was keeping my feelers out for whether you need rescuing," Sarah answered, confirming Jass's suspicion that a parent could never fully untether herself from her child.

"No need to rescue me. She's a good helper."

"You'll make a great mom someday."

Jass cringed. "Oh, I don't know. That would be a long time off for me. For now, my goal is Favorite Auntie." The way Sarah studied her, Jass braced for a follow-up question about whether she actually had nieces and nephews. She did not want to go there, so she directed the conversation back to Sarah. "How you do it twenty-four seven?"

"Not very well, usually," Sarah said.

"How come you do that?" Jass asked before she could catch herself.

"Do what?"

"Well…I've learned so much from you about the importance of positive self-talk. Listening to your show is one of the reasons I can say what I want with confidence. And then I hear you say things like that…" Jass considered mentioning that it made her sad, but she bit her tongue. It wasn't her place.

At the mention of her show, Sarah's professional façade snapped into place, the practiced pose that Jass had so often studied in the online photographs of Sarah. "It takes constant diligence," she said.

"I didn't mean that as a criticism. I just…You're awfully hard on yourself. From what I see, you're doing a great job with Chloe. She's a great kid…And she's waiting extremely patiently for me." Heart hammering, Jass resumed her job. She hadn't meant to challenge Sarah Cooper. What was she thinking throwing her own advice back at her? Luckily, she was almost finished getting the pool sorted, and having Chloe as a helper kept her focused on the job.

Once the filter was running again, Jass gathered her tools to carry to her truck and sent Chloe to tell her mom they were all set. Sarah met her out front. The evening air carried a chill, and she had her arms wrapped around herself, hands on her elbows.

"Should be smooth sailing now," Jass said.

"Thank you…for seeing it through," Sarah said.

Despite her efforts to keep her mind on her work, Jass wanted to wrap her arms around Sarah. If she kept Sarah's pool on her route, would that go away in time? She pushed her feelings aside. "You bet."

"We'll see you next week, then?" Sarah ran her left hand from her elbow to her shoulder, calling Jass's attention back to her smooth skin. What she wouldn't give to touch Sarah again.

Jass knew it was unwise to agree to put herself in temptation's path each week, but she nodded anyway. "I'll put you on the schedule."

CHAPTER NINETEEN

When a bright orange car pulled into the driveway a few steps away, Sarah reflexively placed her hand on Chloe's shoulder. Chloe was lost in the task of feeding the peacocks, Sarah in a replay of Jass's comment about how critical Sarah was of herself and her parenting. Since then, Sarah had been more mindful of not only her thoughts but of her actions. She felt better about her parenting when she separated it from her work and devoted her attention one hundred percent to her daughter. Phone stowed in her pocket, Sarah ripped bread into tiny pieces to hand to Chloe to prolong the outing. A yellow equal sign caught her attention as the car came to a stop in the drive.

In another neighborhood, she would not have been surprised to see the Human Rights Campaign sticker on the back of a Subaru, but given that she was in Revelia, it made her curious. She peeked at the driver exiting the vehicle and was surprised to see the driver staring back at her. This was the house where Sarah had intercepted Jass. Had she told this woman that they had slept together? She glanced down at Chloe. "Almost ready?"

"There's still lots!" Chloe pulled two chunks of bread off the heel Sarah held, gleefully tossing each to the birds. Usually, Sarah enjoyed watching the birds dart about, the sweep of the flock— were they called a flock?—as they scrambled in the direction of Chloe's throw, but she was distracted by the driver who remained in the drive even after she pulled shopping bags from the hatchback.

To her horror, the woman strode toward them before Sarah could set Chloe's feet in motion.

"I see you're enjoyin' the birds," the woman said, her accent surprising Sarah. She looked every bit a California girl with her hair mostly shaved short but floppy long at her crown, a section of which was dyed purple.

Sarah relaxed. This wasn't about her and Jass. She felt like a schoolgirl the way Jass consumed her every thought. Their last conversation had stung. It had not been easy to be schooled by Jass on the importance of positive self-talk, but she'd been right, and Sarah had been trying to keep better tabs on her thinking ever since. She had wanted to thank Jass for reminding her, but in the past weeks, she had serviced the pool in the morning, well before Sarah felt put-together enough to run outside and have a conversation. She'd had only fleeting glimpses of Jass as she first gracefully skimmed the net over the pool's surface and later pushed the vacuum. She had not considered how much athleticism…

"…fine for feeding the birds."

The word "fine" snapped Sarah back to the present. "Excuse me?"

"There's a fine for feeding the birds. I love them, too, but I promised my girlfriend I wouldn't let anyone feed the birds on this property."

"Oh, I'm so sorry! I had no idea!"

Chloe fisted her hands at her hips. "But they're hungry!" she challenged.

"They find plenty on their own. I promise." She raised the bags in her hands as kind of a salute and headed toward the house as a great racket of barking erupted from inside.

"Let's go, Chloe." She had at least an hour until she needed to start dinner and was wondering whether she had it in her to sunscreen her daughter to throw her in the pool. If she did, she'd have to factor a bath in before bedtime, and…

"Look at the big dog, Mommy!" Chloe slammed on her brakes, watching what looked like a golden Rastafarian Muppet creature dance around the woman. "Doggie! Doggie!" she hollered.

The dog swung in their direction and bounded across the lawn. "Elmo! Get back here, you big galumph!" The woman shed her bags and bounded after the dog, grabbing him by the collar as he danced around Chloe. "I'm so sorry. He's still a puppy and has a lot to learn. Elmo! Sit!" she commanded.

Though the dog sat, he strained in Chloe's direction, trying to lick her face. She did not help the situation, throwing herself at the dog as if they were long-lost pals.

"What a sweetheart!" Sarah exclaimed.

"Sweet, yes, but a handful, unlike my well-behaved pup, Bandit." She gestured toward the door where a small white dog sat by the discarded groceries. "Do you have a pet?" she asked Chloe.

"Not yet. I was going to get a cat. Mama said yes, but Mommy said no."

Sarah raised her hand to confess, "And I told you why I said no. Pets are a lot of work." She wanted to say that she could not take on another responsibility as a newly single parent, but even thinking that brought her fear and embarrassment to a boil. She took a breath and grabbed a mental bucket of water to throw on her hysteria. They were judgments she could refuse to internalize. The root of the reaction was shame, and she knew that shame grew more powerful in darkness. She could only disarm shame with honesty. She took Chloe's hand and squeezed it for strength. It was important to be strong for Chloe. "When Mama moved out, I couldn't take on another chore." Sarah raised her chin and met the stranger's gaze, relieved to find compassion.

"Oh, I agree with your Mommy. Pets are a *lot* of work. I have to be super careful when I volunteer at the animal shelter because I want to bring all the dogs and cats home. That's where I got Bandit."

Hearing his name, the little dog licked the air and bobbed his head.

"Can I pet Bandit?" Chloe asked.

"No," Sarah said in unison with the stranger's "Sure!" Sarah did not want to be a nuisance and was uncertain about how much she should allow her to entertain her daughter. "I'm sure Bandit's mom is busy."

"It's really no problem. C'mon. I'll introduce you. I'm Casey, by the way."

"I'm Sarah. And this is Chloe." Chloe bounded ahead of them toward the front door but stopped and looked back at Sarah before touching the dog.

"Hang on a sec. I'm going to throw this one in the backyard." She and Elmo both stepped over the little dog and disappeared into the house. Muffled barking accompanied Casey's return. "Poor Elmo. He thought we were going to play. He demands a lot of attention. This one does, too, but he's happy to be held." She scooped Bandit into her arms and tipped him over, so he was looking at Chloe upside down.

Chloe giggled and reached out to pet his head. Casey stepped out and sat cross-legged on the porch. "Feel his tummy. It's super soft."

Chloe looked to Sarah, and at her nod, sat down next to Casey to pat Bandit's belly. He leaned over and licked Chloe's elbow. She squirmed and giggled. "He's giving me kisses, Mommy!"

Sarah smiled. There was something special about having a pet. There were so many things that Sarah had wanted for Chloe's childhood. She stopped herself, hearing Jass's reminder about negative self-talk. Her mind would do better to focus on the kindness of this neighbor who was now settling Bandit in Chloe's arms.

Chloe beamed as if happiness was about to burst her seams. Sarah snapped a few photos with her phone as Chloe nuzzled the dog and squeezed him around the middle. "Be gentle with him."

"Trust me. He'll tell her if she's being too rough. He grumps at me all the time for sitting too close to him or jostling him, but he's never bitten me. He's a little lovebug. He'd spend all day in my lap if I let him." She stood and they watched Chloe in silence for a several minutes.

Sarah's attention returned to the sticker on the Subaru and how Casey had mentioned her girlfriend. She was curious about the couple and searched for a way to engage Casey in conversation. Remembering how Casey had labeled Bandit "her" dog, she asked, "Elmo is your girlfriend's dog?"

"Yep. He's a real handful. We go peacock hunting every day, so he can work off his beans."

Sarah laughed and tilted her head in Chloe's direction. "I do the same exact thing."

"You know, she seems really good with dogs. Maybe she'd like to chase Elmo around and tire him out for me sometime."

Chloe's head shot up. "Now? Can I chase him around now? I'm really fast!"

"You are really fast," Sarah said. "But we should let Casey put her groceries away. We'll come back another day."

Reluctantly, Chloe let Casey take Bandit from her lap.

"Thank you for letting us meet your dogs. And also for telling us about the peacocks. I promise from now on, we will only watch them. No more feeding."

"Thanks. I appreciate that. See you soon! I'm always here around this time."

Sarah thanked Casey and took Chloe's hand, excited to have met her friendly neighbor. She looked forward to telling Jass about it when she came for the pool's weekly maintenance. At the corner, she looked back over her shoulder, recalling when she'd first seen Jass and impulsively asked her to take a look at her pool. She found it interesting that she had the same warm feeling now that she had had after observing Jass's radiance, like light breaking through the darkness that her divorce had brought into her life.

"Thank you for a nice outing," she said as she and Chloe walked home.

"You're welcome, Mommy." Chloe swung their joined hands, and Sarah felt contentment wash over her. She could absolutely handle the life she had been gifted.

CHAPTER TWENTY

"...These experiences stopped me in my tracks and returned me to some important fundamentals about shame. I have been feeding my shame with secrecy and silence and, because I'm being completely honest with you, far too much alcohol."

While she worked, Jass had been excited and curious to listen to Sarah's new podcast. She had cued it up and jumped into her routine, smiling in surprise when she recognized herself in Sarah's anecdote about positive self-talk. Serendipitously, she found herself working on Casey's pool and recognized her immediately in Sarah's second anecdote. She was tempted to stop the podcast and call Amara, but she was too engrossed in Sarah's exploration of the two neighborhood encounters. At Sarah's admission that she had been medicating with alcohol, Jass sat back on her heels. Sarah was sharing in a way she never had with her audience, and Jass didn't want to miss a word.

"I know the only thing that can eviscerate shame is empathy, but I have been silent because of anticipated judgment. I have been afraid of letting you, my wonderful audience, down. I have been so focused on shielding my daughter from societal criticism of her parents' divorce that I have failed to model positive behavior. I am changing that now by starting with an open apology to all of you. I'm sorry for pretending I was not vulnerable. I'm sorry for putting my professional image before my life truths. I am so thankful for the compassion I've felt in these short encounters with friends. I am truly blessed. I accept the invitation to be my best self today and invite you to stay on the journey with me."

Sarah's words gave Jass chills. She grabbed her phone to back up a minute to listen to the end again. She needed to share what she was thinking and feeling right now! She texted Amara to ask if she'd heard the new episode. No reply. Was Casey home? She frowned in frustration. Casey was a client, not a friend. She only knocked on the door when she had a pool-related question. She thumbed to a playlist of good background music, songs that occupied but did not engage her mind.

Her words had helped Sarah. Granted, they'd been Sarah's ideas, and Jass had worried about overstepping. Now she felt proud of herself for speaking out. It had created a whole new podcast. Why wasn't Amara texting back to say she'd listened yet? She was bursting to explore the fact that Sarah had apologized. Could she text Sarah? She had Sarah's number…But they were not friends. Sarah had made sure to reestablish a boundary that Jass would respect.

That said, if Sarah could let go of the shame she felt about her divorce, could she also change her stance on dating? This was why Jass needed Amara!

Finished vacuuming, she squatted to release the vacuum tube from the return. Elmo raced across her peripheral vision. Yes! Casey was back. She stood, keen to pick Casey's brain about her encounter with Sarah. Had she even known who she was talking to? There was a good chance she wouldn't even know that she was in the latest podcast!

But it wasn't Casey who stood in the grass poised to throw a ball for the quivering goldendoodle.

"Jass!" Chloe called, running to the pool fence.

"Hey, kiddo! You made a friend!"

The confused shaggy dog stood poised behind the youngster, his eyes trained on the ball in her hand. She turned and tossed it for him. He quickly grabbed it and ran back toward the house. That's when Jass saw Casey and Sarah step outside. Sarah was relaxed and unguarded chatting with Casey, and Jass drank her in. She wore dark-blue jeans and a heavy corded sweater that made it easy to imagine cuddling side by side with a cup of warm tea.

"That's Elmo! Are you doing our pool next?" Chloe hopped from foot to foot outside the gate.

"I sure am," Jass said.

Sarah glanced in her direction, her demeanor shifting when she recognized Jass in the pool yard. Feeling hurt, Jass took a sharp breath and raised her hand in the direction of the two women before turning back to her work. There was no way she could talk to Casey now, and she'd most likely be finished with Sarah's pool before she returned, so there was no chance of chatting with her either. That made things easier but also left Jass disappointed.

Jass packed up her cart, rehearsing what she would say when she walked by Casey and Sarah. Could she mention that she had listened to the podcast? Probably not since she didn't know if Casey knew about it. But she would have told Casey had Sarah not been standing next to her. And had she seen Sarah at her house, she would have thanked her for the episode. By the time she was ready to go, she had not resolved what to say. Maybe she could walk right by with only a hello. She took a deep breath and wheeled the cart through the gate.

Where to look? Toward the women? The gravel below her feet?

"Do you know the little one?" Chloe asked, giving Jass an out.

"I don't."

"His name's Bandit. He won't chase the ball." The dog lay still as Chloe stroked his exposed belly.

The contrast in the dogs made Jass laugh inwardly. Her thoughts were more like the big dog chasing after the ball when she wanted them to be calm like the little white dog.

"Oh!" Casey said with a little clap. "Do you have a sec? I'll get you this month's check."

"Sure. My next pool's close," Jass said.

"Yeah! Sarah was telling me. Super that you were able to get it all fixed up!" Casey disappeared inside, leaving Jass with Sarah.

"Great episode," Jass said.

Sarah's hand went to her chest. "Oh! You listened?"

"Of course. I hope that's okay. This was one of your best."

"Thank you," Sarah said. She looked toward the house. "I mean thank you for more than listening. Thank you for reminding me."

"Constant diligence," Jass repeated what Sarah had told her.

Sarah smiled. "Or being surrounded by a supportive community and leaning on them when I need to. I'd forgotten about that."

Casey returned, handing Jass a check which she folded and put in her back pocket. "Thanks."

"I'm sure I owe you," Sarah said.

Why did everything Sarah said feel like it had implied meaning? "I'll send you an invoice," Jass said.

"Bye, Jass!" Chloe held Bandit's paw and waved it in her direction.

"Maybe I'll see you next week!" she replied. She wheeled out her cart and drove a block to Sarah's house. Her phone finally rang as she passed by the plant graveyard on her way to the pool.

"Girl, The Sarapist is *IN*!" Amara sang.

"Oh, am I glad you called," Jass said, getting to work on Sarah's pool. "I have so much to process!"

CHAPTER TWENTY-ONE

"You're sure you're okay with us celebrating with Lydia's family?" Tricia asked eyeing Sarah skeptically.

"You said that her sisters have kids. I'm sure that Chloe will have more fun," Sarah answered. Chloe was finishing her bowl of cereal at the table, and Tricia and Sarah had stepped into the kitchen to talk before Tricia took Chloe for the long weekend. Sarah reined in the urge to explain where she now stood on Chloe spending time with Tricia and her girlfriend.

Tricia continued to study her. "Do you want me to bring her by for pie?"

Sarah remembered how painful it had been to spend half of Thanksgiving with her father and then have to be uprooted to spend the rest of the day with her mother. "She deserves a relaxing holiday. I'm not going to make her eat two Thanksgiving dinners like my parents made me."

Tricia feathered her hair back with her fingers the way she did when she was considering saying something difficult. Sarah had consciously made decisions to avoid anything difficult, so she was utterly surprised when Tricia thanked her. "I know this isn't easy for you, Sarah."

It wasn't, but she vowed to do better than her parents had. She had already failed to provide Chloe a two-parent family. She took a breath knowing she would never tell a client who had divorced that they had failed. Her priority was to make sure that Chloe had a stable childhood despite the fact that her parents could not stay together.

"All done," Chloe said, bringing her bowl to the sink.

"Good job! Are you ready to have a great weekend with Mama?"

Chloe jumped into Sarah's arms and gave her a cereal-soaked kiss on the cheek. "Are you making pie?"

"You know that's what I like best about Thanksgiving."

"Who will help you make it?"

"Believe it or not, before I had you, I had to make it myself. I'll probably remember how to pull it off by myself again." Her voice quavered and she had to blink back the prick of tears that pushed at the back of her eyes. She could not look at Tricia. "Let's get your teeth brushed, so you're all ready." The routine that she and Tricia had created did not ease the hurt when she had to hug Chloe goodbye. Sarah reminded herself that she could push through the hard. She could be strong in this minute and fall apart later.

After they left, Sarah fought the pull to dull the ache with alcohol. Then she remembered admitting to her listeners that she had been drinking too much and had promised to find better coping strategies. That was easier said than done, especially when she was the only one around to police herself. If she had a drink, her house would not be so quiet. One drink would keep her from worrying over whether Tricia was maintaining Chloe's schedule. One drink would make her want another, and she could not afford that slippery slope. She needed to stay away from the temptations in her kitchen.

The day was lovely, the kind that made the desert-hot summers worth it. Instead of returning to the house, she examined her front yard with a stranger's eye. Automatic sprinklers kept the lawn green, and once a week, a crew came by to mow and do some light trimming. She had noticed, though, that Jass had to duck when she came through the side gate each week. She never remembered to ask the crew to trim the greenery overhanging the gate. Tricia had always been the one to work in the yard, but that didn't mean that Sarah was incapable.

She walked around the side of the house and found a pair of hand clippers in the garage and a trash can for the cuttings. Though most of what Tricia had planted had died, the roses had continued to bloom. She didn't know how to prune them or when it was best to do that, but she did know to cut off the dead flowers.

"Hey, neighbor!"

Sarah looked up to find Casey silencing her earbuds. She pocketed the clippers and walked to the edge of her lawn. "Getting a long walk in, so you can eat a big Thanksgiving feast?"

"It doesn't matter what day it is, Elmo always needs a long walk." Hearing his name, the larger dog wagged his tail. Bandit had already taken a seat on Casey's foot. "You have your bird in the oven yet?" Casey asked.

"Oh, no. I'm on my own today. Chloe's with her other mom. I'm entertaining the idea of having pie for dinner."

"No family nearby?"

"They're within driving distance, but this year?" She shook her head. "I honestly need a break."

Casey smiled. "I know exactly how you feel! I used to dread goin' home to Mississippi for the holidays."

Sarah returned her smile. She remembered the years that it had been difficult to return home. Wondering whether Casey experienced the same difficulty with parental acceptance, she said, "It can be tricky, can't it?"

"It's better now, but there were some years I didn't feel too welcome."

"Holidays are so laden with expectations."

"Especially in the South," Casey said. She turned her gaze to the dogs. "I should get back to my walk."

"Happy Thanksgiving," Sarah said.

Casey echoed her words and started up the block before pausing again. "You're welcome to join us. Marv's aiming to sit down at two o'clock."

"Oh, that's very kind of you, but I couldn't…"

"But you can! Especially if you have pie to share! Please join us! One of my former professors and her wife are coming this year. Pops would feel awful if he knew you spent the holiday on your own."

Sarah weighed the invitation against what she had originally planned for the day. The obvious answer was yes. "That's so kind of you. I was going to make pumpkin pie. Is that okay?"

"Perfect. Pops grows apples, so we've already got that covered. See you at two?"

"See you at two. Thank you so much!"

Casey waved as she continued on her way.

Sarah dragged the trash can back toward the house. With great satisfaction, she did so without having to duck. "You're next," she said to the pots with dead plants. New plants would help her keep her mindset positive and would give her something to focus on over the long weekend.

* * *

"I'm confused," Sarah said later as Marv placed the fresh cranberry sauce onto the table, completing an impressive spread. "I thought you were Casey's grandfather."

"She's my roommate and dates my granddaughter." He brushed the front of his button-down shirt, though it showed no signs of the massive amount of cooking the man had done.

Sarah still didn't understand and said to Adrienne, "But you live in Fairfax, and Casey lives here?"

"That's right," Adrienne said.

"It was love at first soaking," Casey's professor friend, Nancy, said, triggering the story of how the two women had met. Sarah hoped that their stories would explain why Adrienne did not also live with her grandfather, but the thread moved elsewhere. Conversation flowed with ease, and the food was delicious. Sarah was beyond thankful to be included. She found that she and Nancy had similar taste in reading, and her wife, Mimi, had so many suggestions of not-to-be-missed queer movies that Sarah had to pull out her phone and take notes.

Sarah cleared dishes with Casey and though she considered asking how Casey had come to live with Marv, she switched topics, saying she could hardly even conceive having dessert after enjoying Casey's sweet corn casserole and sugary sweet potatoes.

Casey painted a vivid scene of how much of Thanksgiving in the South was rooted in butter and sugar as the two tidied in the kitchen in preparation for dessert. When the table was cleared of dinner and stocked with pies and fresh whipped cream, Sarah was surprised when Adrienne did not join them. Instead, she had moved to another room with a puzzle spread out on the table.

"Does Adrienne not like pie?" Sarah asked when it became clear that Adrienne was not returning for dessert.

"She loves pie," Marv said. "But not the sound of this old man eating it."

"Would you rather I wear my noise-cancelling headphones?" Adrienne asked.

"No, no. You're fine where you are. It wouldn't work for every family, but it works for ours," Marv said.

"I wish my parents had thought about what worked for me more than they thought about what our family looked like to our community." Casey cut into the pies and started dishing them around.

"Amen to that," Marv said. He dabbed some fresh whipped cream onto a plate with a sliver of apple and pumpkin and carried it to Adrienne where she worked on the puzzle.

When Adrienne accepted the pie without taking her eyes from the puzzle, it all clicked for Sarah. Her noise sensitivity and the need for her own space—Adrienne was neurodiverse. And yet for this family, it was a complete nonissue. Clearly, everyone had learned what worked best for Adrienne and did not insist that she bend to fit their will. "I wish my parents had thought more about what worked for me than what they wanted for themselves," Sarah said.

Unexpectedly, Nancy leaned over and hugged her. Marv served her pie. "You're always allowed to put what works for you first here. Welcome to the family."

Sarah took a bite of Marv's apple pie. It was the sweetest thing she'd ever tasted.

CHAPTER TWENTY-TWO

"Doing great, Jass. You've got a beautiful cervix. I'm going to insert the catheter now and deliver the sperm. Amara, I'm going to read out the sample number one more time. Ready?"

Amara nodded, and they confirmed the details. There was no turning back now. Jass's heart pounded, and she broke out in a sweat. This was their second month driving into Pasadena to inseminate, and Jass wanted this to happen for Amara so badly. She didn't want to mess anything up. She was so grateful that the clinic would perform insemination on any day but January first when they lost their parking to Rose Parade attendees.

"Okay, here we go, Jass. Remember you might experience a little bit of cramping as I inject the sperm. That's completely normal."

"You feeling okay? Amara asked.

Jass squeezed her hand. "I feel good."

"You're sure?"

"You're squeezing kind of hard. We're going to have to work on what you do when you're nervous."

The doctor chuckled along with Amara. "It doesn't matter who stands there holding a woman's hand. There's always a lot of stress in the unknown."

Jass appreciated that she remembered that she and Amara were not a couple.

"Okay. My part is over. Your job is to relax. I'll be back in about a half hour."

After she'd gone, Amara continued to hold Jass's hand. "She's totally giving you time to masturbate. Do you want me to step out?"

"Amara! There's no evidence that orgasm helps with conception."

"Still. You didn't last time. I didn't know if you wanted to change things up to see if it changed the outcome."

"Do *you* want me to masturbate?" Jass covered her face with both hands. "Delete. Delete. Delete. Please forget I ever said that. There's no damn way I'd be able to get off on an exam table for one, and two, talking about masturbating is not exactly a turn-on for me."

"At least stick a pillow under your butt to keep the goods in your uterus."

Jass lifted her hips and let Amara reposition the pillow.

"You feeling okay?"

"You cannot ask me that every three minutes. How about I'll tell you if something feels different."

"Okay."

Amara spun around on the rolling stool. After a few rotations, she said, "Happy Thanksgiving."

"I would be really thankful if today is the day I get knocked up," Jass said.

"I'm already thankful. You know that, right? I'm so thankful that you're doing this with me." She lay her head on Jass's shoulder, her gaze on the San Gabriel mountains through the window.

Jass threaded her fingers through Amara's highlights. "What did you tell your parents about missing Thanksgiving dinner?"

"That I was spending the day with you and no, that still didn't make you my girlfriend."

"When are you telling them about all this?"

Amara shrugged. "I don't have to. My body won't be changing. You on the other hand won't be able to hide it. When are you telling yours? There's no way you're not seeing your family for more than a year."

There was still part of Jass that wished she could carry Amara's baby and never tell her family. But Jass knew she was right. She also didn't deem it necessary to have the conversation until it was a reality. Amara's question would extend into the issue of custody, but Jass was confident that they had squared everything away in the contract a lawyer had drawn up before they had inseminated the first time. There would be no question that neither Jass nor anyone in her family would ever have a legal claim to the baby she produced.

"This time next year, you might have a baby," Jass whispered.

"I know," Amara whispered back.

"Does it scare you?"

"Incredibly."

"Where do you see yourself next Thanksgiving? At your parents'?"

"I don't know. I want them to know their grandkid, but…"

"You also want your kid to grow up different than you did?"

"I get worried about how much they'll want to be involved."

"Yeah," Jass said. "I can see that." She wanted to ask Amara something but struggled with how to put it into words. They had been clear from the outset that Jass was not interested in co-parenting, that she wanted to be the cool auntie, someone in more of a godparent kind of role. They had not talked about holidays. Would spending holidays together with Amara and her baby blur the lines of who they were to each other?

"Where will you be next Thanksgiving?" Amara asked.

"Holidays are hard, aren't they?"

"Hard how?"

"They're loaded with so many expectations. Norman Rockwell, you know? But whose family even looks like that anymore?"

"You think Thanksgiving demands conforming to that standard?"

"Exactly. It makes people who don't have a 'normal' family feel bad."

"C'mon. Neither one of us has ever held up Norman Rockwell as a goal. Not even Sarah Cooper could say that she lived a Norman Rockwell life, even before she divorced."

"Doesn't matter. That's the image people celebrate. It's a yearly trip-wire reminder that we're different."

"We create our own table. We always have."

"What do you think Sarah Cooper's table looks like this year?"

Amara squeezed her hand. Though talking to Amara about the last time she'd seen Sarah had been satisfying, it did not help her think about Sarah any less. She typically did Sarah's pool service on Thursdays, but she would of course not be there today.

Amara had been surprised that Sarah had not been upset when Jass admitted that she'd listened to the podcast, given her response when she'd first discovered Jass was a listener. Did that mean that Sarah had been successful in expunging the desire she'd felt for Jass and could now treat her like any other listener?

Jass didn't want to be any other listener, and she didn't want Sarah to be just another customer she saw once a week. It seemed like a weird train of thought to follow in the doctor's office, so Jass diverted the conversation to whether Amara had work to do over the holiday weekend. She did tech for a networking company housed in Silicon Valley, which meant she did the majority of her work from home. It offered flexibility but made it difficult for her to maintain work boundaries, and she was always juggling multiple projects.

"I'm sorry," Amara said on their way back to Revelia. "I shouldn't have brought up Sarah Cooper."

"You don't have to apologize," Jass said. She felt self-conscious reclined in the passenger seat, but she knew it made Amara happy.

"You got quiet."

"There was a lot going on in my head even before her name came up."

"Can you see yourself at a table with her?"

Jass closed her eyes. Could she see herself at a table with Sarah? So far, she had eaten chicken nuggets and macaroni and cheese with her and Chloe at a table. The pizza she had been very much enjoying in Sarah's bed before…What did it say that when she imagined Sarah Cooper's table, she could see a place setting for Tricia? She certainly wasn't setting a place for someone new. Jass didn't want to think about that, so she answered with a question. "What do you think she's doing today?"

"You think she has her daughter for the holiday weekend?"

"I don't know how any of that works."

"She's talking about being her best self. I think her best self needs you."

Jass rolled her eyes. "You want me to get laid because you think it will increase the probability of implantation."

"I was not even thinking about implantation. Now that you bring it up, though…"

"You're such a liar!"

"I want you to be happy, and I think you would be happier if you got down and dirty with her again."

If she'd been closer, Jass would have smacked her friend. She closed her eyes, imagining how good it would feel to be back in Sarah's bed. She'd been ready for so much more that night. And then she'd brought up Chloe and the podcast. Neither of those things had changed. "You know what would make me happy?"

Amara glanced at her, her perfectly sculptured eyebrows lifting to ask the question.

"Enchiladas."

"I can at least make that wish come true."

Jass closed her eyes and rested her hand over her uterus. If only all wishes could be so easily realized.

CHAPTER TWENTY-THREE

Sarah walked around the tables of plants and flowers feeling guilty for shopping without Chloe. She loved the local nursery with its two big koi ponds. When they had first moved to Revelia, Sarah and Tricia had made many outings out of a trip to the nursery to let her feed the fish.

She reminded herself that she was not there to recreate the past. She was there by herself to pick out new plants. Those were happy memories, and it would be foolish to spoil her day in reflection. She pulled a three-wheeled cart behind her, occasionally picking up a pot to read the care instructions. She was looking for plants that would add color to her yard but didn't require too much attention.

On Thanksgiving, Marv and Nancy had talked about how forgiving succulents were. That, she decided, was exactly what she was looking for. She quickly lost herself in the variety of plants, some vibrant green and others gray. Others were reddish or tipped with orange. She loved the symmetry of the circular plants and the texture of the spikier ones with white lines. Soon her wagon held a dozen plants. Knowing she had at least that many pots at home, she resisted the temptation to buy more, passing by them quickly on her way to track down potting soil.

It was then that she noticed the selection of potted Christmas trees but more specifically, among them, Jass. Sarah sucked in her breath. Jass's shoulder-length hair was down instead of in its usual ponytail. It felt different to see her in jeans and a three-quarter-sleeved shirt, gray with heather-green arms.

"Jass!" She greeted her without considering what else she would say.

Jass turned, and when she recognized Sarah, smiled brightly. "Sarah! Beautiful day, isn't it? I couldn't stay inside."

"Yes, beautiful," Sarah agreed, though the adjective fit the woman in front of her even better than it did the day. Seeing Jass again made Sarah's skin tingle.

Jass motioned to the trees. "I've been thinking for years that I should get a potted Christmas tree instead of buying another cut tree. I feel so guilty throwing them away. Now that I'm here, though, I'm second-guessing my ability to keep it alive."

"We never mess with a live tree. Prelit artificial tree are the most genius invention ever."

"You don't miss the way a live tree makes your house smell like Christmas?"

"All my favorite Christmas smells are from the things I bake. The house will smell like cinnamon from now through January."

"That sounds lovely, too. You baked for Thanksgiving?"

"It's not Thanksgiving if there's not pumpkin pie."

"Uh, oh. Then I guess I skipped Thanksgiving!" Jass laughed.

"No pie? Not even for breakfast?"

"Who eats pie for breakfast?" Jass asked.

"Everyone I know! Everyone I met yesterday agreed that pie for breakfast was a favorite part of the weekend." Seeing Jass's look of confusion, she added, "Casey invited me for Thanksgiving since I was on my own this year."

"She's who you were talking about in the podcast, isn't she? The one who made you realize that you're not on your own with Chloe? She offered to help in the afternoon witching hour when you're often at loose ends. I remember seeing Chloe playing with her dogs one afternoon."

"Yes. Such fortuitous timing. Not to sound clichéd, but I am so thankful for...well, you know. You listened..." She looked away from Jass, her thoughts skipping from the most recent episode to how she had reacted when Jass had told her she listened to the podcast. What would have happened if it had been different the night they had slept together? It had been clear to her that they had both been anticipating more sex. What would have happened if they had shared dinner and fallen back into each other's arms? Would Jass have stayed the night? Would Sarah have awoken full of shame and regret and used that to push Jass away?

No matter what, she would have had to push Jass away. That's what they would have had time to establish, she told herself. Had they been able to sate their desire, she could have explained that her priorities lay in parenting Chloe. She did not have the emotional bandwidth for dating.

She owed Jass an explanation. For weeks she had been behaving as if she could pretend there was nothing she needed to apologize for. Now, she could see that it was long overdue. She looked back at Jass. She hadn't moved or tried to fill in Sarah's words. Sarah remembered Amara saying that when Jass said she would do something, she did it until it was done. What had her intentions been in accepting Sarah's invitation to bed? Sarah had not given her a chance to talk. She had thrown accusations at her and then she'd thrown her out. She did not deserve this woman's kindness.

She laughed, then, and Jass cocked her head in confusion. "I'm sorry," Sarah said. "You would not approve of my internal dialogue."

"I wish I knew what you were thinking," Jass said quietly.

"I was thinking I owe you an apology and a chance to talk about what happened."

"That doesn't sound like problematic self-talk. Isn't that pretty healthy?"

"I only told you the good part."

"What about the part that made you laugh?"

"I don't know if I'm that brave." Sarah remembered what it had felt like when she had asked Jass to stay for dinner. Her body still wanted Jass. *She* wanted Jass. Was it wise to invite her to talk? They couldn't stay at the nursery. Could they have lunch together? Probably not at her house. "Are you hungry?" she asked.

Surprise blossomed on Jass's face.

"I'm sorry. I'm not thinking very clearly. Can I invite you to lunch? At a restaurant where the two of us can talk like adults?"

"I'd like that," Jass said. "Are you ready to check out?"

Sarah didn't follow until Jass pointed to her cart. "Oh! I need soil. Then I'm ready. Do you mind if I drop everything off at home and meet you somewhere? Your choice."

"That works. Do you want help with all this?"

Sarah appreciated that Jass had asked if she wanted help, not whether she needed help. "I'll pass, if that's okay. This is my first big solo house project, and it feels important to execute it on my own."

"Okay," Jass said. "There's a taco place I like a lot. Do you know Rico's?"

"I haven't been before, but I love Mexican. Do they do a good fish taco?"

Jass's face lit up like Sarah had given the right answer to difficult question. "The best!"

"I'll finish up here and meet you there?" Sarah asked.

"Perfect," Jass said.

Sarah watched Jass turn and walk toward the exit without looking at the Christmas trees again. For the briefest moment, Sarah pondered whether to pick one out as a gift. Then she pushed the idea aside. Jass had understood Sarah's desire to make decisions on her own without her having to explain. Jass glanced over her shoulder as she left the nursery, catching Sarah watching. Chagrined, Sarah turned to complete her errand.

Jass had shifted the trajectory of Sarah's day. Where she usually would have explored the items placed near the register to tempt exiting shoppers, she was singularly focused on paying, loading her car and dropping the plants at her house.

With the plants stowed in the shade, Sarah hesitated. It wasn't a particularly warm day, but she was sticky enough that she entertained the idea of cleaning up prior to lunch. She started to tell herself not to be foolish but quickly caught herself. She acknowledged the nervousness she felt. But this was not a date. It was an apology lunch to resolve what had happened between them. Fretting about changing was yet another stalling tactic. Luckily, with Jass waiting on her, she had no more time to dither.

CHAPTER TWENTY-FOUR

Jass's thumb hovered over her phone. How long would Sarah be? Did she have time to text Amara? But why? She was an adult. She could figure out how to eat lunch with a beautiful woman on her own. Her stomach tightened with anticipation. Sarah Cooper had invited her to lunch. There would be no escaping the overdue conversation. She sipped her horchata, soothed by the smooth drink. She and Amara agreed that it was the best in the San Gabriel valley.

Shutting her eyes, Jass tried to get a hold of what to say. How could she be at such a loss? Sarah so often occupied her thoughts that at first when Sarah had said her name at the nursery, she was sure she'd only imagined her. But now here she was, striding across the parking lot, still dressed in jeans threadbare at the knees and a tight rust-colored tank covered by an unbuttoned flannel shirt. Even dressed for a day of work in the yard, Sarah looked fantastic.

Jass felt the familiar pull when Sarah spotted her. Her gait switched from hesitant to purposeful as she strode to Jass's table. Jass debated standing. Standing would invite hugging. Hugging would very likely light a fuse difficult to extinguish. Jass remained seated and settled for waving hello.

Sarah sat across from her.

"I ordered us both fish tacos. They should be out soon, but I didn't know what you wanted to drink."

"What do you have?" Sarah asked, eyes on Jass's drink.

"Horchata."

"I've never tried it."

Jass extended the cup. "Do you want to try mine?"

Sarah accepted the cup and wrapped her lips around the straw for a pull of the drink.

Jass tore her eyes away from Sarah's lips, far too aware of parts of her body that missed their attention.

"It's so sweet!" Sarah exclaimed.

"You want me to get you one? Or a soda? Or..."

"No. You stay. I'll grab something."

Sarah stepped inside and returned shortly with a fountain drink. A young but thickly mustached employee followed with two baskets of food.

"You weren't lying," Sarah said after she'd taken a bite. "These are wonderful. Thank you for suggesting this place. I've driven by a thousand times, but I've never been brave enough to stop."

"That's the second time today you've talked about not being brave. I would not have pegged you for...What's the opposite of brave?"

"A coward?"

"Well that sounds plain mean. I am absolutely not calling you a coward." Jass took another bite of taco to put her mouth to better use.

"And this impression you have of me is from listening to the podcast," Sarah said, diving right into the hard stuff.

Jass sipped her horchata. "I realize now that I must have come off as a creepy stalker. I'm sorry. I wasn't stalking you. I recognized you, and I should have said so, but I didn't."

"Why didn't you?"

"I don't know. Maybe if I had seen you feeding peacocks and recognized you, it would have seemed logical to say 'Hey, thanks for your show.' But you were asking me to take a look at your pool. It didn't seem relevant."

Sarah set down her taco. "But you did recognize me. And that scared me."

"And yet, you had invited me to stay for dinner. That was brave."

"Some would call it brave."

"But you're not, are you? You're calling it foolish and telling yourself you shouldn't have given in to your desire?"

"How'd you know?"

"You worry about what people will think about you. You said so on the podcast. You think you should be only focused on raising Chloe right now, and you think that your ex should be doing the same thing, so by not dating, you get to be the better person."

Sarah tilted her head as if to study Jass. Had she said too much? Was Sarah trying to put into kinder words what a fool Jass was? Instead, she said, "Did you minor in psychology?"

Relieved that she had not overstepped, Jass said, "I learn a lot of stuff from a great podcast."

"Hmmm." Sarah held eye contact with a sly smile before growing more serious. "You feel okay about what we did?"

"A hundred percent. What's wrong with two consenting adults finding pleasure in each other?"

"One of those adults is a mother with responsibilities."

"My parents got divorced. My mom dated. I was fine."

"How old were you? When they got divorced?"

"Ten." Jass remembered that Sarah's parents had divorced when she was younger. Did years of watching her own parents fight make it easier for Jass to accept that her parents were not staying together? She could see where a younger child might be shielded from the conflict and long for the memory of their family as a unit. She had no such longings, only memories of her father in a drunken rage. "Divorcing my dad was the best thing my mom ever did. It took her way too long." Jass rattled her cup and sipped the milky water. She hadn't intended to get into her family history. This was lunch, not a session with her therapist. "I'm going to get some water. Can I get you anything?"

"Sure. Water would be good."

Jass dumped her trash on the way to get two cups of water. She tried to organize her thoughts, tried to muster up the courage to say what was on her mind. When she returned, Sarah had cleared her own trash. Jass set one of the cups in front of her and drank from her own. "Can I ask a follow-up to the shame podcast?"

Sarah straightened her shoulders in a way that felt like they were shifting to a more formal interview. "Ask."

"You talked about Chloe and the effect trying to hide your vulnerability has on her, but you didn't talk about you. I've been thinking about you…" She couldn't stop her face from flushing red. "If you're shutting out the judgment you feared, does that mean you are thinking about dating differently?"

"I haven't changed how I feel about where a parent's priorities should be. Chloe will always be my priority."

"Isn't that like arguing that the oxygen mask should go on your kid first when everyone says you should put it on yourself and then help your kid. If you're falling apart, how can you be a good parent?"

"Dating isn't going to pull me together. Not dating is getting the oxygen mask on myself, so I can be more together. I don't have the bandwidth for anyone else. That's what I'm saying."

"What about sex without dating?"

"You think if I don't have sex, I'll fall apart?"

"When we were rolling around naked together, I got the impression that sex is pretty important to you."

The way Sarah studied Jass made her feel naked. She leaned forward but turned her head away from Jass, so she was no longer making eye contact. "Are you suggesting that we be fuckbuddies?" Her question asked, she turned her gaze back to Jass.

Sarah's delivery of the question did not offer any insight on her position on the topic. In all the conversations she had imagined, none had ever included Sarah Cooper uttering the word fuckbuddies. The topic felt dangerous, and she wished she could consult Amara. Would she think it appropriate to proposition Sarah about casual sex? Jass crossed her fingers she wasn't making a huge mistake and plowed ahead. "Like I said, I don't think there's anything wrong with two women who are attracted to each other having some fun together."

Jass could see Sarah's training in the calm way she received Jass's words. "Are you thinking about what you want in the long term?"

Jass's heartbeat pounded at her pulse points. What Sarah was asking was fair, but all she could say was, "I'm having a lot of trouble thinking any further than getting you naked again."

Sarah threw back her head with a guffaw. It was a joyous sound that Jass sometimes heard when Sarah invited a friend to her podcast. It lit her up from inside, and Jass drank her in. Sarah settled newly twinkling eyes on Jass and rested her chin in her hand. "You surprise me."

"You don't laugh enough. You have a wonderful laugh."

"Oh! It feels lovely to laugh."

"Why did you laugh at the nursery? Now that you said 'fuckbuddy,' are you brave enough to tell me what you were thinking?"

Sarah chuckled again and pursed her lips in attempt to keep the idea secret. "That I don't deserve your kindness."

Jass remembered that Sarah had said she would not have approved of her internal dialogue. That meant she'd told herself to accept Jass's kindness. That left Jass wondering how much Sarah would allow herself to accept. "You deserve to be happy. I hope you know that."

CHAPTER TWENTY-FIVE

Sarah checked her rearview mirror, confirming that she had, in fact, asked Jass to follow her home. Something had clicked inside Sarah when Jass had said she deserved to be happy. Sarah had an explicit fantasy of everything she could do in her empty house. Essentially, wasn't she single and unattached? What, really, was stopping her from acting on her desire? As she approached her horseshoe drive, she rolled down and waved for Jass to park behind her.

No thinking about neighbors seeing the truck in her drive, she told herself. She rotated the keys in her hand to pull up her house key as she waited for Jass. Her heartbeat thrummed in her ears, and Jass assessed her as if she could hear it too. She walked to Sarah, her purposeful stride mesmerizing, stopping only when her shoulder whispered against Sarah's. She leaned close to Sarah's ear. "You asked me to follow you. Should I keep following you?"

Sarah shivered. "Yes, please."

It took everything she had to rein in the impulse to throw her arms around Jass then and there and pull her into a kiss. She had to wait until they were inside. Jass stayed close at every step. She slid the lock back into place, let her bag fall to the floor and tossed her keys onto the hall table, finally able to take Jass in her arms.

Jass lifted her hair off her neck and covered it with hungry kisses. This was what she wanted. This was what she needed, and she reminded herself that there was no shame in that. She twisted to capture Jass's mouth, tasting a hint of salt, a reminder of her morning working outside. The kiss fanned her want into burning desire. She wanted more and slid her hands under Jass's shirt. She felt no shame, only Jass's warm skin.

"Can we pick up where we left off? Before I let the public flood in here?"

Jass nodded. "That means losing this." She pulled her shirt over her head.

Sarah pushed her overshirt off her shoulders and tossed it in the direction of her keys. She walked behind Jass, kissing her neck and shoulders. She unclasped Jass's bra and slid her hands over Jass's exposed breasts. Jass leaned into her arms, tilting her head to invite more kisses. Sarah kissed her way back around until she stood in front of Jass. "There is so much more I want to do with you." She reached for Jass's hand and led her to her office bedroom.

They needed no words as they stripped and climbed into bed. Sarah found Jass's mouth with the confidence that what they did here together was solely between the two of them. There was no shame in the swipe of her tongue across Jass's lip, no shame in the tangle of tongues that followed.

She surrendered herself to Jass's hands, her skin coming alive wherever Jass touched her. She allowed herself the gift of the beautiful woman in her bed who believed it was okay for two consenting adults to find pleasure in each other.

She reveled in the warmth of Jass's mouth on her breasts, the press of her body. The thrill of being desired by someone as sexy as Jass took her breath away. Her mouth still on Sarah's breasts, Jass ran her strong hand down Sarah's body, over the sweep of her hip and around her thigh. Sarah wanted more. Jass swept by Sarah's curls but did not linger. Sarah reached for her hand and redirected her between her legs.

Jass brought her mouth back to Sarah's. She teased her tongue across Sarah's lips in sync with her fingers at her slick folds. "Inside?"

"You have to ask?" Sarah gasped, pushing against Jass, wanting to feel her everywhere.

"I do," Jass said, still teasing, still testing. "I want to make sure this feels okay to you."

"I want you," Sarah gasped.

"As long as you're sure." Jass circled with maddeningly unhurried strokes.

Her pace conveyed her conviction that there was nothing wrong with their choices. Hurry was a close companion to shame. Sarah would not invite shame back into her bed. "I am sure." She relaxed and pulled Jass closer to deepen their kiss, allowing herself to explore Jass with no thought other than the pleasure it brought her.

Jass broke from the kiss and trailed a quick line of kisses until she was at the apex of Sarah's legs. Her mouth found Sarah's center at the same time she pushed inside. Sarah melted against her, welcoming every emotion that ricocheting inside her. No shame in wanting to be touched. No shame in wanting release which came to her without any effort. No shame in pulling Jass back to her and coaxing the same waves of pleasure from her.

Finally, they lay spent, Sarah's head resting on Jass's shoulder. She traced lazy circles down her arm and across Jass's firm belly. "I've never done something casual like this. I don't know how it all works."

"I hope you're not thinking I do," Jass answered.

"But you're the one who suggested it! Isn't that what you want?"

"Oh, I definitely want you." Her hand traced a similar path over Sarah's sated body. She felt self-conscious when Jass's fingers traced along the scar from her cesarian section. Her body was no longer taut where Jass's was, and she struggled to push away her instinct to compare. Jass's touch communicated that she was beautiful. She would hold that as an affirmation. "When I'm lying next to you like this, it's pretty difficult to think of anything else."

"What about when you have clothes on? What if I am too busy selfishly taking and don't give you what you need?"

"I know your position on dating right now. I am not in any way pressuring you. I have a lot going on in my life. It's not the best time for me to date, either, so if this works for you, it absolutely works for me. You are an amazing, amazing lover. How do you know I'm not just taking from you?"

"You know what's keeping me from dating right now. Why do you say it's not the best time for you to date?" Sarah asked. Relative to her own life, Jass's seemed so uncomplicated.

Jass took a deep breath, and Sarah's head rose and then fell with the long exhale. "It's complicated. Amara needs me."

Sarah propped herself up on her elbow. She liked Jass's friend and worried about why she would need Jass. *Was she sick? In crisis?* "Is she okay?"

"Yeah, yeah. She's okay," Jass said. "Honestly, my friendship with Amara has made it difficult for me to date. The women I've dated have had a very hard time with how close we are."

"Have the two of you ever dated?"

"Oh, hell no!" Jass exclaimed. "That would be like dating my sister. Plus, she was never attracted to women, even before…"

Sarah searched Jass's deep brown eyes. Before what? The reminder of how little she actually knew Jass started to fan Sarah's insecurities. Two adults offering each other pleasure, she reminded herself. If she were a man, would she even be giving it a second thought? She had internalized the stigma and wished there was more support to help her reprogram her thoughts. She was raising a daughter. How would she react if years from now, Chloe was in a sexual relationship that brought her happiness? A responsible sexual relationship, she amended. Wouldn't she strive to accept her daughter without judgment? Unlike the way she had been judging Tricia.

"How long have you two known each other?" Sarah asked.

"We met in the fourth grade. We spent so much time together over the years that by high school, everyone was convinced that we were going to get married someday."

Sarah cocked her head, confused.

"They couldn't accept that our connection wasn't romantic. We were just two queer kids who thankfully found each other." She bit her lip as if she was having trouble finding words. "That was before she transitioned."

CHAPTER TWENTY-SIX

Amara's story wasn't Jass's to share, and it had made falling asleep that night difficult. Jass would reach for her phone to text Amara only to get caught up in all that had happened. If she told Amara she had outed her, she would owe her the whole story, and she wasn't ready to share the whole story yet.

She twisted her net onto the extension pole to scoop leaves from her third pool of the day. Her work was cut out for her after Santa Ana winds had swept in three times the usual amount of debris. These were the days that she followed Dave's advice to set a timer because she would never remove every leaf and would put herself terribly behind schedule if she tried.

Another wave of mild dizziness fluttered through her. Weird. She had felt off from the time she had gotten up but kept thinking that it would wear off. The cup of coffee hadn't helped. The zap she got from reaching into cold pools to set up her vacuum hose hadn't recalibrated her. She didn't feel sick. She simply did not feel like herself. She tipped her head back with her eyes closed and took a deep breath, telling herself that it would settle whatever was going on.

Nothing was going to settle the emotions that still skittered through her belly when she remembered being in Sarah's bed again. In that way, she felt good. Really good. She couldn't stop herself from smiling when she remembered Amara's suggestion that orgasm helped with implantation. If that was the case, she had given it a lot of help.

With seven more pools on her agenda, she needed to stop daydreaming. For a holiday like Fourth of July, she could prepare for the missed week with a chlorine boost to get the pool through a two-week span, but fall holidays were trickier. Pumps didn't do well when the basket filled with leaves and few owners checked them.

Was Sarah one who would keep an eye on her pool and do some maintenance in between Jass's weekly visits? It hadn't even occurred to her to look at the pool when she was there the day before. She'd had other things on her mind. Her body tingled, responding to the mere thought of returning to Sarah's.

When would she see Sarah again? She had said that Chloe was with her other mom for the whole weekend. Should she text to see if Sarah had any plans that evening? Was that too forward? Was there any way that she could continue sleeping with Sarah without expectations of where things would go? And once she got pregnant? What then? Surely pregnant women had sex. What had Sarah's sex life been like when she carried Chloe? She blushed. Could she ask Sarah such a question?

She couldn't go five minutes without thinking of Sarah. Leaves. Chlorine. Water levels. She had to get a handle on herself. If she gave herself a concrete time to think about it, would she be able to regain her focus? She pulled out her phone to text Amara just as it buzzed with an incoming text.

You told me not to ask you how you are. But we usually talk every day and we didn't talk yesterday. Are you okay?

Sorry. You will not believe the day I had. Will you be home later?

Home all day. Come by!

Finally having made a plan with Amara, Jass relaxed. She opened her music app, selected an upbeat playlist and got to work.

"I feel weird," Jass said when she got to Amara's apartment, figuring it would be easiest to get it out of the way. "I've been oddly off-kilter, but it could be what happened yesterday." Jass walked to Amara's bar and slipped onto one of the two stools.

"Hungry?"

"No."

Amara walked into the kitchen, setting glasses of water, a container of Jass's favorite spicy trail mix and a bowl on the counter. She leaned her elbows on the counter, studying Jass. "Why do you feel weird?"

Rip the bandage off quickly, right? Jass thought. "I slept with Sarah Cooper again yesterday, and I outed you. And I'm sorry." She did not say out loud how much she wanted to see Sarah again and how hard it was knowing she was just a ten-minute drive from Amara's.

"Wow," Amara stretched over several beats. "Happy Thanksgiving weekend. What happened?"

Jass filled her in on the nursery, lunch and following Sarah home.

"But you didn't stay for dinner."

"I don't think fuckbuddies eat dinner together. We're not dating."

"No. Fuckbuddies definitely aren't having dinner together. Did it feel different, like something…happened?" Amara tapped her belly.

Jass chewed her lip and then pulled out her Chapstick, applying it liberally. "I've been thinking all day that I feel different, but that's impossible, isn't it? What are the chances?"

"Thank you, Sarah Cooper," Amara exclaimed.

"Are you mad I told her about you? I could have said you're not into girls. I don't know why I went into the rest of it."

"Because she's a therapist. People spill all sorts of things to therapists."

"She's not *my* therapist."

"Maybe you told her because you're not going to be able to keep being pregnant a secret, and knowing I'm trans will make it easier for her to understand your motives. Did she think we were a couple?"

"She asked if we'd ever gone out."

"Gross," Amara said. Then she laughed and came around the bar to give Jass a squeeze. She rested her chin on Jass's shoulder with her arms draped loosely around her from behind. "I worry that you're going to get attached. Sex hasn't ever just been about release for you."

"I know," Jass said. "But this is perfect. She doesn't date. I'm emotionally invested in this baby we're trying to make. It's not like I can date, anyway. It's a win-win."

"What happens when you start to show?"

"Let's get me pregnant before we stress about that."

Amara gave Jass a solid squeeze and whispered, "You are. It's happening. You're already glowing."

"How do you know that's not post-orgasmic bliss?"

Amara studied her. "I don't. I can't explain it. You just feel different."

"It is tempting to ask Sarah questions about when she carried Chloe," Jass admitted.

"She could be a great resource! What an idea! When do you want to pee on a stick?"

"Don't they say to wait a week?"

"But if you're feeling weird…Does it hurt to check?"

"Let's see if I miss my period first."

"I hate the waiting." Amara sat on the stool next to Jass.

Jass leaned her head on Amara's shoulder, her thoughts not of the waiting game but how hard it was to wait to see Sarah again. "Do you think I can text Sarah?"

Amara sat up straight, popping Jass's head from her shoulder. "Like text a booty call?"

"This is embarrassing."

"Weren't you the one explaining to Sarah that there shouldn't be any embarrassment in single ladies having some fun?"

"Right? When I'm there, it makes sense. I'm not thinking, but now, all I do is spin and spin. Is she regretting it? Will we hook up again, or does she think it's too complicated?" Jass pulled her phone out. "What would I even text her?"

Her phone buzzed in her hand and Sarah's name flashed on the screen. She flipped the phone over, resting it on her leg.

Amara clasped her hands together and rested her chin on them. She leaned forward, forcing Jass to look at her. "Who is it? It was her, wasn't it? What did she say?"

Heart pounding, Jass woke up her screen. She opened the message and read Sarah's one-word text.

Busy?

CHAPTER TWENTY-SEVEN

Sarah could not find stillness on Sunday. Typically she savored any morning she did not have to get up and parent, allowing herself to doze past eight o'clock. She had woken shortly after six and found it impossible to fall back asleep. Her bed smelled like Jass, like sunshine and pools, and she itched to touch her again. She grinned like a schoolgirl, recalling how relieved she had been when Jass had immediately answered her text to say that she was not busy.

Being with Jass felt so right. She couldn't explain how Jass intuited precisely how to touch her after so little time together, but oh she did. Sarah's body responded to the memory of being touched. She ran her hand over her belly and down her thigh imagining her hands on Jass's skin while she remembered how glorious Jass's hands felt on her. What would it be like to wake up next to Jass? Sarah sighed. Surely that would complicate things.

Jass had not even stayed when Sarah had offered her dinner. Sarah accepted it as appropriate. Staying for dinner meant talking. Sharing details of their lives would lead to more emotional involvement that they were both avoiding. The problem was that

Sarah did not know whether she could flip a switch on the days she had Chloe and stop thinking about and wanting Jass. Jass had made it clear that casual sex was all she could offer right now. Why? Did it have to do with her professionalism? Her friendship with Amara?

Her brain engaged to the point that she would never fall back asleep, Sarah got up, did a yoga routine and ate breakfast before changing to work on the last of her potting. Tricia would drop Chloe off at ten. Thinking about Tricia activated her muscle memory to reach for the vodka to splash into her orange juice. Remembering that she had shared with her audience that she was using alcohol to help her cope stayed her hand. She ate her toast, drank plain orange juice and reviewed her mantras, the most helpful one of late being to stay in her own lane. She had learned the hard way that she was not in control of Tricia's life. She could not control Tricia's choices when they were married, and she now coped better when she reminded herself to concentrate solely on herself.

Breakfast finished, she returned to her planting. Gardening had proved to be a great distraction for the long weekend without Chloe. Dedicating several hours of each day to rolling around in the hay with Jass had contributed as well. When she stood to fetch a trowel from her garden shed, muscles she had not used in a while whined. What happened next for her and Jass? Could she text Jass during her workday when Chloe was at school, or would she have to wait two weeks until Tricia had Chloe for the weekend to invite her over again? Not a question she could ask anyone about.

Sarah filled a pot partway with soil before adding the succulents and then filling the gaps with more soil. She was not quite finished when she heard Tricia's tires on the drive. She glanced at her watch. Only ten minutes late today. She was making progress. Tricia's unpunctuality had been a major source of tension when they had been together. Sarah had noticed that since Tricia had started dating Lydia, she'd been arriving more closely to the agreed time. Sarah tried not to question why Tricia would be more motivated now. Nothing positive ever came from comparison.

She opened the gate and met them at the car. Chloe wiggled out of her car seat and ran to Sarah's arms. Sarah bent to her knees to fully receive her, a piece of herself returning as Chloe wrapped her arms around her neck.

"How was your weekend?"

"Great!" Chloe said. "Lydia has a real Christmas tree at her house! Can we have a real tree, so our house smells nice too?"

Sarah recalled the trees Jass had been looking at when she had run into her at the nursery. "I was at the plant store this weekend, and guess what! They have Christmas trees in a pot that we could plant after Christmas! Would you like to go get one? What would you think if we had a baby tree this year?"

"Yes! Baby tree! Let's go!"

"Let's start with you putting your backpack in your room."

"Okay!" She turned to Tricia and gave her a hug.

"I love you, kiddo," Tricia said. Eyes closed, she rocked Chloe back and forth before kissing her crown.

"Love you!" Chloe said before tearing into the house, her backpack bouncing on her shoulders.

"Sounds like it went well," Sarah said.

"It did. She had a great time with Lydia's nieces and nephews. Threw a fit when we didn't have pie for breakfast."

"Oh?" Sarah asked, biting back a smirk. She should not find pleasure in knowing Chloe had thrown a tantrum, but it tickled her that her own Thanksgiving tradition was already so firmly engrained.

"Lydia's family hasn't ever heard of that practice. There wasn't any leftover pie to take home. She got over it. Are you really thinking about a live tree? I was so sure you were going to argue about the stability of traditions being important."

Sarah shrugged. "I'm not going to throw the old tree away. It makes sense to alter the tradition this year. Honor that things are different. This is an easy way to demonstrate to Chloe that I hear her and her desires are important. I want to be able to say 'yes' as often as I can."

Tricia crossed her arms and scrutinized Sarah. "Did you end up visiting your folks?"

"Actually, no. I needed a break this year. A neighbor invited me over, and it was one of the nicest Thanksgivings I've ever had. Truly lovely people."

"That's great, Sarah! I'm so glad to hear that you weren't alone here."

Sarah would not think of Jass, would not replay how very much *not* alone she was for the weekend. She visualized a switch in her mind that she could flick to keep that life separate from the one that included Chloe and Tricia.

"You look good," Tricia said.

"Thanks," Sarah said. "I feel good." She was ready for the conversation to be over. Now was when she usually started to think about whether she and Tricia would hug goodbye. The contact made her uncomfortable, but the end of a conversation with Tricia was always so difficult to navigate. "Glad you had a good weekend."

"Yeah. You, too." She took the cue and waved to Sarah as she walked to the car. She rolled down the window as if she had something else to say. The moment passed, though, and she simply waved again before pulling away.

Sarah wiped her hands on her thighs and stomped loose dirt from her shoes before finding Chloe. The stuffed animals that traveled with her, Giraffie, Baby Teddy and Greenie, a silky salamander, were lined up carefully on her bed. Her daughter was home.

"Before we go to the store, let me show you the plants I got. You can help me finish planting the last few, okay?"

"Okay, Mommy!"

"How was the pie on Thanksgiving?"

"Yummy! And Lydia has the whipped cream you can squirt from the can. She squirted some right into my mouth!"

"That's a special treat!" Sarah wished that Tricia had sent her a photo. In the past, though, Sarah had been critical of snaps she had taken when she was with Lydia. Maybe she would text to ask if Tricia had a copy she could share. It stung to hear about memories that Chloe was making without her. Jealousy crept up on her. She feared that Chloe would be disappointed to return to her more mundane scheduled life with Sarah. She reminded herself of the Theodore Roosevelt quotation she loved to share with her listeners: comparison is the thief of joy.

She would not let feelings of inadequacy hijack her day. She tapped her finger on her chin as she thought. "Maybe if you were really still, I could catapult whipped cream into your mouth with a spoon."

Chloe pulled her chin to her chest, leveling her blue eyes on Sarah's. "That sounds messy."

"It sounds like a fun challenge to me! We'll try after lunch. Deal?"

"Deal!" Chloe wiggled with excitement. "But first I want to feed the fish!"

"First the fish," Sarah said, one hundred percent back in the role of mom.

CHAPTER TWENTY-EIGHT

Twelve agonizing days passed by with no texts from Sarah. Jass knew that she had Chloe. The chatterbox had kept her company last week while she tended the pool. She and Sarah had waved and exchanged a handful of inconsequential words, nothing that would betray the hours they had spent in bed together. She had not expected Sarah to be in contact when she had her daughter, intuiting that it would be important for her to keep her two selves separate from each other. Still, as she pulled up to the house, it was difficult to school her body. Her thighs tingled. She rested her head on the steering wheel for a moment and smacked her fists against her legs. "We're here to work. That's it. Stop thinking. Stop remembering."

She pulled air deep into her lungs and held it for several beats to settle her thoughts before she let herself out and hauled her cart to the pool, noticing that the plants along the side of the house were doing well. There was also a new bird feeder hanging across from the window above Sarah's kitchen sink.

She heard the sliding-glass door open and shut with a slam. "Hi, Jass!" Chloe trotted over.

"Hey! You still in school or are you on vacation now?"

"I'm in school next week. Then it's Christmas!"

"So I'll see you next week and then not again until the new year."

Chloe looked confused. "Why?"

"Because I get vacation, too."

"But who will take care of the pool?"

"In the winter the pool barely needs me anyway. I'm already giving it less chlorine than I do in the summer when you're swimming and it's really hot. Unless a bunch of leaves go in your pool, it will be fine until I'm back in January."

"I can get leaves out if it gets windy," Chloe said.

"That's a big help. I wish everyone would keep an eye on their pool and help out like you do. You wouldn't come in the pool yard on your own, though, right? You'll check with your mom?"

"'Course!" The tawny-headed youngster said, running back to the house.

Jass hadn't meant that she needed to ask that second but took the opportunity to twist the net on her pole and start skimming the pool's surface. She scooped the edges first and then started her serpentine pattern. A smell caught her attention. She glanced to the house, seeing that Chloe had left the door open. Sarah must have been starting dinner.

Jass's stomach turned unpleasantly.

She grabbed her water from her cart and sipped until her stomach quieted. She had not skipped lunch and had eaten an apple a few houses ago. Now that she'd stepped further away from the house, she felt better. She swapped out the net for her vacuuming equipment. Chloe returned, eating a lemon yogurt. That smell caught at the back of her throat. She switched to breathing through her mouth.

"My mommy says we'll watch the pool. You don't have to worry."

"Super! What are you doing for Christmas vacation?"

"Put decorations on the tree. We always watch *The Sound of Music* and drink hot cocoa."

Jass remembered the first time she'd seen the movie and smiled. She'd had such a crush on Julie Andrews. She'd have to remember to ask Sarah if she'd ever crushed on her. "That sounds like a great tradition," she said, still breathing through her mouth. She was grateful when Chloe kept talking about the things she would do over her break which included going up to Casey's house to throw the ball for Elmo. It was a good thing Sarah's pool was the last of her day. She really needed to get home and lie down. Something was not right at all with her system. Her stomach turned again when she added half a gallon of chlorine.

She'd skip sweeping the pool. She'd cleared the big debris and would be able to do a more careful job when she returned next week. Thank goodness she had another visit before she skipped two weeks.

"You're done already?" Chloe asked, disappointed when Jass had packed up her cart and called her out of the pool yard.

"I'll see you next week, though!" Jass reminded her. Where she was usually happy to keep chatting for a moment, today she kept her feet moving. She had to put food in her stomach. All she had on the cart was water, and that had only temporarily settled the nausea.

To her dismay, Sarah pushed the door open as she passed as if she'd been waiting for Jass to finish. "Have a minute?" she asked.

Standing this close to the house, whatever Sarah was cooking enveloped Jass. Chicken, onion, garlic. It was too much. Jass's hand flew to her mouth. "I need…" She didn't even finish the sentence, just scooted past Sarah and ran to the bathroom. To hell with what it would look like for her to be running to a customer's bathroom. Plus, she'd been inside before.

She barely made it to the bathroom before emptying the contents of her stomach into the toilet. This had never happened to her. She was mortified. She flushed and cupped her hands under the tap water to rinse her mouth and rinse her face. What would she say to Sarah? She wished there was a way to get out of her house without having to talk to her, but that, she knew, was impossible.

A small rap on the door pulled her attention. "Jass, are you alright?" Sarah asked.

"Did you throw up? Are you going to throw up again?" Chloe called.

Sarah murmured something to her daughter and when she spoke again, there was no chorus. "I have a glass of water for you."

Sheepishly, Jass opened the door and accepted the water. She was scared to breathe through her nose and sat on the toilet lid, not wanting to get closer to the kitchen. Sarah stepped in and rubbed her back.

Conflicting messages raced through Jass. Her stomach was still a mess and on top of that was now knotting with the memory of Sarah's hands on her skin when they had stripped bare in this same room.

"Something you ate?" Sarah asked.

"I don't think so. All I had was a PB&J today."

"Yeah, that's pretty bland." Then Sarah laughed. "It's *such* a good thing I'm not a dude. I'd be so scared I got you pregnant! When I was carrying Chloe, I couldn't do any of the cooking. Tricia did it all because it made me so nauseous!"

Jass's eyes snapped to Sarah's. Was she pregnant? Her heartrate spiked. She'd told Amara she would not think about it until she missed her period, and she had been successful in putting that life question into a very secure box. Sarah's joke ripped the lid off.

"You should see your face right now!" Sarah laughed again. "I promise that as hard as I tried, there is no way I got you pregnant. I was actually coming out to ask whether you have plans this weekend. Tricia is picking Chloe up from school tomorrow, so…"

Jass sipped her water and handed it back to Sarah. "I'll have to get back to you."

"Oh. Of course. Let me know how you're feeling." She glanced toward the door as if checking for Chloe and then shut it. "Am I allowed to say that I'm really hoping you feel better tomorrow? I've been looking forward to my weekend solo."

The wave of nausea quelled, replaced with a swell of desire. "I would a hundred percent like to help you occupy your kid-free time."

Sarah's gaze fell to Jass's lips, but she quickly looked away, a good thing not just because Chloe was somewhere in the house, and her mouth tasted like garbage. She felt considerably better, though, and told Sarah, promising to text her about her availability Friday evening.

Disappointment swept over her face. Had she been wanting more than a text? She pushed the question aside and returned to her cart and the truck. She pulled Amara up on her rapid-dial and stared at her phone without hitting dial. It would only torture Amara if she called. She was probably home. And if she wasn't, Jass would wait. She pulled a granola bar out of her glovebox and inhaled it. The rest of the way to Amara's, she sipped water.

She said a quiet "Thank you" when she spotted Amara's car in her space. She jogged up the stairs to her apartment. "Get a stick ready," she said without preamble.

"Are you serious?"

"You better have a pregnancy test!" Jass said. Since Amara had bought all the ovulation kits, she had depended on Amara to buy the pregnancy test. There was no way Jass was going to test without her.

"Are you kidding? I have at least three different tests." She grabbed Jass and pulled her inside, pushing her toward the bathroom where she quickly pulled a handful of tests out from under the sink. "Which one?"

"Do I care? You pick! I'm too nervous."

Jass could see that Amara's hands were shaking as she opened the package and handed her the stick. "I'll read the instructions in the hall."

Jass did her part and scooted out to the hallway, shutting the door.

"You left it in there?" Amara cried.

"I'm too nervous! Set the timer. We're not looking until it goes off."

"Okay." Amara set the timer. "You said we had to wait till you missed your period."

"That was before I hurled at Sarah's house."

Amara jumped up and down. "You hurled? Really?"

"It is so weird that you are excited about me puking at a client's house."

"But that can be a sign, right? How are your breasts? Tender?"

"They're always tender before my period."

"Okay, but are they more tender than usual?"

Jass considered the question. "They barked at me when I rolled over to turn off my alarm yesterday."

Amara grabbed Jass's hands. "This could be it!"

The timer went off, and Amara opened the door.

CHAPTER TWENTY-NINE

"You have…no idea…No idea…How. Good. That. Feels," Sarah panted, savoring the way her body pulsed around Jass's fingers.

"Oh, I think I have a pretty good idea." Jass peppered Sarah's neck with kisses, enjoying the salt on her skin. When Sarah's breath slowed, Jass kissed her back to breathlessness. When the last waves of Sarah's orgasm subsided, Jass flopped on her back next to her.

Sarah raised herself on her elbow and traced one beautiful curve of Jass's after another, enjoying the way some of the paths coaxed a shiver from Jass. "I am so glad that whatever funk you had yesterday passed quickly."

"Me, too," Jass said. She tipped her head away and stared at the ceiling.

"Are you feeling okay now?" She ran her hand across Jass's flat belly. *What if*, she thought, stroking the soft plane. She was transported to the early days of her pregnancy. Tricia had been as excited as she was. Pregnancy and parenthood were still an exciting abstract idea. Tricia had been a wonderfully supportive partner throughout the pregnancy. She had made Sarah feel like a goddess, worshipping the way Sarah's body changed as Chloe grew. She chuckled inwardly, recalling how Tricia had marveled when Sarah's breasts swelled immediately. She cupped Jass's breast. She had the most beautiful breasts.

Jass covered Sarah's hand with her own. "So I need to be honest with you about something," she said softly.

Sarah rearranged her arm, so she could rest her chin in her hand. Turning her hand to hold Jass's, she couldn't resist saying, "You really are pregnant?"

Never in a million years did she expect Jass to say, "Yes."

She waited a beat. That wasn't supposed to be Jass's answer. Her eyebrows pinched together, and she scrutinized Jass. She couldn't be serious. Sarah relaxed her face. She had to be joking. "You're messing with me."

"I'm not messing with you." Jass sat up, utterly serious. "We inseminated Thanksgiving day. I peed on a stick yesterday. I'm pregnant."

"We? Who is we?" Sarah sat up as well, pulling a sheet over her as if it could shield her from what she did not want to hear.

"Me and Amara. She wants a baby more than anything in the world, but she doesn't have a womb. I do."

These facts, delivered so matter-of-factly refused to compute in Sarah's mind. "But she has no partner! Why would she choose to be a single parent?"

"She's twenty-eight. She's ready to be a parent. You have a whole episode about having kids before thirty."

Yes, that had been a priority for Sarah, one that had driven her own timeline of marriage and pregnancy. And look at where that had gotten her, divorced and co-parenting at thirty-two. "She has time to think through something so momentous more carefully."

"She has thought it through. We've talked to lawyers. We have a contract. This is what I meant when I said that Amara needs me."

Sarah shook her head, her mind reeling. "You think a legal contract will create a barrier between you and the baby you're spending the next nine months with? A baby who will start to move and kick inside of you? You think you'll be able to hand over a baby after forming your own relationship with it?" She remembered so vividly the conversations she'd had with Chloe before she was born and how firmly she bonded with her from the moment they lay her squishy form onto her chest. "What about breastfeeding? Don't you want the baby to have your colostrum? What happens after that? Are you going to pump breast milk for Amara to feed the baby? Who will you be to this baby? And how could you not tell me?"

At this she threw off the blanket and scooted off the bed to reclaim her clothes. She shoved her head and arms through her shirt not bothering to turn it right-side-out. She angrily pulled on her panties and jeans before facing Jass again. "You did this on Thanksgiving? And slept with me the next day? You didn't think to tell me that you'd just been *inseminated?*"

"We talked about this being casual! You used the term fuckbuddy! I didn't think that level of intimacy called for disclosing that there was a chance I could get pregnant. It didn't work the first time, so I didn't mention it. It didn't seem relevant."

"Unbelievable." Sarah stomped out of the room to the kitchen. She went to the pantry and pulled out a bottle of wine. Learning that her casual hookup was knocked up called for alcohol, didn't it?

She'd told her audience that she would stop self-medicating with alcohol. She put the bottle back and drew a glass of water from the sink. She drank it all and filled it again. Jass was still in her bedroom. Was she dressing? Would she leave? This felt awfully reminiscent of the first time she had thrown Jass out. She tilted her head back recalling how difficult that evening had been after Jass left. She heard footsteps behind her.

Jass appeared at her elbow and took a glass from the strainer and filled it with water. She walked to the table and sat. She wasn't leaving. What was she supposed to say? Jass had a point about their hookups being casual, but that didn't make the enormity of what Jass was taking on easier to process. "Do you need something to eat?"

"That would be amazing. I eat all day long now."

"Your body is demanding calories. Eating to dampen the nausea is your body's way to make sure the baby gets enough nutrients."

"What were your favorite snacks?"

"Almonds and raisins. I had a baggie of them with me at all times." She rummaged in her refrigerator and the cupboard before returning to the table. She placed a sleeve of crackers and a cheese stick in front of Jass and refilled her water. She hesitated by the table, worried that her actions could be interpreted as supporting this wholly irresponsible venture. She leaned against her counter instead.

Jass took a bite of the cheese stick. "Cheese sticks! This is a genius snack! Thank you!" She shoved a cracker in with her bite of cheese. Clearly she did not have a handle on things. Could she not see what she looked like sitting at Sarah's table having a child's snack? The last thing Sarah wanted to think about this weekend was mothering, and here she was caring for a future mother. Not mother. Jass had to be delusional if she believed she would be able to part with the life she was creating.

Every time Tricia had Chloe for the weekend, it felt like a piece of her was missing. She did not see how having a contract would keep Jass's heart from splitting in two after she birthed the baby and handed him or her to Amara.

It was too much. Sarah sat and covered her face with her hands.

"I told you I'm not in a position to date right now. This is what I meant. Amara almost backed out of the arrangement because she worries about the impact this is going to have on my life, but she's my family. I know you probably feel like I dropped a ton of bricks on you, but can you understand why I didn't say anything earlier? When you have Chloe, you are one hundred percent Chloe's mom. That isn't going to change. And we had no idea whether Amara's goods were going to work with IUI."

"Wait, Amara's goods?"

"Her sperm. She froze before she transitioned in case she ever wanted to do intrauterine insemination or in vitro fertilization. Her doctor recommended it even though at the time she was not thinking about children. He wanted her to have options. I'm guessing you and Tricia used a donor?"

Sarah got up and fetched the wine, her listeners be damned. If this was really the way the conversation was going, she needed help. She pulled out the cork and poured herself a glass, leaving the bottle on the counter. "We did."

"Did you choose a willing-to-be-known donor?"

Sarah snorted. She should have taken the difficulty she and Tricia had experienced with even that conundrum as a sign that they were not ready to enter into parenting together. Tricia had insisted that they choose a donor that was not willing to be known. She did not want their child tracking down the donor at eighteen. Sarah should have read Tricia's insecurity. She had won the argument about at least giving their child the option to find the donor at eighteen, but ultimately she had lost in failing to recognize that Tricia simply wasn't ready to parent. She did not understand all it entailed. She liked the concept of a perfect family with two moms and a cute baby, but she was not up for the actual work of it. Sarah told Jass all of this, explaining how they had prioritized the donor profiles. "I have a few baby pictures of the donor somewhere. Chloe has his eyes." She got up to refill her glass and, standing at the counter, said, "Amara will be able to identify all sorts of features her child gets from you."

Jass nodded. "Chloe did something the other day that reminded me so much of you that it sucker-punched me. I know that I'm signing up for a lot here, and I know that there's a whole lot I'm not prepared for."

"Where are your families on all this? Are they supportive?"

Jass broke their eye contact. "We haven't told them yet. Again, until it was a reality, it didn't seem necessary. And I have the first trimester to get through. I mean, I'm not out of the woods yet."

"Oh, Jass," Sarah said, dropping back into a chair. "What happens if you make it out of those woods only to be thrown into a den of lions when you tell your families?"

"That's a possibility with my mom and Amara's dad. He's not much a part of her life these days. He treats her like she's his wife's adult child, not his. He wants nothing to do with her. But her mom…She cried when Amara transitioned because this isn't the family she envisioned, but now I think she'll worry less about her being lonely. And she'll have another grandkid to spoil. My mom won't understand. To her, kids ruin everything, but I think Dave will be there for me. We're definitely taking a risk with all of them. But the baby isn't for them, so it has to be worth it. I know how naïve that sounds." She smiled ruefully. "Amara and I…We just keep reminding each other that we'll always be there for each other. That's what counts. We always have been, and we always will be. That'll have to be enough."

Sarah tipped the empty stemless wineglass. What did anyone know about having enough?

CHAPTER THIRTY

"What do you think I should say?" Jass asked before taking a bite of apple. When she finished work for the day, she was definitely picking up almonds and raisins. And cheese sticks. She took another bite of apple wishing she'd sliced up some cheddar to go with her snack that morning.

"This doesn't sound like a hard question," Amara answered. "She asked how you are. You tell her. How *are* you?"

"Hungry. And tired. I can barely move I'm so tired." She was not even halfway through her day, and she was ready to be home on her couch. Once she had done five pools, could she find a place to park in the shade and take a short snooze?

"So text her back that you're hungry and tired."

When Sarah's text had come in, Jass had started to type in how she truly felt, but before she hit send, she decided to check in with Amara and called on her way to her fourth pool. "What if she's asking because she hopes I'm up for stopping by after I'm finished for the day?"

"Jass," Amara said, and in the way she said her name Jass could hear everything she already knew.

"I know." She tapped nervously on the steering wheel with her thumbs. "I should answer honestly. If I'm beat, I have to tell her I'm beat. But if I say I'm beat, I'm saying I'm not interested in messing around, right?"

"That's not how I would read it. How did it feel when you left yesterday? Is she still game for messing around with a pregnant lady?"

A whoosh bottomed out Jass's stomach as if she'd driven over a big dip. She was pregnant. It hadn't seemed real when Amara had whispered *positive* after reading the pregnancy test. Jass had imagined the moment and had anticipated that they would jump up and down, hugging each other, giddy with excitement. But Amara had whispered the word and handed the test to Jass. Two lines. They sat—Amara on the toilet lid, Jass on the edge of the tub, their knees touching. Nothing was different, but everything had changed. "We didn't talk about it," Jass said.

"So the real question is what is best for you right now. And I say that completely unselfishly. I am not going to tell you what to do."

Jass groaned. She was really dragging. She had never experienced this level of exhaustion. "My last pool has a great outdoor living space, and I fantasized about taking a five-minute snooze on the couch."

Amara laughed. "That wouldn't be good for business. If your fantasy has you snoozing on a couch instead of meeting a naked Sarah Cooper there, I'm pretty sure you already know what you need to text her."

"I know. But I don't want to admit how tired I am."

"Because then no sex for you."

"Because then no more sex for me. What if that's it? I thought we had come to an adult agreement, and now I feel like I ruined it."

"It's not like you would be able to hide it. Better to have told her now than for her to find out when you start showing."

"Okay. I'll tell her I'm tired. I'm at my next pool. I gotta buck up and get through my day."

"You're not going to listen, but remember what your dad says. Set a timer. The pool doesn't have to be perfect, and if you're moving more slowly, you might get less done. It's okay to cut yourself some slack today and make it up next time."

"Thanks," Jass said. She unloaded her cart and hoofed it up the steep drive. The houses north of Sierra Madre were built into the foothills which meant many of the properties were hilly. She paused at the gate to catch her breath and take in the amazing view of the valley below. She did her chores weighing where she would feel comfortable cutting back to preserve energy. One pass with the skimming net instead of multiple passes until the surface was free of debris? She knew many of her colleagues skipped emptying the secondary basket after they vacuumed. It had never felt right to her. She had a fixed idea of what got done each week and would not allow herself to fall short of the norm she had established with each client.

That was what gave her pause.

Sarah's text had moved beyond what they had established Thanksgiving weekend. Had Sarah asked if Jass could stop by after work, she would not have worried, but Sarah had not texted *Busy?* or *See you after work?* She had texted *How are you feeling?*

That was emotional, not physical, unless she was reading too much into it, and Sarah really was just asking if she was up for sex. She was overthinking. Ruminating was not going to help. Better to send a reply. She took Amara's advice and answered honestly. *Tired and hungry.*

Sarah's reply came immediately. *Yep. First trimester is all eat and sleep.*

I finish a snack and want another snack.

The baby wants a snack.

It's not even a baby yet.

Your body is working hard!

Jass shoved her phone away. She needed to stay on track with her checklist, not keep texting with Sarah. This family had a hammock, and again, Jass fantasized about lying down for just a moment. When Sarah had carried Chloe, would she actually nap when she was tired? Or did she have to push through at work? She did not need to text Sarah. The last text was a statement, not a question. She should let it sit and keep herself on task, but more importantly to keep herself focused on what she and Sarah had agreed was a casual relationship. They had not fired many texts back and forth, but they were building something different.

The problem with her job was that for the most part, she did it by rote. She did not need to think about any of it. To stop her endless circular thought patterns, she needed to occupy her mind. She'd listen to music to stop thinking about Sarah.

When she pulled out her phone to cue up a song, she hesitated on Sarah's text. She should not keep the conversation going. But Amara had said that Sarah could be a good resource for pregnancy questions. She couldn't resist typing her question. *How does anyone get through the day feeling this tired without any caffeine?*

She turned on her music but still heard the ping of Sarah's reply. What was she doing that she was always responding so quickly? *Don't push yourself. Nap when you are tired.*

Don't think my clients would take to me crashing in their yard.

I wouldn't complain.

Jass hesitated. That was flirty. Did that mean that Sarah had, in fact, texted to feel out whether Jass would be stopping by? *You're not my typical client.*

I would hope not.

The text made Jass swoon. *No swooning!* she scolded herself. But she read it again, not quite believing that Sarah Cooper directed such words at her. She was going to have to be very careful to not allow herself to get too attached. Sarah's words about how difficult it was going to be to give up the baby rang in her memory. What did it mean that she was far more concerned about whether she was getting too attached to Sarah than she was about being able to hand over the baby she was making for Amara?

"I'm pregnant," she whispered to herself. And she still didn't know where Sarah was coming from. Did she feel differently about their arrangement now that Jass was pregnant? For that matter, did Jass feel differently about sleeping with Sarah now? She rested her palm on her tummy. She needed a pause, some time and space to acclimate to this new state of being. *If* she made it through the first trimester, she reminded herself. She had to make it through the first trimester. Her life had become complicated enough without having to backtrack to "not pregnant" again. Staying pregnant would ground her in something certain, something to see through. She was good at seeing things through.

Sarah was not her typical client, but she was not a certainty, either. As tempting as it was to flirt with Sarah to see where it would go, Jass couldn't see herself going there today. Sarah hadn't asked a question, but her text was flirtatious, and Jass felt like she should answer it. The problem was that she didn't know if she had it in her to flirt back. It took her two more pools to formulate her response. *I'm sorry about the shitty timing of all this.* She typed it and stared at it so long that her screen went black. Should she hit send? If she did, Sarah would know not to expect her, and she would have Chloe again through another whole weekend. They could not keep texting. It would inevitably lead to Jass getting too attached. Better to maintain some autonomy and keep things simple.

She hit send.

When her phone buzzed in her pocket, she left it in her pocket. Keep it simple. That would be her motto.

CHAPTER THIRTY-ONE

Sarah checked her phone for the umpteenth time. Her last message sat there unanswered. Was Jass at home napping? Sarah had not been lying when she said that the first trimester was all about eating and sleeping. She had been seeing clients at that time, and if she had a cancellation, she would set a timer and snooze on the couch in her office, waking in a puddle of drool and befuddlement and just enough time to run to the bathroom to pee and splash water on her face.

She shouldn't have asked how Jass was feeling. She'd thrown the dynamics so far off-kilter that it ended up feeling awkward to ask whether Jass might stop by after work. Now it was almost dinnertime. Two weeks ago, Jass had declined her offer of dinner, but she had happily occupied the time that it took to make, eat and clean up after herself reviewing how wonderful it felt to be touched again.

A knock at the door startled her to her feet. Had she missed the sound of Jass's truck? She set down her book and jogged to the door with a huge smile.

"Casey! Hello!" She had been so certain it would be Jass that she searched up and down the street.

Casey looked over her shoulder. "Sorry to stop by unannounced. We realized that none of us have your number, and I had a question for ya, so I figured I'd pop on down to ask. The dogs are always game for a walk. At least Elmo is." Both dogs sat patiently at her feet. "Chloe's not here?"

"No. She'll be so sad to have missed seeing Elmo and Bandit. She's with her other mom for the weekend."

"I was wondering if you might be interested in Drag Queen Story Hour."

"That sounds fantastic! Who does it?"

"Adrienne's library has been doing it, and she brought it up with the library staff here in town. They told her in a town like Revelia they didn't think any families would come."

"Chloe loves story time, and we would definitely support a drag queen reading."

"Great! Know any other queer families in town?"

"I wish! I'll feel out some of the other moms at Chloe's pickup. Is Adrienne a children's librarian?"

"She's actually a library clerk, but she's super good with kids and super crafty, so she ends up working in the children's section quite a bit."

"I am the furthest thing from crafty. I could use project ideas to occupy Chloe over Christmas break. I run out of ideas so fast."

Elmo snuffed around Sarah's garden clogs by the front door, and Casey pulled him back close to her. "I'll text her. I'm sure she has stuff on hand she can bring the next time she drives out."

"Oh, that would be amazing." Sarah paused. Casey's words brought to the surface many unanswered questions for Sarah. She understood that Marv needed light caregiving after suffering a ministroke but could not understand why Adrienne lived in Fairfax. "Can I ask you a question?"

"Sure."

"You wouldn't prefer to live with Adrienne all the time?"

The purple chunk of hair fell across Casey's face. She tucked it behind her ear. "She needs her own space. Knowing she can get away and recharge is what makes dating work for her. I like it best when she spends the night next to me, but if I asked for all her nights, we wouldn't be together. That would be a deal-breaker for you, wouldn't it?"

"It would. I'm feeling so old-fashioned these days. I don't know when I got so old!" Sarah laughed. Her head ached from the amount of wine she had consumed to try to make sense of Amara's choice to be a single parent and Jass's agreeing to carry the baby. As if Casey could follow her internal train of thought, Sarah asked, "Would you blink if your friend decided to have a baby on her own, without a partner?"

"Is this for your book?"

Sarah waved her off. When she had mentioned her podcast at Thanksgiving, Casey's friend Nancy had said she should write a book. When Sarah had insisted she was no writer, Nancy challenged her to try and suggested a book by Anne Lamott. Sarah took down its title as she was always interested in new podcast material, and while the book was about writing, much of it also applied to life. She was getting ideas, but for a book of her own? That she hadn't figured out. "No. I'm curious and looking for another perspective."

"Would I blink? That's an interesting question. I mean, everyone pictures marriage and then baby, but relationships aren't for everyone just like kids aren't for everyone. If one couple can say they don't want kids, why can't a single person decide they do? It's not like they're saying I have to have a baby. As long as it works for them, then I guess I don't see how it's any of my business," Casey said. Bandit lay across her feet and sighed.

Sarah could not understand Casey's lack of concern about whether a single parent had sufficient resources to support a child. Her years of counseling focused Sarah on the long-term impact of big choices like starting a family. But her answer vividly reflected the discussion at Marv's about putting what works for the individual first. Sarah had let what society says is right reinsert itself. "Do you and Adrienne talk about kids?"

"Oh, no! We already have our two pups, and both of them were unplanned. For now, they're plenty to keep us busy!"

"You two are young. You have time. And I've taken up too much of yours. Let me give you my contact info, though, so you can text if Adrienne has craft ideas for us."

Casey obliged and immediately shot Sarah a text. "Now you have my number, too, so you can text me if Chloe is interested in playing with the dogs. Or if you need a break."

Sarah thanked her and promised to follow through on her kind offer. The time in between the weekends that Chloe spent with Tricia could be gruelingly long. She knew the importance of self-care but it did not feel acceptable to hire a babysitter because she could use some uninterrupted time. Was it different for parents who could drop their children off with grandparents? Did it feel less selfish when a grandparent longed to spend time with their grandchild? Her mom didn't have time for that. The few occasions she had tried to ask her mom for help, all she'd received was a lecture on her life choices.

Her concern for Amara choosing to have a child on her own was rooted in how little support she got from her family. It didn't seem like either woman had a family who was going to step in to support them. That was legitimate, wasn't it? Not her being judgy? Tricia had often complained about Sarah being judgmental.

She'd thought she'd done a good job of setting aside her reservations about the baby and had texted Jass from a place of support that morning. She'd been sincere in answering Jass's apology with permission to do what was best for her. And then Jass hadn't responded. Maybe she had decided that it was best if she did not spend time with someone so obviously conflicted about her life choices. It surprised Sarah how melancholy that made her feel and she wished that she could have accepted Jass's revelation as breezily as Casey had.

A cloud passed over the sun and dusk was fast approaching. Sarah should water her plants before she made dinner. She slipped into a flannel shirt and gardening clogs. She loved watering her plants, the way it all smelled after she watered. Once outside, she discovered many chores to squeeze into the end of the day, one task leading to another. Getting the birdseed from the garage to refill the feeder, she noticed leaves floating in the pool and checked the leaf trap. Once she'd emptied that, she discovered that the water was low, so she pulled the hose.

She'd walked back to the garden area to turn on the hose when she saw Jass's truck slow at her drive. Heat rushed through her. She'd come after all! "I'm out back!" she called when Jass stepped out of her truck.

Jass lifted her hand in greeting as she strode to the gate. Sarah loved watching her walk, the confidence she radiated as if wherever she was, was exactly where she was meant to be. Her sunglasses pushed up on her head held her hair away from her face and accentuated her cute bangs. She let herself through the gate, and Sarah couldn't help herself—she met Jass and wrapped her arms around her.

"I wasn't sure you'd be up for coming over," she said.

Jass returned the hug. "I wasn't either. I got all caught up in my head and couldn't figure out how to reply earlier. But I couldn't stop thinking about you."

Jass felt so good in her arms, and her breath near Sarah's ear nearly undid her. "Same."

Once they stepped out of the hug, they stood close. Jass cocked her head. "You can't stop thinking about me carrying Amara's baby, or you couldn't stop thinking about me naked?"

Sarah laughed. "Honestly?"

Jass held her gaze steadily. "Always."

Sarah wet her lips. "Both. But I just read this quote in a book someone recommended about how when you drive at night, you can only see as far as your headlights, but you can make the whole trip that way. Maybe instead of worrying about the whole trip, we could stay focused on what we can see right now in front of us. And right now, I see you."

"I like that idea," Jass said. "I'd like it even more if it included fewer clothes."

Sarah kissed her. "For that, we move inside."

"Lead the way," Jass said against her lips.

CHAPTER THIRTY-TWO

Chloe galloped across the patio and up into the lawn area beyond the pool and did several laps before she stopped to watch what Jass was doing. Her little sides heaved. "You look like a pony turned loose!" she called.

"I *am* a pony," Chloe said. "Mommy says I have to run around until I can control myself."

"Can you do any tricks?" Jass asked. "When I see ponies running, it seems like they jump and twist like they are practicing how to buck off little kids."

"Like this?" Chloe tore around the yard again, adding a few little hops.

"That looks like a bunny hopping. That's not going to get a kid out of the saddle."

Chloe jumped higher.

"Now you look like a kangaroo. Put some twists in! Kick your feet out!"

She kicked like she was playing soccer with an imaginary ball. Jass stopped and did a quick Google search for bucking ponies. She let herself out of the pool yard and jogged up to the grassy area with numerous trees. "Watch this," she said, sitting on a cement retaining wall.

Chloe sat down next to her and took the phone, and together they watched a small white pony tuck in its head and kick its feet. Chloe poked the phone's screen and got to her feet. Now she snaked her head from side to side and tried her best to kick both feet while she twisted to the side. She cracked up and fell to the grass. "That's hard!"

"Well, they're working with four feet. I'm sure that makes it easier."

Chloe sat down and poked the screen again to watch the rest of the video. "What are those?" She pointed to little jumps in the field.

"Those are fences the pony can jump over. Haven't you seen a pony jump?"

Chloe shook her head and pouted her lower lip. Jass searched for jumping ponies and pulled up an adorable montage of kids jumping the tiniest, scruffiest ponies she'd ever seen.

"I want to be a jumping pony!" Chloe said.

"You can jump over anything." When Jass was the surliest of teens, her mother had dated a man who had a daughter who was a few years older than Jass. His daughter took riding lessons, so Jass's mother had found a barn and enrolled her own daughter. Jass remembered being dropped off in the morning and picked up hours later. She ran with the other barn rats like they were a second herd of ponies. She had loved running around the arena when there were no lessons, jumping the obstacles on foot. She searched around the yard for things suitable to jump and spotted a pile of toy trucks in the dirt. She loved that Chloe had a fleet of trucks as much as she loved that she had on gender-neutral jeans and a navy blue sweatshirt. "These trucks will do. Watch."

She lined up four trucks and jogged over them. When she turned to see Chloe's reaction, she laid eyes on Sarah standing next to her daughter, the back of her wrist pressed to her mouth as if she was trying not to laugh. "What in the world are you doing?"

Jass couldn't take her eyes off Sarah. She wore loose jeans rolled at the cuff and a charcoal turtleneck sweater. She looked as if she was ready to curl up by a fireplace. Jass thought of how nice it would be to lean back into Sarah's soft embrace. Sarah would wrap her arms around Jass and rest her chin on her shoulder while they watched flames flicker in the fireplace. She was trying to remember if Sarah had a fireplace when Sarah's gaze shifted from her to Chloe. Right. Chloe. Sarah had asked what they were doing. "Chloe wanted to learn how to jump her pony."

"It's not the same as the pony in the video," Chloe grumped.

"They had poles," Jass explained. "I bet you could make jumps out of bricks and garden tools."

Sarah gestured to Jass's abandoned equipment. "I didn't mean to interrupt you sending Chloe out to run off her beans."

They had not figured out how to be around each other when Sarah had Chloe. Her words didn't feel as if she was pushing Jass away. Would it be weird for her to stay beyond her pool duties? She welcomed a distraction from spending another night of sitting on the couch focused on what was happening in her uterus. "I don't have plans after work. I don't mind."

Sarah didn't answer immediately. What was she thinking? Was she weighing whether allowing Jass to interact with Chloe was overstepping the firm boundaries she had in place to protect her? Was she worried that letting Jass do things with Chloe would complicate their arrangement?

"Please, Mommy?" Chloe said. "Jass already taught me how to buck. Watch!"

As she took off across the lawn, Jass stepped closer to Sarah. Their shoulders brushed, and Jass longed to lean into Sarah, but she respected Sarah's boundaries and was not going to push. She worried that Sarah would interpret her playing with Chloe as angling to have Sarah accept her as more than a casual hookup.

In a low voice that warmed Jass to her core, Sarah said, "Whenever I'm around you, I want to let my inner pony free like that."

How was Jass supposed to respond to that? She snuck a look at Sarah whose eyes never left Chloe. Jass knew that Sarah felt her gaze, though, because the corner of her mouth pulled into a smile. Jass could tell that although she was watching her daughter, she was remembering the things she and Jass did when they were alone. Jass longed to help Sarah fully explore her freedom but settled for bumping her hip against Sarah's.

"Sadly my days are filled with bridles and saddles," Sarah said as Chloe ran back.

"Did you see me, Mommy?"

"I did! You look like one happy pony!"

"And now I can jump?"

Sarah looked at Jass. "If you really have the time."

"Let's set up one for today, okay? And you can practice while I finish up the pool." Jass looked at Sarah. One jump. Fifteen minutes to finish the pool. She'd be pushing to finish in the fading light.

"And then two next week?" Chloe asked.

"In the new year. Remember I get a vacation at the same time you get your vacation."

Surprise filled Sarah's eyes. "I take off two weeks around Christmas and New Year. You can always text me if there's an emergency."

Chloe pushed into her mother, and Sarah's arm naturally draped across the child's shoulder, pulling her into her warmth. Jass wanted to add *or if you're alone.* Sarah crossed her arms and raised her eyebrows. She knew.

"So. Bricks and garden tools?" Jass asked.

"I have tools in the shed, and there are some bricks and broken pavers stacked behind it." Sarah led the way to a metal structure in the back corner and pushed open the door. Both Sarah and Chloe looked at Jass, making no move to enter the dark space. Jass ducked and let her eyes adjust to the dark, quickly finding a rake and a shovel. These she handed to Chloe. She stacked four bricks and carried them to the middle of the yard.

"We'll start with an X shape to practice with. If you were on a real pony, we'd set up trotting poles in front, but since you're not, we'll skip that step."

"You must have ridden before," Sarah said.

"I took lessons for almost a year."

"Lessons?" Chloe's eyes gleamed.

Sarah held up her hands. "We're not talking about lessons!"

Chloe crossed her own arms, mimicking her mother's earlier pose. Jass quickly stacked two bricks as far apart as the tools were long and rested the head of each tool atop the brick, its base at the bottom of the other brick, crisscrossing in the middle. "Okay, you're all set. Let's see you trot over this. After you jump it, go all the way around your arena…"

"Arena?" Chloe asked.

"That's where you ride a pony. When you're training, we'll call your yard the arena, okay?"

Chloe nodded.

"Okay. Let's see!" Jass said.

Chloe ran and hopped over the X. She continued running around the yard and hopped over it again.

"You've got it! Let's see you do that five more times while I finish the pool."

Sarah walked with her as she returned to the pool. "Thank you for helping her burn off some energy. She'll definitely sleep tonight."

"No problem. It's fun remembering my pony-riding days!" Jass said.

"Maybe you'll tell me about them sometime," Sarah said.

Sarah's words brought to mind the image of their sharing stories with their naked bodies intertwined. She suppressed a shudder of desire. "Shoot me a text if you're free over the holiday," Jass said as nonchalantly as she could. She entertained the idea of finding a place to take Chloe riding but quickly reined herself in. She was not dating Sarah Cooper. That meant no planning outings with her kid. "I'll be around."

"Tricia and I haven't ironed out how we're going to work the holidays," Sarah said. "I've been trying to keep my head above water, getting as much work done as I can before she's out of school."

"I get it. No pressure," Jass said. "If you've got free time, great."

"Jass! Watch me jump!" Chloe called from the yard.

"That was a wonderful thing you did for Chloe. Thank you," Sarah said.

"You're welcome," Jass said. She turned her attention back to Chloe as she ran through the yard toward the jump, but her body stayed tuned into Sarah's movements. Her opening the door and then shutting it. She grabbed her windbreaker from her cart and zipped into it, the night having grown colder without Sarah by her side.

CHAPTER THIRTY-THREE

"Flexible is exactly what I'm trying to be." Sarah pinched the bridge of her nose.

Tricia continued to outline details of her holiday plans with Lydia that were inconsequential for Sarah. Sarah increased the volume of the show Chloe was engrossed in and stepped onto the back porch to continue their call, sensing that it was not going to get any easier.

"I hear you," she said as she slid the back door closed and sat on the outdoor couch. "You want to get away with Lydia for the weekend. I'm saying I'm willing to have Chloe two weekends in a row, but you owe Chloe your presence Saturday morning. You and I talked about this. I know we can't maintain every tradition, but opening presents in the morning is second only to her birthday. This isn't about me. It's about Chloe, and she comes first. Bring Lydia if you have to, but you're here until we finish the aebleskiver." For Sarah, it was the food that made Christmas more than the gifts, and for her whole life, breakfast had consisted of the Danish pancakes covered with powdered sugar and served with special jams.

"Bring Lydia? Me, you, Lydia and Chloe sitting around a Christmas tree opening presents? I don't think so."

Sarah rolled her eyes. "So you come in the morning by yourself and have Lydia wait for you or drive yourself to the resort. Ultimately, this is your conflict, one you created when you decided to date Lydia. You told her you have Chloe for New Year's Eve, didn't you?"

"New Year's! But New Year's is for couples! I planned on getting her New Year's Day!"

"Friday to Sunday means you have her for New Year's Eve."

"You're talking about how Christmas is important for kids. New Year's is one of *the* most important days for couples, and I have plans!"

Tricia sounded like a child trying to get out of chores. It had been a major contributor to the divorce and one problem Sarah had hoped divorcing would solve. Unfortunately, she continued to find herself in the role of enforcer. "You could hire a babysitter for the evening."

"For New Year's? How am I going to find someone now for New Year's that won't cost me an arm and a leg? Why can't you watch her one extra night? It's not like you're dating anyone! You're just doing this to punish me for dating."

"I'm not punishing you, Tricia! You and I had a child together, a child who deserves to have a relationship with both her parents." Sarah's phone pinged, and she glanced at the screen to see if Casey was changing the plans for Drag Queen Story Hour. Her brow furrowed when Jass's name flashed on the screen with the text. She'd check after she got things squared away with Tricia.

"Why do you have to be like this? You think if you're not getting laid, nobody should be having any fun?"

"My sex life isn't relevant here," Sarah said, acutely aware of the text she had waiting from Jass. She poked the call to speakerphone and opened Jass's text. *Can you talk?* she read as Tricia launched into how Sarah must not have any recollection of sex. Sarah cut her off. "I need to go. I've got to get Chloe ready for the day. But we'll see you Tuesday for the big cookie-making day."

"That I have on my calendar."

"See you at eight, then." It never hurt to remind Tricia of the agreed time, especially when being able to record with Joshua depended on Tricia picking Chloe up on time. "It's one of Chloe's favorite activities," she said to soften the overall tone of the conversation.

"I know. Lydia thinks it's sweet we make cookies from scratch. She's not against me spending time with my kid. Believe it or not, she was asking why I only do every other weekend."

Sarah wasn't expecting that and while she would like to explore a different co-parenting schedule, she sensed that Jass needed her. "Let's revisit our schedule in the new year, okay?"

Tricia agreed, and Sarah ended the call. She stepped inside to check on Chloe. "Still okay in here?"

"Is it time to go?" She stood up on the couch.

"No, not quite. I'm going to get some snacks together. Five minutes?"

Chloe slipped back down the back of the couch. "Okay, Mommy."

She dialed Jass. "Sorry for the delay," she said when Jass answered.

"It's okay. I didn't know whether to ask you. I've been spinning all morning not knowing what to do, and I didn't know whether to call you, so I texted you."

"Jass, what's wrong?" She did not sound herself at all.

"I had bleeding this morning. Bright red, like I'm starting my period. Can that happen? I Googled it, and some sites say it could be implantation bleeding, but I thought the egg was already implanted if I had a positive on the pregnancy test. I'm freaking out, and when I freak out, I always call Amara, but I can't call Amara and tell her that I'm bleeding because it would *really* freak her out."

"Jass, take a deep breath," Sarah said calmly. "Are you sitting down?"

"No. I can't sit still. I don't know what to do with myself."

"Can you take a deep breath? You sound like you're about to hyperventilate. Count in for five and hold for five," Sarah instructed. She held her breath for five beats as well before instructing Jass to release the breath and repeat. She sat and counted out breaths with Jass for several minutes. "The Internet is correct. Bleeding can be completely normal, especially if it looks like the spotting you get before your period. If it continues, you'll need to see your ob-gyn. But right now, the best thing you can do is relax and try to get your mind off it."

"I can't relax. If I stop, I worry, but if I get up to do something, I feel like the baby is going to fall out."

Sarah shook her head even though Jass couldn't see her. "If that baby is growing normally, it's not going anywhere. If something is wrong and the baby is nonviable, there is nothing you can do to stop your body from bleeding."

"Wow."

"Too blunt?" Sarah wished she could see Jass's face.

"No. That's exactly what I needed to hear."

"Are you serious?" Sarah couldn't tell if Jass was being sarcastic, but she sounded sincere.

"Yeah. You're saying what I do has nothing to do with whether the little bean sticks. That's kind of comforting."

"I'm glad." Sarah bit her lip. She needed to get Chloe ready for their outing. Did she dare invite Jass? "Do you need to be with someone? Chloe and I are on our way to the first ever Drag Queen Story Hour at our library. Casey invited us. Maybe it would be good for you to get out. Try to stop worrying about what you can't control."

"Who are you talking to?" Chloe asked from behind her, causing Sarah to jump. "Is Mama coming to hear the story?"

Sarah tipped the phone away from her mouth. "No, it's Jass, not Mama."

Chloe hopped up and down. "Yay! Jass coming with us?"

"I don't know, sweetheart. Run and get your shoes on." To Jass, she said, "Sorry about that. She was in stealth mode."

"It's okay. You're nice to offer, but I think I'll stay home and rest."

"Okay." Sarah felt strangely disappointed. It was probably for the best, though. If Jass continued bleeding, she would probably want to stay closer to home, and it wasn't like she could comfort Jass without Chloe asking why Jass was sad. "Would you text me later to let me know if you're okay?"

Jass didn't answer right away, and Sarah worried that she had overstepped. "Sure," she finally said. "I'll text you tonight."

"Why is Jass worried?" Chloe asked as they walked to the car.

"What?" Sarah was still thinking about the pause after she had asked Jass to text her later. She was the one who called to ask about the spotting in the first place.

"You said Jass needed to stop worrying."

"Oh. Grown-up stuff."

"That's what you always say," Chloe grumped as Sarah strapped her into the car seat. She tickled Chloe's chin, and the girl giggled and squirmed, hopefully forgetting that Sarah had not explained why Jass was worried. It occurred to her that if Jass didn't miscarry, there would come a point where Chloe was going to ask about the baby. She hadn't the first clue about how she would answer that.

CHAPTER THIRTY-FOUR

"Are you sure you're okay, Jasmine?" Her mother, Esther, leaned over and pressed her cheek to Jass's. "You don't seem like yourself." Esther was every bit herself, dressed for midnight service in a black and red dress that reminded Jass of the poinsettia gathered by the fireplace. Her curly black hair perfectly framed her face.

"Ma. Stop. I'm fine. I'm eating! You're always on my case about not eating enough, and this year, I eat and you're still worried about me? I never win!"

"Did you and Amara have a fight?"

"No, Ma. She'll be at Mass tonight. But she had other plans for dinner." Amara often joined Jass on Christmas Eve, but they were certain that if they were together for too long, one of them would reveal the pregnancy.

"You better not be tired because you've been running your route this week," Dave said, a plate balanced on his stomach, beer in hand.

Jass usually found it difficult to take time off, but this year, she was glad that she had listened to Dave and had told all her clients that she was taking the holiday weeks off because she was absolutely beat. So beat that she happily sat next to Dave on the couch staring at but not watching the football game he had muted with the subtitles on. "No, you're right. They don't need me, and I need the break."

One of her aunties heard this and turned a doubtful expression toward her mother. "Jass needs a break? She must not be feeling okay."

Jass slouched under the scrutiny. Christmas Eve, Nochebuena to her mother's family, wasn't something she could miss. She had hoped that the dip in her energy would be masked by the sheer volume of family and friends that her mother liked to gather around her, but these days her mother missed nothing. When she was married to Jass's dad, they were too busy fighting to notice her. After the divorce, her mother focused solely on dating. It was only after she settled in with Dave that she decided she needed to parent Jass. These days, that consisted of her pointing out how many cousins were getting married and pressuring her to settle down. She tried to take control of the conversation by roping Dave in. When he took a vacation, he always had a home improvement project queued up. "What's this year's project?"

"Found a bunch of stuff on the roof I've gotta do. I got up there to tar around the skylights and…"

Jass's strategy worked. Her mother and aunt drifted back to the kitchen, and she was able to half-listen to Dave as he described the domino effect set off by one small job. "Always something to keep me busy." He finished his beer and scooted forward on the couch. Instead of standing, he narrowed his eyes. "You got anything to tell your ma and me?"

"No!" Jass snapped to attention. "Why would you say that?"

"You seem wiped out is all, like after you took that ridiculous job stripping the fiberglass out of that vinyl pool."

"Nope. I'm never saying yes to a job like that again."

"Good. I coulda told you that was a crap job better to skip."

"I know."

"You're really okay? You'd tell me if you weren't, if you were in trouble?"

Dave watched Jass, and she felt her news deep in her belly. He had given her the perfect window to tell him she was pregnant, and she knew if she did, he was not the kind to stand and make a formal announcement. In a house full of people, he could keep it to himself, but for now, it didn't feel real enough to share. She still couldn't quite believe it was possible to hear a heartbeat at five weeks. The first ultrasound had offered comfort that Jass's pregnancy was viable. Still, Jass hadn't figured out what she would tell her parents. "Yeah. I'd tell you."

"Good." His gaze returned to the TV, but he still looked like he was thinking. He stood. "You want a beer?"

"Naw. I'm good."

"You sure you're not pregnant?"

"What?" His words surprised Jass. "Why would you say that?"

"Something's different, and pregnant women don't drink. I hope you know you could talk to your mom and me if something's going on. I always thought having a lesbian for a kid meant I'd never have to worry about 'em turning up pregnant, but...assumptions. Ass out of you and me. I thought I should ask."

"You're the best, Dave."

He raised his empty beer can. "I know. Back atcha, kid."

She was glad that after she thanked him, he left her to go get another beer. She escaped to her childhood room that was now decorated as a generic guest room. She had to call Amara.

"I was just going to text you!" Amara said. "I was reading about the sixth week on that website Sarah sent you, and it says the baby is making hands and feet. Hands and feet! You're making hands and feet."

"No wonder I'm so tired," Jass said, lying down across the comforter. "Dave asked me if I'm pregnant."

Amara gasped. "He did not!"

"He did. I said no when he offered to get me a beer."

"How did you explain that, lady?"

"I don't know. I threw a lame question back at him. He was so serious, saying I can talk to him if there's something wrong. But nothing's wrong..."

"...so you're not lying to him." Amara picked up on Jass's train of thought.

"I think you should be here when I tell them."

"You know I'll be there. I'll even explain how I got you pregnant."

"Oh, no," Jass said firmly. "We're skipping the details."

"Fine. Fine. So, no talking about hands and feet at the church, and no looking at your belly."

"We can do this," Jass said.

"We *are* doing this!" Amara said. "Hands and feet. Thank your woman for the website. When are you seeing her again?"

"I'm not sure. She has Chloe again this weekend. But honestly, I don't know if I'm up for more than making your baby these days. Sarah wasn't lying about this being the time of eating and sleeping. I had a big dinner here, and now all I want to do is crash."

"You rest. I'll see you at Mass." Amara ended the call with a kiss.

Jass lay her phone against her chest and closed her eyes, hoping nobody would miss her. She rested her hand on her stomach, picturing hands and feet. They probably looked like fish fins. She pulled up Sarah's last texts. She'd thanked Jass for letting her know that she hadn't had any more spotting. Then she had texted the link Jass had shared with Amara where she could plug in the date of conception and read about what was happening with the baby each week. The website had already greatly allayed Jass's fears when she read that light bleeding was normal in their rundown of the sixth week, and now it was fueling Amara's excitement.

Hearing the rapid whoosh whoosh whoosh of the life inside her and then seeing the gestational sack had made everything significantly more real for Jass. She'd asked Sarah what it had been like for her and Tricia, and they had gone back and forth more like classmates sharing notes than the hormone-driven teenagers they turned into when together.

In a blink, her hormone-driven self had been replaced with an always nauseous one. Why did they call it morning sickness when it lasted all day? Jass was especially uncomfortable at night, crawling out of bed to eat saltines at all hours. Strangely, she slept better during the day and fought the drowsiness pulling at her now.

Thank goodness she had another whole week where she could crash on her couch whenever she wanted. She had no clue how she would manage her schedule when she felt so utterly depleted doing absolutely nothing.

"Jasmine!" someone called from another part of the house. She would get up. In just one minute, she would swing her feet over the bed and get to her feet. Her eyes felt like they were glued shut. Her breathing slowed and she drifted to sleep, vaguely aware of someone entering the room and covering her with a throw. She would have to explain how tired she was, but even that wasn't enough for her to offer a protest to the blanket and return to the party.

CHAPTER THIRTY-FIVE

Sarah was dithering. She hated that she dithered. She wanted to be decisive and have what she wanted without guilt. She wanted to go to the movies. It was the new year, and there were interesting movies she could see since Tricia had Chloe. She would rather go to the movies with someone, and she would like that person to be Jass.

She enjoyed Jass's company. She sat with that for a moment. Wanting to spend time with Jass was different from hooking up. Friends hung out, and before she would not have called Jass her friend. Jass's pregnancy had changed that. She was curious about how Jass was doing and felt comfortable texting to check in. Asking her to a movie felt different. Wanting to invite Jass made her defensive. She probed beneath her feeling and was unsurprised to hear Tricia's voice asking how Sarah's seeing Jass was any different than her dating Lydia.

Jass had said she was in no place to date either, Sarah reminded herself. She was emotionally invested elsewhere, not poking at Sarah for more time or commitment. That was the difference. So asking her to go to a movie was not leading Jass to believe she could offer more than she was prepared to. Besides, maybe she didn't even like going to the movies, or maybe she wasn't even interested in seeing what was playing.

Having found a sliver of clarity, she texted Jass. *Would it be weird if I invited you to the movies?*

As in would it make me feel weird or would it be bad for you to be seen at the movies with me?

If it would be weird for you. Or if it feels like I'm sending mixed messages.

Amara and I were tossing around ideas of what to do. Can I invite her?

Sarah had not seen Amara since she had helped Jass with the pool. She knew a lot more about Amara now. Did she know that Sarah knew? Sarah couldn't imagine Jass not letting her friend know. It would be interesting to see her now that the picture of who she was to Jass was clearer. *That sounds fun. Had the two of you picked a movie yet?*

Stuck between two.

Her text was quickly followed by blurbs about two rom-coms, neither of which had been at the top of Sarah's list. Nevertheless, she was curious to hear about why they appealed to Jass and Amara. *I lean toward the love triangle.*

Me too! Jass texted. *Do you mind doing the matinee? I can't stay up late anymore.*

Sarah agreed to the matinee and offered to drive. Jass accepted and told her they would meet Amara at the theater as Amara was coming from the Rose Parade in the opposite direction.

"Wow. I really ended up liking that. It was not what I expected at all!" Amara said as the three exited the theater.

"Since when does a woman stay married and keep her lover on the side with her spouse's approval? I don't think anyone expects that!" Jass said.

They stood on the patio outside the theater. Amara had dressed in layers for the early-morning wait for the parade and was more prepared for the cool evening than Jass and Sarah.

Bouncing on her toes, Jass grimaced in Sarah's direction and said, "Did the ending bother you?"

"I can't say I understand it or find it believable." Sarah buttoned her long black coat. Jass, instead of zipping her thin green denim jacket, moved closer to Amara who threw her arm around Jass.

Sarah envisioned the mixture of their genes. Would the baby favor Jass's rounder face or Amara's more angular features? Or would they be able to identify whose eyes the baby got, whose nose... She, of course, saw much of herself in Chloe, but there were features that clearly came from the donor. Being able to share those observations with each other was going to deepen the bond between the two who were clearly already fused to each other. She felt no jealousy that Jass had leaned into Amara. They reminded her of Chloe's hugging-pandas stuffed toy.

"Hungry?" Amara asked. She immediately bumped Jass's hip with her own and said, "Stupid question. You're always hungry now. Does anything on the plaza appeal to you?"

"I love the Italian place. Sarah?"

Three, according to the children's song she had loved to sing to Chloe, was a magic number. First there are two parents and then baby makes three. But three felt more like a third wheel than a magic number tonight.

Amara surprised Sarah by linking their arms at the elbow and walking toward the restaurant. "We need to talk about that movie. I won't make you eat, but I won't let you go without talking about why the ending isn't believable, and if we don't eat soon, Jass will pass out. So you're coming with us."

"You sound like you're kidnapping her," Jass said, falling in line with them.

Amara dropped her arm, chagrined. "You are free to make your own choices. I hope you will join us."

"In for a penny, in for a pound right?" Sarah said.

She said the phrase in response to the dinner invitation, but as they settled into their seats, she wondered whether joining the pair of friends for the movies was redefining her intentions when it came to Jass. At the table, they assessed each other wordlessly, and when Amara and Jass settled in the chairs across from her, Sarah felt a pinch of sadness setting her bag on the empty chair next to her.

With little talk, they focused on perusing the menu and ordering. The moment the waiter retreated to the kitchen, Amara leaned forward low, her body resting on her arms folded on the table, and looked from Sarah to Jass. "I have to know whether you would have stayed."

"That depends. Do you mean as the wife staying in her marriage or the girlfriend staying as mistress?" Sarah asked.

Amara shrugged. "The girlfriend. It's historical, so I get why she chose to stay with her husband. Could you..."

"Whoa, whoa, whoa," Sarah said. "It was the eighties. That's not historical!"

"For me, anything before gay marriage being legal is historical," Amara said.

"But the eighties was post-sexual revolution. It was the era of women's festivals. There was a community for them. She could have left her husband," Sarah argued.

Jass jumped in. "So you wouldn't be a mistress. You would have left your lover in her sexless marriage and gone off to find true love at a women's festival?"

"Or I would have left my husband and run off to a music festival *with* my lover. There isn't room in a relationship for three. Someone is going to get jealous," Sarah answered.

"But she loved her husband. She didn't want to leave him, and her mistress got her no-strings-attached sex," Amara said. "She said herself that she didn't believe in marriage."

"There's no such thing as no-strings-attached sex," Sarah said.

Amara looked pointedly from her to Jass. "No?" She sat back, her gaze settling on Sarah. "Are you saying there are strings?"

Sarah opened her mouth and then shut it, not sure what to say. She looked to Jass who waited for her answer with an unreadable expression. Having reached out to her for something other than sex had shifted things. Was it Jass's being pregnant that had shifted things? But strings? She did not feel a desire to commit to Jass. Did she? She pushed the thought aside. "I'm talking about the long term. Something sustained, like the end of this movie implies. What if the couple decides to have children? What are they supposed to tell the child about the lover her mother has on the side?"

"Here is another adult who loves you and is invested in you growing up to be a wonderful person," Amara said.

The waiter returned with their food, giving Sarah room to think. With a few simple sentences, Amara had given her a lot to process. Jass devoured her manicotti and was happy to steal bites of chicken parmesan from Amara as well as bites of Sarah's lasagna. Though they commented on the quality of the food, Sarah continued to discuss the movie. "I'm having trouble processing the ending because for me a relationship is between two people. Someone told me once that it's the person in the relationship who wants the least who gets what they want. The only way it works is if the other person is satisfied with what is offered. Speaking for my own relationship, I was not fulfilled with what Tricia could offer, but I would never have sought out someone on the side to satisfy what Tricia could not. I can't imagine her going for that, either."

"I think it was a brave ending," Jass said. She sipped her water as if she were considering saying more. "You have a more traditional sense of marriage and family. I'm guessing for you that marriage and family included one if not more kids. Some couples don't want kids. Some singles do." Here she reached out and squeezed Amara's hand.

"To be clear here, I would have loved to share this parenting experience and would happily be set up with any bi or pansexual friends you have." Amara placed her hand in the middle of the table as she delivered her truth.

Sarah surprised herself by reaching out to cover Amara's hand with her own. "Please don't think that I am sitting here judging you. It was difficult for me to wrap my brain around everything when Jass told me what she is doing, but I am getting there. You two and my friend Casey have shown me how very much I have to learn about what makes a family."

She caught Jass's gaze moving from her hand on Amara's to her and then to Amara. The two friends shared a long enough look that Sarah wondered what they were communicating. Were they rolling their eyes at Sarah? Should she not have said anything about the pregnancy? Less talking, she told herself. More listening. "Tell me what family is for you." She leaned forward.

CHAPTER THIRTY-SIX

Jass settled into the passenger seat of Sarah's mom-car, a sensible Ford Escape that invited her to fall asleep on the spot. She tipped her head in Sarah's direction. "Thanks for driving. And for coming out with us."

"I am so glad I did," Sarah said.

"You're sure?" Jass asked. "The conversation went a direction I didn't anticipate at all."

"I am absolutely sure. I was the one who tipped the vote in favor of the love triangle movie, so the conversation didn't surprise me in the least."

Jass moved her gaze to the road ahead. Sarah may have been prepared for the discussion, but she had said some things that surprised Jass, namely her position that sex always included a level of attachment. She wasn't ready to ask Sarah what she imagined would happen with them. She had said that no strings attached didn't work in the long term. Did that mean she had an expiration in mind for her and Jass? After Amara's baby was born, Jass would not be satisfied with casual hookups. The more time she spent with Sarah, the more she was sure she wanted a life partner. She could do with a partner now, she mused, someone to feed and take care of her. "What did you do for New Year's Eve?" she asked to keep the conversation light.

"Don't judge me," Sarah said, turning ever so briefly to Jass to offer a smile.

"Never," Jass said.

"After Tricia picked up Chloe, I put on my pajamas, ate popcorn for dinner and went to bed at eight."

"That sounds like an awesome night."

"You don't think it's sad that I didn't even make the east-coast new year?"

"I didn't either," Jass said.

"You, at least, have a great excuse. How are you feeling? Are you tired of me asking?"

"I'm not tired of it at all. It's so nice to be able to talk to someone about it. My stepdad guessed I'm pregnant at Christmas, and if it had just been him and my mom, I might've told them then, but I wasn't ready to tell the whole extended family."

"Huh." Sarah quirked her head to the side. "For some reason, I thought you and Amara were estranged from your families."

"Oh, no. I see my mom and Dave at least once a month. Amara sees hers less, but they expect her to at least check in with a call. We've been talking about filling them in on our project. Amara said she'd go with me when I tell my folks. I'm not sure how they're going to take hearing that I'm having a baby, and that it won't necessarily make them grandparents."

"You're not sure?"

"Legally, I've done my best to protect Amara's parental rights, but it's not like I'm going to hand over the baby and disappear. I'll be helping Amara out, and if her parents are too upset, maybe mine will do grandparent kind of stuff. A few weeks ago, Chloe did another thing that reminded me so much of you. It made me realize that you were right about us not thinking everything through. That's why we want to talk to our parents together, to feel them out and see where they fit into the baby's life. Like Amara said tonight, someone doesn't have to be a blood or legal relative to be invested in a child's life."

"My concern is about consistency. Going back to the movie, if the couple has a child who grows up with the mother's lover as someone invested in her, what happens if she disappears? We're supposed to protect our children from that kind of heartbreak."

"Marriage isn't a guarantee against heartbreak. I spent the better half of my childhood wishing my dad *would* disappear. All he did was make me and my mom miserable."

"I'm sorry."

"You don't have to apologize. At least it wasn't my whole childhood and my mom found Dave. Genetically, he's not my dad, but he's more of a father than my bio dad ever was."

"I was apologizing for falling back into my perception that the best families always have two parents and at least one child. I spent a great deal of my childhood wishing I could fix my broken family, and now as a parent I'm stuck in the same place trying to figure out how to navigate single parenthood with Chloe and co-parenting with Tricia. We made promises when we got married."

"Amara and I are making a promise, too, just not ones that the government has a paper for. At the end of the day, if you model resilience and flexibility, doesn't that prepare Chloe for the inevitable heartbreaks ahead of her?" Jass regarded what her mother had modeled, codependence for ten years followed by an inability to cope without a boyfriend for three years before she finally found Dave and was able to demonstrate any semblance of stability.

"Oh, no!"

Jass snapped upright, looking for trouble. The drive had lulled her into deep relaxation, and she didn't know what she had missed. Sarah had stopped the car on the street at her driveway.

"I was so caught up in our conversation that I drove home out of habit."

"Not out of hopefulness?" Jass asked, resting her hand on Sarah's knee.

Sarah covered her hand with her own. "I didn't want to presume. I don't know how you're feeling in your body right now."

Jass glanced at Sarah's house. Did she admit how much she wanted to go home with Sarah? Though the evening was far from what most would consider a date since it had included Amara, it had given Jass a peek at what lay beyond sex. If she went inside with Sarah tonight, it would deepen her feelings for Sarah. Did she dare risk that when Sarah had not expressed a change of heart about dating? Jass searched Sarah's eyes, trying to determine what she was thinking. Did she want Jass to come in? Would she agree that extending their evening would move them to a place beyond a physical connection? In the shadows, she could not read Sarah's expression. "Can I be honest?"

"Always," Sarah said without hesitation.

Always. That one word carried so much weight. Always sounded like a long time, and yet they had not laid out any expectations of how long their arrangement might last. "There are a few things. One is that if I get into bed with you tonight, I will not be able to get out."

"Chloe doesn't come home until eleven tomorrow. You can stay the night."

Jass blinked in surprise. "You'd be okay with that?"

The way Sarah nodded made Jass bite back a laugh. It looked as though her mind had not caught up to her body, and her body was answering before her mind could create a reason she should say no. "It would be lovely to wake up next to you. We could get breakfast together before I drop you off."

Jass could not hold back a smile at how nice that sounded. "Okay, then. The other thing is that I am not prepared to stay the night. I don't have any pajamas."

"You haven't had pajamas any of the other times you've been in my bed."

"All the other times, we were getting in bed for a specific purpose. I'm not sure that's in the cards tonight. I wouldn't want for you to be disappointed if you were hoping to get lucky on the first day of the year."

Sarah reached across the console and threaded her fingers through Jass's hair. "I already got lucky when you let me invite myself along on your movie date."

"Yeah?" Jass asked.

"Yeah," Sarah said. "So you'll stay?"

"I'd like that."

Sarah parked. Looking at the empty car seat, Jass felt Chloe's absence. Tricia must have her own car seat in her vehicle. Would Jass drive Amara's child around enough to need an extra car seat? Questions like these made her understand Sarah's comment about their not fully thinking their plan through.

She followed Sarah into the house, accepting the offer of a spare toothbrush. They didn't speak as they readied themselves for bed, and Jass felt like she was in stealth mode observing Sarah in such a domestic state. When Sarah made one last trip through the house to check the doors and fetch a glass of water, Jass stripped off her clothes and slipped in between cold sheets, scissoring her feet in place to warm herself.

"I hope you don't mind that I turn off the heat at night."

"I won't once you add your body heat to the mix here."

Sarah undressed as Jass watched. She had thought that she was worn out from the day, but by the time Sarah slipped in beside her naked, her insides had coiled tightly. Jass settled easily with her head on Sarah's shoulder and her right thigh tucked between Sarah's. She was so tired, and yet, when Sarah's hand ran from Jass's shoulder down to her hip, she felt herself come alive. She sighed into Sarah's kiss and pressed herself close, moaning when Sarah's fingertips traced the edge of her breast. Sarah's hands and mouth distracted her from the questions she had about what exactly she and Sarah were doing. Even better, her attentions overrode Jass's persistent nausea.

They warmed the sheets together, and for the first time in a long time, Jass fell into a deep and restful sleep.

CHAPTER THIRTY-SEVEN

Sarah pressed herself to Jass's naked back, relishing her warmth and smooth skin. She could spend all day in bed with this woman, but not this day. She hated to wake Jass, but she did not have all day to give over to these pleasures. Tricia would be there to drop off Chloe in a matter of hours. They needed to get up, get breakfast, get back to real life. She stroked Jass's shoulder, and Jass stretched. She could sense the moment Jass registered Sarah behind her, the pause as she woke in an unfamiliar place. Jass relaxed, pushing herself back against Sarah more fully. She reached for Sarah's hand and pulled it around her middle.

"Good morning," Sarah whispered, kissing Jass's neck.

Jass turned enough that Sarah could reach her lips for a kiss. "What time is it?"

"After eight. We should really get up." Sarah ran her palm from Jass's hip to hip, imagining the cells dividing and growing within her. She recalled the mornings Tricia had run her hand over her own belly when she had been pregnant. She had meant to create so much more than a baby. She had believed they were putting down deep roots that would help them weather any storm.

Instead, despite all her efforts, they had withered. They were like a plant she didn't understand. Was it too much water? Too little? Not enough sun? Too much? And then there were the plants that belonged, like the succulents she had recently bought. She gave them so little attention, and yet they were thriving. Jass felt like that in her arms, in her bed. She belonged. Something had happened without her permission. Jass was a plant she thought she had contained in a pot that she now discovered establishing itself throughout the yard. She had said the night before that there was no such thing as no-strings-attached sex. Waking up with Jass in her bed was the perfect illustration. For so many weeks, she had believed that if she kept her real life with Chloe separate from her physical relationship with Jass, she could avoid strings.

And then she had invited Jass to spend the night. Now, holding her, all she could think about was how much she missed waking up next to someone. Sex was lovely, and so far, she had enjoyed the certainty of Jass. They had been on the same page when it came to getting the most out of her Chloe-free days. But what would it be like if she wasn't worried about getting up and getting Jass out of the house before Chloe came home? It was so easy to imagine more with Jass until she remembered Chloe. Then she froze.

"Did you fall back asleep?" Jass asked, turning to face Sarah. She propped herself on her elbow, gently tracing Sarah's jawline and collarbone. "You stopped touching me. Are you worried about getting me out of here before Chloe comes home?"

Sarah's chest tightened at Jass's words. "Sorry. It's not that I'm ashamed of this, of wanting you."

"I'm glad to hear that. And I want to hear more, but if I don't put food in my belly in the next two minutes…"

"Now I'm really sorry!" She placed her palm back on Jass's abdomen. "I got caught up thinking about this when I should have been planning on what to feed you."

"As much as I'd love to hear more about that, I am desperate for food."

"I'm on it!" Sarah rolled out of bed and grabbed a robe. "I wanted to take you to my favorite bagel place for breakfast. Do you want a piece of toast with peanut butter first?"

"That sounds so good," Jass said.

Sarah started for the kitchen but had to backtrack to kiss the sleep-rumpled version of Jass. "How are you this beautiful first thing in the morning?"

"I don't feel especially beautiful at the moment."

"Trust me, you are." Sarah lingered a moment more, her lips pressed to Jass's, before she shuffled to the kitchen, turning on the heat on her way.

She had not even finished applying the peanut butter to toast when Jass entered the kitchen, fully dressed. "It felt funny to have you wait on me," she explained, sliding onto the barstool.

"I've really thrown things off-kilter, haven't I?" Sarah asked, sliding the finished toast across the counter. "Orange juice? Water?"

"Juice," Jass said, taking an enormous bite. "Did waking up together bother you?"

"Absolutely not!" Sarah looked up to make sure Jass understood her sincerity. "I was actually caught up in how wonderful it felt waking up with you and what it would be like to spend a lazy morning in bed instead of fretting about getting up and getting you home. But then I imagine Chloe here, and I don't know how to be her mom and be involved with you simultaneously."

"Involved," Jass repeated. In her voice, Sarah could hear how vague she sounded.

"Let me get dressed, and we'll get real breakfast and talk more," Sarah said.

"Trust me," Jass said when they were well into their bagel breakfasts. "I know how hard a kid can be on dating. I was that kid, and I met a lot of guys before Dave, and I didn't like who my mom was with the majority of them."

Sarah appreciated that Jass returned to the sticky topic. As a therapist, her instinct was always to lean into hard topics, but she had to be careful to try to reserve that for her clients, so her friends and family didn't feel psychoanalyzed. "Did you wish she hadn't dated?"

"That's a hard question because if she hadn't dated, she wouldn't have met Dave, and I got lucky with him. Did your mom date a bunch and disappear as a parent to be the girlfriend?"

"My mom never disappeared. She was always my mom, but she didn't expect anyone she dated to be my dad. I didn't want another dad. I wanted my dad, but he left, and I hardly ever saw him again. He had no interest in being a part of my life, and she didn't hold him accountable. I don't know if she thought having a daughter would scare off potential partners, so she never invited anyone to form a relationship with me. She basically allowed everyone to ignore me."

"You've never gone into detail on your show about how your parents split. That sounds really painful."

"It was. It still is." Sarah's throat constricted. She took a sip of her coffee, unused to divulging that much about her past.

"I'm sorry," Jass said. "Your parents' divorce was different for you. I didn't absorb any of the stigma. I was too busy being disappointed in my mom to even think of what people might be saying about us."

Sarah sat with this. Finally, she said, "My mom was trapped in a box that said family was made up of the two people who created you. There was no framework to help her accept that her relationship with my dad wasn't meant to be forever, and there wasn't anything wrong with that. Your mom was angry with your dad, and from your description, it sounds like she was focused on herself and never internalized her failed marriage the way my mom did."

"Yeah, my mom has never cared what other people think about her. Sorry. That sounded judgmental."

"Please don't apologize for giving me a new perspective, especially stuff I could turn into a podcast."

"So I might be hearing you processing this all in a few weeks?"

"If you're okay with that." She did not want Jass to feel like she was using her. For sex or podcast material.

"No! Of course! I loved recognizing myself and hearing you process the conversation. Amara is enjoying them, too. Don't tell her I told you, but she used to skip your episodes on family. She's been critical when you seem to perpetuate normative society. She tried to explain how you've bought into homonormative expectations, but I didn't really absorb it."

"Homonormative? Not heteronormative?"

Jass held up her hands. "It has something to do with how gay marriage upholds the structure we need to dismantle. Beyond that, you'd have to ask her."

"I would love to talk to her about that. And marriage. When she said I could set her up with a bi or pansexual friend, she didn't say that she was interested in marriage. Does she not support marriage?"

Jass pursed her lips. "She's not against people committing to each other, but she is critical of how the whole structure creates an expectation that fulfillment for a woman comes from being married and having children. That's what led her mother into marriage. By society's standards, she did everything right. She found her husband and had children. Her parents have more than their fair share of problems, but her mom either won't or can't leave, and unlike my dad, hers never left. What's her mom supposed to do? If she leaves, she's a bad mom and a bad wife. There's no other story. She's trapped in a bad marriage, and it ripples out."

"I can see that," Sarah said, considering how she had once regarded marriage as a milestone of personal success. She was still struggling with loss—her marriage *and* her self-esteem.

"Do you think you'll get married again? Or your ex?"

Sarah laughed. "Talk about a hard question. I want to do what's best for Chloe. I thought that Tricia was getting pretty serious with her girlfriend because she introduced her to Chloe, but then she didn't bring the girlfriend Christmas morning, so I really don't know where they stand." They sat in silence, the obvious question hanging between them. Sarah looked at her watch.

"Speaking of Chloe," Jass said, pushing back from the table.

"Wait," Sarah said. Jass stilled and held Sarah's gaze. "Where do *we* stand?" she asked quickly, before she lost confidence. "We've said that this isn't a good time for either one of us to date. What happens after you have the baby? Do you and Amara have plans to co-parent? Does creating a family with her mean you are happy to just have casual relationships, or are you looking for something more permanent? A committed relationship? Marriage? Maybe kids of your own?"

Jass held her gaze. "I'm ready for commitment. A spouse. Maybe a kid. I want the whole package."

She stood then, clearing her place. Sarah followed, wishing they had more time to talk. Was Sarah a convenient stopgap while Jass waited to have Amara's baby? Or could they be something more? Sarah had meant what she'd said about the next part of her life being dedicated to what was best for Chloe. But again, she found herself questioning her stance on single parents and dating. What would it look like to parent with someone like Jass?

She glanced at her watch. Ten thirty. She'd be pushing it to get home to meet Tricia. Now was definitely not the time to have this conversation.

CHAPTER THIRTY-EIGHT

"Are we excited to see this baby?" The ultrasound tech bustled into the room, smiling at Jass and Amara.

Jass's stomach fluttered so wildly, she wondered again whether the baby was moving. She'd read online that week thirteen was the earliest women could feel fetal movement, but that was typically for a second pregnancy. Google predicted that she wouldn't feel the baby move until week twenty-five. "I'm excited!" She reached for Amara's hand.

"So excited," Amara echoed.

"Are you hoping for a boy or a girl?"

On this, Jass deferred to Amara. In Jass's eyes, it was Amara's pregnancy. Amara squeezed her hand. "All I care about is having a healthy baby."

"A surprise, then! I'm seeing more and more of that these days. Personally, I think it's lovely to focus on the life instead of the sex."

"I couldn't agree with you more," Amara said.

"For today's ultrasound, I'm taking measurements to make sure that the baby is meeting projected growth milestones. We'll confirm the due date, check the placenta, lots of fun stuff, but for most parents, this appointment is all about the images, seeing your baby for the first time."

The constant need to correct people exhausted Jass. Each new nurse or tech understandably assumed that Jass was carrying her own baby, and if Amara was with her, that they were a lesbian couple. She appreciated the friendliness that they typically encountered, but it didn't make explaining how she and Amara were different any easier. Before she could decide whether to clarify her position with the tech, Amara spoke.

"Do you feel like we're checking up on your work?"

"Hey, I'm doing the best I can with the materials you gave me. Trust me," Jass riffed back. "And you'd better be happy. I'm working really hard on this."

The tech was quiet as she applied the warm gel to Jass's belly and began pushing it back and forth. Both Jass and Amara knew that the tech was trying to read their banter. Jass decided that staying quiet kept the focus on the life growing inside her.

These appointments were a strange in-between place for Jass. She had to be present for the nurses and doctors to check on the baby, but she one hundred percent felt like she was there to support Amara. She watched Amara, not the screen, reading her wonder as she listened to the tech identify what she was seeing. She could hear the baby's heartbeat through the monitor, but this more rhythmic beat was not the thing that made her insides swell. It was the look on Amara's face, how the sound and images made the baby real for *her*.

"Here's an arm. And fingers."

Jass glanced at the screen, finding it a distant second to watching Amara's face. "You see fingers?"

Amara shook her head. "So far, I don't recognize…Wait! Was that a foot?" Her face radiated joy.

"It is," the tech confirmed.

Jass looked at the frozen image on the screen. "Is that a big toe?"

Amara squeezed her hand before releasing it to swipe her phone to life. When she aimed it at the screen, the tech assured her that she would print out the clearest images for them.

Hours later, they had used those images to tell both of their parents that Jass had begun her second trimester. Amara drove Jass home and gave her a long hug. "I'd offer to buy you a drink after all that, but…"

"I'm knocked up," Jass provided.

Amara pushed away from Jass and held her by the shoulders, adopting the shocked expression her father had worn when they first stopped by Amara's parents' house to drop the bombshell. "But how!"

They dissolved into laughter because it was no use wasting any more tears on Amara's father's ignorance. "My parents asked the same thing. Why is it so different?"

"Because they listen. They asked because they're actually interested and they care about you. Mine asked because I'm no longer his son and only his biological daughters have a chance at having a normal life, and my mom is too cowed to stand up to him."

"But she looked happy."

Amara nodded. "Now for the sisters."

"Ask them if Dave's right about how much more work they are when they're 'toothless and helpless.'"

Amara's face turned serious, and she asked how Jass had felt about her mom's reaction.

Jass's mom's fixation on the toll pregnancy would have on her body didn't surprise her. Her mother was obsessed with her being partnered, and if the baby didn't mean that she and Amara were finally a couple, her mother was convinced that post-pregnancy dating was going to be even more difficult. "Reminding her that I date women and women who date women don't tend to be so caught up in fitting a nonsensical ideal did the trick, though!"

Amara rolled her eyes and pursed her lips in sympathy. "Speaking of women who date women…"

"Do not ask me about Sarah Cooper."

"You haven't talked to her about what the whole package entails for you, have you?"

"We talk."

"About the long term?"

Jass shoved her hands in her pockets. "Hypothetically."

"We went to the movies, what? A month ago? That's a long time to let an elephant like that sit in the room."

"She hasn't said anything," Jass said, hearing how childish she sounded. "It's not like we've had any time together. You know how much working has sapped me dry."

"That's bullshit."

Jass pressed her hands to her sides as if she was covering the baby's ears. "You're going to have to work on your language before this one is born."

Amara rolled her eyes. "Don't deflect. I'm trying to make a point here. After the movie, she said there's no such thing as no-strings-attached sex. She's still having sex with you. Clearly there are strings by now."

"That's what I thought. I keep expecting us to talk about whether there could be an us after this." She motioned to her belly. "Not when I'm there doing the pool, obviously, but you know, I've stayed over a couple more times now when Chloe's with Tricia, and she hasn't brought it up."

"So you bring it up."

"She's still a single parent. I only see her when she doesn't have Chloe. It's not worth bringing up because she doesn't want to change the dynamic with Chloe."

"*You're* pregnant and wiped out. What if she's sitting there wanting to talk about it but assuming that you don't want to broach the subject again until you're done cooking my baby. You want more with her, don't you?"

Jass thought about how magical it felt to wake up in Sarah's arms. She wanted so many more mornings like that, and she could easily imagine waking up to Chloe bouncing around. "I can see it," Jass admitted. "I don't think she can, though."

"And that, my friend, is why you should be calling her."

"But she doesn't want strings. What we're doing is short term, and if I say I could do more, she'll probably end things."

"Call her. We're in the second trimester, baby! This is when you're going to get your big energy boost and start glowing."

"I am not going to glow."

Amara hugged her and walked to her car. "I'm pretty sure you already are, but you should call Sarah and ask her."

"You're relentless."

"I'm romantic, and I want you two to work out."

Jass climbed the stairs to her apartment. Did she have more pep in her step? For the last month, the stairs had been a cruel obstacle at the end of her day, but that was when she was in her first trimester. Now she was officially in her second trimester, and she was going strong even after the doctor's appointment and parental check-ins.

She was checking her fridge for food when her phone chimed. Dave's name flashed on the screen, and she laughed out loud at his text asking if she was eating enough protein. She keyed back that she was an adult and could be trusted to eat well even though her fridge had little to offer. Dave could read her so well. She had to admit that she wished that the weekend was one she could spend with Sarah. Dinner was the most difficult meal for her pull off. She hated cooking for herself.

Did Sarah ever think about what it would be like to have Jass over when she had Chloe? So far, Sarah's concrete boundaries kept Jass at a distance. Could Amara be right in suggesting that Sarah might feel like the boundaries were for Jass? Unfortunately, there was only one way to find out. She slathered peanut butter on a piece of celery and imagined what Sarah's Friday evening might look like.

Jass drafted a message and scrolled through the pictures she had taken after the ultrasound. She selected the one of the baby's foot and wrote *Look what I'm making!* And then *Chat later?*

She stood with the fridge door open, willing something more substantial to appear. When it was just her, she didn't bother with whether what she was hitting all the appropriate food groups. Now, especially with Dave's message, she spent more time considering vegetables and protein. She eyed her peanut butter and celery, knowing it wasn't what any medical professional would consider a meal.

CHAPTER THIRTY-NINE

Jass's text stopped Sarah in her tracks. The broccoli was ready, and Chloe didn't like it mushy. Usually, she was better about ignoring her phone during the dinner hour, but Chloe hadn't been able to find Greenie, the stuffed salamander. Chloe could not remember if she had brought it home from Tricia's last weekend. They had texted Tricia to ask her to look for it and had been waiting for her reply. Instead, she opened her phone to an ultrasound image. Jass had told her about the appointment, and it touched her that she was sending an update. She enlarged the image, tracing the delicate toe with her thumb.

"Did she find him?" Chloe snatched the phone from Sarah.

"Chloe!" Sarah reprimanded.

But it was too late. Chloe was already studying the image. "What's this?"

Sarah took a deep breath. "It's a baby's foot. See the big toe here?" She traced it again.

"Why is it all black?"

"It's a picture of the baby inside the mommy. It's called an ultrasound. Doctors use the pictures to see if the baby is healthy."

"Is Mama growing a baby?" The hurt and confusion on Chloe's face brought all Sarah's fears to the surface.

"No, no. Mama hasn't texted yet. This baby…" This was not her news to share. How would she explain the dozens of questions that would surely follow if she identified Jass as the one carrying the baby? "Let's talk about that later and get the broccoli out. It's time for dinner."

She set down her phone and turned her attention back to dinner, plating the chicken and putting butter and honey on slices of hot cornbread. Impressed that everything was hot at the same time, she decided to reward herself with a glass of wine. Was that true? Or had the ultrasound stirred up feelings she was trying to suppress? It was so easy to fall back on that familiar crutch. Firming her resolve, she poured some sparkling water for herself and a cup of milk for Chloe.

"Wash hands for dinner, Chloe!" Where had she gone? Sarah walked to the hallway to Chloe's room and found her daughter sitting in her bed. Sarah thought she was talking to her stuffed animals until she noticed the phone in her hand. "Chloe?"

Chloe's eyes widened.

"Who are you talking to?"

"My mom wants to talk to you." Chloe held the phone out and scuttled to the bathroom to wash her hands.

Sarah put the phone to hear ear and followed. "Hello?"

"Am I really invited to dinner?"

"Jass? What in the world?"

"Chloe called me. I take it she knows about the baby. Hope it's okay that I mapped it out for her."

"Mapped it out?" The words came out in a squeak that brought her daughter's gaze to her. She held a hand towel out to Chloe and told her to run to her place at the table. "I'm so sorry, Jass."

"She's going to know when I start showing anyway," Jass said matter-of-factly.

"True." Sarah walked to the dining room. She had thought she'd have a private talk with Jass, but it sounded like there was no need for it. "And she's invited you to dinner?"

"According to her, babies need more than celery and peanut butter."

"She's right about that." To Chloe she whispered, "She's eating celery and peanut butter?"

"For dinner!" Chloe exclaimed, wide-eyed.

"You'd better come over here. I'll put a plate together for you," Sarah said. "See you soon." Sarah ended the call and set the phone back on the counter. "Chloe Adele," she said.

Chloe's gaze dropped to her food. "I wanted to know about the baby. It's not Jass's baby. She's cooking a baby for her sister because she doesn't have an oven."

Interesting that Jass had called Amara her sister. She was curious about what Jass had said about her role in the child's life. Sarah filled a plate and a glass with water for Jass before joining Chloe at the table. "What do you think about that?"

"I think she's so nice she could cook a baby for Mama, too because Mama doesn't want to cook a baby in her oven."

This was news to Sarah. Was she talking to Chloe about her pregnancy, or were Tricia and Lydia talking about babies? "When did you and Mama talk about babies?"

"Before," Chloe helpfully supplied.

"Eat your broccoli before it gets cold," Sarah said. Suddenly her stomach swirled nervously as she anticipated Jass joining them. She had eaten with them before, of course, but that had been before they'd slept together. She knew that she and Jass needed to return to the conversation they had started back in January, but she'd been avoiding it, afraid to ask if Jass's definition of the whole package might include Chloe. But that question implied she could see herself partnered again. Could she take a risk like that when it wasn't just her heart on the line? She'd been so careful to keep Sarah-the-mom separate from the Sarah she was with Jass. Would Chloe be able to sense the shift that had occurred between them if she was in the same room with Jass?

There was a knock at the door. She took a deep breath, about to find out.

"We're already at the table," Sarah said. They stood awkwardly for a moment before Sarah leaned forward for a quick hug. "Thank you for sending the picture. It's so exciting!"

Jass covered her belly with her hand. "The pictures make it so much more real." She walked to the dining room without waiting for Sarah. "Hey, Chloe! Thanks for inviting me to dinner!"

"Can I see more pictures of the baby now?"

"No phones at the table, remember?" Sarah returned to her place at the table and motioned to Jass's plate. "She can show you after dinner."

"Happy Friday! Are you doing anything fun this weekend?"

"Maybe we'll go back to the library tomorrow," Sarah answered. "We have some books to return."

"Is the pretty lady going to read again?" Chloe asked.

"Not tomorrow. She only comes once a month."

"Do you like to read stories?" Chloe asked Jass. "I like the stories the pretty lady reads. She does funny voices!" Chloe balanced a bite of cornbread on her fork, holding it there until it reached her mouth.

"This is the best chicken I've ever had in my whole mouth," Jass said, rolling her eyes back.

"That sounds funny," Chloe said.

"Well, it's true! It's what my family says when something is really, really good."

Sarah swallowed hard as a wave of emotion crashed over her, touched by the way Jass brought her own family to her table. "I'm glad that you like it!"

Jass's eyes stayed on her for several beats. "I know I need to get better at feeding myself, but it's so much easier to be fed." She turned to Chloe and said, "Being a grown-up is hard, and being a mom is even harder. Your mom's rocking it!"

"Mommy makes the best dinners, but Mama makes the best cookies."

"Mama's definitely the baker..." Sarah swallowed the *in the family* that always followed the comparison of her strengths to Tricia's.

"I sure can't compete for best chef or baker, but I'd be happy to read a story with you tonight." Jass turned to Sarah, her eyes questioning whether that was okay.

"I'm finished with my dinner. Can I get them now?" Chloe asked.

"Two more bites of chicken. Then you can grab them and take them to the living room and wait for Jass."

Chloe ate her two bites and carried her plate to the counter next to the sink before disappearing down the hall.

"You don't have to read if you're too tired," Sarah said, sipping her water.

"I'd like to. It's sweet that she asked. I couldn't believe it when it was her on the other end of the line!"

Sarah chuckled. "I had no idea she'd swiped my phone. She's a sneaky little thing!"

"Is it okay I told her about the baby and about Amara?"

"Of course it's okay. Like you said, eventually, it's not going to be a secret. We've always been open with her about her own birth story, and it's very different from her peers. It's good for her to hear about other kinds of families. I love the Drag Queen Story Hour at the library. They read different kinds of books and she gets to meet other kids with two moms or two dads."

"I'd like to check it out with you sometime. The days are getting longer, so I could work in the afternoon instead of the morning. I mean, if that's okay with you. We haven't talked about doing things together with Chloe."

Sarah was touched that Jass deferred to her position on whether they would spend time together with her daughter. It meant, though, that she needed to figure out how she felt about it. "It's really scary for me. Having you over for dinner scared me. It's so easy to be with you, and when I see how you are with Chloe, it's tempting to make plans. But one dinner, an outing here and there, that's not parenting, and to be with me means being a parent, and I don't know if that's something you think about."

Jass looked like she was going to respond, but Sarah held up her hand to stop her. She needed to finish her thought. "And even if you'd be on board with that, I don't know if that's where I am. I trusted that Tricia was ready for the commitment of a child and found out that she isn't up for the everyday grind of parenting. She barely makes it through every other weekend. The only way to find out if someone is in it to the extent that I am is to have them here twenty-four seven, and that…Well, it scares the hell out of me because what if I break Chloe's heart again?"

"That's a lot," Jass said. She looked at Sarah's hand but didn't take it.

"I know. I've been thinking about it for a month now, but I didn't risk admitting any of it out loud because I don't want to lose the weekends I have with you."

"Come read, Jass!" Chloe called from the living room.

"I have two more bites," Jass shouted back. More quietly she said, "Not a lot of time to respond to you."

"Welcome to my life, my real life," Sarah said. She felt defeated.

"You said I could see pictures of the baby when I finished my dinner!" Chloe whined.

"Be patient," Sarah called.

Jass finished her dinner and followed Chloe's example, taking her plate to the sink. She looked toward the living room as if she was torn between Chloe's demands and wanting to say more. "She'll learn about relationships from you, too, don't you think? Whether they work or don't work. She'll learn about taking turns and having to be patient. And she might learn about heartbreak as well. But if that were to happen, you could teach her about the healing properties of chocolate." She shrugged and gave Sarah's hand a quick squeeze. "I'd better get over there to read. I don't want her to think I'm ignoring her."

Sarah's heart swelled and ached at the same time. What she said, every part of it, was so true. And yet, Sarah couldn't let go of the fact that for now, things were easy. Even weighing whether Jass could integrate with Chloe and Tricia felt tenuous, but it wasn't just Jass and Sarah's complicated life with an ex. Even if Jass wasn't a co-parent to Amara's child, they were still part of Jass's package, and Sarah could not see how all those components fit into one picture.

CHAPTER FORTY

Amara fidgeted nervously as they approached the library. "Are you sure it's okay that I'm here too?"

"Sure, I'm sure. They want to attract people." Jass's stomach flip-flopped anticipating seeing Chloe and Sarah at the Drag Queen Story Hour. She felt so comfortable with Sarah now that she worried about doing something that would reveal their relationship to Chloe. "You're nice to come with me," Jass said.

"Are you kidding me?" Amara said, nudging Jass with her hip. "I'm going to get reading tips from a drag queen *and* get to spy on you and your Sarah Cooper. I would not have missed this for anything."

"She isn't *my* Sarah Cooper," Jass whispered. "Can I trust you to keep that locked in the vault of your brain?"

Amara rolled her eyes. "Can you trust me? I'm trusting you to cook my baby, and you're seriously trying to talk to me about trust?"

"Not a word, Amara. Chloe is sharp and sneaky."

"And will be fixated on you and my baby. Don't worry so much. Isn't this about listening to a story more than talking, anyway?"

Jass exhaled her anxiety and inhaled calm. It was a good thing she had centered herself because the moment they moved into view of the children's room, Chloe rocketed to them and wrapped her arms around Jass's legs.

"Jass!" she said at a very un-library-like volume.

Jass took in her purple leggings, her hoodie covered in rainbow unicorn heads and butterfly wings flopping behind her. Sarah was equally decked out in a sky-blue jumpsuit and a jacket made of hundreds of small multicolored patches that looked like a stained-glass window. "We are so underdressed!" Jass whispered to Amara.

"Is she your sister?" Chloe asked, clinging to Jass.

"This is the baby's mom, Amara," Jass said. "And this is my favorite short person, Chloe."

"Thank you for inviting us to story time," Amara said.

Sarah smiled in greeting and hugged both Jass and then Amara. "I'm so glad the two of you could make it!"

"Come sit with me, Jass! Mommy says the floor hurts her back. Can you sit on the floor?"

Jass made a worried face. "We can give it a whirl. I might be able to sit down, but I am not so sure about the getting up part."

"We'll get you a lily pad!" Chloe skipped across the room and grabbed a green padded circle she placed next to the one she had been using. Jass let out an oomph as she settled on the tiny cushion. Sarah and Amara were talking on the other side of the room. Jass wished she could hear what they were saying as it definitely had to do with the baby. Within minutes, the star appeared and sashayed through the few seated children and the handful of adults.

"Bumblebee!" Chloe clapped her hands together in delight.

"Hello, hello, my lovelies! I am so happy to see some familiar faces and some new ones, too!"

Bumblebee wore a fabulous wig, black streaked with yellow, mounded up in a beehive with some long strands left to frame her face. She wore a form-fitting blue sequined dress with the highest heels Jass had ever seen. She perched delicately at the edge of chair and introduced the first story she would read, *The Rainbow Fish*. She leaned forward as if sharing a secret and asked who in the audience had heard the story before. All the small hands in the room went up.

"Well, my lovelies. Today you get a different ending where the Rainbow Fish gets…" Bumblebee covered her mouth dramatically. "Maybe I should just read the story."

The children cheered.

Chloe smiled, wide-eyed, at Jass, and she reached out to grasp her hand. As the story progressed, Chloe scooted closer and closer until she had climbed all the way into Jass's lap. The way Chloe settled in melted Jass's insides. She rested her chin on Chloe's head and inhaled slowly and deeply. She closed her eyes and listened as the Rainbow Fish learned how to recognize and acknowledge what was special about the other sea creatures.

Something stirred inside her. Week seventeen. Could it be the baby? She wrapped her arms around the child in her lap, stricken by the enormity of what she and Amara were doing. The story ended, and Chloe squirmed in her lap to smile up at her. "You liked it?"

"Loved it!" Jass said. "You could tell?"

"I thought you were going to squeeze out my stuffing."

"Oh! I didn't mean to. I'm sorry!" It was that feeling inside her, like her heart was expanding to encircle Chloe. She glanced back at Sarah, and when their eyes met, her heart expanded again. Chloe and Sarah made her feel full in a way she never had before. She wanted to stay in this circle with Chloe and Sarah, but it wasn't up to her. Sarah's circle had already broken once, and Jass understood her need to protect Chloe. She forced herself to loosen her hold on the little girl, but Chloe took hold of Jass's arms and wrapped them around her middle again.

Now Jass's eyes met Amara's. She was watching, too, and Jass understood what moms talked about when they said that children were like having a piece of their heart walking outside of their body.

Bumblebee was holding up another book and asking who in the audience liked to play with trucks.

Chloe's hand shot up, and Jass smiled, picturing the collection of trucks she had seen in the yard. Again, she took Jass's hand, this time raising it in the air.

"How do you know I play with trucks?" Jass asked, amused.

"C'mon. You *drive* a truck!"

Having heard Chloe, Bumblebee smiled broadly and asked Jass what kind of truck she drove.

"Just a pickup. I don't know if it counts."

"Of course, of course!" Bumblebee said. "It would fit right in. You two are going to love this story."

She loved the story about each of the trucks preparing to sleep on the construction site. Later, when the three adults stood by the park adjacent to the library while Chloe climbed on the jungle gym, she learned that Bumblebee had changed that one as well, though she hadn't mentioned it.

Having checked out the library's copy of the book, Sarah slowly turned the pages. "I've read this book to Chloe a hundred times and always went with the male pronouns that are on the page. It never occurred to me to change the pronouns to she and her. I wonder about changing all the pronouns, though. What do you think about alternating from one truck to the next? The crane truck is she, but the cement truck is he?"

Amara caught Jass's eye.

"Are you rolling your eyes at me?" Sarah bumped her shoulder to Jass's.

The contact released a flood of sparks in Jass that she hadn't felt in weeks, and her thoughts immediately turned to how Sarah might want to spend her next weekend. "Of course not!" she assured Sarah.

"Then what was that look?" Now she turned to Amara whose gaze flicked from one woman to the other.

Amara smiled. "It is a treat to see how you work your way through things. I am used to your polished podcasts. Now, knowing you better, I can see that you are always thinking and processing. It's exciting, and I wish more people approached the unfamiliar like that."

Sarah turned another page. "Would you read the dump truck with female or male pronouns?"

"I think I'd read it different every day. You never know, some days the dump truck might wake up feeling more masculine and the next day more feminine. Maybe I'd use they-them pronouns," Amara answered.

"I wonder why Bumblebee didn't use they-them pronouns at all," Sarah said.

"Interesting," Amara responded. "But using different pronouns has made you think differently about this book, and I can see you percolating a podcast that I'm eager to hear because it's going to shape the way people react when their loved ones talk about changing pronouns."

"You're putting a lot of faith into my podcast's reach."

Chloe ran to the swings, and Jass automatically crossed the playground and positioned herself behind Chloe while she wiggled onto the seat. "Ready?"

"Ready!" Chloe said.

Jass took hold of the two chains and backed up until she could lift Chloe no higher. Then she let go, smiling at Chloe's squeal of delight. She pushed Chloe on the return and looked up to catch Sarah's eye. *Thank you*, she mouthed. Jass shrugged, not needing thanks for doing something that she was happy to do. She felt swirling in her middle again. Could it be the baby moving? She rested one hand on her belly and used the other one to push Chloe.

It felt like a family day at the park watching her best friend continuing her conversation with her lover. But Jass yearned to be recognized. She was beginning to feel suffocated, not just by keeping her distance from Sarah when Chloe was around as she was doing now, but also because they never did anything in public to threaten Sarah's professional persona.

The February day was too beautiful to brood. Jass filled her lungs with the cool winter air and enjoyed the warmth of the sun on her back. Really, what did she have to complain about? Pregnancy was probably messing with her hormones, making her feel like she needed to nest or something. A gentle breeze played with Sarah's light brown hair, and she quickly pulled it back and tied it in a knot, reminding Jass of the first time she'd seen her in person. Jass had called her a hot mess that day. Today, none of what had made Sarah so frazzled was present, leaving Jass to sigh over how beautiful she was.

Chloe started to scooch forward on the seat, so Jass grabbed the chains, slowing her to a stop. Chloe jumped from the swing and ran across the park to throw her arms around her mother's legs. Jass followed, tucking her hands deep in her pockets, so she would not be tempted to do likewise.

CHAPTER FORTY-ONE

"What do your pools look like today?" Sarah leaned forward and rested her chin in the palm of her hand, full in all senses of the word watching Jass putter in the kitchen. It wasn't having someone else to take care of the never-ending dishes. It was the familiarity with which Jass moved through her space that filled Sarah's emotional cup.

"Four will be quick, but one needs a filter change. Too bad I don't have Chloe to help me. This one is starting to make bending difficult." She pressed her hands to her belly, and then her eyes went wide and her jaw dropped open.

"What?" Sarah asked, sliding from the kitchen stool and rounding the counter to stand with Jass in the kitchen.

"I think I felt a kick!"

"What are you, week twenty? I felt Chloe move right around the same time." She watched as Jass turned her attention deep within, her introspection magnifying her radiance. Sarah moved behind Jass and wrapped her arms around her shoulders. "She was always busy after I ate, especially if I had a breakfast like this." She'd made Jass one of her favorite breakfasts: waffles, eggs, and sausage, and she had laughed when Jass asked if she could have peanut butter for her waffle.

"There it was again! Holy shit! That is so wild! I have to tell Amara!"

Jass leaned against the counter and started thumbing a text. Sarah took over at the sink. She told herself not to feel left out. This was Amara and Jass's moment, not hers.

Jass set her phone on the counter and placed both hands on her belly, accentuating her baby bump. "When could Tricia feel Chloe?" she asked.

"Oh, not for a few more months. The baby has to be bigger to push to be felt from the outside." Those months had felt so special to Sarah, her time to create a unique bond with Chloe. That was a major reason she had had her doubts about Jass being able to carry a baby without becoming attached, but her focus never seemed to stray from the fact that this was Amara's baby. Her unwavering conviction carried to Sarah as well, so it felt natural for Jass to bust out her phone to share the latest news. Too bad logic had such a bad track record for communicating with her emotions.

Jass's phone chirped, and she quickly replied, smiling radiantly.

"You are glowing," Sarah said, setting aside her mixed emotions.

Jass put her phone on the counter again and put her palm to her cheek as if to check for a fever. "Am I?"

"Absolutely. You are the epitome of vibrance, and your baby bump is adorable."

Jass's hands returned to her stomach. "It's so trippy how my body is changing. Amara's taking me to get maternity clothes because I've had to start wearing my stretchy pants with the waistband below my tummy."

"I should pull out my stuff!" Sarah said. She paused. Was that overstepping or taking something away from Amara? "Or would that be weird?"

"It's not weird to help us save some money," Jass said. "Unless you wore a bunch of dresses. I am not wearing a dress."

Sarah laughed. "Noted. I had a pair of jeans I loved. They'd be long on you, but cute with the cuffs rolled up. And overalls! Oh my god, you'd look adorable in the overalls. I loved them, especially when I got bigger and couldn't stand anything hugging at my waist. When are you going shopping?"

"After the ultrasound this week."

"Oh!" Sarah clasped her hands together. "The gender reveal. Does Amara want to know?"

Jass eyed her phone as if she'd rather Amara answer the question herself. "She goes back and forth. She never identified with her birth sex, so it seems, not pointless, but…"

"Inconsequential?"

"That's a better word. She knows that a sex will be assigned at birth, but she also wants to give her child the opportunity to be themselves. People find out sex beforehand to think about names and what color to paint the nursery and what color clothes to buy or toys. This baby will have dolls and trucks in a bright green room because Amara loves the color green."

"I wish I'd considered that before Chloe was born. I am embarrassed by the amount of pink she has and that it never occurred to me to change the pronouns in books."

"But you're not prescriptive. She has a construction site in the backyard! You let her get dirty and run around the backyard like a pony, and she has a lot of different colors in her wardrobe. There's nothing wrong with pink or dresses. I don't want you to think I'm being critical of you if you wore dresses when you were pregnant. You look great in dresses, and maybe Chloe will grow up feeling beautiful in dresses. That's allowed, too."

"Okay. You get ready. I'll go dig in the garage for my pregnancy stuff." She wrapped her arms around Jass and kissed her. "You're coming back after your pools, though, right? I got all the stuff to make that chicken enchilada casserole you told me about."

"I will always say yes to food."

"I hope you're coming back for more than the food."

Jass let her arms fall to Sarah's hips and leaned back to catch Sarah's gaze. For a moment, something like sadness tinged her expression, but then she kissed Sarah, her full lips igniting a fire within Sarah that she hoped they would fan into flames when Jass's workday was through. "For so much more than the food," Jass whispered.

Then she was gone down the hall to get dressed. Sarah slipped into the garage and started moving bins. She was up on the ladder and had almost gotten her hands on the right box when her phone rang. Grumbling, she descended the ladder without the box to check the screen. Tricia.

Tricia was sobbing.

"What's wrong? Is it Chloe? Is Chloe okay?"

"She's fine. She's watching TV."

"God, Tricia. You can't do that to me! You almost gave me a heart attack!"

"I don't know what to do! I don't know what to do!" Tricia kept repeating the phrase over and over, and Sarah could easily visualize her pulling at a lock of hair.

"First off, take a deep breath. If you're not sitting down, sit and put your head between your knees. You're going to hyperventilate." Knowing it would take her a few minutes, she put Tricia on speakerphone and climbed the ladder again.

Tricia switched to repeating "Okay," and Sarah told her to breathe in for four beats, and then exhale for six beats between each *okay*.

By the time Tricia had calmed down, Sarah had retrieved the box and was quickly weeding out the dresses. "What's going on?"

"Lydia and I had a huge fight, and she left, and I need to go after her, but I've got Chloe, so I'm stuck." She sobbed again. "I'm stuck!"

At that moment, Jass entered the garage looking for Sarah. Her eyebrows shot up in surprise. Sarah mouthed *Tricia*.

"Chloe?" Jass whispered.

Jass's concern warmed Sarah to her core. Sarah shook her head and took the phone off speaker. "She's okay. Tricia and Lydia had a fight."

Jass made an *eeeek* face and motioned that she would text Sarah later. Sarah placed her hand on Jass's chest and mouthed *Thank you* before leaning in to kiss her lightly. She leaned forward to whisper next to Jass's ear, "Sorry about this." While she was talking, she missed what Tricia said. "Hold on," she said into the phone. "No, I'm listening. Just give me a sec." She closed her eyes and took a deep breath. Holding the phone away from her, she said, "She's a wreck. I wouldn't be surprised if she's calling to ask if I can come get Chloe."

Jass nodded without betraying any emotion. "Raincheck on dinner?"

Sarah's free hand curled into a fist, frustrated with Tricia's intrusion on her weekends off. That was on her, too, though, for always being willing to rescue her. But she couldn't leave Chloe stuck there if Tricia couldn't pull herself together. "I'd like you to come back."

Jass studied her. "You're sure?"

Chloe herself had invited Jass to dinner before. It wasn't that big of a deal, Sarah told herself. "Yes, I'm sure."

"Okay. See you later, then." She delivered a quick kiss and headed toward the door.

"I'm back," she said.

"Is someone there?" Tricia said.

"Just my pool tech," Sarah said.

"On Saturday? This early?"

How was Sarah supposed to answer that, especially when Tricia was calling about a fight with her girlfriend? "There was something weird going on with the pump," she lied.

"You could've asked me to look at it. Such a waste of money."

"What's going on with you and Lydia?" Sarah asked, steering the conversation back to why Tricia had called.

This brought a new flood of tears. This was going to take a while. Sarah went inside to brew some coffee, listening to Tricia talk about how having Chloe for the weekend had brought up the topic of how serious Lydia was about creating her own family.

"I can't," Tricia sobbed again. "I already let you down, and I'm doing my best to not let you down more by having Chloe when it's my weekend, but Lydia wants so much more, and you know me. I'm shit with a newborn."

Sarah couldn't help but laugh. At least she could own how bad things had gone for them after Chloe arrived. "I don't know what to say, Tricia. I'm not arguing with you."

"I know. But could you take Chloe today? I need to talk to Lydia."

"Maybe she needs space and that's why she left. Can you shift gears for Chloe? You just said you're trying to not let me down. And you know that I worry about Chloe. It's disruptive when you change the schedule."

Tricia's tears answered her question. Sarah was going to have to rearrange her whole day. Ever since Jass had built jumps for Chloe in the backyard, Sarah had been planning to take Chloe riding. She could pick up Chloe from Tricia's and take her to Griffith Park. No doubt she was worried about Tricia and confused about what was going on. She would need some special time with a mom, and today Sarah was the one who could give her that. *Again* the part of her that felt like Tricia would never grow up whispered. No. She could not let that into her brain space. She was doing what was best for Chloe and her day. She needed to feel out how Tricia's emotional state was affecting Chloe. "I need a shower. Can you hold it together for a half hour?"

She heard the huge exhale on the other end of the phone. "Thank you, Sarah. I owe you. Again. I'm sorry. I'm a work in progress."

"We all are. I'll be there soon."

What was she doing, she asked herself. She was granting Tricia grace. And keeping her dinner date with Jass? Was it selfish not to cancel? Or risky given what Chloe was watching her other mom go through? She didn't have the answer, but if she could grant Tricia grace, she might as well extend it to herself as well.

CHAPTER FORTY-TWO

Jass waited as Chloe rearranged the stuffed animals on her bed, at once making space and creating an audience for the books she had chosen. Jass watched Chloe closely as she had been all night, trying to read whether she was feeling abandoned by Tricia's choice to chase Lydia.

Sarah had texted during the day to let Jass know that she'd been right about Tricia asking her to take Chloe. Jass knew that Tricia was trying to salvage things with Lydia, but she didn't quite see the point. Lydia's wanting kids sounded like a dealbreaker. She admired Tricia for being honest about whether she could have more kids, but she noted the irony of her choosing to spend the day trying to repair things with her girlfriend rather than maintaining her relationship with Chloe. Jass had spent years knowing that her mother's boyfriends came first. Was that because she was older, or was Chloe feeling the sting of coming second today? If Chloe were twelve, Jass would ask.

Being asked to spend time with Chloe had given Jass hope that Sarah might see something more than a sexual exchange. Hearing her lie to Tricia about the pool tech being there to fix her filter had cut her deeply, and she had wrestled with it all day, vacillating between confronting Sarah about it and opting out of dinner.

She was glad that she hadn't canceled. She loved hearing Chloe talk about the ponies at Griffith park during dinner and having Chloe request that Jass read her bedtime stories was heartwarming.

Ready for Jass, Chloe patted the bed and snuggled in under her arm. "This one is for the baby," she said, handing Jass *Owl Babies*.

Jass read through the story of the three owl babies who missed their mom while she was gone from the nest. Two of the owls were confident their mother owl would return. The third was a worrier. Had Chloe picked the book because she felt abandoned by Tricia, or was Jass reading too much into her choice? "Which owl are you?" she chanced asking when she and finished.

"The oldest one, Sarah."

"It's a good name."

Chloe giggled. "But I can't be Sarah because I don't have a brother and a sister."

"Would you like to have a brother or sister someday?"

"Yes!" Chloe set the first book aside and handed Jass a book with a bunny standing under a toadstool on the cover. "But Mama doesn't want another baby."

"Maybe just not right now," Jass said.

"Amara's your sister. Do you have another sister or brother?"

"Nope. Only Amara. For a long time, it was just me and my mom after she and my dad got divorced."

Chloe sat up and turned to face Jass. "Then what happened?"

"My mom met a guy she really liked and married him. He's my stepdad."

"So you had two dads."

"Kind of. But one at a time."

"You could be my stepmom."

Jass's heart skipped a beat. Had Chloe said what she thought she said?

"You like my mom, don't you?" Chloe pressed.

How was Jass supposed to answer that? "I do like your mom…" She tried to gather her wits to explain how she and Sarah were not doing what Tricia and Lydia were doing, but Chloe had already snuggled back into the crook of Jass's arm with a simple, "Okay. These are my other picks."

Though Jass read the stories, her mind was elsewhere. What was Sarah going to say about it? Because she certainly had to tell her. By the time she finished reading *Once Upon a Cool Motorcycle Dude*, she peeked at Chloe who had been especially quiet during the story. Fast asleep. She put the books on the bookshelf but hesitated to move the arm wrapped around Chloe for fear of waking her. She bent to kiss the top of Chloe's head and then relaxed back against the headboard for a minute. She should get up. She knew she should. But she couldn't yet. Getting up would mean being alone with Sarah, and she didn't know if she had the courage to admit how deeply Sarah had hurt her. This didn't feel like being just the pool tech.

She startled awake and opened her eyes to discover Sarah smiling down at her. She was threading her fingers through Jass's hair. That was what had woken her, but now the repeated motion threatened to lull her back to sleep. Her fingers felt so good. Sleep felt so good. She closed her eyes and felt Sarah lean over her.

"C'mon. You can't fall asleep here."

"I'm already asleep," Jass mumbled.

"What am I going to do with you?"

Jass looked up. Sarah continued to stroke her hair. She looked at her with such tenderness, Jass could barely breathe.

She shifted and snapped off the small reading lamp. Plunged into darkness, Jass could no longer read Sarah's expression, but she felt her hands on her body and moved toward them until she was standing.

She watched as Sarah rearranged Chloe underneath her covers. As she had done with Jass, she smoothed Chloe's hair away from her forehead. She leaned forward and kissed Chloe's cheek before turning to take Jass's hand to lead her from the room.

Jass was not sleepy anymore. It was such bad timing to want Sarah the way she did. And she wanted her. All of her. She wanted to fall asleep with her and wake up with her. She wanted dinners and reading stories to Chloe. She wanted to take her to ride the ponies. She wanted Chloe to ride her route on Saturdays and learn how to take care of pools. She wanted it all, and when she kissed Sarah, she poured everything into the kiss, desperate for Sarah to want her in the same way.

"Whoa," Sarah said when they came up for air. "I thought you were asleep."

"Not anymore," Jass said, stroking the soft skin beneath Sarah's ear. Sarah closed her eyes, emboldening Jass. Jass ran her fingers up through Sarah's hair from the base of her neck and felt Sarah shiver. Her mouth next to Sarah's ear, she whispered, "I want you."

"Jass," Sarah whispered.

Jass peppered Sarah's neck with kisses. "Be with me."

Sarah's hands tightened on Jass's arms. "I can't. Not tonight. Not with Chloe here."

Jass kept her face at Sarah's neck. She closed her eyes and breathed Sarah in, the peachy sweetness of her. She wanted to take a bite. "I want it all, Sarah. I want to stay. I want to make pancakes with you and Chloe in the morning. I want all of it. You. Chloe. The whole package."

"Stop. Jass. You can't. I can't."

Jass did not stop kissing Sarah's neck. She kissed all the way around to Sarah's right ear, making a necklace of kisses. Chloe saw what Jass did—that they could be a family. Sarah had let her stay for dinner. Did that mean that she could see it, too? Jass returned to Sarah's lips and kissed her deeply, her whole body electric with desire. "Why couldn't we be a family?" she whispered when she came up for air.

Sarah took a step back and put her hand on Jass's chest. "How can you ask me that tonight after Chloe watched Tricia and Lydia splitting up?"

"She's not upset, Sarah. She picked out books for the baby, and we talked about stepparents and siblings. She's fine."

Sarah took another step back, her brows pinching together. "Why were you talking about stepparents?"

Jass heard a protective tone Sarah's voice. This wasn't the Sarah Jass experienced when Chloe wasn't there. This was the mama bear protecting her cub. Jass had to tread carefully. "That *Owl Babies* book got us talking about siblings, and I was telling her I didn't have any and asked if she wanted a brother or a sister like the owls in the book."

"Jesus, Jass. Tonight? You really felt like that was an appropriate topic after seeing her mom fall apart?"

"She asked me questions. I answered them. She asked if I like you, and I do! I more than like you if you want to know the truth of it. I love you, and I wish you would let me take you to bed, so I can show you. You said the only way to know if I could be a parent to Chloe was to be around more. Let me be here. Let me love the both of you."

"I can't do this, Jass. Not tonight." Jass reached for her, but Sarah held out a hand. "Please don't."

An icy wave barreled into Jass, and she took a step back. "I am just the pool tech, then?"

"What?"

"This morning. When you were talking to Tricia. You said you were just talking to the pool tech. Is that all this is to you, some weekend fun?"

"Tricia was in a state. She didn't need to know that I had someone here."

"Your fuckbuddy. I forgot."

"You are obviously more than that."

"Sorry, it's not obvious. I spent all day trying to figure out which one meant more, your lying to Tricia or your letting me have dinner with you and Chloe. Selfishly, I decided having dinner was more important. But it wasn't, so I should go." The words nearly caught in her throat. She cleared it and bit her tongue to focus her emotions. She was not going to cry. She would definitely not cry.

"I'm sorry that what I said made you feel minimized. That wasn't my intention at all. I don't want to invite Tricia into this yet."

"What is this, Sarah? I need to know."

"This is still great. But it's not the right time to spring more on Chloe."

"She knows, Sarah. She asked me if I like you after I talked about my mom finding Dave."

Sarah's hand went to her throat, and she hooked her thumb over her mouth. She lifted her chin to rest on her thumb. "And you said?"

"That I do. She said okay, and we read more stories. I love the *Motorcycle Dude* one, by the way."

That did not make Sarah smile.

Things settled into place for Jass. The stories had helped her. She wanted the happily ever after. "I don't like being a secret. Does anyone in your life know about me?"

Sarah's silence spoke volumes.

Jass stepped forward and put her arms lightly around Sarah. She breathed her in again. It would be so easy to fall completely for this woman, but would she ever be able to give herself fully in return? Where Jass was ready to leap in, Sarah seemed content to sit on the side of the pool dangling only her toes in the water. "I'm going to go," she whispered.

Sarah didn't stop her when she gathered her things. At the door, she paused again, but Sarah had not moved. Jass knotted her lips. She would not cry.

Yet.

CHAPTER FORTY-THREE

Sarah had been right to let Jass go. It had been hard enough to have Jass deliver her take-me-to-bed kiss when they had just stepped away from a sleeping Chloe, but then to hear that she wanted more? The declaration of love?

It had been too much.

And then Tricia had been on the porch at ten a.m., needing Sarah's comfort after Lydia had not bent on the issue of children. She'd sat uncomfortably next to her ex who had no idea of the boundary she was pushing. When she was a sobbing mess was not the time to explain that she could not be her emotional support anymore, but Sarah needed to make that boundary crystal clear, and soon. She did not want Chloe to see her holding Tricia and infer that they were getting back together. She did not need Jass stopping by unexpectedly to see her with her arm around her ex, either. She scooted to put an inch between their bodies, patting Tricia's shoulder as she cried.

Thank goodness Jass hadn't stayed. What would she have told Tricia had she arrived to find Jass at the stove flipping pancakes? She did not need that kind of confrontation in front of Chloe. She would need to tell Tricia. But only if there was something to tell, and she was not so sure what she would say now. For the third week in a row, she found herself waiting to see Jass's truck pull up for the weekly pool service, so they could talk.

She had hoped to clear the air the weekend Tricia had Chloe again, but Jass had not accepted her invitation to spend the weekend together. She closed her eyes against the sting of Jass's refusal. It brought a clearer picture of how Jass had searched her eyes before saying that she could not fuck around anymore. She had asked whether Sarah was happy playing at being a couple twice a month or whether she ever wanted more. Sarah was good at compartmentalizing. She could set aside her needs for the times she could be with Jass wholly. Didn't that count for anything?

Jass insisted that she wanted Sarah and Chloe. She wanted to be a family. But what would that even look like when she had the intimate tie of a child with Amara? And then there was Tricia.

Again. As if her thoughts had conjured her ex, Tricia's silver Pilot swung into the drive. Sarah preemptively rolled tension from her neck.

Chloe looked up from her after-school snack of peanut butter on crackers. "Why's Mama here? Am I going to her house tonight?"

"No, sweetheart. I didn't know she was going to be here. You eat your snack."

Tricia walked toward the house, a package wrapped in brown paper in her hands.

"This is unexpected," Sarah said at the front door.

"You're always saying you want me to be more present for Chloe."

"When you have her, Tricia. As in be prepared to be with her one on one without the TV on."

Tricia rolled her eyes. "I had a job that took me by that farmers' market this morning." Remember when we took Chloe to their pumpkin patch? They had a sign out front saying fresh strawberries."

She paused, waiting for Sarah to speak. The problem was that when Lydia had held firm about breaking up with Tricia, Sarah should have said that it was not her job to provide emotional support, but she had not. She had let Tricia in and had been there for her while she cried. Instead of having pancakes with Jass, she had fed Tricia breakfast, and sat at the table wondering what her life would have been like if Tricia had never left them.

Tricia would have been complaining about the number of chores to be done. The laundry. The grocery shopping. The pool.

Sarah's gaze went to the street. Jass would be arriving soon. Was there any quick way out of this trip down memory lane? She took a deep breath. "I remember."

"Chloe loved all the bounce houses. Why didn't we take her this year?"

Why hadn't they? Sarah hadn't wanted to go because that was something families did. Selfishly, she didn't want to stand there and watch all the other parents with their children. But was that how Amara would feel? Not likely. Tricia was waiting for an answer, and Sarah did not want to fall into the spiral of social pressure. "Because it's a racket," Sarah said, remembering how much they paid and how she had quieted the discomfort by rationalizing that they were paying more for the experience than the attractions and pumpkins. An experience for Chloe, not for the parents.

Tricia extended the package. "Well, I remembered how much Chloe loves strawberries, so I stopped. They smell amazing."

Having heard her name, Chloe came running. "Berries!"

Sarah clenched her teeth. "Let's wash some to have with your snack."

"Berries! Berries! Berries!" Chloe danced in the hall.

Tricia ducked by Sarah as if she sensed and was avoiding the annoyance Sarah was trying to keep in check. She appreciated the gesture, but why did she have to come on the one day of the week she could see Jass?

As she was about to shut the door, she finally saw the flash of red she had been waiting for. She closed the door with a quiet click, doubting that she would be able to hustle Tricia on her way before Jass was finished servicing the pool.

At the sink, Tricia was already rinsing the berries in a colander and had cutting board and knife at the ready to cut off the stems. She would always be part of their life. Isn't that what Sarah wanted, for Chloe to have a relationship with both her moms?

Jass was at the pool gate, her attention directed toward the yard. Sarah turned to put her back to the window, resting her back against the counter.

"Too tempting?" Tricia said with a wink.

Sarah looked at the strawberries, not following when Tricia tipped her head toward the window. "Your hot pool chickie. She could be a fun distraction." Tricia waggled her eyebrows.

"Don't be crude," Sarah whispered.

Tricia handed a bowl full of strawberries to Chloe. "Here you go, kiddo. Take them to the table."

Chloe taken care of, Tricia turned and rested her elbows on the counter. "It's not crude to admire a beautiful woman. There is something seriously wrong with you if you have not been enjoying a weekly ogle of this woman."

Sarah's stomach did a loop-the-loop remembering how much more than ogling she had done. She missed Jass's touch. She'd been ready to explode by the time her free weekend came up.

The realization that she was thinking about Jass in the same way as Tricia hit her so suddenly, she almost smacked herself in the head. Because it was more than the way that Jass touched her. It was falling asleep next to her and waking up with her. It was the way Jass brought her cuttings from her other clients' homes and helped Sarah propagate them. Jass had said she wanted to make pancakes with Chloe. She wanted more of those mornings, not just the two Sarah was offering twice a month. She had not been fair to Jass.

"Again, crude. You're what? Three weeks out of your relationship, and all you can think about is getting someone else into bed?"

"Humans are not meant to be solitary creatures, Sarah," Tricia said.

Sarah rolled her eyes. "I was actually hoping to catch Jass today. So. Thanks for the strawberries..." She circled the kitchen counter and paused to give Tricia the opportunity to leave.

"Oh..." Tricia looked to Chloe and back to Sarah.

"What?"

"Can we talk after that...About this weekend?" Tricia sat next to Chloe and asked about the strawberries. *All about you*, Sarah thought in anticipation of what Tricia had to say. It was bad enough that she was going to flake on Chloe yet again, but she couldn't at least ask her daughter what she's doing at school?

The pool was framed by the sliding glass doors. Tricia was going to be watching the interaction with Jass. Sitting next to Chloe who had talked to Jass about being a stepmom. She didn't talk to Sarah about Jass, but would she share with Tricia how Jass sometimes joined them for dinner?

Sarah couldn't send Jass a text. Jass had been slow to respond to Sarah's texts and when she did, Sarah could feel that she was being held at arm's length. "Be right back," she said and slipped out the back door.

Though it was warm, Sarah wrapped an arm around her middle and with the other, she absently ran her fingers from her elbow to her shoulder. She stopped at the pool fence. Jass was kneeling by the return. When she stood to coil her hose, she caught Sarah's eye.

"Hey," she said evenly as she continued her work. Sarah's pool was the last on Jass's Thursday, so she wasn't typically rushing to wrap up but today she appeared to be in a hurry. "Everything okay with Tricia?"

Ah, that explained it. She'd seen Tricia's car. "She brought strawberries for Chloe. I wish she'd thrown them in the fridge and surprised her tomorrow. This is her weekend."

"She's at a loose end without Lydia?"

Tricia's observation about Jass echoed in Sarah's ears. "I think so. She picked up the strawberries where we had a family outing years ago. It's important to me that Chloe doesn't get the impression that her moms are going to get back together. And that you don't think I'm hoping she'll come back because her relationship with Lydia is over."

"I hadn't given that any thought," Jass said.

"I always wished my parents would get back together again."

"These warm days are bringing the temperature of the pool up nicely. If you had a solar cover on it, you could be swimming in a week." She glanced at Sarah and then away. "Chloe could be in soon."

"I don't..." Why was Jass changing the conversation? She wanted to talk about the distance between them. She needed to have her arms around Jass that instant, not a pool fence and acres of awkwardness between them. She allowed herself the flash of a fantasy of opening the gate and closing the distance between them, knowing exactly how shocked Tricia would be. But that wasn't fair. She owed Tricia an adult conversation, not a childish move like the one she now pushed out of her mind. "Would you be able to get us a cover?"

"Sure. I'll add it to next month's invoice. I'll take measurements today. I'm guessing it'll be somewhere between two-fifty or three hundred. That okay?"

"I don't like this."

"You just asked me…"

"No. The money is fine. Buy the cover." She could turn around and go back in the house. She probably should, given that the longer she talked to Jass, the more curious Tricia would be. She shut her eyes and slid a finger and thumb over them, pausing to pinch the bridge of her nose. "I came out to talk to you because I was hoping this weekend we could see each other, but now…"

"Tricia's got other plans this weekend?"

"I'm guessing so. She said she needed to talk when I'm done talking to you. It's not hard to guess what she's here to talk about."

Jass shrugged. "You know it doesn't matter to me. I love Chloe. I'd love to spend time with the both of you. But I'm done pretending that I'm not in love with you when she's here."

She had finished packing up her cart and wheeled it through the gate that Sarah held open. For the briefest of moments she paused, and Sarah knew the words Jass wanted to hear, but she could not find her voice.

"If you were a listener , what would The Sarapist tell you to do about this?" Jass asked in parting.

It could have felt like a punch, but it didn't land that way, and Sarah returned to Chloe and Tricia with most of her attention focused on Jass's question. What would she tell someone in her situation to do? It was no longer a question of dating. Jass had used the word love again. She deserved a thoughtful and honest response. All Sarah had to do was sort herself out. After she dealt with the letdown Tricia was about to deliver.

CHAPTER FORTY-FOUR

Thursdays brought equal parts of anticipation and dread for Jass, and she spent much too much time fantasizing about what she wanted from Sarah. Some of those fantasies included Sarah waiting by the pool in a bikini, so to see her sitting by the side of the pool with her feet in the water sent a ripple of hope and desire through Jass. Then Chloe's head popped up out of the water with a squeal of glee.

"I take it the pool cover is working?" Jass called from the patio to avoid startling her girls.

Sarah looked over her shoulder and smiled at her, and Jass wished she could stop time and imprint that image forever.

"It's so warm on the top and sooooooo cold on the bottom!" Chloe called out, bouncing across the shallow end Sarah had exposed by pulling the cover from the deep end.

"I wasn't sure how to get the cover off, but someone refused to wait until you got here."

"It's easier with two, anyway," Jass said.

"Isn't that the way with everything?" Sarah asked, still smiling at Jass. Her tone was heavy with suggestion. Had something shifted in the last two weeks?

Jass scolded herself to snap out of her fantasies. Just because Sarah was flirting did not mean anything had changed. This was her free weekend, and she was probably just thinking about hooking up. Jass demonstrated how to fold the cover at the end of the pool, trying her best not to let her eyes linger on Sarah's cleavage or the smooth expanse of belly the striped blue bikini exposed. Sarah looked exceptionally good in blue, and it was too easy for Jass to imagine what she would look like out of it and what her naked body would feel like in the pool.

"Thank you for suggesting the cover. It makes a world of difference."

"Kids and pools go together like peanut butter and jelly. You should get the most use out of it as you can. If I had this pool, I'd be swimming laps all the time."

"You're welcome to use it anytime."

Her words hung in the air, and Jass did not know how to respond. Thankfully, Sarah's phone rang. She looked at the screen. "Oh, shoot."

"Tricia?" Jass guessed.

"No. It's my…I've been trying to get in touch with this therapist, but I keep…" She gestured to Chloe. "I can't hustle her out just to take this call." Her thumb hovered over the phone symbol.

"Take it," Jass insisted. "I'll keep an eye on Chloe. She can help me with the pool." Sarah searched her eyes. Was she thinking about Jass's words? Did they sit on her tongue demanding to be echoed?

Sarah broke their eye contact and swiped the screen. "Elodia! Thank you so much for your patience…Hold on one second while I get Chloe settled." She lowered the phone to her chest. "Are you sure?"

"We're good. Take your time."

Sarah squeezed Jass's shoulder. *Thank you*, she mouthed.

"Where's Mommy going?" Chloe asked, climbing out of the pool.

"She needed to take a phone call, but I thought you would rather stay in the pool. If you don't want to, it's okay. But I promised your mom that you could hang out with me while she talked on the phone."

"She can talk on the phone a long time," Chloe said seriously.

"Good. Because it can take a long time to get your pool looking spiffy. Do you want to help or play in the water?"

"Do I have to help?"

"Nope. As long as you stay on the steps while I run the vacuum, you're fine. That should help mix the warm water on the surface with the cold water underneath. You know what works better, though?"

"What?"

"Cannonballs!"

Chloe's eyes went wide. "I can't jump without a mom in the pool!"

"Oh. What if I was in the pool?"

"Do you have a swimsuit?" She rested her wrist on her cocked hip, looking so much like a preview to her teenaged self that Jass had to smile.

"It's kind of a requirement of my job. I keep a suit and a change of clothes in my truck. A suit in case I have to grab something I can't scoop up with a net and a change of clothes for if I ever fall in."

"But you've never fallen in."

Jass loved that Chloe remembered. "Nope! But you'd better knock on wood now!"

Chloe giggled and rapped her knuckles against her head.

"Let's go get my suit. You'll have to come with me. I can't leave you in the pool yard. And then you can show me where I can change."

Chloe asked a million questions about what Jass carried in her truck, and Jass happily answered them. She stayed parked on the patio couch while Jass ran to change into her suit. It didn't fit properly. The way her belly protruded tempted her to back out of the deal, but she couldn't be that person. She threw her new large tee over her suit—she would take it off when she was ready to get in the water. "Hope you're okay with this," she said, rubbing her tummy.

By the time Sarah had ended her call, Jass had finished the pool chores and had waded in, teeth chattering but ecstatic to see the way Chloe flung herself into the pool to swim the short distance to Jass.

"Mommy, watch this!" Chloe said when Sarah returned to sit by the steps. She backed up as far as she could and then ran and jumped to Jass, her little hands trying to pull her knees to her chest.

As they had been practicing, Jass guided her out of her float and turned her around, so she could swim back to the edge.

"You went so high!" Sarah said, high-fiving Chloe when she reached the stairs. "Are your lips blue?"

"No!" Chloe said, preparing to launch herself again.

"Jass's lips are turning blue. You didn't have to swim. I said you could anytime, but I didn't expect you to get in. It's better than it was a few weeks ago, but it's a long way away from being warm enough for me."

"The baby likes it. They're moving like crazy in there!" She dropped her voice and said, "And yours is going to sleep like a rock tonight!" She pushed away from the wall and got in position to catch Chloe again. "How'd your call go?"

She was disappointed that Sarah had changed out of her bikini but also appreciated the faded jeans and a well-loved red tee Sarah had changed into. She'd rolled up the jeans to her knees and rested her feet on the first step. Elbow propped on her knees and her chin in the palm of one hand, she tipped her head. She was simply herself, Jass realized, not the person worried about her reputation. "Really good. Thank you for letting me take that. We were finally able to Zoom, and she was extremely helpful."

"I want to feel the baby move!" Chloe said, her arms hugged around Jass's neck.

"Too early. The Internet says it'll be another three weeks or so before other people can feel what I'm feeling."

"What's it like?"

"Like my body is a trampoline, and someone is jump, jump, jumping in there."

"Did I jump, Mommy?"

"You sure did. And when I could feel you on the outside, I would push against your arm or leg or whatever you were poking me with, and you'd poke back. I'm pretty sure that's why you could count so early. I would go push, push, push, and you would go poke, poke, poke."

They stayed in for another fifteen minutes, Sarah's gaze sending a whoosh of warmth through Jass's belly every time it focused on her. When Sarah said it was time to go in, she set Chloe up on a towel spread over the warm cement. Jass climbed out, painfully aware of how far she was from a classic beauty. Still, Sarah's eyes lingered on her exposed tummy in a way that made her feel sexy.

"You're amazing," Sarah said, stepping close to wrap a towel around her shoulders.

Jass kept her voice low. "Did your therapist tell you to say that?"

"Maybe. There are a lot of things that need to be said. Will you stay for dinner, until Chloe is out?" She looked away from Jass when she asked.

Jass's heart fluttered. "I'd like that."

"Me too." Sarah's hand found Jass's for the briefest moment, and she squeezed.

Jass wanted it all to mean that Sarah was ready to let her into her life, or at least acknowledge the possibility, but the brevity of the gesture felt like a warning to keep up her guard. Be happy with what she can offer, a voice inside whispered. You're worth more than every other weekend, another voice said. Jass wanted to lose herself in the deep desire she felt, but as badly as she wanted to kiss Sarah, she couldn't yet.

She sighed and followed Sarah and Chloe at a safe distance into the house.

CHAPTER FORTY-FIVE

"When did your bulb burn out?" Jass asked when she returned to the kitchen in dry clothes. Sarah cringed. Distracted by helping Chloe rinse and change, she'd forgotten about how she'd been getting by with a camp lantern to light her bathroom.

"A few days ago. I should have gotten up there to figure out how to get the cover off."

"Could I have a look or do you need help with dinner?" When Sarah's eyes dropped to Jass's belly, Jass rolled her eyes. "Don't even suggest I can't get on a stepladder. I'm pregnant. I don't have a sprained ankle."

"It's not that. I'm trying to not feel inadequate letting a pregnant woman fix something for me."

"I know this great podcaster who did a whole episode on not 'shoulding' on yourself. Saying you *should* fix it, that you *shouldn't* let me do it. I'm sure I could find it." She pulled out her phone like she would really look it up.

Point taken, Sarah said, "If you're seriously offering, that would be lovely." With a satisfied smirk Jass tucked the phone away. It might have made her feel defensive, but it didn't. Instead of landing like a "gotcha," it felt more like an "I've got you," the satisfaction stemming from Sarah allowing herself to be caught.

"C'mon, Chloe. Can you show me where your mom keeps the stepladder?"

"Yep!"

"You sure you don't mind the extra help?" Sarah asked softly as Chloe scampered out of the kitchen.

"I could use an extra pair of hands."

Sarah shook her head. "Are you trying to impress me, or is this who you are?" Jass's expression shifted, making Sarah regret her words. She should not question Jass's kindness. There she was *shoulding* herself again.

"It's good for kids to learn stuff like this."

"You're right." Ever so briefly, Sarah wrapped her arms around Jass's shoulders. She pressed herself against Jass. "It's also good for me to learn how to accept help. Thank you for reminding me."

Jass rested her hand on Sarah's, and it felt like the snap of a clasp finding its home. In a flash, Jass was following Chloe down the hall to grab the stepladder from the garage, leaving Sarah to study how easily she inserted herself in Sarah's life. She sneaked past every one of Sarah's protective barriers.

Ten minutes later, Jass and Chloe stood triumphant in the kitchen, a strange-looking bulb in hand. None of the bulbs in the closet would fit.

"Do we have time to run to the hardware store?" Jass asked.

It wasn't actually the timing of dinner that was the issue. Letting Jass go to the hardware store for her meant acknowledging the place she was establishing in Sarah's heart and life. She had talked about this with Elodia. It was one of the things she wanted to talk to Jass about. "I haven't done the vegetables, and I have cheese to grate, lettuce to rip…" she stalled.

Chloe climbed onto a chair and surveyed the counter. "Are we having triceratops tacos?"

"Yes."

Chloe cheered. "They have Cheetos on top!"

"Sweet!" Jass said before Sarah could clarify that grown-ups were not required to consume the cheesy puffs. With one word, Jass disarmed her fear of inadequacy.

"I have about a half hour left."

"Plenty of time for a run to the hardware store. You in?" She held her palms out to Chloe, and Chloe quickly low-fived her.

"Yes!" she squealed.

"Are you sure you want a helper for that step?" Sarah asked, knowing how much Chloe slowed down a routine errand.

"I'm a good helper," Chloe argued.

Sarah smiled. "So I've heard." She played with Chloe's hair but had her eyes on Jass. "You won't be nearly as quick…"

Jass frowned, and Sarah wished they were not talking in front of Chloe. She didn't know what exactly she was reading in Jass's expression. "We're only looking for one thing."

Sarah found it difficult to concede, focused on how if it were her, she would prefer to run an errand on her own. Doubt crept into Chloe's eyes.

"With two pairs of eyes looking for the right bulb, we might be twice as fast," Jass argued.

Chloe lit up.

Sarah could hear her therapist advising her to let Jass in. Jass was offering. Again. Why didn't it get easier to accept it? "If you're sure…"

"Trust us." Jass winked at Chloe, reigniting the sparkle in her eye and reminding Sarah that when she let Jass in, she put Chloe's heart as well as her own on the line.

"Okay. Let's get you the car seat for your truck."

Once Chloe was secured, and they were off, Sarah pulled up a grown-up playlist as she continued to prepare dinner. These moments Jass gifted her brought home how much easier days went when she could pass off the baton momentarily. It felt different when Chloe was away for the weekend. There was pressure to decompress. Even the ten minutes it had taken for Jass and Chloe to figure out how to remove the lightbulb had been such a wonderful breather. The give-and-take with a second adult in the house was different. Shorter sprints instead of a marathon.

In no time, she was ready to plate, but Jass and Chloe had not returned. Weird. Feeling anxious, Sarah considered a glass of wine, just a small one to keep her from watching the clock. The phone rang and her heart squeezed tightly. Something was wrong.

"So my truck battery died," Jass explained.

"I'll come get you," Sarah said immediately, walking toward the door.

"That's silly. We're fine here. I just didn't want you to worry."

"But what are you going to do with Chloe?" Sarah asked, picturing the meltdown Tricia would have had if faced with the same inconvenience.

"We've got stuff we can do," Jass assured her. "I'll text you when we're on our way back."

Yet again, Sarah felt like she was putting Jass out. "I should come and get her."

"And by the time you get back, I'll probably be all squared away here. It probably won't take twenty minutes for the roadside assistance to get here. Why don't you enjoy the quiet?"

"Because I feel guilty that I let you do something nice and look at what it got you!" Sarah tried to vocalize her anxiety.

"Some time hanging out with my buddy. We'll let you know when we're on our way back."

She hung up. That was it. No swearing under her breath, no manipulative pauses or punishing tone. Simply the courtesy of knowing Sarah would be wondering why they weren't back yet. Sarah sat on one of the barstools, slowly turning her unfilled wineglass.

* * *

"Ready for sleep?" Sarah asked Chloe when she'd finished the third story.

Chloe breathed deeply, and Sarah almost got up, thinking she was asleep. "Do I have to go to Mama's tomorrow?" Chloe asked.

"It's your weekend with her."

"I know," Chloe grumped.

Sarah stroked her back. "Why don't you want to go to Mama's?"

"I want to play with the gliders."

"You could take them to Mama's."

"Jass flies them the best. I want to play with Jass. Can't you ask her to come tomorrow? She likes it when you make her dinner, and I like to play with her."

"I know you do."

"Did she go home?"

"Not yet."

"She could stay over. Then we could do the gliders before school."

Sarah sucked in a quick breath. Did Chloe know that she and Jass were together, or was she just focused on getting what she wanted? She was not prepared to talk to Chloe about Jass. What would she call Jass? Her girlfriend? It didn't feel like the right label. She wasn't in her twenties anymore. Bedtime was not the time to unpack any of that. "She has work, and I have work, and you!" Sarah stood and poked the covers in tight around Chloe. "You are officially tucked in!"

"Tell Jass good night."

"I will. I love you."

"I love you, too."

Sarah paused in the doorway to take a deep breath, letting it out slowly before she joined Jass in the living room. She plopped down on the couch beside Jass. "What a day."

"You could say that again."

Sarah reached out and threaded her fingers through Jass's hair. "I'm sorry about your truck."

"What? Please. No. This was way better than have it slow down my workday."

"This really is who you are, isn't it?"

Jass held Sarah's steady gaze. "I don't understand why it's so difficult for you to let me help out."

"I told my therapist about you, and she said you sound like a dream. I realize that she meant it as a compliment, but you know me. I think, when am I going to wake up and find you gone? Or when are you going to wake up and decide that I'm too much, that we're too much?"

"Like you were for Tricia? You think I'll leave like Tricia did?"

The corner of Sarah's mouth turned down. "I'm not comparing you to Tricia." She laughed. "Tricia would not have turned waiting for a battery replacement into something fun."

"I'd already had my eye on the gliders. I loved those things when I was a kid and wanted to get them with the replacement bulb, but I didn't know if you'd be okay about me buying them for Chloe. Then when we had all that time to kill…"

Sarah had not planned on kissing Jass. They had things to talk about, a whole list of things she had explored with Elodia. She could not think of a single thing now, only the need to kiss this kind and wonderful and sexy woman who had walked into her life. She scooted closer and cupped her hand behind Jass's head, pulling her for a deeper, more intimate kiss. She felt Jass hesitate for an instant, and in that instant, Sarah realized there was no door to shut. If Chloe got out of bed, she would see them on the couch. While she was weighing the risk, Jass pulled away.

She kept her eyes closed, and Sarah hated knowing that she was responsible for the inner struggle Jass was trying to sort out. She had no right to kiss Jass like and hold her at arm's length when they were with Chloe. How was she so brave? Sarah reached over and placed her hand on Jass's waist, tracing the circle of Jass's belly. God, she wanted this woman, wanted to be able to trust that everything was going to work out the way that Jass trusted her arrangement with Amara was going to work out.

Jass opened her eyes, and they mirrored Sarah's desire. The intensity frightened her. She took a steadying breath and searched for the bravery she had felt earlier.

"My therapist says that I'm allowed to be happy. She asked if I was really willing to martyr myself for my podcast. And now I'm seeing that it's not just me, it's Chloe. You make her happy, too. When I was tucking her in, she was asking why she has to go to Tricia's this weekend. She wants to stay here and have you come over to play with the gliders. I'm so scared, though, that I'll let people down. I've told so many people to focus on their kids instead of their own happiness. Won't they be angry if I admit that I fell in love with someone? It negates everything I've stood for."

Jass held Sarah's gaze. "Not everything, though."

Sarah tipped her head, trying to think from the listener's perspective.

"One of the reasons I listen to your podcast is because I know that you'll be real. You've shared difficult things before. You shared your divorce. You shared that you weren't coping so well. And your listeners love you for that. I love you for that. I agree with your therapist. You're allowed to be happy."

There was that word love again. Jass said it so easily. Sarah bit her lip. "I want to be able to love you."

"You have my permission."

This made Sarah laugh, and it felt so good. The tension and uncertainty with which she'd been wrestling slipped away, and all she wanted was to kiss Jass, to feel her skin, to fall into her. "I want you so badly," Sarah said.

"I'm right here."

"But I haven't told Chloe. As much as I want you, I can't have you stay over."

Jass whispered. "Are you going tell Chloe?"

She wanted to. But she could not fathom what she would say or when she would say it, and she did not know how she was going to feel in the morning. Right now, right now she could see the wisdom in Jass's honest approach. "I want to. I don't know how to. It seems like such bad timing with everything that happened with Tricia and Lydia. But I want to. I really, really want to."

Jass bit her lip. "It is so hard to be near you and not be able to touch you or look at you or be affectionate."

"Believe me. I know," Sarah said. She held out her hand. "Let me show you?"

"What about Chloe?"

"This is why doors have locks." She imagined shutting imaginary doors in her mind as well, ones that would keep out voices of fear and doubt. "Let me show you."

She knew that she was asking Jass to step onto a precarious branch, but it was all she could offer at the moment with the hope that it would hold them both for the night.

CHAPTER FORTY-SIX

Jass looked over her shoulder at the clearly wired Chloe and then quickly to Sarah in the driver's seat before returning her gaze out the window. Her heart fluttered, and her belly flip-flopped. She toed the bag at her feet, crossing her fingers in hopes this first outing as Sarah's girlfriend would go well. Sarah assured her that the conversation she'd had with Chloe had gone well, but Jass remembered so many of her mom's boyfriends and how things had gone back then. She was prepared for Chloe to turn into someone unrecognizable now that Jass was a potential threat to the relationship she had with her mom.

"Was Vasko a real bandit?"

"Vasquez." Jass turned in her seat to see Chloe better. "A hundred percent, Tiburcio Vasquez was a real bandit. He robbed all sorts of wagon trains and then hid out where we're going. You'll see why."

"And your dad took you there?"

"Yep."

He had, and it was one of the reasons Vasquez Rocks came to mind when she and Sarah called to say that she had asked Chloe about the three of them spending time together. The way Dave had included Jass was one of the things that had made him different from the other men her mom had dated. The hour-long drive meant it was no small gesture. She wanted both Sarah and Chloe to know that she was genuinely invested in them both.

Sarah smiled at her, and Jass reached across the console. When Sarah's fingers curled around her own, her stomach fluttered again. She pulled down the visor, using the mirror to look at Chloe. If she had noticed that Sarah had taken her hand, she wasn't showing it.

She celebrated her choice of destination when Sarah and Chloe wore twin expressions of wonder when they caught sight of the jagged rocks jutting dramatically at a forty-five degree angle from the ground. As she predicted, Chloe scampered up the sandstone happily exploring the nooks and crannies that had made it a such great hideout from law enforcement. If not for her protruding belly, Jass would have played sheriff. Sarah took that role, giving Chloe time to hide before announcing that she was there to haul any fearsome bandits off to jail.

While Sarah climbed with Chloe, Jass wandered the base of a formation looking for a perfect hiding spot. She moved quickly, so she could get back to the trail where she was certain Sarah would return once she captured Chloe. She heard and then saw them coming, inching down the rocks, holding each other's hands for balance, grinning broadly. Jass pulled out her phone and captured them in the other-world setting used in so many movies and TV shows.

"Fun?" she asked as Chloe scrambled off the rocks.

"Yes! But Mom says it's time for lunch."

"Good idea. The baby's hungry, too."

"The baby's always hungry," Chloe chirped.

"Always. And when they're born, all they'll do is eat, sleep, and poop."

"Really?" Chloe looked to Sarah for confirmation.

"Sounds about right," Sarah said.

"I want to feed the baby when it's born."

The adults stared at each other. Jass was still uncertain about overstepping with Chloe. "I'm sure Amara is going to be super tired and need lots of help," she offered.

"New moms do need a lot of help," Sarah agreed.

"I could use some help, too," Jass said.

"With what?" Chloe asked.

"Well, if this was where Vasquez came to hide after he robbed wagons, there should be treasure."

"Treasure!" Chloe clapped her hands.

Sarah tilted her head in question, and Jass answered with a *trust me* expression. "If I was looking for treasure, I'd look for a creek bed, wouldn't you? Where water might wash it out of its hiding place."

They continued, Chloe occasionally pointing off the trail. "Like that?"

"Exactly like that! Let's look!" Jass said, following Chloe off the trail.

It didn't take long for Chloe to spot the box Jass had set between some exposed tree roots. "Mommy! Treasure!" Chloe squealed.

"What in the world?" Sarah asked, joining her daughter to uncover the same fancy cigar box Dave had planted for her years ago. It still had his pocket change. Even though at ten, she had known what he'd done, it had touched her. She remembered poking him with a question about why, if Vasquez was robbing stagecoaches, there were no watches or necklaces, so she had added items from the thrift store for authenticity.

When she saw Chloe's face as she opened the box, she was glad she had. Blue eyes big as saucers went to Sarah and then to Jass. "Treasure," she whispered. She bit her lip. "We need to take it to the police. They'll know what to do."

Sarah bit back a chuckle. "We can let them know and ask them what to do."

Satisfied, Chloe carried the box to the picnic area where they had lunch as she arranged and counted coins and studied the costume jewelry and watches Jass had added. Absorbed in watching Chloe inventory the contents of the cigar box, Jass herself was startled when Sarah said, "Chloe, sweet, remember how we talked about how I'm spending more time with Jass?"

"Yeah. Dating. Like Mama and Lydia when Lydia made her happy."

Jass couldn't hold her surprised laughter, and she coughed to cover it up when she saw the stern look on Sarah's face.

"We talked about how you and I aren't going to change. The number of days you're with me isn't going to change. I would like for Jass to have dinner with us more often."

"So she won't eat cereal for dinner?"

"That's one reason."

Sarah sounded so level-headed, and it was taking all of Jass's resolve not to giggle at Chloe's perspective.

"I told you that you can always ask me questions or ask us questions. Do you have any today?"

Chloe paused the way Sarah did when she was really considering a question. "You said that you and Jass are dating like Mama dated Lydia. But Lydia left and Mama cried a lot. You smile a lot with Jass," she said, turning to her mom. Then she leveled her most serious face at Jass. "Are you going to make her cry?"

"Me? No!" Jass swore, her hand up like she was in court. "I mean, not if I can help it." She tried to think of how to explain the uncertainty of the future with Chloe. She needn't have bothered because Chloe's mind had already moved ahead, just as it did when they were reading books and Jass was in a panic to explain the way she liked Chloe's mom.

"Will this make the baby my cousin?" Chloe asked.

"Um," Jass said. She'd told Chloe that Amara was her sister, so if Jass and Sarah were together… "Yes?"

"Yes!" She pumped a little fist in the air. "That's almost as good as a sister or brother."

Jass had her arms folded on the table, and Sarah reached across to place her hand on Jass's forearm. Jass covered Sarah's hand with her own, and then Chloe added her little hand to the pile.

"Does this mean we can have slumber parties?" Chloe asked.

"If your mom says it's okay," Jass replied. "I brought my Dora the Explorer jammies."

"You did not," Sarah laughed.

"Would I lie about something like that?" She made a face at Chloe who erupted into giggles.

CHAPTER FORTY-SEVEN

As Chloe's eyes were getting heavy, Sarah's phone pinged. Regretfully she had forgotten to leave it in the kitchen for tuck-in. She crossed her fingers that Chloe had settled down enough that she wouldn't notice.

"Is it Mama?"

No such luck. "Let's see," Sarah whispered. "I'm sorry I had my phone in here."

"Thank you for your apology," Chloe said. Sarah cringed inwardly. She loved that Chloe did not feel obligated to say it was okay when it was not, but it stung to be held accountable by a five-year-old.

Sarah was even sorrier when she saw Tricia's text. *Can you talk?* Tricia wasn't calling to say good night to Chloe. She hadn't asked if Chloe was still up. Wanting to talk at seven forty-five on a Saturday night most likely meant she was having some kind of meltdown. Chloe didn't need to hear that. "It's someone from work. I'll call them back later." She tucked her phone in her pocket and stroked Chloe's forehead until her eyes grew heavy again.

"Sleep tight," she whispered. "I love you."

"I love you too, Mommy."

Down the hall, Sarah found Jass changing into her pajamas.

"You weren't lying," she said, wrapping her arms around Jass from behind. "These are adorable. How do you manage to be adorable and sexy at the same time?" She brushed Jass's hair to the side, so she could pepper Jass's neck with kisses.

"I wouldn't exactly call this sexy," Jass said, turning and pointing to her belly, the pajama top fanned out to the sides with only the top two buttons fastened.

Sarah had to laugh.

"I thought a large would cover more than this," she said sheepishly. "But they're way too long and not working at all here. Sorry."

"Don't be. Like I said. Adorable." She kissed Jass on the cheek. "Would you mind if I made a quick call?"

"Is everything okay?"

Sarah sighed. "Tricia texted me. I'll make it quick. I promise." She leaned against Jass, who despite it being early spring, already smelled of summer. "I have so many other things on my mind."

A slow smile crept across Jass's face. "I'm happy to hear that." She kissed Sarah deeply. "Do you need privacy?"

"No. Stay." They sat on the daybed, resting their backs against the wall. Jass took her hand, and Sarah took a deep breath, preparing for the whirlwind that was Tricia.

"Sarah!" Tricia boomed into the phone, a cacophony of voices and music competing with her voice. "I need your help so bad!"

"It's bedtime, Tricia. Were you calling to say good night to Chloe?"

"No. I came out to Club Tempo tonight, and fucking Lydia is here with someone. I can't…"

"Stop. No more words, Tricia," Sarah said firmly. If she didn't stop Tricia, she'd pick up momentum, and Sarah would be calming her hysterical ex for a half hour, minimum. "If you didn't call to talk to Chloe, I'm going to hang up. I can't talk to you about Lydia."

"But, Sarah! This is seriously gutting me! You have to help me!"

"No, Tricia. I don't. I cannot be your emotional support anymore. I can't be your therapist."

"I'm not asking you to therepitize me! I'm asking for some compassion!"

"I can't, Tricia."

"Yes, you can. You just won't. Why are you shutting me out?"

"Tricia, we aren't a couple. We are co-parents. I responded to your text in case there was something that would impact Chloe. Clearly, that isn't the case. So you need to call a friend or find a therapist you can talk to about how to cope with your hurt. It isn't my responsibility anymore, and I can't let it take any more of my energy."

"What? All of a sudden I'm not allowed to call you anymore?"

"I didn't say that you can't call me. I said I can't be your emotional support."

"Un. Fucking. Believable," Tricia swore.

"I'm sorry that you are hurting. Chloe would love to talk to you before bedtime sometime this week, but before seven-thirty, okay? She does best with a consistent bedtime."

"Can I say good night to her now?"

"It's almost eight, Tricia And we've had a big day. Talking to you would wind her up again."

"What does that mean, you had a big day?"

Why had she said that? Sarah leaned against Jass, trying to find the right words. Though Jass could not hear the conversation, she shifted, wrapping her arm around Sarah's shoulders. *You okay?* she mouthed.

"Sarah?" Tricia snapped her attention back to the conversation.

Sarah nodded to Jass. "We went to Vasquez rocks today. We hiked all day, so she needs her sleep." Sarah's heart pounded as she kept eye contact with Jass. She could leave it at that. She took Chloe on trips by herself all the time, but now was also a logical time to tell her about Jass. It would sting given that she'd seen Lydia with someone, but how long was she going to make excuses to not tell Tricia about Jass? How long did she plan on denying Jass that validation? "Jass invited us," she said.

"What? I couldn't hear you over the music."

"I said we went with Jass. On a date. To Vasquez rocks."

"Wait. You went where with who?"

"Jass took us to Vasquez rocks. We wanted to talk to Chloe about us."

"Hold up. You're telling me you can't talk to me about Lydia and in the very next breath, you're telling me that you're screwing the pool chick?"

"Her name is Jasmine."

"You fucking hypocrite!" Tricia yelled into the phone. "This is rich. You don't have time for me because you've got better fucking things to do? What happened to parents needing to focus on raising their kids, huh?"

"I was wrong," Sarah said. Jass rubbed gentle circles on Sarah's shoulder with her thumb.

"What? Now that you've ruined my future with Lydia, you can all of a sudden change the rules? Fuck that, Sarah. Fuck you!"

She hung up.

Sarah stared at the phone, not quite believing that Tricia had actually disconnected.

"What did she say?" Jass asked.

"She dropped a few f-bombs and called me a hypocrite." Sarah shrugged. "About what I expected."

"Do you want to talk about it?"

No, she did not. She wanted to take Jass to bed. She wanted to put Tricia and her meltdown behind her. "I can't yet. Give me a minute."

"Sure. Okay," Jass said.

"I'm not freaking out about telling her we're together."

Jass's head bobbed as she took a big breath in. "Okay. Thanks for telling me that."

Sarah had planned out a much different evening. Her conversation with Tricia had derailed it all, and she struggled to recenter herself. "Come with me," she said, scooching off the bed. It was ridiculous to share the small bed in the guest room that she'd been using. She retrieved clean sheets from the hall closet and walked to the master bedroom. Without a word, Jass followed and helped her make the bed.

Sarah tried to find words to express what she was feeling. Tricia did this to her, threw her into an emotional tangle that she had to pick at carefully, like she would a knotted necklace. She had learned that she had to approach the task unrushed. She was thankful Jass didn't push her to talk before she was ready. They worked together until the last of the covers were in place and they were ready for bed.

"I should've tumbled the sheets in the dryer," Sarah apologized when they had crawled in.

"They're fine," Jass said. "Are you really worried about the sheets? We could go back to the other bedroom if it's bothering you."

"No," Sarah said, tracing her fingers down Jass's arm. "I want to be here with you. My head is just a tangle. I wanted tonight to be about us. I wanted to talk about you being here, about Chloe and your cute pajamas and whether there was a chance of me talking you out of them."

"Always," Jass interjected.

Sarah pushed her head against Jass's with a smile. "I wanted to ask what you'd like to do for breakfast tomorrow and prepare you for how much energy Chloe is going to have in the morning. She's going to be so excited to have you here. I'm so excited that you're here."

"Is that why you're talking so much?" Jass leaned forward and kissed her lightly.

"I'm nervous."

"What about?"

"About how my life isn't lavender-scented sheets and uncomplicated mornings. Tricia will always be a part of our lives. It's complicated. I've been thinking about how I need to be firmer with my boundaries. I've been tiptoeing around Tricia because I'm afraid that if things are unsettled between us, she'll bail on Chloe. But it makes me so tired worrying about her."

"She's not your worry," Jass said.

"I think I figured that out today."

Jass sighed. "I wanted my dad around more when I was a kid. I wanted to spend time with him, but when we did end up doing something together, it felt like a punishment. My mom couldn't make him want to spend time with me."

Sarah let Jass's words settle and then said, "I thought it would be easier if we stayed together because I could make it all work. Then I had to admit I couldn't fix the relationship. Now I have to accept that even the law can't make Tricia grow up and be responsible."

"Nope. She's got to want it."

"If we do this, if we're together, I come with all this."

"Yep. And I come with Amara and this baby. I know it's not the same as Tricia, but…"

"No. I get what you're saying. It was hard for me to understand at first, but I'm starting to grasp that this is who you are. Giving and kind, caring and reliable, and loving, oh so lovable..."

"And this is who you are, someone who can sit with things that make you uncomfortable and grapple with them until they make sense to you. And you are loving, and oh so lovable."

"Thank you," Sarah whispered. She reached across the pillow and played with Jass's hair. Exhaustion, both physical and mental, settled onto her like a blanket. "I had other plans tonight."

"I'm happy to be held by you. I'm enjoying the afterglow of you telling your ex that you and Chloe went on a date with me."

"We did. And it was a good one. A memory day." Jass turned on her side, and Sarah spooned behind her, stroking her back as her breathing slowed. She kept waiting for the conversation with Tricia to spike her anxiety, but it never did. Why did she live waiting for the other shoe to drop instead of trusting what felt right? As she felt herself start to drift, she slid her arm around Jass's middle, resting her hand on her belly.

She felt a bump.

Had she imagined it?

No. There it was again, like a faint fist bump from Amara's unborn child, congratulating her for her progress at being human. Did Jass feel it? "Jass?" she whispered. But Jass was already fast asleep.

CHAPTER FORTY-EIGHT

"Ugh. I'm so glad we only have one more class." Jass grunted as she lowered herself into the passenger seat of Amara's car. As she grabbed the door handle, she guiltily looked around the parking lot, afraid one of the other couples might have overheard her.

"I'm sorry," Amara apologized. Again.

"It's not your fault this teacher is so clueless. I hoped after we talked to her last week that she'd lay off the…"

"Kissy, kissy!" Amara interrupted.

"I cannot be the first unpartnered woman to take this class. What if my mother was bringing me?"

"Gross," Amara agreed. "I hoped it would be better this week."

Jass shook her head. The woman obviously had retained nothing after the couples introduced themselves. Tonight during the relaxation exercise, she had awkwardly tried to correct herself. "Let's have our ladies lean back against their husband"—and with a befuddled glance in their direction—"or…person." She hoped the nurse did better with other nontraditional families.

It made for a difficult dynamic. Jass wished there was a class specifically for surrogates, someone to talk to about it. Jass felt some camaraderie with the other mothers who were in the third trimester and experiencing exhaustion. At week thirty-two she was starting to wonder if maybe the umbilical cord was like a charger because as the baby's energy increased, Jass's plummeted. But when the conversation moved to the hypothesis that disrupted sleep prepared new mothers for breastfeeding during infancy, Jass felt isolated.

Did any surrogates think about breastfeeding? Or once the baby arrived, did they hand the baby over and wait for their milk to dry up? How long was that going to take? Would it be painful? The class might have made her uncomfortable, but it also brought up the issues she and Amara needed to talk about. "The content was pretty good tonight, though. I had no idea there was such a thing as a lactation consultant!"

"Or that babies can have trouble latching! Who knew!"

"Do you want the baby to breastfeed?"

Amara's head whipped toward Jass and then back to the road. Then she looked at Jass again. Her gaze dropped to Jass's chest and then her own.

"Sorry. I mean do you have an investment in the baby having breast milk? It sounds like there are good pumps available."

"You're already doing so much. I didn't want to ask."

Jass shrugged. "You definitely want the baby to have colostrum, don't you? And if that brings in my milk, why wouldn't we keep doing that? I'm not saying I'll breastfeed. I know it's important for you to do the feeding and create a bond with the baby." In the dark of the car, she couldn't read Amara's body language or facial expression well. They had to communicate even if it was difficult. "Is it hard for you to be there with all those couples?"

"It really sucks," Amara said. "The way she talked about moms pumping to help dads feel more connected to the baby..." She blew out a long breath. "I'm scared about what it's going to be like. Of course I want the baby to have colostrum, but then what if that bonds them to you? What if that makes it harder for them to bond with me? And then I feel like an asshole. You're doing all these amazing things, and I'm worried that the baby will only want to be with you."

"This is *your* baby," Jass said, unwavering. She wished her emotions were as stable as her voice. Spending hours around the other couples who were talking about nesting and maternity leave and how baby makes three had her mind spinning and spinning on what it was going to be like to hand over the baby and walk away. What if she felt like a piece of her had been lost forever? Sarah had warned her that they had not thought it through, but in reality, who could think through every aspect of something like that? Jass was constantly trying to keep control of her thoughts, focusing on what it was going to be like and trying to shut the door on her worries. She snort-laughed.

"What?" Amara asked.

"I'm thinking about how Sarah says to shut the door on unproductive thoughts. I'd like to keep the "what if" door about what it's going to be like after the baby comes shut, but maybe we didn't think everything through."

"How could we, really? Some things you have to do on faith."

Jass reached for Amara's hand. "I have faith in the baby adoring you."

Amara squeezed. "Thanks. I don't know what I was thinking signing up for that class. I should have at least signed us up in West Hollywood instead of throwing us into this heteronormative vat."

"Isn't it a given since it's where I'll have the baby? It was good to talk about the birth certificate, and I don't know if you've been doing research on birth plans, but I sure haven't. How do we feel about drugs?"

Amara swung her car into her parking space and busied herself getting out. "Come see the room."

Jass heaved herself out of the car. "Does this mean no epidural for me?"

"Totally your call, lady. You want an epidural, you get an epidural."

Jass took out her phone and texted Sarah. *Did you get an epidural with Chloe?*

"Asking your woman?"

"Is that okay?"

"She's a good resource," Amara said, but there was something in her voice.

"What?"

"It's nothing. It's stupid." Amara unlocked the door and immediately started up the stairs. Jass followed, now convinced it was definitely something.

Standing in the nursery, she couldn't ask what Amara was feeling. Amara walked to a table by the crème-colored rocker and snapped on a lamp. Amara's photos did not do the room justice. The light-green walls were calming but bright. On the wall with the delicate white crib, a mural of a tree-branch extended protectively. Delicate leaves suggested early spring. "Amara! It's amazing!" Jass turned to take in the dresser with changing pad at the ready. She opened a drawer organized with rows of diapers and tiny, neatly folded clothes.

"This is what they're wearing home from the hospital." Amara pulled out a forest green garment that looked like a gown. "No feet. Just slide it on and knot it at the bottom. Good, right? It's got to be easier than getting arms *and* legs poking through the right places."

"It's perfect. The room is perfect. It's *all* perfect, and this is why you're the mom. And now I have to sit."

"Try the rocker!"

Jass did. She closed her eyes and rocked. "Yes," she said, drawing the word out over many syllables. "You did good." Jass's phone chimed.

What am I, a cavewoman? Of course I did drugs!

Jass smiled.

"What did Sarah say?"

"How do you know it's Sarah?"

"Who else makes you smile like that?"

"That's fair. She said do the epidural."

Amara sat on the ottoman and chewed her lip.

"Would you rather I not talk to Sarah about the baby?"

"No!" Amara said a little too quickly.

"What, then?" A text came in, and she read it quickly, Sarah asking how class went. She tapped out that it was fine and that she was at Amara's. She tucked her phone in her pocket and turned her full attention to her best friend.

She shrugged. "I said it's nothing." Jass wasn't letting her off the hook. She put her feet in Amara's lap and closed her eyes. Someone should really talk to the person who decided a birthing class should start at six. Jass was exhausted. But she wasn't going anywhere until Amara talked.

Amara pushed off Jass's shoes and rubbed her feet. "Oh, honey. Aren't you sweet listening to what the teacher said about taking care of Mom."

They stared at each other, said "Kissy, kissy" in unison and then burst into laughter.

The tension broken, Amara sighed. "I'm just jealous. I feel like the baby only moves for Sarah and Chloe."

"They move for you, too!" Jass reached for Amara's hand and stretched it to her round belly. "I'm sorry I made you feel jealous. I loved how Sarah described it like a fist bump, and Chloe was so ecstatic when she felt the baby move. I thought you'd want to know."

"I know. I did. I appreciate how you text me so much."

"It's been hard with you doing all the work on the room. I'll see you more now that it's done, right?" Jass asked, but it felt hollow. Yes, she'd been careful not to visit Amara when her place was full of paint fumes, but the reality was that she spent most of her free time with Sarah and Chloe. This made her feel terrible. She didn't want to be the friend who ditched her for her girlfriend, especially when she was Amara's baby mama. "I'm sorry we haven't been spending more time together."

"I get it," Amara sighed. "I'm happy for you."

Jass knew there was more. "But…"

"But the baby spends all this time with Sarah and Chloe. You look like the families we see at the birth class."

"I told you what Chloe said when Sarah told her about us, didn't I?"

"That she wanted to know if the baby would be her cousin."

"Exactly. She knows this isn't my baby."

"Would you have a baby with Sarah?"

"Whew. Now there's a tough question. I don't know if she wants more kids. I don't even know if she ever wants to get married again. It scares me to ask."

"But it's what you want."

"Yeah. I want to be like the couples in class. I want my life completely entwined with someone. Like we're starting a new life together."

"We're starting a new life. Doesn't that entwine us?"

Jass smiled and tickled Amara's side with her toes. "Of course we're entwined. You and I are for always, but…"

"Not like the couples at the class. I know. I feel it too."

"C'mere." Jass took Amara's hands and pressed them to her belly again. "They're starting to bump around. Sing a song."

"Like what? I don't know any baby songs."

"Sing anything. Or tell the baby about the room. Or your day. Or how awesome their *tìa* Jass is."

"You really are awesome." Amara fanned her fingers out across Jass's tummy like she was holding a basketball. She aimed her face to the ball shape and said, "You're awesome, too, baby." Like knocking on a door, the baby thumped against Jass's womb. Amara's eyes flew to Jass's. "I felt that!"

"We've got this," Jass said, keeping her focus on certainties instead of things beyond her control. Amara was right about their being entwined. Would there still be room for Sarah and Chloe when the baby came, or would this baby inevitably make a family out of Jass and Amara? She sat in the baby's room thinking about how Chloe had asked if Jass would bring the baby back after it was born. Jass wasn't sure how Sarah would feel about that. She knew Amara, sure, but she also knew that Amara wasn't *really* Jass's sister. Did that matter? Or could they be a new kind of family tree?

Jass stared at the tree painted on the wall and recalled how branches could be grafted. There was a tree on her route that looked like any other tree until the springtime when it flowered. Some branches had deep plum blooms while others had snowy white ones. How long did it take to know whether a graft had taken?

The baby bumped against Amara's hands again, their blossom getting closer to bloom.

CHAPTER FORTY-NINE

"Here we are!" Sarah said, pulling up at Tricia's apartment.

Chloe unbuckled and jumped out of the car without protest, but the quiet worried Sarah. Sarah's dropping Chloe off was a new strategy, one that Sarah hoped would quell the need to remind Tricia about the importance of being on time.

"When are the fireworks?" Chloe asked the instant Tricia opened the door.

Tricia looked surprised by the outburst. "Not until it's dark. You're going to have to be patient."

"I'm not good at patient," Chloe grumped.

Sarah laughed. "We know where you got that!" She echoed both Chloe's desire for fireworks and frustration at having to wait. It had been more than a month since she had had an evening free to spend with Jass. After she had told Tricia about their relationship, she had been even less dependable when it came to taking Chloe every other weekend. With Jass at the house more often than not, she had found that it was easier to tell Tricia to "pick it and stick it" than insist she maintain having Chloe overnight every other week.

Now Tricia suggested an outing, like taking Chloe to see the fourth of July fireworks and had much better follow-through.

"Are you sure you're not interested?" Tricia asked. "It's all queer families, and they walk over to the Colorado Street bridge to watch the fireworks at the Rose Bowl. It sounds like it's going to be great!"

"Can you? Can Jass?" Chloe asked, her eyes full of hope. Sarah gritted her teeth at Tricia's asking in front of Chloe.

"I appreciate the invite, but it won't work this year." Sarah knelt to give Chloe a big hug. "Remember, Jass isn't supposed to go too far when the baby is so close to coming. Maybe next year."

"Okay!" Chloe squeezed her back and ran into the apartment.

"Worried about being spotted with your new girlfriend out in public?" Tricia asked when Chloe was out of earshot.

Sarah was sorry that her being with Jass still caused Tricia pain. She had an all-too-clear memory of how badly it had hurt when Tricia had started to date again. They had invested so much in each other when they'd married. Would they ever be able to be around each other and not feel a pulse in the old wounds? When she and Jass had first started sleeping together, she would have answered Tricia's question defensively. Today, she answered with care. "No. It really does sound like fun, and someday, I see all of us being able to do that. But not today."

Tricia pulled her brows together. "You really see that happening?"

"Absolutely. We're going to blink and it will be Halloween, and Chloe will want all the grown-ups in her life to see her costume. And then it will be Thanksgiving and Christmas. I'd like for Chloe to not have the shuffle from house to house on those important days."

They stood in silence, negotiating their new boundaries. As much as Sarah was happy to have a free evening, it was difficult to leave Chloe. As far as she and Tricia had come, there was still quicksand that Sarah vowed to avoid today. Sometimes Chloe was more receptive to a fist bump than a hug. Sarah held out her fist. Tricia looked confused for a second but then bumped her knuckles against Sarah's.

On impact, Sarah popped her fingers out like an explosion, wiggling her fingers as she retracted her hand. "Enjoy the fireworks."

"Yeah. You, too," Tricia said. "They'll be over late. You sure you don't want her to stay over?"

"She didn't pack for that, and it's fine. I'll be up." Sarah trotted down the stairs to her car, leaving Tricia with whatever she was wrestling. It felt a hundred times better to Sarah to have this new arrangement. Chloe no longer argued about spending time with Tricia. If it worked for her, that was what mattered.

The house was quiet when she returned. She moved carefully through the house in case Jass was taking a nap. When she found both the bed and the couch empty, she stepped outside. In the midday heat of July, Jass could only be one other place.

Sarah's heart warmed when she spotted Jass on her favorite pool float. Sarah kicked off her flip-flops and dangled her legs into the pool.

Jass tipped her head in Sarah's direction and smiled.

It filled her, that smile, as did the question that followed.

"How'd the drop-off go?" She paddled until the float bumped up against Sarah's knees.

"Good." Sarah threaded her fingers through Jass's wet hair.

Jass sighed deeply. "I'm staying right here for the rest of this pregnancy."

Sarah laughed. "Sounds good to me."

"You coming in?"

"I hadn't planned on getting wet," she said without thinking about her words.

Jass splashed in Sarah's direction. "That's too bad. I've been cooking up such a good fantasy while I waited for you."

"Did you? And it involved me getting wet?"

"Oh, it did."

Jass's words were already working their magic on Sarah. She tingled in anticipation of Jass's touch and didn't have to wait long for Jass to run a cool, wet hand up her calf and thigh, stopping at the cuff of her shorts.

Sarah leaned forward and captured Jass's lips with her own. She kissed her, unhurried, knowing she had hours and hours to soak in the deliciousness of wanting Jass. Jass reached her hand behind Sarah's head and pulled her closer. Sarah gasped as Jass's wet hand lifted her hair from her neck. Jass took advantage, sliding her tongue along Sarah's, stroking until Sarah was breathless with desire. "You've already made me so wet," she whispered when they had to break for air.

"We should do something about that." Jass dipped her hand

into the pool and dripped water onto Sarah's thigh. Eyes holding Sarah's, she pulled the raft out from under her, stripped off her top and tossed it onto the deck next to Sarah. She waggled her eyebrows before she went underwater, emerging with swim shorts that joined her top.

Sarah's heart pounded. "What about the neighbors?"

Jass waggled her eyebrows again. "Incentive to practice being quiet?" She pushed away from Sarah then, moving gracefully through the water.

The neighboring yards were quiet. She rationalized that the only people outside would be in pools. She stood and as quickly as possible shucked off her clothes, jumping in with a shriek. The water wasn't cold, but Sarah's whole body came alive as she moved naked through the water to Jass.

Jass moved away from her. "How does it feel? You asked me once about swimming naked. What do you think?"

"Amazing," she said, trying to catch Jass. She ached to touch her. Jass was a stronger swimmer and easily kept out of her reach.

She submerged again, but this time instead of swimming away, she emerged in front of Sarah, sweeping her hands up Sarah's hips and grazing her breasts before she guided Sarah to the wide stair. There, Jass wrapped her arms around Sarah, pulling their bodies flush. Sarah's body went molten in Jass's hands that felt silken on her skin. "Do you know how many times I have imagined you naked in this pool?"

"A few?" Sarah breathed as Jass kissed her neck.

"More than that." Jass lowered her mouth and circled her tongue around Sarah's nipple before scraping her teeth across its surface. Water ebbed and flowed across Sarah's skin as Jass nipped and touched until the ache between her legs begged to be touched.

"I want you to touch me."

"I know." Jass continued to tease her, sweeping her hand from Sarah's knees up along the inside of her thigh, just skimming the patch of hair before continuing up Sarah's belly.

"Jass," Sarah growled.

She could tell her impatience delighted Jass in the way she made eye contact when her hand reversed direction. "Sarah," she said.

In this moment, she could see the promise of more than days, of years, of decades. She trusted Jass. Could that last a lifetime? Their connection felt like it could weather the ebb and flow that came with commitment. For years, Sarah had resisted divorce because she did not want to fail. The way Jass looked at her made her feel like there was an opportunity to succeed.

She caressed Jass's heavy breasts, ran her thumb across the darkened nipples and down around her round belly. "I've loved watching your body change. Have I told you lately how wonderful you are?"

"You're wonderful," Jass said. She slipped her fingers through Sarah's folds. Sarah arched her head back and raised her hips, begging to feel Jass inside. Jass continued to tease, circling Sarah's clit with steady pressure. Sarah gripped the side of the pool, Jass's hand keeping her from floating away.

"That feels so good," Sarah whispered.

"I have an idea." Jass pulled Sarah's earlobe with her teeth.

"So far, I have really liked your ideas."

"Let's go inside where we don't have to worry about being quiet."

"Yes, please."

They toweled off as they ran to the house. They did not have to wait until dark for fireworks.

CHAPTER FIFTY

Jass surely hoped that she would have more minutes in the day after the baby came. As it was, she and Sarah had been trying to find a moment to sit and talk about something that had come up on her show, but the only time they had alone was right before bed, and by then Jass was half asleep.

Thus, she found herself at the end of her Thursday route at Sarah's with her thumb hovering over the play button of the latest podcast. She'd promised Sarah she wouldn't listen until they had talked.

But Sarah's request had thrown a spark on Jass's tinderbox of anxiety. Her heart sank a bit guessing that it was about whether they could fully be a couple. It felt better that Chloe and Tricia knew, but Jass felt like she remained a guest in Sarah's home, not a member of the family.

She looked toward the house. Since Chloe hadn't burst out to help Jass with the weekly maintenance, they were probably out together. Maybe she and Sarah would have time to talk when they returned. She'd waited three days to listen. She was itching to know what Sarah was exploring.

She hit play.

"Hello, everybody! I'm Sarah. I'm a licensed marriage and family therapist which makes me The Sarapist, and in today's episode I'm going deeply into what it means to be a family. Remember the neighbor who helped me work through my shame about my divorce? We had the most interesting conversation I've been mulling over ever since…"

Jass relaxed into her routine, Sarah's voice filling her with warmth as it always did. She moved more slowly than usual. In another week, Dave and his employees would be taking over her route. The day it hit her that she would need maternity leave, Dave texted to ask for her route and the dates she wanted covered.

Though Sarah had changed their names to maintain their privacy, Jass could easily identify Casey and Adrienne when Sarah explained that they were not married, so technically Adrienne's granddad, Marv, was not Casey's family. Casey's parents were still married, but Adrienne's parents had divorced. Adrienne was not interested in marriage. Casey was struggling with wanting to meet her girlfriend where she was but also fulfill her desire to have a recognized partnership.

"It's an interesting question for the queer community," Sarah was saying. Finished checking the chemicals, Jass grabbed the skimmer net. "Now that same-gendered couples have the right to marry, there's an argument that joining this failed institution is assimilation. I see truth in this, both in how I thought that marrying would validate my experience and how I felt defined as a failure by my divorce. My neighbor put me in an utter tailspin when she asked me whether I would ever marry again."

Jass pressed the button on her headset to pause the episode. This was why Sarah wanted to talk to her before she listened. Should she wait? She finished skimming and changed the vacuum head. She poked her phone on the cart to see how much of the episode was left. More than half. She should listen to music. She picked up her phone and texted Amara. *Have you listened to the new The Sarapist is In?*

Undulating dots kept Jass in place. *Not yet. Is it good?*

So far. Scared to listen to more. Sarah said to wait, but I couldn't. Shit.

Right?

What are you going to do?
Wait?
Want me to listen at 2x speed?
No! You don't get to listen first!

Jass set the phone on her cart and pursed her lips. Sarah would be home soon. She couldn't imagine Sarah wanting to listen to it together. She would understand Jass's curiosity, wouldn't she? But what if she was going to say she never wanted to get married again? Maybe that was why she wanted to talk beforehand, to soften the blow. Jass busied her hands setting up the vacuum tubing, her stomach heavy with doubt. She might as well face whatever it was Sarah was thinking.

Feeling a bit like she was reading Sarah's diary, she clicked her earbud back to play.

"Marrying would of course mean dating, and I've been very clear about my position on single parents and dating."

Despite the July heat, Jass felt cold.

"For me to even consider marrying again, I'd have to be dating, and I've given all sorts of professional reasons to explain why single parents shouldn't date. I adopted a position that I now realize was based in fear. Fear of hurt and rejection. Fear of judgment. Talking to my neighbor it's clear that, married or not, my neighbor's girlfriend's family is my neighbor's family. This sounds a lot like my girlfriend who is carrying a baby for her friend because, though they are not related by blood, they are family."

Wait. Jass wished she could back up from her earpiece. Sarah said girlfriend. But the way she said it, her audience could see it as Jass being a woman Sarah knew who, like Casey, had a different idea of family. She pressed play again.

"This makes for a complicated relationship when I already have a child, an inquisitive child who says, 'who is this baby to me?' A child who has been saying, 'who is your girlfriend to me?' She has a Mommy and a Mama already, and she is trying to find the language to explain this new relationship..."

Chloe was trying to label her? How did Jass not know this! She tucked her hand under her belly. Once the baby was Amara's, would the tie she had to Sarah and Chloe be less clear somehow?

Sarah had been talking parallel to Jass's thoughts, so she missed some of what she said but startled when she heard the word marriage.

"…marriage back on the table. It isn't something that I'd thought about until I was able to recognize that it wasn't so much that getting divorced made me a failure. It hurt me, and I didn't want to hurt that way again. Not to sound clichéd or like some country song, but this woman came along and opened my eyes to see that to love and be loved is to risk hurt. My neighbor's girlfriend said she doesn't need the government to legitimize their relationship. She needs only the promise that her girlfriend will hold her heart with as much care and tenderness as she holds her own. I'm ready for that too.

"I'm ready for the branches of my family to stretch further. I'm ready to find a name for who this new woman is to me and my daughter. And even though there's no law that connects me to the baby she's carrying, they are my family. So this is me being my best self, my fallible self, my learning self. I hope you will stay on this journey with me."

Jass stood dumbstruck, on information overload. If this was how Sarah felt, why had she told her listeners before she'd told Jass? Sure, she'd said she wanted to talk about the episode, but couldn't she have held the episode until she'd talked to Jass first? Was this really how she felt or simply something to explore for podcast content?

"Jass!"

The screen door slammed, and Jass turned toward the house, not remembering that she was vacuuming with the skimmer box open. Her foot dipped through the hole, throwing her off balance.

With her heavy belly, there was no way to avoid going down, and she wasn't going down on cement. Windmilling like crazy, she pitched herself right into the pool.

CHAPTER FIFTY-ONE

"Mommy! Mommy! MommyMommyMommyMommy!"

Sarah paused on her way to the bathroom. They had been home for all of thirty seconds. Could she not have one minute to herself to pee? Chloe had been so excited to see Jass's truck in the drive that she'd hoped she was going to have a minute to catch her breath after a long day. She shut the bathroom door. She was allowed a moment to herself, wasn't she? Chloe pounded on the door. Apparently not.

"Mommy! Jass fell in the pool!"

Sarah jerked open the door. "She fell in? Are you sure?"

"I said hi to her, and she did..." Chloe whipped her arms around in circles. "You have to save her!"

Chloe grabbed her hand and took off at a run. Sarah followed. By the time they got to the pool, Jass was climbing the steps, sopping wet.

"Jass!" Sarah threw open the gate and took her by the arms. "What in the world?"

"I fell in!"

"That's what Chloe said! Are you okay?"

"I'm fine. I'm fine."

"Are you sure? Did you hurt yourself?" Sarah ran her hands over Jass's body, searching for anything amiss. "We need to get you a towel."

Jass grimaced when she took a step.

"You are hurt! We need to take you to the hospital."

Jass examined her ankle. "I don't need a hospital. I scraped my ankle when I fell. It's no big deal." She removed her earbuds and held them up to Sarah. "You said you wanted to talk about your last episode. What did you want to say to me?"

Sarah looked at Chloe and then back to Jass. "Towel first."

"No." Jass took a step back instead of following Sarah toward the house.

"Jass? What is it? Did you listen to it already? I asked you to wait. Chloe, could you run and get Jass a towel?" She opened the gate, and Chloe looked from one adult to the other.

"Are you fighting?"

"No. We're talking," Sarah said.

Chloe took a step back. "What about?"

"About some things I said on my podcast." Sarah found herself smiling at how Chloe's posture paralleled Jass's. Didn't Jass see what she meant about their being a family already despite not having adopted any labels? "I asked Jass to wait to listen to it."

"You didn't listen to Mommy?" Chloe asked, now scrutinizing Jass.

"I always listen to them when they drop! And I couldn't understand why you would say not to listen. And then I did, and I find out that you told the whole world about us. Why would you tell them and not me?"

"I wanted to tell you!" Sarah stepped to Jass and wrapped her arms around the dripping woman. "Welcome to my life where something I've put at the top of my list of priorities can get knocked off. I wanted the first time I said I can't lose you to be special, but it's been one thing after another pulling me in a different direction."

"We sleep in the same bed every night."

"I know. I should have just said 'I love you, Jass, and I want all your days.' But I didn't. And I'm sorry. I shouldn't have asked you not to listen. I should have waited on the episode, but I was so excited. I *am* excited. You make me dream all sorts of new possibilities. I want us to name that. Can we?"

Chloe squealed. "Do we get to keep Jass?"

"You make me sound like a lost..."

Jass didn't have time to say *kitten* before Chloe slammed into her legs for a group hug. Jass wasn't expecting Chloe to lunge for her and took a step back forgetting how close she was to the side of the pool. For the second time in minutes, she lost her balance. She tried to right herself by grabbing Sarah but only managed to throw her off balance as well.

The three tumbled into the pool together.

Sarah came up with a gasp. "Oh, no! Oh, no!" She reached for Chloe. She grabbed at Jass. Chloe was already surfacing in the float as she had been taught at eighteen months old, her safety training kicking in. Jass emerged from the water with a glorious smile, laughter pouring from her.

"You fell."

Sarah splashed her. "You pulled me in!" She tapped Chloe's hand, and the girl turned and swam to Jass, wrapping her arms around her neck.

"Whoa! Whoa!" Jass swam to the edge with her barnacle firmly in place. Again, she said to Sarah, "You fell. And you told everyone."

Sarah understood now. "I did. Head over heels, I fell for you. And I told everyone."

"I fell, too!" Chloe announced, placing one of her tiny hands on Jass's cheek. "Will you be my Jass forever?"

Sarah rested her hand against Jass's other cheek. "You have to share. Will you? Be ours, Jasmine? Forever?"

Jass reached around Chloe to pull Sarah into the hug. "I'm already yours. I have been all along."

Sarah stretched to kiss her on the lips, and Chloe kissed her on the cheek. "How did I get so lucky?"

"I could ask the same thing," Jass said. She made a face.

"What is it?"

"Nothing."

"Are you okay? Are you in pain?"

"No." She shook her head. "A funny twinge is all. I didn't hit anything going in the second time. I'm sure I'm fine."

"We should call Amara."

"Don't be dramatic."

"I'm not. Come on. Out of the pool. Let us take care of you."

They hoisted themselves out of the pool, laughing at each other. "You all get dry. I'll be in after I finish the pool."

"Nonsense. The pool can wait. You're coming in now." Sarah was not going to walk away from Jass, not with the grimace she'd made. She worried that Jass wasn't being honest about how she felt.

"I'll get the pool hose out!" Chloe said, squishing across the pavement in her sandals. She reached into the skimmer and pulled the tubing free from the pump.

"That kid's got a future." Jass used the net to retrieve the pole on the vacuum.

"She's learned so many good tricks from you, case in point." Sarah took the pole from Jass. "Tell me what to do."

"I'm not helpless!"

"I'm worried about you. While we clean this up, you're texting Amara. She needs to know what happened. And then you're putting her number in my phone, so I can make sure you told her."

"Aye, aye Ms. Bossypants," Jass grumped to Chloe.

Chloe giggled, but Sarah noticed a slight gimp when Jass retrieved her phone. Chloe told her how Jass wrapped the hose, and they were finally able to go inside to get into dry clothes. Sarah kept a keen eye on Jass, but she insisted through the evening that she was fine, that her scraped ankle was her only ailment. Despite Jass's assurances, she texted Amara to have her hospital bag at the ready.

Finally, Sarah climbed into bed and nestled into Jass as best she could around her enormous belly and the multiple pillows she used to help her sleep. "I love you. I should have told you days ago."

"This was more memorable." She squeezed Sarah. "I love you, too."

"You're really okay?"

"Stop worrying about me. I'm more than okay. I'm perfect."

"That you are. Sweet dreams."

Jass was already fast asleep. Sarah lay awake beside her for a long while listening to her breathe and to the sounds of the night, wondering again how she had gotten so lucky.

CHAPTER FIFTY-TWO

Jass loved the animal-shaped pancakes Sarah made for breakfast. She loved sharing a table with Chloe.

"Full yet?" Sarah flipped another golden pancake out of her frypan.

"Still eating for two!" Jass said, scooching forward to hoist herself up for one more pancake. Something didn't feel right. She looked down as she felt the whoosh of water spill from her body. She sat. It was happening. The baby was coming. She couldn't move or speak.

"Jass?" Sarah said.

"I think my water just broke," Jass whispered.

Chloe looked confused. "But you have orange juice."

"Jass is saying the baby is coming." Sarah rushed from the stove. "Are you in pain? Have you been having contractions?"

"I don't feel a thing. But all of a sudden…" She looked down at the puddle by her feet.

"Come on! Let's get moving. I'll grab your hospital bag while you call Amara. Tricia will have to meet us at the hospital."

"Tricia?" Jass asked, confused.

"To pick up Chloe."

"I want to stay with Jass and the baby!"

"Chloe, honey. We don't know how long it's going to be. You don't want to sit in a hospital waiting room all day."

"Neither do I," Jass said. "I'm not ready to go yet. I'm not even having contractions! Why can't I stay here?"

"Your water broke! That means you go to the hospital."

"I don't remember that part."

Sarah pulled out her phone, dialed, and showed it to Jass. Jass was not surprised to see Amara's name on the screen before she put it to her ear. Feeling oddly like a leaky faucet, she carefully made her way to the bathroom.

"Sarah? Is everything okay?" Amara answered.

"It's me. Sarah says I have to go to the hospital if my water breaks. Is that true?"

"Did your water break?" Amara shrieked.

"Yes?"

"Am I picking you up, or are we meeting at the hospital?"

"Nothing's even happening yet," Jass complained. "Can't I finish my breakfast?"

"*Yet* is the key word in all that. Brush your teeth. I'm coming to get you."

Jass sat in the bathroom with her hands on her belly. "I don't know if I can do this," she whispered.

"I've got a change of clothes for you. Can I bring them in?"

Jass knew all sorts of people were going to see her parts today. Resigned, she rested her elbows on her knees and cradled her head. Something pulled deep inside. Jass let out an "Ooof."

Sarah set the clothes on the counter. "There's a box of pads in the drawer. I'm guessing you need one."

Jass looked up and saw a worried Chloe behind Sarah. "I'm fine," she said. "Amara's taking me to the hospital. I'll be back once I push this baby out."

"You're not going without us," Sarah said.

Chloe's face lit up.

"I'll get Jass's bag," Sarah said. "You get yours."

"I don't want to go to Mama's. I want to stay with Jass."

"We'll talk about it at the hospital. No matter what, you need fun things to do while you wait. It might take Jass's body a long time to…"

Jass gripped the counter and sucked in a breath through her teeth.

Sarah stepped closer to Jass and rubbed soothing circles on her back. "You can do this."

"What if I can't? What if it's too hard?"

"I did it, and there's really not a choice. That baby's coming out."

Jass nodded. "I'm scared."

"Well, it's a scary thing, but think of the millions of women who have done it before you, lots of whom went out behind a bush and just squatted the baby out. At least you don't have to do that! Let's get you into dry clothes. That's step one. One step at a time, okay?"

"Step one," Jass agreed, reaching for the clothes in Sarah's hands.

In no time, they were waiting for the elevator to take them up to Labor and Delivery. Amara punched the button repeatedly as if it would bring the elevator more quickly. Jass held Sarah's hand, and Sarah held Chloe's. The doors opened.

"Mama!" Chloe said.

Jass whipped her head around. She knew Tricia was coming for Chloe but was not prepared to actually have her at the hospital. Jass rarely saw Tricia, either because Sarah was dropping Chloe off at Tricia's apartment or because Tricia no longer came inside when she dropped Chloe back at the house. Jass did not want any animosity on her delivery day.

Amara stepped inside the elevator and held the door. "Let's go!"

Jass crinkled her brows at Amara. Whose side was she on? Tricia hung back from the group.

"You, too," Amara said. "Y'all are going to have to suck it up for three minutes. We'll get everything sorted out once we're upstairs."

Chloe took Tricia's hand and pulled her in, a grin stretched from ear to ear. She bounced on the balls of her feet as if the elevator would be delivering them to Disneyland. Sarah squeezed her hand, pulling Jass's attention. *You're okay*, she mouthed.

Comforted by Sarah's words, Jass nodded and her insides pulled, and not just because of the contractions. Everything would change today.

The doors opened, and there was only one thing to do. She gathered her courage and waddled to the nurse's station, still clutching Sarah's hand. Amara had called ahead, so the staff was ready for her. Jass handed over her insurance card.

"It looks like someone's ready to have a baby today!" a male nurse said, approaching the group. "I'm Àngel. I'll be your delivery nurse. You brought a whole fan club!"

The Spanish pronunciation matched his relaxed posture and immediately put Jass at ease. "How many people are allowed to be in the delivery room?" she asked. When she and Amara had done the birthing classes, it had never occurred to her to ask if Sarah could be there with her, but now she could not imagine leaving her in the waiting room.

"That's up to Mom," Àngel said.

Jass turned to Amara. "I know we didn't talk about it, but would it be okay for Sarah to stay?"

"I've told you a gazillion times. I get a baby at the end of this. You get whatever you want."

"Will you stay with me?" Jass squeezed Sarah's hand.

"Tricia?" Sarah asked. "You're good with Chloe?"

"I want to see the baby!" Chloe whined.

Sarah knelt down. "Of course you do. It's so exciting right now, but it's going to take Jass's body some time to get ready. I'll text Mama when the baby is here, okay?"

Chloe crossed her arms.

Tricia scooped Chloe up. "Trust me, babies take a long time. You took forever! Let's go do something fun, and I'll bring you back as soon as Mommy texts, okay?"

"You won't forget?" Chloe said seriously.

"Promise," Sarah and Jass said together.

"Sweet kid," Àngel said as they made their way down the hall to the room where Jass would deliver. "Your niece?"

"Oh, no. I'm her bonus mom." Jass beamed as she shared the label Chloe had bestowed on her. She cupped her belly with her hands. "And I'll be this one's favorite *tìa*."

Amara added her hand to Jass's belly. "I'm flying solo with this one."

"Looks like you've got great support, though."

"The best," Amara said.

"Okay, let's get your vitals and see where you are."

Hours later, Amara sat in awe as Àngel placed her baby girl in her arms for the first time.

"How does it feel?" Jass asked, sweaty and exhausted.

"I can't find words," Amara whispered.

"What are you naming her?" Sarah asked.

"I was thinking Cecilia Jasmine. What do you think, *Madrina?*" Jass's eyes widened. "You want me to be her godmother?"

"The two of you would make pretty awesome Fairy Godmothers, *Hada Madrinas.*"

Sarah leaned over and wrapped her arms around Jass's shoulders. "I'm game if you are."

"I'm in. She's perfect, isn't she?"

"Just like you," Sarah said.

Jass covered Sarah's hands with her own. "As long as I'm perfect for you."

Sarah bent to kiss Jass tenderly. "There's no question about that."

CHAPTER FIFTY-THREE

Sarah started to wake when Jass rolled away from her. She loved the way Jass's body fit against her sans baby bump. Jass settled her with a hand to her shoulder. "You should sleep. I won't be long."

She turned for a kiss and pulled one of Jass's pillows to her, listening to the familiar sounds of Jass slipping away to pump in the office. After only three days, Sarah should not have felt so exhausted, especially given the fact that she was not the one who had pushed out a baby and didn't have to interrupt her sleep to keep her breastmilk in. Though Jass assured her that she didn't need any help with the nighttime pump, it was difficult for Sarah to quiet her mind without Jass next to her.

After several minutes, she gave up trying to go back to sleep and padded down the hallway, pushing open the door Jass had shut most of the way to trap the light of the small table lamp.

She startled, swiping quickly at her eyes when she saw Sarah.

Sarah rushed to her. "Hey, are you okay?"

Jass nodded wordlessly, but another tear slipped down her cheek. She had been holding her phone and quickly turned it off and set it on the table.

"Talk to me," Sarah said. She grasped Jass's hands, so glad she'd insisted Jass have a bra that held the pumping apparatus. "What are you feeling?"

"I'm not sad," Jass said.

"It's okay to be sad, you know. Postpartum hormones are no joke for any mom. I still remember being bombarded with all sorts of emotions after Chloe was born, the highest highs of euphoria with being a mom and then crashing into the panic of the enormity of it all. I can only imagine how it feels to have these major changes in your body and nothing tangible to attach them to."

Jass pushed out a long breath. "I am so happy for Amara and Cecilia."

Sarah squeezed Jass's hand.

"It's so weird not to have her knocking around inside me, you know?"

"I know." Sarah feathered Jass's bangs from her forehead.

"But I also feel relieved. Is that terrible to say? Almost...relieved to have done what I said I would do for Amara? That was a big project, and I completed it." Now she beamed at Sarah.

"You sure did. I remember when she told me you always see things through." Sarah felt blessed to have witnessed the magic and wonder of Amara becoming a mother. Remembering Amara's expression when she had first held Cecilia skin to skin after the delivery still made her misty-eyed. Had they not had the excuse to drop off breastmilk each day, she might have worried about intruding, but Amara's home had become an extension of her own. It brought her joy to do dishes or make Amara lunch. She watched Jass closely, trying to imagine what Jass must be feeling if she herself was so emotional.

"I'm sorry. I'm trying to find words. There are so many things spinning in my head right now."

"Honey, it's been three days. Be gentle with yourself."

Jass swallowed hard and whispered, "I miss her." Her eyes flicked to Sarah's and then away. "Not in an I-want-her-back kind of way, but...I can't stop thinking about her." She scrunched up her face. "I can't stop thinking about what they're doing."

"Why don't we text Amara?"

"At one in the morning?"

Sarah shrugged. "She could be up giving Cecilia her bottle. If she's not up, I think she's smart enough to turn off her phone."

Jass eyed her phone.

Sarah held out her hand, and once Jass had acquiesced and given her the phone, she shot off a quick text.

You up?

Three dots appeared. Sarah tipped the phone in Jass's direction, so she could see. Jass frowned. "They went away. Now they're back."

Sarah tipped the screen back toward herself. "This is silly." She hit video call, and seconds later, Amara came into view.

"Thank god!" she whispered. "I've got my hands full of baby and couldn't figure out how to text."

"What's going on?" Jass asked.

"What isn't? Cecilia won't sleep tonight. She wakes up hungry and then she barely eats. It's like three sips of the bottle wipes her out, and she goes back to sleep, but then she's up an hour later. I can't function like this! The lactation consultant said she should be taking a few ounces each time I feed her, but she barely has a few sucks."

"Oh, sweetie. I know!" Sarah pulled the ottoman around, so she was sitting next to Jass, squeezing them both into the frame.

"Sarah! Oh, am I glad to see you. I wanted to call you so bad, but I didn't want to wake you to ask if this ever happened with Chloe. What if I can't do this?"

"Take a breath!" Sarah laughed. Her heart swelled knowing Amara had thought of her in a moment of vulnerability. Jass must have been feeling something similar. She reached for Sarah's hand again.

Amara closed her eyes and took a deep breath.

"Did you change her diaper first?"

"Yes. But even that barely wakes her up."

"Have you tried taking her out of the sleep sack? Take off her outfit if you have to, especially get her feet, so she feels air on them. Tickle her to keep her eating. That usually did the trick for Chloe."

"Can we see her?" Jass asked.

"Oh my gosh, yes! I'm sorry! She angled the phone so they could see the sleeping baby in her arms.

Sarah slipped her arm around Jass's shoulder, wishing baby smell came through the phone. She had loved nuzzling Chloe's head and breathing her in. Jass breathed deeply and relaxed. Seeing Cecilia was what she needed. They had been talking about getting some of the newborn photos printed. She would do that later, so Jass would be able to look at Cecilia each time she pumped.

"You've got this." Sarah held Jass tight. "Both of you."

Jass swiped at her eyes again.

"Jass, what's wrong? Are you crying? Why are you crying?" Amara sounded alarmed.

"Just experiencing a lot of feelings. I'm fine. I needed to see the both of you is all. It was so quiet here."

"Be thankful for that in an hour when this one will be waking me up again to eat."

"But then you'll really get her awake," Sarah reminded her. "And then you should get a decent chunk. We'll be over in the morning to give you a nap. Hang in there, okay?"

"You're the best. Jass, your woman is the best."

"Don't I know it!" Jass said. "Hope you get some sleep tonight!"

Sarah ended the call. Jass turned off the pump and held up the plastic bottles. "You're amazing. I never got that much milk when I pumped for Chloe. Want me to take care of them?"

Jass gratefully accepted the offer.

After she stored the milk in the refrigerator and rinsed the pumping apparatus, Sarah crawled back into bed, this time spooning Jass. "Feel better?

Jass sighed and pushed back flush against Sarah. "So much. I really am thankful that we get to go back to sleep and stay asleep."

"Me, too."

"Thanks for getting up with me."

"Anytime. I love you."

"I love you, too."

Jass relaxed in Sarah's arms. Sarah lay awake longer, imagining Amara parenting on her own. She held the woman she loved and imagined what it would be like to parent an infant with her. She startled when Jass took her hand and moved it under her nightshirt.

"I miss you," she whispered. "How many more weeks until we can have sex again?"

Sarah chuckled into Jass's neck. "At least six." She wiggled her hips against Jass's to let her know how much she missed their intimacy.

"I guess I can wait that long." She turned enough to give Sarah a kiss that would make it very difficult to fall asleep.

CHAPTER FIFTY-FOUR

Six weeks later, Chloe sat with her arms crossed on the countertop, her chin resting on her forearms, not taking her eyes off Jass. "But it's not your birthday."

"Nope." Jass handed Chloe a beater covered in chocolate frosting.

Chloe licked the beater, painting a chocolate smile on her cheeks.

Jass turned to extend the other beater to Sarah who was preparing lunch at the counter opposite and found her watching. Her body warmed under Sarah's gaze. That look told her Sarah knew exactly what they were celebrating. Jass waggled her eyebrows suggestively.

"No thanks. A taste now will just make me want more." She licked her lips, making Jass want to kiss her.

Turning to block Chloe's view, Jass suggestively licked chocolate from the beater. "But a small taste is such a fun way to anticipate what you'll have later," Jass purred, crossing the kitchen to wrap her arms around Sarah. She rested her chin on Sarah's shoulder and then kissed her lightly on the neck.

"I don't need a taste to know I want more," Sarah whispered. "Especially when it's you I want."

Sarah pressed herself against Jass, savoring the closeness. It felt like an eternity since she had felt Sarah the way she wanted to. "I want you," she whispered.

"And I want you," Sarah whispered. "Are you sure it's a good idea to amp Chloe up on sugar given what we're celebrating?"

"Doesn't that mean that she'll crash hard?" Jass winked at her as she returned to finish frosting the cake with Chloe.

"It's not Mommy's birthday or my birthday," Chloe said, still trying to name the celebration.

"Nope," Jass answered, spooning chocolate frosting onto a chocolate cake.

"It's not Valentine's Day or Easter or…what's the green food day?"

"What *is* green food day?" Jass asked.

"I made green mashed potatoes on St. Patrick's Day last year. We should do that again!"

"Yes!" Chloe agreed. "And green eggs for breakfast, too!"

"What about green pancakes?" Jass asked.

This time Chloe's *yes* drew out for at least ten syllables. Sarah finished her chicken salad and stowed it in the fridge until they were ready to make sandwiches when their guests arrived. She wrapped her arms around Jass from behind, resting her chin on Jass's shoulder as Jass ran the wide spatula over the frosting. Jass's life felt sweet.

"So what are we celebrating?" Chloe asked, truly perplexed.

"You have to wait for *tìa* Amara and Cecilia to get here."

"Text them and ask when they'll be here!" she pleaded, impatiently.

"They'll be here when they get here. Why don't you pick out some of your favorite stories to share with Cecilia?"

The moment Chloe disappeared, Sarah kissed Jass, and she thought she might melt. "After a kiss like that, how am I supposed to get through the rest of this day?" Jass moaned.

"That was supposed to hold you over!" Sarah swatted her. "You're the one making it hard moaning like that!"

"They're here! Mommy! Jass! They're here!"

Sarah and Jass joined Chloe at the car. Sarah swooped in and relieved Amara of the carrier, as was usual. When Sarah was present, both Jass and Amara deferred to her with her years of parenting. Whenever Jass saw Cecilia, she was hit with a slew of emotions. In part, she was worried about handling such a tiny living being. Thrown in the deep end, Amara had to overcome that hesitation a lot faster, but Jass also kept some distance to make sure she did not cross the line between aunt and mom.

Sarah crooned to a fast-asleep Cecilia before leaning to plant a kiss on Amara's cheek. "You're looking great!"

"Wouldn't believe I had a baby a month ago, would you?" She lifted an arm to show off her figure and winked at Jass before kissing her cheek. "You look awesome."

"Doesn't she?" Again, Sarah scorched Jass with her gaze.

Amara ooed at them like they were middle school kids on the playground. "Somebody likes you!" she said, drawing out the word like for at least four syllables.

"C'mon! C'mon. Come see the cake!" Chloe said.

"What are we celebrating, anyway?" Amara asked when the youngster had run ahead.

"Me having my body back," Jass whispered. "But don't tell Chloe that."

Amara threw her head back and cackled. "I wondered at that look Sarah gave you. I'd offer to take Chloe to give the two of you some privacy, but what I really want to do is lie down in your guest room."

"Go. Sleep." Once inside the door, Jass nudged Amara down the hall.

"Only if you're sure," she mumbled, her feet already carrying her toward a nap. "With the nanny coming during the week, I have no reason to be this tired."

"You're parenting by yourself. If you weren't exhausted, I'd be worried."

"But Chloe wants me to look at the cake." Amara could barely keep her eyes open.

"I'll explain to Chloe." Sarah handed the carrier to Jass.

Jass set the carrier down by the couch and sat to unbuckle the straps. She carefully maneuvered Cecilia onto her lap, smiling at the shimmy that rippled through the baby. She opened her eyes for a second and then settled right back to sleep, balanced on Jass's thighs. "Hi, sweet pea." She stroked Cecilia's cheeks and fingered her perfect ears. She marveled at all the complicated design of an ear and how perfect both were.

"Is she still asleep?" Chloe asked, bouncing into the room.

"Use a little voice," Sarah reminded her, pulling Chloe into her lap as she sat down.

Chloe reached out to hold Cecilia's hand. "All she does is sleep," she complained.

"It takes a lot of energy to grow," Sarah explained.

"If I get a sister or a brother, I want one to play with."

Sarah and Jass shared a smile over Chloe's head. She was used to seeing Sarah in Chloe. Gazing at Cecilia, she searched for her own features. Right now, they shared coloring, dark skin and dark hair in contrast to Sarah and Chloe's pale skin and blond hair. Coloring would always tie her more to Cecilia than to Chloe, but Dave's whiteness had never made him less of a parent to her. Did he ever wish people in public could pair the two of them, or was it enough that the two of them felt like family?

"Can I watch TV?" Chloe said.

"In Moms' room, so you don't disturb your cousin," Sarah said.

"Was that a singular or a plural 'mom' you just did there?" Jass asked.

Sarah stroked Cecilia's thick hair. "Plural? Can we talk about how it doesn't make sense for you to pay rent on your apartment when you're always here now?"

"Sarah Cooper! Are you asking me to move in with you? And Chloe? What will your listeners say?"

"Oh."

"Did I break your brain?"

"No!"

"What's spinning around in there?" Jass asked. She sat patiently as Sarah sorted through her thoughts, each one reflected in her expression, the last of which was surprise.

"I wasn't thinking about my listeners. I was only thinking about what works for us. For this family."

"Wow. Sounds like a podcast."

Sarah pursed her lips. "Maybe. Like I said, my mind is very much on other things right now."

"Does pumping milk get me out of packing?"

"Absolutely not!" Sarah laughed.

"Okay, okay. I'll get started on it." She leaned into Sarah, and the two of them sat in silence for a long while. Jass's mind spun on all pieces of her life, as one of the responsible adults in Chloe's life, as the girlfriend of a woman she couldn't wait to get her hands on and the aunt who could gift her friend a nap while she held her baby. Her life was incredibly full.

"Think you'll ever want one of your own?" Sarah whispered.

Jass could not even fathom it. "Ask me again in a year." She leaned forward to kiss Sarah. "Right now, all I want is you."

EPILOGUE

One year later

Sarah sat shotgun as Jass drove to Pasadena. "I like the sound of Amara's church, but I don't know if I could make this drive every week."

"Amara's been managing it for six months now *and* with an infant. It's not like there's a church in Revelia that would welcome her like this one has."

"I know, and I'm tempted to enroll Chloe in that sex-ed class that Adrienne talks about. But I hate giving up sleeping late with you." Sarah squeezed Jass's thigh and left her hand there.

Jass looked over from the road, her glance traveling briefly from Sarah's eyes and then to her lips. It had been difficult for her to leave Sarah's embrace this morning. She rested her right hand on top of Sarah's, her thumb rubbing the ring on Sarah's left ring finger.

"Does Amara finding such a cool church make you wish we'd had a big traditional wedding?"

Sarah shook her head. "Not for one minute. What we did was perfect."

Sarah rested her head against the seat with her gaze still on Jass, still surprised by the feeling of absolute faith Jass gave her in their commitment. After they got their marriage license, they went to City Hall, taking Amara and Casey as their witnesses. They went to lunch afterward, and when Chloe announced that her moms had just gotten married, the small café delivered complimentary champagne to the table.

Jass parked next to Amara's car in the parking lot, so they knew they had the right place. Chloe was unusually quiet as they walked through the campus to the sanctuary to find Amara.

She stood at the front of the sanctuary. The choir was still practicing which made Sarah feel conspicuous as they entered the large room, chairs in an arc with two center aisles. Amara looked to have staked out the entire front center row.

She greeted them all with hugs and kisses applied to cheeks, able to move freely as another church member had an eye on Cecilia.

"I told you about Evan," Amara said, waving him over. "These are Cecilia's godmothers, Sarah and Jass."

"So nice to meet you," he said with a smile. He stood several inches shorter than Jass. He had long hair pulled back in a ponytail and a neatly trimmed goatee. His jeans and button-down shirt made Sarah feel overdressed in her suit jacket, but Amara's sweet blue dress that showed off her amazing legs put her more at ease.

She and Jass took seats in the front row. By the time the service started, the first two rows were filled with guests who had come to support Cecilia's dedication. Amara had explained that the church did not do baptisms.

The minister, a woman to whom Sarah had warmed instantly with her short, frosted hair and easy smile, invited Amara and her family forward to the pulpit. Sarah agreed with Jass about how welcoming the church felt. She could not picture any minister in Revelia wearing a stole with a progress flag pattern on it, and she had noticed that the church members had pronouns printed under their names. Sarah and Jass stood holding hands, smiling as Amara introduced them to the congregation. Chloe bounced on the balls of her feet, waving when she was identified as Cecilia's cousin, to which the congregation laughed warmly. Sarah recognized Amara's mom and guessed the younger woman with her preteen kids was a sister. Dave could not have looked prouder and Jass's mother less interested. Sarah was touched to see that several members of Jass's extended family had come to support her. Casey and Adrienne smiled at her from the second row, joined by Marv. It even felt right for Tricia to be there with her new girlfriend, Dee, who seemed good for Tricia. She was patient with Chloe and also very clear about having zero interest in having a baby of her own.

The minister held up a single rose which Cecilia immediately snatched. Gently extracting it from Cecilia's hands, she said, "This rose is a symbol of life's beauty. I touch your brow, your lips and your hands to dedicate your thoughts, words and deeds to the heritage of good."

She talked more about the role the church community played in the life of a child and the joys Cecilia would bring to the congregation, ending with a call and response where those gathered promised to support and love Amara and Cecilia. The minister then took Cecilia and walked down one aisle, introducing the little girl to the congregation.

Sarah noticed how Amara's gaze lingered on Evan before she continued to track her daughter as the minister wove through the congregation and made her way back. Sarah felt the building filled to the brim with love. She squeezed Jass's hand.

"I love you," Jass mouthed.

"Love you, too," Sarah silently returned.

Though neither of her parents attended the service, Sarah knew she stood there with family, that her life was surrounded by love. Her loved ones supported her and Chloe. They were not on their own anymore, the Two Musketeers taking on the world alone. Now she was part of an ever-growing tribe.

She tried to convey all that she was feeling and thinking as she held Jass's gaze. She bumped their joined hands against Jass's hip, eliciting the smile that had captivated her from the start. Ever so slightly, Jass raised her eyebrows. Her eyes sparkled with mystery. Every time Sarah looked into those soft brown eyes, she fell in all over again.

If you enjoyed meeting Casey, I hope you will check out *Birds of a Feather*, the story of how she met and fell in love with Adrienne.

Bella Books, Inc.

Women. Books. Even Better Together.

P.O. Box 10543
Tallahassee, FL 32302
Phone: (800) 729-4992
www.BellaBooks.com

More Titles from Bella Books

Hunter's Revenge – Gerri Hill
978-1-64247-447-3 | 276 pgs | paperback: $18.95 | eBook: $9.99
Tori Hunter is back! Don't miss this final chapter in the acclaimed
Tori Hunter series.

Integrity – E. J. Noyes
978-1-64247-465-7 | 28 pgs | paperback: $19.95 | eBook: $9.99
It was supposed to be an ordinary workday...

The Order – TJ O'Shea
978-1-64247-378-0 | 396 pgs | paperback: $19.95 | eBook: $9.99
For two women the battle between new love and old loyalty may prove
more dangerous than the war they're trying to survive.

Under the Stars with You – Jaime Clevenger
978-1-64247-439-8 | 302 pgs | paperback: $19.95 | eBook: $9.99
Sometimes believing in love is the first step. And sometimes it's all
about trusting the stars.

The Missing Piece – Kat Jackson
978-1-64247-445-9 | 250 pgs | paperback: $18.95 | eBook: $9.99
Renee's world collides with possibility and the past, setting off a tidal
wave of changes she could have never predicted.

An Acquired Taste – Cheri Ritz
978-1-64247-462-6 | 206 pgs | paperback: $17.95 | eBook: $9.99
Can Elle and Ashley stand the heat in the *Celebrity Cook Off* kitchen?